Sailors ran and armed themselves, readied the heavy weapons, and took shelter behind the deck railing. The new ship flew neither sails nor flag to identify its origins, but at least fifty oars sprouted from the sides of it like the legs of a centipede. The deck sported no heavy weapons like their ballista or catapult, but at least a dozen large creatures crowded against the rails.

They were massively muscled, humanoid in appearance in that they stood on two legs and had a pair of arms, but their heads looked like that of a bull. Huge horns topped the bovine heads and fur covered their bodies. In their enormous hands, they wielded massive battle-axes and swords that would take a normal man two hands to swing.

"Minotaurs! Damn those creatures!" Zeb cursed.

"Do you think they sent the storm?" Azerick asked.

"Minotaurs despise magic, so I doubt it. They must be working with someone; as if they weren't dangerous enough!"

"Are they pirates then?"

"Worse, they're slavers. They'll board our ship, take as many of us alive as they can, and use us or sell us as slaves. Look alive, lad, because here they come."

The Sorcerer's
TORMENT

BROCK E.
DESKINS

To my readers: Like a car without wheels, no matter how grand the vehicle, I can go nowhere without you.

CHAPTER I

Once again, it seemed the fates conspired against the young sorcerer, taking away his home, his friends, and anything that brought him happiness. Azerick had already lost his father, home, and the future he had planned because of someone's greed and thirst for power. He lost his mother, his friends, and his second family to evil men with nothing but avarice in their hearts. Just when he thought his life was back on the proper path at the Academy, he had to leave his home, education, and friends behind.

Had he meant to kill Travis? Azerick certainly felt he had reason and possibly justification, but in his heart, he knew it was an accident. He would not mourn Travis' death. Azerick took every loss and every hurt inflicted upon him like a hot sword under the hammer of a blacksmith. Every ringing blow tempered him, made him stronger, harder, and more lethal to those who sought to harm him.

Azerick crossed the night-shrouded city and went straight to the docks where a handful of ships stood moored. He had to make several inquiries before he finally found one leaving this night. Most outbound ships had set sail with the coming of the tide, but the *Sea Star* had been delayed when the large cargo hoist had to be repaired after snapping its boom. The crew was hastily loading the rest of the cargo so the ship could set sail the instant the tides became favorable. Azerick approached one of the sailors assisting with the loading of the last few crates needing stowed.

"Excuse me. Do you know where I can find the captain of this vessel?" he inquired.

"He be checking the storing of the cargo below decks. Best you wait until he is done a'fore pesterin' him, boy," the sailor responded.

Azerick waited patiently, constantly casting looks over his shoulder as he half-expected the Watch to run him down as the sailors hoisted the last cargo net full of crates over to the open hatch of the ship. Several minutes passed after the last load was stored in the ship's belly before a man swung over on the returning boom clutching onto the limp cargo netting. When the arm reached the dock, he released his grip and dropped lightly to the wooden planking.

"One of my mates says you want to see the captain," the man stated.

The ship's captain looked to be in his mid-fifties and sported a thick, but well-groomed beard going from blond to mostly grey. He wore oiled, knee-high leather boots with the tops rolled down below the knee. His face showed the harshness of years of abuse from the sun and saltwater, but he was surprisingly fit and agile.

"Yes, sir, my name is Azerick, and I would like to request passage on your vessel."

"This isn't a passenger ship, boy. It's a merchant ship—my merchant ship."

"I've sailed before, Captain, and I will work as hard as any man on board."

"I've got a full crew and need no more hands, and more importantly, no more bellies to fill for this trip."

"Sir, it is very important I leave tonight on your ship. You can put me on half rations. I brought a lot of my own food and can catch fish if I run out."

"Sounds to me like you're running, lad. You wanted by the Watch, is that it?" the captain asked, a hard frown deeply creasing his face.

"No, sir," Azerick answered honestly since the Watch probably was not looking for him yet, "I just have urgent business I must attend to."

"And where might that urgent business be?"

"Where are you sailing?"

"North Haven, after a roundabout loop through the Inner Isles," the captain answered.

"Perfect, that is where I have business."

"I don't know what kind of trouble you're in, boy, but I don't need it on my ship, and I want no part of it." The captain turned to retire to his ship.

"Peg knows me well and will vouch for me, Captain!" Azerick called at the departing sailor's back.

The captain turned back and eyed the young man standing before him to see if a lie hid behind the youth's eyes. "You say you know old Peg, do you?"

"Yes, Captain, I do. He sailed with my father."

"Wait here and I'll go have a word with old Peg. If you are lying to me, boy, you had best not be here when I get back. I don't much appreciate having my time wasted, particularly when I'm already behind schedule."

Leaving his warning hanging in the air, the old sailor walked toward the row of shops and buildings facing the docks and the open ocean. Azerick hoped Peg would vouch for him. It was a stretch claiming he knew Peg, but he said he had sailed with his father. Hopefully it would be enough. Nearly thirty minutes passed before Azerick spied the captain reappear out of the darkness.

"You might have saved me some time by telling me straightaway who your father was, lad," the captain grumbled. "Although, if my brain wasn't so full of seawater I suppose I would have picked up on the name. Darius talked about you all the time. He was a good captain and a good friend. Grab your bag. I'll show you where you can store yourself and your gear. The name's Captain Zeb, by the way."

"Thank you, Captain," Azerick said as he shook the boat captain's calloused hand.

"You'll still work, make no mistake. I don't allow no freeloaders, no matter who their father was."

"Yes, sir! It will be my pleasure to work on your ship."

"If you think it'll be a pleasure then you haven't spent much time on a boat; especially mine."

The captain gave Azerick a footlocker and showed him to a bunk in a tiny room under the forecastle. He was forced to live in the cramped space since all other bunks on the ship were accounted for, but he did not mind. The space had no porthole for fresh air, but he enjoyed the privacy. He could conjure a light that would allow him to study the few books he had brought with him when he wasn't working the decks.

As soon as he stored his gear, Azerick was ushered back onto the deck and instructed to help pull in and stow the mooring lines. Once the thick ropes were secured and the ship was underway, Captain Zeb assigned a sailor to break him in and literally show him the ropes.

He recalled how Peg had been teaching Bran about knot tying, which apparently was a vital skill for any sailor working aboard a ship as it was the first thing a sailor named Balor showed him. Perhaps if the night's events had not frayed his nerves so much he would have recognized the captain's name as the same man Bran had shipped with on his quest to rescue Andrea.

Azerick enjoyed the salty air and the wind in his face. Memories of sailing with his father flooded his mind and elicited a rare smile until he remembered he would never again sail with him.

Rusty stood before the headmaster, the entire teaching cadre, the chief constable, and Travis' father.

"Now, Franklin, tell us everything you can about what happened last night, if you would, please," Headmaster Dondrian instructed.

Rusty took a deep breath and collected his thoughts. "I talked to Azerick earlier yesterday. He said if anything should happen to him he wanted me to have his alchemic set. It was an odd thing to say, and it is a very expensive set, so I asked him if anything was wrong. He said he had to leave to take care of some things and that he might be gone for a while."

"Did he say where he was going or what he had to do?" Chief Constable Lazlo asked.

"No, sir. I asked, but he said he didn't want to get me involved, and then he changed the subject."

"Tell us more of what happened last night in the clearing," the headmaster directed.

"I knew something was wrong, so I waited until Azerick left and followed him out to the clearing. Azerick and Travis faced each other in mutual combat. Azerick's spells were completely absorbed by

Travis' ward. He must have been wearing an enchanted item because no spell he knew could protect him that effectively."

"I object to that statement, sir. This student could not know what kind of power Travis could weave into his casting. He is a Beaumonte. Unlike others, the blood in our family has run pure for generations," Lord Beaumonte insisted.

Magus Allister's gruff voice filled the room as he interrupted the nobleman. "No, Franklin could not, Lord Beaumonte, but as one of your son's teacher's I can assure you that a spell shield with that kind of power was far beyond the abilities of all but the most experienced students here. Travis was only a mediocre wizard at best, despite the purity of his blood."

Lord Beaumonte jumped to his feet and shouted. "I will not stand by and have my son's memory slandered, sir!"

"Truth is not slander, My Lord," Magus Florent said in support of Magus Allister. "Go on, Franklin, what happened next?"

"Azerick must have realized that none of his lesser spells were able to touch Travis, and having been struck several times by his magic, he used a more powerful spell. He cast a lightning bolt and knocked Travis to the ground. He then turned to face those three over there." Rusty pointed at Travis' friends. "He knew they would shoot him in the back if he got the upper hand on Travis."

Several shouts of protest erupted from the accused student wizards, but the headmaster hushed them.

"I was watching from the cover of the trees, and when I saw all three preparing spells, I cast a spell to disrupt them."

"He set our shirts on fire and burned me!" one of the boys protested.

"Be still, Ronald," the headmaster ordered. "I will deal with you three in a moment."

Rusty continued. "Azerick turned back to Travis who was on his feet and pointing his wand at him. Azerick told him to put the wand away and admit defeat. Travis told him he was going to kill him and then me. Again, Azerick warned him not to use his wand or he would be sorry. Travis did not listen and triggered his wand. When he did, it blew up, killed him, and did all the damage you saw in the clearing."

"It sounds like Azerick knew the wand was going to malfunction. Is that true, Franklin?" the headmaster asked.

"Yes, Headmaster. Azerick cast a spell on it one day after Travis and his friends beat him up in the halls, but he didn't know it would react so violently. He told me he thought it would just break."

"Do you know why Azerick met Travis in the clearing last night?"

"He told me he had stopped Travis from raping a girl the night of the ball, and Travis challenged him," Rusty replied coldly as the room burst into shocked mutterings.

"Objection, Headmaster; that is hearsay! Three other witnesses have discounted the accusation, and the girl refuses to speak of it!" Lord Beaumonte said in defense of his dead son.

"Lord Beaumonte is correct. Without another actual witness, anything Azerick allegedly said must be discounted until he appears to give testimony," Chief Constable Lazlo affirmed.

"Do you know where he went after the incident, Franklin?"

"No, Headmaster. He refused to tell me or even hint as to where he was going or what he was going to do."

"Would you tell us if he had?"

"No, Headmaster, not even under the threat of torture," Rusty swore and meant every word of it.

"Well, let us just see about that, young man!" Lord Beaumonte snarled; his voice thick with malice.

Magus Allister rose from his chair once again, his anger evident on his wrinkled face. "Threaten one of my students again, Lord Beaumonte, and any protection you may enjoy from being related to the duke will not be sufficient to protect you!"

Travis' father hastily backed away, pointing a quaking finger at the old wizard. "My son is murdered in your academy, and now one of your instructors dares to threaten me! This is intolerable! I demand he be arrested at once."

The chief constable looked from the duke's cousin to the very formidable and supremely angry archmage. "My Lord, I'm sure we are all terribly upset at everything that has happened. Tempers are of course running high, but I am certain the magus does not truly wish to cause harm to anyone. Let us just calm ourselves as best we can and see that justice is served. Given all the testimony we have heard, I feel it is best to hand this case over to the magistrate for further review. We can do nothing until the accused is located anyhow."

"There may be nothing you can do, but I assure you that my resources do not lack your magistrate's limitations!" Lord Beaumonte shouted as he left the meeting, slamming the door behind him.

"What is going to happen now, sir?" Rusty asked.

"It's in the hands of the magistrate's office now, Franklin. At this time, you are considered nothing more than a witness. Any punishment that would normally be incurred from casting offensive spells with intent to cause harm to another student or citizen will be dismissed given the mitigating circumstances," Headmaster Dondrian assured him. "Let it be known however, that any aggression between you four young men will not be tolerated and will be grounds for immediate dismissal from the Academy. Is that understood?"

The young wizards all swore that it was, and Rusty shuffled out of the headmaster's office with his head down and returned to his room. Rusty's emotions were in turmoil, as he feared for his friend while trying to process what had happened last night. He had never seen anyone killed before nor magic used in a way that caused so much damage. He had never really taken his studies seriously, but seeing the awesome, destructive force for what it was, he vowed to change that. A knock at his door startled him from his ponderings.

"How are you, Franklin?" the magus stepped into the room and asked.

"I don't know. I'm scared, and I'm worried about Azerick."

"I'll be honest with you; of all the young men I have ever met in my very long life, Azerick is the last person I would worry about. If anyone can come out of this on top, it will be him. Did he ever tell you of how he and I met?"

Rusty and the old wizard laughed themselves to tears as the magus detailed the accounts of their first few encounters. Both young wizard and old held their stomachs, afraid they were about to burst open as Magus Allister regaled him with the story.

"By the way, don't you dare repeat what I said."

Rusty promised that his secret was safe with him and went back to thinking of his friend, but with a bit more hope for his success than he previously had.

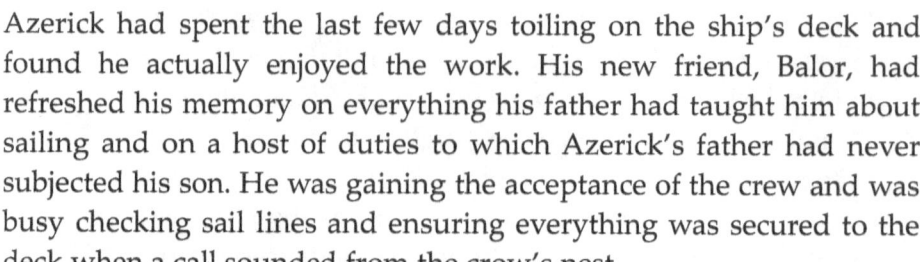

Azerick had spent the last few days toiling on the ship's deck and found he actually enjoyed the work. His new friend, Balor, had refreshed his memory on everything his father had taught him about sailing and on a host of duties to which Azerick's father had never subjected his son. He was gaining the acceptance of the crew and was busy checking sail lines and ensuring everything was secured to the deck when a call sounded from the crow's nest.

"Sails, four points off the starboard bow!"

Azerick scanned the horizon and finally made out the white sails against the blue sky.

"Unknown vessel on a definite intercept course! Make that two ships!" cried the lookout.

"I have a bad feeling about this," the captain said as he came up behind his newest crew member.

"Who do you think it is? What do they want?" Azerick asked.

"It's pirates, or I'm a one-legged milkmaid. Ready the scorpions and deck catapults! I want every man to the armory to draw swords and crossbows!"

Men scrambled everywhere across the deck and into the rigging with cutlasses stuck through their belts and gripping crossbows. No sailor wanted to face a battle at sea, but the treacherous waters made the prospect of doing so a very real hazard, and they all trained for such eventualities.

"I hope you aren't afraid of a fight, boy."

"No, sir. Not at all."

"Then you better be ready to fight like a demon, because we are outnumbered, and it's win or die out here."

Azerick crossed to the armory, thrust a couple of dirks through his belt, and retrieved his staff. *Your odds are better than you might think, Captain. I bet they do not have a sorcerer on their ship.* He just hoped he would be enough to turn the battle to their favor. Azerick would only use magic if forced. The general populace was wary of magic, and sailors were more superstitious than most.

As the two ships cut toward the *Sea Star*, Azerick was able to make out more details. Both were two-masted schooners, but they carried extra sails for speed. They were lighter ships than the *Sea Star* but still sported a catapult on the bow and several scorpions along the rail. Captain Zeb ordered deck shields locked in place. The deck shields were simply iron-banded, wooden shields that slid into slots on the deck and tied to the railings to provide cover from all but the heaviest projectiles.

The men scrambled to follow the captain's orders and crouched behind the shields with their crossbows cocked and ready. The minutes turned to hours as Zeb tried to outmaneuver the pirates, but the wind and current favored their foes. Their separation dwindled until there was less than two-hundred yards of open water between them. The pirate vessels began flinging chain into the rigging using deck-mounted catapults. The steel links fouled the lines and tore holes through the sails. The ship began noticeably slowing as the ruined rigging lost the wind. The sailors aboard the *Sea Star* returned fire with their own catapult, but the pirates continued to gain.

The first pirate vessel closed to within a hundred yards, and the captain ordered his men to loose their crossbows at will. Dozens of quarrels flew from the *Sea Star* like a swarm of angry hornets. Azerick saw a few pirates drop to the deck and lie still or writhe in pain, clutching at the shafts lodged in their bodies. The *Sea Star*'s crew hunkered down to reload, and the pirates returned the assault.

"Pull us to port and do not let them catch us between them!" Zeb ordered.

Azerick watched as the second ship tried to maneuver to their other side. If the pirate vessels caught the *Sea Star* between them, the flanking assault was sure to tear them to shreds. Already quarrels clattered to the deck or found the backs of men as they shielded their fronts from the first ship. The *Sea Star* swung hard to port, cutting straight across the path of the second enemy ship, but their maneuver caused them to lose a lot of precious wind, and they fell closer to the pirate ships.

"Prepare to repel boarders!" Captain Zeb shouted as the ships cut the distance by half. Azerick stepped up from behind one of the shields, and the captain tried to pull him back down. "What are you doing, you fool? Get down!"

"Don't worry, Captain, I know what I'm doing," Azerick said with more confidence than he felt.

He wanted to wait, but Azerick knew they were grossly outnumbered, and hesitating would only result in more of his crew's death. He gathered in the Source knowing that his use of magic would create a rift between him and some, if not most, of the crew. Zeb would likely drop him off at the next port if he wasn't forced to toss him overboard.

Several crossbow bolts flew at the offered target, but they dropped harmlessly to the deck when they struck Azerick's magical barrier. Captain Zeb and the nearby Balor looked on in shock at what should have been a very dead young man. Their faces shifted to downright awe as Azerick raked a bolt of lightning across the deck of the nearest pirate ship.

The brilliant azure bolts tore into the pirates, scattering those nearby and setting fire to spare sailcloth and wooden crates. Azerick then launched a barrage of arcane bolts and sent two more pirates sprawling to the deck and the rest diving for cover. The crew of the *Sea Star* snapped out of their astonishment, took advantage of the pandemonium on board the other ship, and fired their crossbows, scorpions, and catapult once again.

"Swing that cat toward the second ship to keep them on their toes!" Captain Zeb instructed while the rest of his crew continued to assault the spell-stricken pirate ship.

Azerick let loose with another round of magical darts followed by a second bolt of lightning. The second lightning bolt cracked the forward mast and set it aflame. As it burned, the weakened wood split, toppled to the deck, ignited more fires, and trapped and crushed several of the pirates milling below in a tangle of rope and sailcloth. Azerick and most of the crew turned their attention to the second ship which was now close enough to start hurling grappling lines in an attempt to board the *Sea Star* and overwhelm her crew.

The young sorcerer released another eye-searing bolt, possibly his last given his fatiguing body, at the pirate vessel to great effect. Most of the pirates had been crowding the rails, ready to swing over on ropes or run across boarding planks as soon as they were able to draw the two ships together. Over a dozen pirates fell to the powerful blast, but Azerick refused to give them even a moment of respite.

He sent a barrage of fiery bolts into the faces of three pirates, followed by a lancing strike that speared through one pirate and killed another man behind him.

The sailors aboard the *Sea Star* shot their crossbows at nearly point-blank range into the massed pirates as Azerick sent a gout of fire similar to the one Rusty had used during his duel with Travis. Between the crossbow bolts, the devastating magical assault, and the burning wreck of the first pirate vessel, the pirates of the second ship lost their nerve. They threw down their weapons and begged for mercy from their would-be victims.

"Take their weapons and set them in longboats. See that they have fresh water and a bit of food. If they run out, they can damn well eat each other. You other men, put out that fire over there before we lose our prize," the captain ordered upon seeing a pile of tar-cured rope burning near the mast, a victim of one of Azerick's spells.

Captain Zeb approached their young savior as the sailors ran about following his orders. A few others paused long enough to give Azerick a clap on the back, but most gave him a wide berth.

"That was quite a bit of work you did there, son. You have any other secrets I should know about?"

"None I think you need to know of, Captain. Nothing like this, to be sure," the exhausted young sorcerer replied.

"I never would have taken the son of Captain Giles as a wizard. Is there anything you need, lad?"

"Sorcerer, and yes, a nap. I am completely spent. Oh, and food. I am starving. Casting spells works up a mean appetite."

"I'll take your word for it, lad. Go lay yourself out in my cabin. I'll have the cook make you something and have it brought to you."

"Thank you, Captain."

"It's us who owes you thanks, lad. We owe you our lives."

Azerick did not reply to the praise as he shuffled off to the captain's bed, so weary that even the gentle swaying of the ship threatened to knock him from his feet. He let out a sigh of relief when his back sank into the surprisingly soft and comfortable bed.

After an indeterminate amount of time, the noise of someone entering the room stirred him to full alertness from a semi-slumber. Captain Zeb brought in a tray laden with a slab of roast beef, mushroom gravy, warm bread, steamed carrots, and a mug of ale. Azerick sat up straight as his nose caught the scent of the delicious food.

"Here you are, lad. Cook went all out on this. I hope you enjoy it. You earned it," Captain Zeb said as he set the tray down on a table bolted to the floor in the center of the room.

"How is the crew doing?" Azerick asked as he pulled up a seat and dug into the proffered meal.

"We lost four men, nine more were wounded, but only three will be staying below decks for more than a couple days. It's not just the injuries you are thinking of though, is it?"

"No, sir. I'm glad to know we didn't lose more, but how are they taking everything else—what I did?"

"Most everyone knows you saved their hides. There are always a few who are a bit more ignorant and superstitious than others, and they're apt to say stupid things. But I wouldn't worry myself. The others stamped out any negative words anyone felt they needed to say about you, and I told everyone that if they didn't like sailing with you then I could drop em off with the pirates in their longboats. There was only a couple hardheads, and I put them on the boat we salvaged."

"So the other ship is still seaworthy then? That's good."

"I got men repairing the rigging, and we'll be back underway in a couple hours. You know, your father was going to make me captain of the *Storm Runner* before everything happened. I never thought his boy would be the one to end up giving me my own ship," Zeb said and smiled.

"You sailed with my father. Were you with him the day they took him?"

"Aye, that I was. I was his first mate on the *Storm Runner* on that last voyage. We had left Lazuul and were headed back for Southport when the pirates waylaid us. Your father had us dump a few barrels of demon fire over the side. As soon as the pirate ship ran into the slick, we set it alight and burned it to cinders."

"Like father like son," Azerick commented under his breath.

"Your father's quick thinking saved us all that day. I owe him my life, as does every man who sailed with him on that voyage. He was a good man and a damn fine ship's captain. None of us knew he had been taken until they started hauling in the rest of us. He never told us anything about taking on any other cargo neither. I thought he had rushed home to you and your mother. It was all he talked about the entire trip back. He said he wanted to spend some time, a couple years maybe, with his family, have another child, and offered me the helm of *Storm Runner*."

Captain Zeb paused and took a deep breath before continuing. "The rest of us were brought in about a week after we arrived in port. It was then we found out they had hauled in your father and killed him in his cell a few days later. The duke's men managed to round up most of the crew. Only a few had caught a berth on another ship before they ran the rest of us down while we enjoyed our shore leave.

"They started askin' about your father and artifacts. I told them what I knew, that your father was a good, honest, loyal man and I didn't know anything about any artifacts or illegal goods on the ship. I guess that wasn't the answer they wanted to hear, so they asked us a bit more firmly, if you know what I mean. For weeks they whipped us, beat us, broke bones, cut our flesh, kept us awake, and starved us. A couple men died in that prison, but they eventually let us go when it became obvious that none of us knew anything."

Captain Zeb took another deep, shuddering breath. "When they let us go, we all caught the first ships out of Southport. Me and most of the boys got on ships going to North Haven and signed on with a shipping merchant up there. It's a bit colder, but the work is good. When we make a run to Southport those of us who were questioned try not to even get off the boat, and when we do, we never leave the docks. I should have thought about you and your mother, but we were all so scared we ran as far and fast as we could. I'm sorry I wasn't there to help you, son, but you're here now and going to North Haven. You have a friend up there, and I'll do anything I can to help you. You are more than welcome to sail on any ship I'm in charge of. You make one hell of a pirate weapon, but something tells me being a sailor isn't in your plans."

Azerick shook his head as he looked past Zeb's shoulder, not focusing on anything in the room. "No, Captain. I appreciate the offer, and I will certainly take you up on your hospitality, at least until I get myself settled, but I have a different path to follow."

"I figured as much. Well, let me leave you to your supper and rest."

Zeb left him alone and headed deckside. Azerick wolfed down his meal and fell asleep for what seemed like days, days of dreams haunted by the dead he tried to leave behind but who insisted upon following him wherever he went.

When he awoke, there was a platter of bread, cheese, and smoked meat on the table as well as a pitcher of water with a good shot of sterilizing rum. He finished the simple meal and headed up on deck, eager to stretch his legs and get some fresh air. Several of the sailors greeted him warmly and knuckled a salute as he passed. He returned their greetings, glad that none seemed too upset or nervous over his display of spellcraft.

"Hey, Azerick," Balor called out to him, "nice to see you back up with us working folk!"

"You know me, always sleeping on the job." He found the captain at the wheel and approached him. "How long have I been asleep?"

"About fourteen hours. It's mid-morning right now, and we've been under full sail for about eight hours," Zeb replied.

"How's the sailing been while I've been out?"

"It's been real smooth. We have a good wind at our backs and a clear sky over our heads."

"I guess I better get back to work then and return your cabin to you. Thanks for the soft bed. I needed it."

"It's the least I could do. I want you well rested in case we run into any more pirates!" Zeb said with a good belly laugh.

Azerick put himself back to work scrubbing decks, mending sails, tarring cracks in the hull, and just about any other task better suited to the greenest crew members. Whatever Azerick's part was in saving them all from the pirates, ship's rules and duties trumped just about everything, even the heroics of young sorcerer's.

The skies remained clear and the winds favorable for the next several days. Azerick was up in the rigging tightening a few lines when dark clouds rolled in far faster than could possibly be natural. He shinnied down the lines and ran across the deck to the wheelhouse.

"Captain, those clouds coming in—" he started to say.

"I see 'em, lad, and I don't like the looks of 'em one bit," the captain remarked.

"It's not just the looks, Captain. I don't like the way they feel."

"Feel—like in a wizard kind of way?" Zeb asked, the color draining from his face.

"Yeah, I don't think they are natural at all."

"I'm inclined to agree with you, boy, but real or not we're going to have to ride 'em out unless you got a trick up your sleeve to deal with a storm."

Azerick shook his head and went back to the main deck. The wind intensified, and the ocean's swells began undulating up and down in huge, rolling waves. The relatively smooth, blue sea became a roiling mass of menacing grey swells almost without warning.

"Lower the mainsails! This is going to be a hard blow, boys!" the captain ordered.

Azerick and the crew raced to lower the mainsails, batten down the cargo and crew hatches, and secure any loose items on the deck. The men in the crow's nest zipped down the lines and reached the deck nearly as fast as a man falling. Sailors took shelter below decks or tied themselves in so the waves now breaking over the gunwale did not sweep them out to sea. The wind raged with a fierceness Azerick had never experienced before. Fat, heavy raindrops began pouring from the black sky onto the deck with a force that stung as if he were being pelted with gravel.

Massive swells slammed into the side of the ship until Captain Zeb was able to point the bow into them and ride up and over the aqueous hills. Shifting swells still hammered the ship as they crashed over the gunwale and bow. Breaking waves swept men from their feet and washed them across the deck. The force of the water and winds batted the unlucky ones over the side and they then had to be hauled back up by their safety line.

Zeb ordered all but a few essential hands below decks. Azerick rode out the storm down in the hold with the majority of the crew until it was his turn to switch out with the men topside to give them a much-needed rest from fighting the massive waves and wind.

Azerick could not believe his eyes when he climbed out onto the deck and clipped on his safety line. Waves and swells five times the height of the deck rolled under and around them. The ship creaked ominously every time it was forced to climb over one of the gigantic swells or was bashed in the side by a large wave. He was certain they were all going to die and that the merciless ocean in all its vast power would smash their tiny, fragile ship to splinters.

All afternoon and night and late into the next day, waves swamped and battered their ship. The wind howled through the rigging and tore the small lateen sails to shreds where they whipped in the wind like a soldier signaling his surrender. Men below decks kept a wary eye out for damage to the hull from the inside. They erected several braces to keep the power of the waves and the twisting of the ship from breaching its wooden walls. They made patches with thick tar and canvas fibers to try to stop, or at least slow, the leaks that sprang between the abused planking of the ship's hull. Several sailors took turns cranking the arms of the bilge pumps to force out the water that unerringly found its way into the ship.

Through his exhaustion, Azerick thought he finally felt a slowing in the rhythm of the huge swells. He concentrated on the rolling of the ship and the sound of the wind above and could detect a definite easing in both. Over the next hour, the storm above blew out, and the ship slowly began to settle into the gentler gait to which he was more accustomed.

He and the rest of the crew climbed out of the hold for a much-needed breath of fresh air. A storm as powerful as that could upset the stomach of even the most hardened veteran sailor. The clouds were breaking up, and Azerick could see patches of blue between the fluffy, floating mists. The sea had calmed considerably, and men started to take up their work without prompting. One sailor climbed up to the crow's nest as others began repairing lines and hauling out the heavy canvas mainsails. Azerick looked around, but he was unable to see the captured ship anywhere. He prayed they had been able to ride out the massive storm as his ship had, but he knew there was little hope for the smaller vessel.

He started repairing lines and securing any items that had come loose during the storm. Azerick heard the captain shouting orders as he worked to help set the ship aright.

"Balor, take a few men below and report back to me with an assessment of the damage," Captain Zeb ordered before going to his cabin to consult his maps in an attempt to determine where the storm had blown them. "Azerick, follow me, if you please."

Azerick followed the captain into his quarters. Zeb pulled a large map from a rack of deep pigeonholes, rolled it out on his table, and weighted down the corners to keep it flat.

"Do you know where we are, Captain?" Azerick asked.

"There's no way to know precisely. I can only make an approximation by knowing what direction we were blown and estimating our rate of travel. It's not that we're lost. I can turn the ship due east and run into Valeria's shoreline. I just don't know how far north it blew us. If we see floating ice, then we went too far. Now tell me about that storm."

"There is not much I can tell you, sir. It was definitely formed by magic though. I could detect the emanations holding it together like wards used to trap doors and things. It would take someone far more powerful than me to conjure up and create a storm, especially one that size."

"If someone purposely made it, I have to wonder if it was meant for us, or did we just get caught in someone else's trap?" Zeb asked rhetorically.

"Ship off the starboard bow!" the lookout called from the crow's nest.

"That may be our answer right there, Captain," Azerick answered.

Both men went up on deck to find out what was happening now.

"Is it our sister ship? What kind of sails is she flying?" Zeb asked.

"It's not flying any sails, but it's moving toward us at a fast clip! I think it has oars, Captain!"

"Oars? You can't use oars alone this far out at sea!" Zeb exclaimed.

"It's definitely oars, Captain, and it's moving fast—really fast!" the lookout called down.

"Every man to the arms room! Boy, I hope you're well rested, because whoever that is I'll bet my right leg they're the ones who set that storm on us."

Sailors ran and armed themselves, readied the heavy weapons, and took shelter behind the deck railing. The new ship flew neither sails nor flag to identify its origins, but at least fifty oars sprouted from the sides of it like the legs of a centipede. The deck sported no heavy weapons like their ballista or catapult, but at least a dozen large creatures crowded against the rails.

They were massively muscled, humanoid in appearance in that they stood on two legs and had a pair of arms, but their heads looked like that of a bull. Huge horns topped the bovine heads and fur covered their bodies. In their enormous hands, they wielded massive battle-axes and swords that would take a normal man two hands to swing.

"Minotaurs! Damn those creatures!" Zeb cursed.

"Do you think they sent the storm?" Azerick asked.

"Minotaurs despise magic, so I doubt it. They must be working with someone; as if they weren't dangerous enough!"

"Are they pirates then?"

"Worse, they're slavers. They'll board our ship, take as many of us alive as they can, and use us or sell us as slaves. Look alive, lad, because here they come."

With their sails torn to shreds, the *Sea Star* was a sitting duck. Azerick heard the twanging and the loud crack of the sailors firing their crossbows and scorpions followed by the heavy whoosh and thwack of the catapult. The minotaurs aboard the oncoming ship simply ducked behind the rail and raised large wood and iron shields over their heads. Stones and quarrels rained down with little effect. The brute strength of the massive, shaggy creatures was enough to ward off even the fist-sized stones flung from the catapult. Such an impact would have broken the arm of a normal man.

The minotaur ship continued to bear down on the *Sea Star* with such velocity that Azerick was sure it was going to ram them. Azerick let loose a stream of arcane missiles at the oncoming ship as it came near. One minotaur took all three bolts in the chest, but it appeared largely unfazed by the magical assault other than brandishing a sneer of contempt.

Azerick sent a blast of lightning into several of the beasts crowding the bow of the enemy ship. The bolt hurled two of the huge creatures back while the one that had taken the three magical bolts let out a bellow and crumpled to the deck, his sharp-toothed sneer wiped permanently from his muzzle.

The swift oncoming ship reversed its oars and back-paddled, swinging its stern around to slam into the side of the *Sea Star*. The shaggy minotaurs threw grapnels over to lock the two ships together while men and beasts met at the rails to do battle. The crew of the *Sea Star* outnumbered the fighters so far on the deck of the minotaur ship, but those odds would turn if the rowers swarmed up from below.

Even at the current odds, the brute strength of the minotaurs was more than a match for the human sailors, and Azerick knew at once that it would be up to him to swing the battle in their favor again. He leapt onto the rail and straddled his legs across both ships, letting loose another blast of lightning along the length of the battling, bull-like creatures. His bolt caught half a dozen of the beasts in its path and started a fire near the stern of the minotaur ship.

Azerick thought if he could set the minotaur ship aflame, the men could chop at the ropes and separate the two vessels lashed together and give them a chance. He was readying a fire burst when he spotted a horrific figure stroll onto the deck of the minotaur ship. It was nearly seven feet tall but extremely thin. Its head was a grey bulbous mass which looked like a large brain with no skull beneath the clammy skin to protect it. Its thin, lipless mouth was set between large mandibles that sprouted out of its cheeks.

Azerick completed his spell and sent a jet of flame toward the abomination. The smell of burning hair filled his nose as the fur of a minotaur in the path of the blast was singed across its huge torso. The sickly, grey-skinned creature screeched out in either rage or pain. The repulsive monster focused its gaze on the sorcerer, and Azerick felt a massive weight press in on his head as if someone were reaching into his skull and squeezing his brain. He blocked out the tremendous pain and focused on his next spell. He knew if he could not get a lightning bolt off on the monster, all would be lost.

Concentrating through the pain, he brought his hand up before him, ready to loose the powerful bolt just as a massive, invisible wave of force swept over him. The spell he was about to release dissipated in his mind as he lost his hold on the Source. He felt himself falling and saw the wooden planks rushing up to meet him. As he thudded boneless onto the deck, he was able to remain conscious just long enough to see every sailor in his field of view collapse in a similar fashion. The hideous abomination had them all. What it would do with them now, he did not want to contemplate. His eyes closed and blackness took him deep into the embrace of unconsciousness.

CHAPTER 2

Azerick woke to the gentle rocking of the ship and discovered that someone had bound his hands behind his back and tied a gag in his mouth. As his eyes cleared, he also realized he was no longer on the *Sea Star*. Through the throbbing haze and pain in his head, he could make out the trussed-up forms of Captain Zeb, Balor, and several other men from his ship. He shook his head from side to side in an effort to clear the fogginess and immediately regretted the action as a wave of pain and nausea washed over him. It was only with the greatest effort of will that he kept from vomiting, which would have been an extremely unpleasant and dangerous action considering the gag in his mouth.

He turned his head with far more care and scanned the deck of the ship. As he had surmised, he was on the deck of the minotaur ship. He saw several of the beasts wrapping up the one he had killed in the battle. Once they had securely enfolded the beast in sailcloth, three of his comrades stood to each side and carried their dead burden to the rail. The six bearers then heaved the body over it and into the sea.

Having executed their duty, the funeral contingent walked toward the prone sorcerer. For a moment, Azerick was sure he was going to receive a brutal beating in retribution for killing their comrade, but the creatures simply walked past without so much as a look down at him. He wondered where the hideous creature was that had so easily immobilized him and the entire crew. The silent appearance of the vile monster answered his unspoken question a moment later.

The monster was even more hideous close up. It's bulbous head looked like a giant tick atop a pair of scrawny shoulders. Large, yellowed mandibles protruded from its lipless mouth and looked at the immobilized humans as a spider would a fly caught in its web. Azerick was about to learn how apt an analogy that was.

The long, gossamer-robed creature glided up to one of the humans. Without a single word being uttered, at least not one Azerick's ears could detect, one of the hulking minotaurs lifted a sailor up to a standing position and held him firmly before the monstrous creature.

It lowered its head toward the rigid form of the sailor almost like a lover soliciting a kiss. With a sickening suddenness, the mandibles of the hideous monster clamped down and pierced the doomed sailor's head at the temples. A stomach-turning sucking sound filled Azerick's ears as the horrible thing made large gulping motions, sucking out the man's brain.

After several minutes, the mandibles were withdrawn, and Azerick could see they had holes at the inside curve much like a viper's fangs, but instead of injecting poison, these were used to suck out the brain of the victim. Azerick was near to vomiting as the minotaur carried the dead sailor to the rail of the ship and casually tossed his lifeless body overboard as if it were no more than common rubbish. He could only stare dumbly at the creature he would forever refer to as a brain sucker. Captain Zeb was not so easily shocked into silence.

"You sick bastard! Let me loose and I'll cut that ugly glob of fish guts you call a head right off your skinny shoulders!"

Azerick was sure one of the minotaurs would thrash the furious captain for hurling such insults at the ostensible leader of this ship and crew. However, his ignorance of the situation was made apparent once again when the brain sucker simply turned toward the cursing human. Captain Zeb let out a piercing shriek of agony for several long seconds before falling silent, twitching slightly with a thin rivulet of blood running from his nose and ears.

Azerick was shocked into motion at the sight of his captain being laid low and rolled over until he brought himself up next to Zeb's quivering form. Now one of the minotaurs moved and landed several solid blows from its large feet, bruising ribs and forcing Azerick away from the injured captain. Injured, not dead, Azerick had time to see before he was batted away.

Fortunately, the brain sucker seemed to have satiated whatever hunger it had, or perhaps it simply wanted to put on a demonstration, because it did not return to the deck for several hours. The prisoners were not offered any food or water in that time, which was probably a good thing considering it did not appear they would be untied to relieve themselves anyhow.

For hours the hulking minotaurs rowed, propelling the boat at an impressive speed: a speed Azerick had to assume was magically assisted. Even given the obvious strength of the shaggy creatures, he did not think they could move a boat this fast without the help of some other unseen force. Were his head not still spinning he could probably sense if there was magic in use.

The deck rail was not a solid wall like the ones on the ships he was accustomed to seeing in Southport. It was more like the handrail of a flight of stairs or banister in which wooden columns spaced about a foot apart supported a solid rail. Azerick was able to see the ocean ahead and a few points off to one side. He spotted what first appeared to be several grey specks in the distance. Those resolved themselves into a natural stone formation thrusting up out of the sea at least thirty feet above the rolling swells. The ship adjusted course slightly in order to pass between two of the granite pillars, which could not have left more than a few feet of space to each side of the ship for it to thread its way through.

Azerick briefly wondered why they were maneuvering between the columns of stone instead of simply going around them. The brain sucker returned to the deck of the ship and glided up to the forward deck as they neared the structure. The grotesque creature lifted its hands over its bulbous head, and Azerick felt a sudden wave of magical energy wash over him as the air between the pillars erupted into a shimmering screen of glimmering light.

Azerick saw the runes carved deep into the stone pillars just as the ship passed through the soap bubble-like screen. He once again felt his stomach become queasy as the world twisted and distorted around him. For several seconds, he felt as if the ship had dropped out from under him and he was falling in uncontrolled flight, his body plummeting into an eternal void.

Reality snapped back into focus, but when he opened his eyes, it was not a land he had ever before seen or even imagined. The sky around him was gloomy like an overcast day early in the morning just before the sun has peeked over the rim of the world. He looked beyond the rail and tried to make sense of the environment around him. All he could see was a dark grey, but whether it was the grey of clouds or distant stone, he could not tell. The scene felt gloomy, lifeless, and colorless.

Ahead of the ship, he could see land of the same cold greyness growing closer as the ship rowed on toward an equally colorless city of tall towers and strangely shaped buildings. Minotaurs, brain suckers, humans, a few dwarves, and beings he had never seen before wandered the streets and worked the docks.

Several minotaurs threw ropes out to the awaiting beings as the ship pulled up parallel to a large dock and secured the mooring lines. Minions extended a gangplank, and the brain sucker lightly strode across, stepped onto the dock, and was greeted by another of its kin. They seemed to confer even though Azerick did not hear a single word and could not see either of the creatures' mouths moving.

More workers rolled several carts with large cages on them out onto the dock. Minotaurs carried Azerick and the other sailors across the gangplank and carelessly tossed them inside the cages. Azerick was glad to find he was sharing a cage with Captain Zeb and that his friend was conscious once again, although he still looked pale and a little bewildered.

"You all right, son?" Zeb asked in a slightly slurred voice.

Azerick nodded, unable to speak due to the gag still in his mouth. The wagons lurched forward, pulled by humans wearing tattered clothes and blank, lifeless faces.

"Here, let me see if I can get that gag out of your gob," Zeb offered and used his teeth to pull the tightly wound strip of rough cloth off Azerick's mouth and down around his neck. Azerick spit out the filthy wad of cloth stuffed into his mouth then tried to work up some saliva to moisten his arid mouth and throat before trying to speak.

"Thanks," he was finally able to gasp out. "Are you all right?"

"My head feels like it was used as a catapult stone and my stomach sent along for the ride, but I'll live, for a while at least," the captain replied darkly, looking around at his surroundings. "Think you can cast any spells to get us out of here?"

"Not with my hands tied. I can't form the weave to craft the spell."

"I'll take it that means no, since I really don't know what you're talking about."

Azerick was heartened to see that Zeb was able to make a small joke and knew he would be all right as long as no one decided to change their condition. A shudder coursed through Azerick's body as the image of the desiccated sailor passed through his mind.

The carts rumbled down the cobbled streets, pulled by the human slaves and guided by the brain sucker from the ship. The workers, likely slaves from their appearance and bearing, led the captives through streets thronged with the glazed, lifeless-eyed denizens of this strange place. The prisoners were rolled into a large, squat building. Barred cells holding prisoners of various races lined the walls of the interior. The ship's crew was unloaded and herded into the vacant cages.

They placed Azerick in a lone cell, separated from the rest of the crew, with empty cells to each side, likely to prevent anyone from freeing his hands. A minotaur gestured for the sailors to turn around and put their hands between the bars. When the humans complied, the creature cut their bonds, freeing their hands. No one afforded the spellcaster such freedom. His hands remained tightly secured behind his back.

"What do you think they are going to do with us?" Balor asked, nervously massaging his wrists.

"I don't know. But I'm sure that whatever it is, it doesn't bode well for us," Zeb answered despondently. "It's my guess we'll be sold into slavery. It looks like this whole city is run by slaves."

"Why don't the slaves revolt? one of the sailors asked. "There must be a hundred times more of them than those ugly monsters from what I saw."

"They obviously have some way of controlling them. There are spells capable of dominating a person's mind or compelling their actions. It is possible they employ some such method, although I know of none that would work on a scale like this," Azerick supplied. "Even if that's not the case, look how easily one of those things overwhelmed our entire crew. The body count of an open revolt would be horrendous."

Several human slaves walked in bearing trays with bowls of some sort of grey gruel. They passed them through the narrow bars to the prisoners, but they did not supply any utensils, so the sailors were forced to eat with their hands. Azerick could not even manage that small dignity with his hands secured. He was forced to kneel down and lap up the bland, odorless, tasteless porridge like a dog. He decided to suffer this ignominy to maintain his strength. So long as he drew breath, he had a chance to escape his captors and free his friends.

As the hours passed, Azerick tried to sleep, but there was no possible way to get comfortable enough to enjoy any decent rest. He sat with his back to the wall, and exhaustion eventually pulled him into a restless slumber. He awoke several times during what he assumed was the night, his cramping muscles never allowing him to sleep for long. He awoke once again to the sound of someone sliding a wooden bowl under his door. Again, he had to eat like an animal from the bowl. Spots of the gruel stuck to his face as he licked the bowl clean. He swore someone would pay for this insult one day.

The bowls were taken away a short time later, and the prisoners were left alone, with the exception of a single hulking minotaur wielding a stout cudgel sitting on a wooden stool near the door. He would occasionally get up to walk the corridor of cells, smacking the bars of the prisoners' cages with the club when someone came too close to them. Other than the guard's occasional rounds, they were left to themselves.

A few hours after their morning meal, the guard snapped to attention as the outside door opened. Several guards of human and minotaur races walked in ahead of two brain suckers. The spider-faced creatures seemed to be conversing in a language that sounded like someone trying to chisel stone with a dead fish.

"Master Xornan, I am sure you will be most impressed with my newest acquisitions. I have one in particular I know will please you immensely," the slave master promised silkily, if the word could apply to such a liquid and grotesque language.

"We shall see, Slave Master Valinquar. You have disappointed me before," the psyling lord reminded the subordinate.

"It was bad luck the ogre was slain in the Games, Lord Xornan. Surely your lordship cannot hold me responsible for simple ill fortune?"

"I hold you responsible for selling me a creature too stupid to move out of the way of a charging Aragonax. You managed to find a creature that even its own dull-witted kind would label as feeble-minded."

"I assure you, this one is different. He is a human wizard, and very smart as humans go."

"A wizard you say? It has been some time since I fielded a magic user in the Games."

Azerick watched the exchange, feigning indifference as he sat in his cell with his back pressed against the far wall. He could make out nothing of the squishy conversation of the two psylings, but the way they looked at him gave him the impression that he was the topic of their conversation.

Come stand before me, human, so I may look at you, a voice commanded.

Azerick heard the command but could not see from where it came. It took him a moment to realize he did not hear the order with his ears but inside his head.

Yes, human, I need not sully my mouthpieces with your crude language to communicate with your primitive mind. Now, come closer. Do not force me to command you. Your cooperation is requested, not required.

Azerick decided that such trifling defiance at this point was futile and did as the monster bade him. He would play the part of the subjugated, obedient, and compliant slave. He would let these disgusting creatures think they dominated him until they let down their guard. Then he would make them pay.

You may play whatever games you like, human. They will avail you nothing. I know everything you think as you think it. Resistance is less than futile; it will no longer even be possible once I bond you. So, you are a sorcerer not a wizard. How delightful. I do not think Valinquar realizes what a catch he has. Yes, you will serve me well, human.

"He is not much to look at, is he, Valinquar?" Xornan said to the slave master, noting the dried gruel stuck to Azerick's face.

"He is merely soiled from his captivity. Do not judge him so hastily. Had I not subdued him, he would have wreaked great havoc on my hunters and ship. It was he who killed one of my minotaurs and seriously injured several others with a most powerful display of wizardry."

"These other humans," Xornan asked, gesturing to the sailors in the other cells, "they were with him? They are his shipmates?"

"Yes, Lord Xornan, I was fortunate enough to capture most of the ship intact. A very fine haul: all quite healthy and strong."

"Very well, I will take the lot if we can agree on the price."

The slave merchant wrung his long-fingered hands together in anticipation of a profitable sale. The two bulbous-headed psylings haggled for several minutes in their indecipherable language before striking a deal. Minotaur and human guards secured the sailors' hands once again and marched them out, prodding them along with their weapons into wheeled cages similar to the ones used by the slave master.

Several of the newly acquired slaves were ordered to pull the carts under threat of force, encouraged by a minotaur wielding a scourge. The indentured sailors had no recourse except to grumble their objections and pull the carts. Even those protestations were subdued lest they invoke the minotaur's displeasure and feel the scourge upon their backs.

Xornan climbed into a silk-curtained palanquin hefted by four minotaurs as the humans were pulled through cobbled streets past various single and two-story buildings. Azerick spied a huge circular stone structure dominating the center of the large bustling city, obviously an arena of some sort.

The plain, blocky buildings began to dwindle, replaced by larger, mauve-colored structures of much more elaborate design. These fanciful buildings were unique, not just for the color of the stone but also for the fact they appeared to grow from the rock itself and were not constructed of cut blocks. The walls blended smoothly with the ground, lacking any sign of seams or mortar. Eventually, these manor houses gave way to even taller towers. These too were of the same hue as the manor houses and looked to have sprouted from the very earth like the stalks of some massive amethyst plant or tree.

The carts halted inside the courtyard beneath a huge tower reaching over a hundred feet in height. The slaves were hustled out of their cages and made to stand before their new master.

Take them to the cells below. I will indoctrinate them later. Leave this one to me, Xornan projected to his guards.

The guards escorted the humans through a door at the base of the tower, down several twisting flights of stairs, and into the cells below. Azerick was left standing before the repulsive Xornan.

You belong to me now, sorcerer, fully and completely. I am your master in all things. You will obey my commands, you will not attempt to flee, and you will not resist. The lives of your comrades hinge on your compliance. Do you understand?

Azerick simply nodded in affirmation of the instructions as a human guard cut the bindings restraining his hands. Azerick rubbed his chafed wrists and looked at the creature who thought to be his master.

"I understand," Azerick began, "that you completely underestimate my compassion for others."

Azerick lashed out with a swift right cross, catching the psyling in the side of his soft, swollen cranium. The sorcerer felt the satisfying smack of yielding flesh crush deeply beneath his fist. He did not bother to stand around to witness the results of his attack, but Azerick was certain the blow caused significant if not lethal harm. He spun around on the follow-through of his swing and sprinted past the surprised guard who had cut his bonds.

He knew that if he showed compassion for his friends the psyling would forever use them against him. Azerick would return to aid his shipmates if he could, but his best chance of helping them right now was by escaping.

Azerick dashed through the open gate of the tower courtyard and into the streets beyond. He could hear the cries of pursuit behind him as he ran blindly down the stone-cobbled avenues. He ducked down a long, narrow alleyway created by two closely built buildings and spun around when he reached the far end.

The sorcerer paused for only a moment as several human and minotaur guards ran toward him in pursuit. Azerick unleashed a powerful bolt of lightning into the close confines of the alley with devastating effect. The narrow walls afforded no place for the hunters to avoid the strike and they took the full brunt of the blast.

Humans toppled lifelessly to the ground and minotaurs bellowed out in pain and rage and were momentarily stunned by the jolt. Azerick made another quick incantation, let loose a barrage of magical strikes into the lead brute, and dropped him to the cobbled street. He then turned and fled into the crowded streets of the city with the guards chasing him once again and bellowing for support.

He shinnied up the pole of an awning support, clambered onto the roof of a single-story building, and darted across the rooftop. The guards followed on the streets below as Azerick leapt up, grabbed the edge of a taller building, and pulled himself onto the roof. Several guards found a stairway attached to the side of one of the buildings and now pursued him across the rooftops while a dozen more chased after him by way of the streets.

The young sorcerer saw a gap ahead of him where another alley intersected the building he was on and the next one. He lowered his head and pumped his legs with steady determination. Azerick planted his foot on the edge of the rooftop and leapt the span between the two buildings, achieving the far roof with only inches to spare.

He then spun around and gestured, shaping the weave while speaking out the words of magic to another spell before fleeing once again. The guards pursuing him across the rooftops hit the slick area the sorcerer had conjured up and slid over the edge of the building, many of them suffering significant injuries from the twenty-foot plunge onto the unyielding stone street.

Azerick's rooftop ended at the corner of a large, open plaza. He hung by his hands from the ledge and dropped into the bed of a wagon below, tumbled when he hit, and rolled out onto his feet. He sprinted across the plaza to another alleyway, chased by the shouts and curses of the guards pursuing him along the streets.

Azerick ran out onto the street and scanned the area for his next route of escape. A shout from his left stripped away most of his options as another guard contingent bore down on him. He turned right and sprinted down the street as the lesser denizens of the city scuttled out of his way.

A stabbing pain bit into the back of his left thigh, ending his headlong flight. The sorcerer tumbled to the street and rolled hard across the cobblestones. He glanced down and saw the fletching of a crossbow bolt protruding from the back of his leg. He realized his chances of escape were gone now, but he would sell his life dearly before being made into the psyling's plaything. He brought his hands up and was beginning to prepare another spell when the twang of the crossbows sounded again.

One bolt caught him high in the right shoulder and another low in the gut. Pain filled him like none he had ever experienced before or could have even imagined. His legs failed him, and he dropped to the cold, hard street, barely able to catch his breath. Azerick knew such a wound was lethal without swift aid from a cleric. He squeezed his eyes closed against the intense pain as tears ran down his face, as much from the pain as from anger at being beaten before he could kill the one who enslaved him.

He forced himself to his feet with a great effort of will, determined to inflict one last blow upon his attackers before death took him into its remorseless embrace. Azerick concentrated on his spell, opened his eyes to find a target, and found himself staring into the hideous face of Lord Xornan.

Azerick discovered that he was still standing in the courtyard of the lofty tower. No wounds were evident anywhere on his body. Only a phantom pain of the memory of the attack remained. Azerick stared in uncomprehending disbelief into what he presumed to be the smiling face of the psyling.

Excellent. I am now much more familiar with your abilities, determination, and cleverness. Now you see, sorcerer, your mind belongs to me. I know what you think as you think it. You cannot escape. You cannot oppose me. You will not attempt to flee. You will follow my orders exactly.

The command hit him like a physical force, and his knees buckled. Azerick recognized the mental attack as being similar to what magic users call a geas spell. The target of such a spell is forced to obey the commands of the spellcaster.

I can make you experience anything I want, and you will never know it from reality. Every memory you possess is mine to use as I wish.

Azerick found himself in the room of the inn he shared with his mother after Duke Ulric's men had forced them out of their home. He stood in the corner unable to move as he watched the large drunken sailor grab his mother and force her onto the bed. Deep down, Azerick knew it was not real, that he had not been in the room to see the attack, but the psyling manipulated his memory as he saw fit.

Azerick's screams went unheard as the man's knife flashed in the light of the burning oil lamp. He felt the blood splash across his face as it jetted from his mother's severed throat. He closed his eyes against the horrific scene. Even knowing it could not possibly be real did nothing to dampen the fear and anguish the memory produced. When he opened his eyes, he once again stood face to face with the psyling. His throat was raw from screaming and he sobbed uncontrollably.

You see, I need never resort to anything as crude as a whip to punish you. I have far more effective methods of control. Do you understand now?

"Why don't you just completely control my mind if you are so powerful? Why leave me any form of resistance or free will?" Azerick asked as he regained control of himself.

I could dominate your mind completely, have no doubt, but I prefer my subjects to be able to think and act on their own, within reason, of course. This is why I have placed those basic commands in your mind. An arena fighter in particular needs to be able to think clearly and independently in order to function at their most effective level. You also have a strong mind and spirit. It amuses me to watch your futile efforts at resistance and thoughts of vengeance.

Azerick was furious at his impotence to resist the psyling's power and the creature's usage of his most private and painful memories. He would fight him somehow. Somehow, someday, he would make this creature pay, he vowed.

Yes, that's it. Use that anger, your hatred of me, in the Games. Unleash your awful power against your foes for me.

"What do I call you? I don't think you would care for me to just call you brain sucker," Azerick asked, trying to ignore the psyling's taunting.

I am known as Lord Xornan, but you will call me master.

"The hell I will, you brain-sucking, overgrown leech!"

At least that is what his mind said. What actually came out was a simple "yes, master." His inability even to curse this creature made him even more furious.

You are most certainly proving to be amusing. Come, slave, I will show you to your quarters. You are fortunate. As my favorite pet, I will afford you luxuries far beyond that of your friends. Keep in mind my previous warning about their continued good health. You claim not to care overmuch about them, but your mind betrays you. It would be a shame if your disobedience were to blame for my selecting one of them for my feeding, particularly the ones named Zeb or Balor.

The sorcerer shuddered at the image of Xornan feeding on his friends' brains. The psyling lord led him inside the vast tower. Opulent furniture with soft velvet-upholstered chairs, couches, and sedans furnished the main floor along with massive glittering chandeliers, gold inlaid murals, and marble floors. A grand circular staircase wound along the wall up to the upper levels of the tower.

Azerick followed his master up several flights of stairs before stopping in front of a sturdy wooden door. Xornan opened the portal with a gesture and stepped through. The room was simple, resembling Magus Allister's chambers at the Academy but with nicer furniture, carpets, and stonework.

This is your room. You may explore the tower, although some areas are blocked to your passage. I will show you to the library shortly where you will find many tomes to assist you in your magical studies.

The evil creature's generosity surprised Azerick, but Xornan corrected his assumption.

My aid in your studies is purely selfish, I assure you. I plan to make a great deal of money, and more importantly earn prestige, from your battles in the Games. It is the only purpose you serve. Should you do well and please me, I may find further use for you. Should you cause me to lose gold or status, your usefulness and my hospitality ends. Come.

The psyling led him up another flight of stairs. The next landing opened directly into a spacious room lined with shelves filled with books.

You are free to use the library, take books to your room, or visit the kitchens should you require sustenance, but you are not to leave the tower for any reason unless under my direction. I have a laboratory located in the sublevels of my tower that I will show you. You are free to use the equipment therein so long as it does not interfere with your combat studies. I will leave you now to see to my other duties and arrange your first bout. Ensure that you are prepared.

The young sorcerer stared at the vast library in awe. The promise of unlimited study surprised and pleased him, but no matter the gilding, a cage was still a cage, and he would be no one's willing slave. He scanned the rows of shelves and found the books arranged by subject. Most were in foreign languages and completely incomprehensible to him, but many were written in his own tongue as well as the language of magic.

Azerick picked several books largely at random and sat down to read by the light of the numerous glowing globes sprouting from the walls of the library and the rest of the tower like luminous pimples. He would study, he would learn, and he would one day destroy the creature who dared to be his master.

Days passed before he saw Zeb and several former members of his crew. He spied them performing mundane tasks in and around the tower grounds. Some were given the duties of guards, others, gardeners and servants. He found Zeb overseeing a group of his men scrubbing and polishing the marble floor of the grand entrance level.

"Zeb, it is good to see you are well," Azerick shouted as he descended the stairwell.

"Aye, well enough, but not so well as yourself from the looks of it," his friend and former captain replied, looking at his finely woven clothing.

"Yeah, I guess so. That brain sucker has me pampered like a prized hunting hound."

"Don't feel no shame in that, lad. We brook no resentment for ya. From the sounds of it, you'll be earning whatever luxuries are afforded ya. Heard you'll be fighting in some big arena. You watch yourself and keep safe. The only fair fight is the one you win. You remember that now. No matter who or what you face, it's his life or yours."

"I'll remember, Zeb. How are you and the men being treated?"

"Fine enough. We're fed, not abused, and given a bunk, but that creature's messed with our minds. He's sapped any desire to flee or fight him. I don't really understand it myself. Ain't seen one of my men since we came here neither. I don't like to think about what may have happened to him," Zeb said with a shudder.

Azerick knew as well as Zeb what likely happened, but Lord Xornan glided into the room without a sound, instantly cutting off all conversation.

Attend me, my pet. We have much to discuss.

Azerick followed his master up the stairs and into a well-furnished study. The room had a fire blazing in a massive stone hearth. The flames flickered and danced like ballerinas within the stone stage with no sign of wood or any other fuel source. Paintings and statues adorned the walls, and plush high-backed chairs sat back from the radiating fire.

I have arranged your first bout. If you are successful, you will fight many more. I have the utmost confidence in this first match. He is a simple brute and has no chance against your magic. It is only an exhibition to introduce you to the Games and gain a ranking. After that, much gold and prestige will be wagered. As you progress, the stakes, as well as the difficulty of your foes, will increase. I expect nothing less than your attaining the rank of Grand Champion.

"I imagine the only alternative is death. When is my first bout?"

In one week. You will face a simple ogre. None know of your magic-wielding abilities as of yet, so even on this match I stand to make a decent profit. And you are correct; you will win or you will die. It is quite simple.

Lord Xornan dismissed Azerick with a simple, wordless thought. He returned to the library to pass the time studying. He found a book on ogres and read everything he could about the creature he would be facing. There was very little in it that afforded him any useful knowledge. Ogres were big, rather stupid, foul-tempered, and extremely strong. They had skin as strong as leather armor; beyond that, they possessed no real additional strengths or weaknesses than any normal living creature.

There was little Azerick could accomplish in a week, so he whiled away the time with his usual studies and focused on tactics. On the day of the event, Xornan sent a human slave to fetch him. The man led him out to the courtyard where his master awaited him in his palanquin.

You will ride with me as a pet of special privilege.

Azerick climbed into the large palanquin, which was hoisted up onto the shoulders of four minotaurs as soon as he entered the silk-covered transport. If the load strained the huge creatures in the least, they did not show it. They carried the loaded litter as easily as a man might shoulder a sack of flour.

Azerick was uncomfortable sitting in such close proximity to the foul creature. Its puckering mouth, clacking mandibles, and distinctive smell unnerved and repulsed him. Once the palanquin was underway, Xornan provided his pet with his instructions.

Once we arrive at the Games, I will occupy my seat in the arena as befits a lord and owner of a gladiator. One of my minions will lead you below where you will remain until it is your turn to do battle. Once it is your turn to fight, you will be led up a ramp to the surface to stand within the fighting grounds. You will face off against your opponent at a distance of a few score of yards. This will give you an enormous advantage to strike first.

Once the Master of Games announces you, he will drop a cloth as a signal to commence the battle. This is a standard match. No magical or special items are permitted. Only the innate abilities of the fighters and their choice of weapons and armor are allowed. Once you are taken beneath the arena, I want you to select a weapon from the ones provided. This will give the appearance that you are just a typical fighter brought in for slaughter. This will provide me with several last-minute bets and increased wagering odds. You will not fail me.

"No, master, I won't," Azerick replied, nearly choking on the word.

It was not a question.

CHAPTER 3

The palanquin smoothly navigated the streets of the city, borne on the shoulders of the four minotaurs who kept perfect step with one another, creating a smoother ride than any coach could achieve. It took about twenty minutes to reach the enormous stadium. The denizens of the city already congested the streets as they converged on the arena for the big event.

Master and slave came to a halt outside one of the arena entrances. A stout dwarf ran up as Azerick and Xornan climbed out of their transport. The dwarf wore a woven blue linen shirt, a broad leather belt secured with a large silver buckle, brown leather pants, and hobnailed boots. His black hair swung in a ponytail and his thick beard flapped in the wind as he ran up.

"Master Xornan!" The dwarf came to a halt and bobbed several bows. "Your seat is waiting and everything is prepared for your entrant. Um, is this it?" he asked looking questioningly at the young sorcerer.

Yes, Braunlen, do take good care of him.

Xornan glided off with two of his litter bearers toward a private entrance reserved for the elite to avoid the press of the common rabble. The remaining two minotaurs stayed with the ornate palanquin as Braunlen took Azerick by the elbow and pulled him toward another gate.

"The name's Braunlen. What's yours?"

"Azerick," the sorcerer replied shortly, not in the mood to supply any more small talk than necessary.

"I'm Lord Xornan's personal arena assistant. I provide weapons, armor, training, and management for all his fighters. I gotta tell you,

you're the smallest one he's ever brought me. That tells me you're either really good, or he doesn't like you and wants to watch you die."

The dwarf led Azerick through a gate and down a long ramp that ran beneath the arena.

"He made it very clear that I am not to die. I'll do my best not to disappoint him."

"That's good. You definitely don't want to disappoint him. I've seen him do some pretty horrible things to those who do," Braunlen said, shaking his big bearded head.

As the pair hustled down the ramp, Azerick could hear the sounds of metal striking metal, the grunts and curses of men, and a general cacophony of noise up ahead. They emerged into a large chamber with several thick stone columns supporting the ceiling. The walls and ceiling were all made of stone and, like the towers and grand manors, appeared to be grown instead of chiseled and set. Racks of weapons, wooden and straw training dummies, armed men, and other creatures filled the area.

Several antechambers and passageways branched off from the main area. Inside these, Azerick spotted more weapon racks, training aids, and gladiators with whom he assumed were their trainers. From somewhere in the distance, the smell of animal pens wafted through the already pervasive and nearly overpowering smell of sweat and blood.

"Hey, Braunlen, bringing us some fresh meat, are you?" a voice called out as the dwarf led Azerick past several antechambers before pulling him into one that was unoccupied.

"This is my area. This is where you'll train and equip yourself. Go ahead and pick out your weapon of choice. If you don't see what you need, let me know and I'll try to get it. If I can't get it before your fight today I'll have it before the next one, guaranteed. Assuming ya live to see another battle, that is," Braunlen explained as Azerick examined several racks of weapons.

"All those weapons are top quality. I inspect and maintain every one of them myself," he assured his young charge.

Azerick selected a light spear he could swing like a staff and use to stab should it prove necessary. He hefted it and brought it through a few attack routines. The steel head threw the balance off a bit and forced him to adjust his grip to compensate, but it would suffice.

"Spear, eh? Not a popular weapon for skilled fighters, but if that's what you want I won't gainsay you," the dwarf rumbled. "You'll be fighting Gragnoc. He's an ogre of typical brute size and strength. He's only had a few fights, but he's dominated them pretty thoroughly. He's as dumb as any ogre, but he's a crafty fighter, so don't underestimate him. Do you want to take some practice or spar a bit to warm up? You have at least an hour before your bout."

"No, I would like to just meditate and relax for a while if it is all the same to you," Azerick answered coolly.

"Suit yourself. You know best how to prepare yourself. I'll be around if you need me." Braunlen ducked out of the alcove to busy himself with some task or other.

Azerick found a simple wooden chair, sat down against the wall, and closed his eyes. He thought about his parents, how they died, how he had killed the man in the alley, the men in the guild house, his mother's murderer, Travis, and the pirates. Was he nothing more than an instrument of death? Could he do nothing other than steal and kill?

If that was the case, then so be it. He had not asked to lose his parents, his home, or live in the streets. He had not asked to be attacked by that man or Travis. He would kill this ogre, he would kill everyone and everything he faced in the arena, and then he would kill Xornan, his so-called master.

"Hey, kid, you the one fightin' Gragnoc?" a voice shouted and interrupted his reverie.

He opened his eyes and stared into the face of what must have been an orc. On closer inspection, he revised his assessment to him being a half-orc. The man was big, muscular, and covered in chain mail. Small tusks sprouted up from his large jaw and curled over his upper lip causing him to slur his words a bit.

"That is what they tell me," Azerick replied calmly without getting up.

The half-orc laughed uproariously at the prospect. "You think you can take him on? He's gonna swat you with that big club of his like a fly, kid."

Azerick felt his temper rising. He was nearly eighteen now, and he had not felt like a kid in a long time. The streets turn a boy into a man quickly—at least the ones who survive.

"I'll kill him," Azerick replied, staring the pig-faced gladiator in his beady, bloodshot eyes.

"With what? That little pig sticker?" the half-orc taunted as he looked at Azerick's short spear.

"No, an ogre sticker. I'll bring a pig sticker when it's time to kill you."

The half-orc reached for his sword and bellowed his outrage. Before he could draw the heavy blade more than halfway from its scabbard, a strong, calloused hand grabbed his wrist and shoved the blade back down.

"No fighting outside the arena, Rangor! You know the rules," Braunlen warned the furious gladiator.

Rangor spit on the floor before spinning around and stomping off, letting his rage out on a wooden practice dummy.

"You sure make friends fast. Watch yourself. He may not be as big as Gragnoc, but he's three times more skilled. He's an experienced gladiator and a crowd favorite. Treat him with respect. You can't judge every gladiator by their size or look."

"That's good advice. I'm sure a lot of people are going to learn that lesson before long," Azerick said darkly.

Braunlen looked at his new gladiator for a moment, wondering if maybe he was guilty of underestimating this young man. The boy did not look like much, but he sat there as cool as could be. Sure, he handled the spear well enough, but not nearly so well to see it carry him through many bouts. It would take far more than that just to survive this first one.

Braunlen did not care for this match-up. Gragnoc was already blooded in the Games. This lad was a first-timer. He should have been matched with another new human fighter or animal before being paired against a beast like the ogre. Nevertheless, he was not in charge of such things and could only shake his head and wish the young man luck.

A runner appeared and informed Braunlen that his gladiator was up in a few minutes. "Up and at 'em, kid. It's time. What kind of armor do you want?"

Azerick got to his feet and grabbed his spear. "No armor."

The dwarf could only stand and blink for several seconds as he saw the finality of the answer in Azerick's eyes. "No armor. I'm surprised even though I know I probably shouldn't be. Are you sure you're not going out there intending to die? Lord Xornan will skin us both if you make him look like a fool."

"I'm better without it."

"All right then, let's go."

Braunlen led him up a different ramp from the one he came down. A metal portcullis stood open at the top leading directly onto the dirt floor of the stadium. The dwarf paused at the top of the ramp and turned to Azerick.

"All right, boy, just stay nimble and don't get hit. I wish I could offer you better advice, but I really don't know what to tell you until I've seen you fight. I normally have at least a few weeks to feel out my new fighters and train them, but Lord Xornan wanted you kept a secret. I hope it was worth it—for your sake."

The dwarf gave him a small shove, and Azerick walked several paces into the arena. As he ambled forward, he discreetly cast his armor spell. The arena was packed, and the crowd cheered and jeered loudly as Azerick stepped into the open area. He watched as a huge ogre strode arrogantly into the pit from the opposite side. The crowd roared their approval as the favored gladiator entered the fighting grounds. The huge beast raised his hands and turned to the adulations of the crowd. There were about fifty yards of dirt floor separating the two combatants as they squared off.

The ogre wore a steel breastplate, greaves, a helmet, and vambraces and wielded a huge wooden club banded at the end with iron. The creature stood nine feet tall, and his huge muscle-corded arms whipped the tree limb-sized club around as if it were no more than a willow switch.

Azerick scanned the crowds seated in the arena. The majority of the spectators were psylings, but he identified several other races in attendance as well. Abyssal elf wizards and priests, human wizards and priests, and other planar travelers Azerick could not identify by name sat eagerly awaiting the spectacle. A psyling wearing brilliant silk robes stood in a boxed area with plush seats centered on the arena floor. His voice rang out loudly in an introduction of the current fighters.

Azerick was surprised that the presenter spoke in his own language before he picked up the telltale signs of magic lacing the announcement. He first dismissed it as no more than the magical amplification of his voice, but he realized that it also translated the psyling's words into the language best understood by the listener. He briefly wondered if it was a spell that allowed the mass translation or a magical construction built into the box seat. Then he thought it best to stop speculating on this trivial matter and focus on not being killed in the next few minutes.

After a thunderous round of applause and cheering, the announcer raised a red silk handkerchief, and then let it drop. As soon as the fabric left his fingers and began its fluttering descent to the arena floor, the huge ogre burst into a charge at the same moment Azerick began his incantation. The speed of the brute astounded the young sorcerer. The ogre had covered over half the distance between them by the time he released his spell.

For a split second, the ear-splitting thunderclap of Azerick's lightning bolt drowned out the roaring of the spectators. The magical attack caught the rushing ogre completely by surprise. He made no attempt to dodge the electrical bolt as it caught him fully in the chest, blackening a large scorch mark on his shiny steel breastplate.

What surprised Azerick even more than Gragnoc's speed was the fact his lightning bolt did nothing more than elicit a roar of pain and anger from the monster. The ogre did not even falter in his charge. He barreled toward Azerick and raised his club, hurling it at the spellcaster before the sorcerer could launch another powerful magic attack. Azerick dodged nimbly to the side, interrupting his hasty attempt to blast Gragnoc a second time.

Azerick tumbled to his left and rolled several times, hoping to put a little space between him and his opponent. He leapt to his feet already prepared to cast another spell, but the ogre decided to forego his club and kill the puny human with his massive bare hands. Azerick tried unsuccessfully to back away when Gragnoc wrapped one hand around his thigh and the other around his throat, lifting him several feet above the ground.

The crowd screamed its approval as the ogre tried to choke the life out of the human. Azerick gasped out the words to a short incantation and grabbed the thick wrist of the hand cutting off the supply of air and blood to his brain. A powerful jolt of electricity shot through his hands and into Gragnoc's arm. The shock stunned the ogre and forced him to release his opponent. Azerick kicked against the metal breastplate of the ogre at the same time as he felt its grip slacken, and launched himself several feet away from the stumbling monster.

Azerick jumped to his feet and waved his hands through another complex casting. Gragnoc spun around and retrieved his fallen club. The ogre turned back to face his opponent and charged, intent on bashing the life from this puny human who dared to cause him so much pain. Azerick completed his spell as Gragnoc began his short charge, and half a dozen illusory duplicates appeared around him. His phantom images were identical in appearance and movement to himself, and his opponent had no way of identifying which images were real and which were illusion.

Gragnoc decided it did not matter. He would simply crush them all. The enraged ogre stormed forward and swung his massive club into the nearest image. His weapon passed harmlessly through the sorcerer and caused the image to disappear. The club swung again in a powerful backhand blow that destroyed a second of his illusions. The four remaining images extended their hands, and another powerful lightning bolt leapt from the group of identical sorcerers. However, only one bolt was real, and it struck the ogre in his broad chest again and threw him hard onto his back.

Azerick was not about to allow the deadly ogre to regain the offensive. He sent a trio of magical strikes to slam into Gragnoc as he tried to climb to his feet. The bolts staggered the ogre, but they did not put him back on the ground. Gragnoc stumbled toward the sorcerer, his arms outstretched, roaring in fury. Azerick sprinted away and picked his spear up off the ground.

The damage he had inflicted on the ogre was noticeably taking its toll. Gragnoc's moves were clumsy and sluggish now as his muscles protested the abuse the sorcerer had inflicted. Azerick thrust his spear as the ogre turned and charged him. The steel point pierced the charred and weakened breastplate and stabbed deep into the monster's chest. Gragnoc's momentum carried him forward and he fell on Azerick with all of his considerable weight. Azerick felt the air forced from his lungs and heard several ribs crack when the ogre crushed him beneath an avalanche of flesh and bone. He pushed against the dead weight with all his might and barely managed to roll the creature off him enough to crawl out.

The crowd roared its adulations as Azerick stood upon shaking legs. Booted feet stomped and hands clapped at his unexpected victory. Azerick wrapped his arm across his chest, holding his injured ribs as he shuffled back toward the gate and the waving Braunlen.

"Great victory, kid!" The dwarf congratulated him as he passed under the portal and started walking down the ramp. "I tell ya, I never thought you would beat that big ogre, but I'm glad you proved me wrong."

Azerick did not speak as he returned to the equipment room with Braunlen.

"Are you feeling okay? Any major injuries?" he asked. "Gragnoc fell on you pretty hard from the looks of it."

"I'm all right. It's just a few bruised ribs, is all, and I'm pretty tired."

"You'll be fine. Lord Xornan has a girl who's pretty good at patching folks up. If it is an emergency, there are healers here who will put you back together if your owner is willing to pay for it. C'mon, Lord Xornan is probably waiting for you outside, and you don't want to keep him waiting."

Azerick let the dwarf guide him up the ramp and back outside to the waiting palanquin. All four minotaurs were standing by the poles, so Azerick figured Xornan was already waiting inside the curtained conveyance. Sure enough, as the two approached, the curtain slid open to reveal the hideous visage of the psyling.

Is my pet well, trainer Braunlen?

"Aye, master, he's a bit bruised up, but he'll be fine," the dwarf replied.

Excellent. Join me, my pet, and we shall return home.

Azerick stepped into the palanquin, and the minotaur slaves hefted the carrying poles onto their broad shoulders and swiftly made their way through the city.

You have pleased me immensely, my pet. I have made quite a good profit from your victory. You are now an established arena gladiator and, as such, you will provide an opportunity for even greater profits as your rankings increase. Moreover, as your ranking increases, so does my prestige; and that is what is truly important. Your next match will not be for another month. Ensure that you do everything in your power to train and study. As you progress in rank, your opponents will become more challenging. Do not disappoint me.

Azerick felt no need to respond to the creature. He knew his words were unimportant to the psyling lord, and Xornan probably knew what he was going to say before he said it anyhow. He kept his thoughts blank as the palanquin wound its way through the streets and back to Xornan's tower. The minotaurs gently lowered the box to the ground in front of the tower steps.

I will send someone to tend to your bruises. You may await her in your room.

Azerick wanted to go down to the laboratory and brew some of his own healing draught, but he followed the psyling's command and returned to his room. Several minutes later, there came a soft knocking on his chamber door. Azerick opened the door, and in the entrance stood a somewhat attractive, brown-haired girl of about seventeen. She had a heart-shaped face and a full figure, but she came well short of being plump.

"Lord Xornan bade me to see to your wounds, sir," she informed him shyly.

"Um, sure, come on in," Azerick invited as he overcame his surprise. "My name is Azerick, by the way."

"I'm Delinda. I tend Lord Xornan's garden and treat any injuries or illnesses his servants may acquire. Where were you injured?"

"My ribs got bruised a bit. It is nothing serious."

"Take off your shirt, please, and I will take a look at them."

Azerick blushed as he disrobed. He could see several dark splotches marking his chest. Delinda gently probed along his chest and around the visible injuries with her slender fingers.

"Breath in deeply and let it out," she ordered. "Just as I thought. You have a few cracked ribs and some deep bruising. Fortunately, none seem to be broken or displaced." She reached into a leather satchel and pulled out a mortar and pestle and several pouches of herbs. "Please hand me that water pitcher over there."

He retrieved the water as she ground several herbs in the small stone bowl. She then poured in some water and soaked a long linen strip in the bowl. When she finished, Delinda wrapped the poultice snugly around his chest, covering his bruised ribs.

"This will help heal the bruises and take away some of the pain."

Azerick enjoyed the soft touch of her hands and the kindness in her eyes. He found that his heart was beating faster and his stomach fluttered. She smelled of rose petals and the herbs with which she worked. He felt the stirrings of emotions he had never experienced before, and it made him strangely uncomfortable, but also warm and pleasant.

"I was going to go down to the lab and brew up a few healing potions. Would you like to come? I could show you how if you want," he offered.

Delinda's eyes widened slightly and her breath caught in her throat. "I don't know if I am allowed to go down there. The master never gave me permission."

"I have permission, and I am sure he would not mind since you are learning something that will help you perform one of your duties better."

"I suppose I could do that then, as long as you are with me."

"Great, let's go." He donned a clean shirt before leading her down the stairs to the laboratory.

Azerick winced from the pain caused by his rush down the stairs, but he did not lose the smile gracing his face. They came to the sturdy wooden door sealing off the underground chamber. It opened at his touch, and he ushered Delinda through the doorway and closed it behind him. Several of the glowing globes provided ample light that glinted off the numerous glass and copper tubes and vessels. A large bookshelf held rows of jars filled with dried ingredients, strange liquids, and preserved body parts.

"You know how to use all of this?" Delinda asked as she looked at the complex equipment.

"Most of it. I brewed a draught to help speed healing once with my own equipment. Before I came here that is."

"It looks quite complicated. Do you think I can really learn to use it?"

"I'm sure you can, and I'll teach you. It can come in very handy. There are stronger healing potions to heal even severe wounds almost instantly, but they take a lot of distilling and concentrating. I have never made one before, but I have always wanted to. We can try one of those another time if you want."

"I would like that very much."

Azerick's heart leapt in his throat at the way she looked up at him with her soft brown eyes.

"Ahem...okay, let's get started then. First, we need to make sure we have all of the necessary ingredients," he said and hurried over to the shelf containing numerous jars of reagents.

He told her everything they would need, and then set her to crushing and mixing the different plants. He then showed her how to work the oil burner and how much water to add to the flask before setting it over the fire to boil. Once the water came to a boil, he poured in the ground herbs and turned down the flame on the burner.

"Now we just wait and let it simmer for a few hours then drink it down. It tastes terrible, but it speeds up healing a lot."

"How fast does it work?"

"It will mend my cracked ribs in a few days, five at the most," he answered.

Delinda's face brightened. "That's incredible!"

"So how did you come to be here?"

Delinda morosely related her story to Azerick. "Some men rode into my village and killed many of our men. They captured a lot of the younger women and older children and put us into cages. They took us far from our village and put us on a boat. We floated several days downriver before reaching the ocean. After two days at sea, we came to an island and were unloaded at a slave market. The slave master purchased me and several others then sold us to Lord Xornan."

"How long have you been here?"

"Four years, I think. You start to lose track of time after a while. How did you come to be Lord Xornan's favored pet?"

"I am nobody's pet!" Azerick exclaimed more vehemently than he intended. "I'm sorry. I did not mean to shout like that."

"That's all right. I should not have called you a pet. That is all we are to him. All of us, we are nothing more than animals to him and his kind."

"I will change that one day. One day this pet is going to turn on his master and tear his throat out."

"No, you mustn't say that! You must not even think it! He will punish you terribly for any thought of dissidence."

"Don't worry. I don't think he will do anything unless I actually manage to act against him, which so far seems highly unlikely."

"So how did you come to be here?" she asked, clearly needing to change the subject.

"I was on a ship, a huge storm came up and blew us off course, and when it cleared we were attacked by a minotaur ship. I killed one of the minotaurs, but a psyling did something that rendered us unconscious. Then we were brought here and bought by Xornan."

Azerick then told her about his parents, Jon Locke, the Academy, and the death of Travis. He didn't know why he was telling her so much. He was accustomed to holding everything in and keeping others out, but as he talked to Delinda everything just poured out of him and it made him feel almost relieved to share so much.

She laughed a pleasant, light-hearted laugh at his tale of how he and the younger students beat Travis and his friends and the pranks they set on each other, but she became somber when he told her about his part in Travis' death. He left out the fire at the guild house, the man who attacked him in the alley, the innkeeper, and the details of how he killed his mother's murderer. Those things were too dark for him to share, and he feared it might make her afraid of him.

"That must have been terrible for you," she told him and laid a sympathetic hand on his arm. "You must not blame yourself. You did what you had to do. They gave you no choice. Much of your life sounds just like the arena, only an arena of a different sort."

He greatly appreciated her understanding. The last thing he wanted was for this young woman to think he was a monster. He turned off the oil burner to allow the potion to cool while they continued to talk about their lives. Delinda told him about the psyling city, at least what she knew of it, and Azerick told her all about Southport.

The potion was finally cool enough to drink and he downed the bitter concoction with a grimace.

"Well, that should do it. Would you like to learn how to make a real healing potion with me some time?"

"I would like that very much. Do you think I could practice making the fast-heal draught? It would be very useful."

"Of course. How about tomorrow? I can take an inventory of all the ingredients down here to see if I need anything else for the healing potion," he said, ecstatic at the thought of spending more time with her.

"I must tend the garden tomorrow, but perhaps when I finish?"

"That sounds fine."

As they stepped out of the stairwell and into the parlor, Lord Xornan stood in the center of the room with his hands tucked into his voluminous sleeves.

"Lord Xornan, Azerick was teaching me how to brew a potion to aid in the healing of wounds," Delinda explained nervously.

"I thought it would be prudent, given her duties, Master," Azerick added.

Of course, I knew this before you made the top of the stairs. Go about your duties, Delinda. Follow me, pet.

Azerick did as he was told and trailed Xornan up the winding stairs of the tower. He thought they were going to the library or perhaps his room for some sort of talk regarding his fight today. This notion was dispelled as they came to the floor where the library was located but continued ascending the stairs. Azerick had never been any higher in the tower than the library floor. The only rooms he knew of above the library were his master's chambers. What could be there that required his presence?

On this floor are my private chambers. You will not enter here. Our destination lies at the top of the tower, Lord Xornan informed his slave as they continued the winding, upward trek.

They reached the top of the stairs and stopped before a thick oaken door. The psyling placed his long, delicate hand against a silver plate mounted on the wall near the door. At his touch, the door opened inward without a sound.

Place your hand upon the plate.

Azerick pressed his hand firmly against the cold polished metal and, for a moment, felt a slight static-like prickling that quickly subsided.

You now have access to this room so that you may carry out the duties I shall prescribe.

Xornan glided into the chamber with Azerick in tow without further explanation. Azerick could not hold back a gasp as he looked about the room. The chamber appeared to be a vault of some kind in which a vast hoard of precious objects and knowledge was stored. Gleaming weapons, staves, wands, and unknown objects lay almost carelessly strewn throughout the room. Some of the objects were intentionally displayed on shelves or mounted on the walls while others lay in seemingly haphazard piles around the chamber.

Rolled up scrolls filled several cabinets whose shelves were divided into numerous small pigeonholes. Bookshelves lined with ancient tomes, some slowly disintegrating with age, lined the walls. Crystals, some as large as his own head, were lined up on a shelf sharing the same cabinet as stone and bone carvings. However, the thing that drew Azerick's eye was a large, circular stone arch atop a short set of marble steps. Carved runes gilded with a shining silver metal covered the entire structure. Perfectly cut gems adorned one section on the right-hand side of the arch. They were laid out in a veritable rainbow of three concentric rings with a palm-sized diamond set in the center.

Xornan's intrusive mind speech broke Azerick's enthrallment. *In this chamber resides my collection of lore and objects of power. This is my vault for storing the things I acquire during my travels. I travel to various worlds and planes by use of this archway. It creates a stable gateway to wherever I wish to go, but that is something with which you need not concern yourself. Your task is to research, catalog, and organize my acquisitions. You will not use or remove any object from this room nor attempt to activate the arch.*

This last statement was a magically reinforced command that hit him like a punch. Azerick staggered under the mentally intrusive assault, but he composed himself as the pressure on his brain subsided.

Azerick simply nodded in supplication as he regained his composure. It was not the first time the psyling had forced his compliance, but the experience always left him queasy and slightly disoriented.

Satisfied his slave would obey his orders to the letter, Xornan left Azerick alone to work on his task. Azerick slowly walked through the cluttered chamber, navigating his way past several objects, picking up a few here and there when they caught his eye for a closer examination. He walked over to one of the bookshelves packed from floor to ceiling with dust-covered books and selected one at random. He carried it over to an equally dust-covered table and carefully opened the leather-bound cover. The pages were yellowed and slightly brittle but perfectly readable as long as he handled it with care.

Azerick pulled out another book and flipped through a few of the pages before returning it to the shelf. He decided the first thing to do was to create some sort of organization for the various objects, books, and scrolls before even contemplating any kind of actual research. Several tomes were stacked on the floor while wooden chests held even more books, scrolls, and other items. He would definitely need more shelves. For now, he would make do with what he had.

The books on the floor were a travesty. He cleared several knick-knacks, that appeared to be little more than curiosities, off a shelf to make room for the books. Then he began browsing each book and listed its title, contents, and author in order to create a catalog and method of organization. It was extremely late by the time fatigue convinced him to call it a night. He had managed to catalog the contents of half a bookshelf by the time he retired for the evening and was moderately pleased with his achievement.

The next day, with Lord Xornan's permission, he had the materials for four more shelving units delivered to the vault room landing. Since he was the only one allowed in the room, he had to cart the lumber inside and construct the shelves himself. Azerick did not mind the manual labor. It actually felt good to work with his hands for once instead of simply burying his nose in a book. He made space against one wall where he stacked the boards that would eventually become bookshelves before diving back into cataloging the waiting books.

Every few hours, he took a break from reading and organizing the books and put one of the shelving units together. Once constructed, he went back to the books for a time and repeated the process. It only took two days before he had put together all four bookshelves. He had also completely organized and cataloged one entire cabinet of books.

He was midway through the cataloging of his second rack of books when Lord Xornan glided into the room with six humans and four minotaurs in tow.

I may be gone for several days. Inform anyone wishing an audience with me that I will see them upon my return. Handle any other business that comes up as you see fit in accordance with my previous guidance. Continue your work here, but be prepared for another bout in the Games when I return.

Without waiting for a reply, Lord Xornan strode onto the dais of the arch and touched several of the colorful crystals in sequence. After a short pause, the large diamond in the center glowed with a bright white radiance. The psyling brushed the illuminated gem with a finger, and the golden runes on the arch flared with light.

The inner area of the stone arch shimmered for a moment before resolving into inky blackness like the pupil of a giant eye. The psyling raised a hand, and a glowing orb sprang to life. It hovered just over the party's head and showed the cold grey stone of a cavern wall.

Azerick watched the small group walk several paces into the tunnel before the gate wavered once more and the mauve stone wall of the vault was once again the only thing visible beyond the arch.

Azerick spent most of his days and evenings locked inside the vault, but he endeavored to spend at least lunch with Delinda and occasionally dinner. He had to force himself, with her urging, to take the time to make good on his promise to show her how to brew the healing draught. He spent a couple of hours each day talking to her and teaching her to create the potions. Delinda was very bright and made a quick study. She was gifted in the use of plants and herbs and showed great promise as a master herbalist and healer.

He stood over her shoulder while she ground several dried leaves into a fine powder. The smell of lavender from her hair mixing with the crushed herbs in the mortar drove him to distraction. His mind began to drift from the task of creating potions to what it would be like to hold Delinda in his arms and feel her deft hands caress his skin.

"Are these ground up fine enough?" she asked, looking up at him over her shoulder.

It took all his resolve to keep from bending down and kissing her passionately right then as she smiled up at him.

"Uh, yeah that's fine," he breathed out heavily, unaware until that moment he had been holding his breath.

"So, what's next?"

He looked over to where a glass flask sat over a flame, its contents steadily boiling. "You mix the other three components you ground previously and drop them into the water."

Delinda dumped the contents of the mortar into a ceramic bowl, poured the crushed ingredients of three other bowls into the first one, and then mixed them thoroughly while Azerick turned down the flame under the flask so the water went from a rapid boil to a slow simmer. Once he declared the components properly blended, she carefully poured them into the flask.

"Now stir it with the glass rod until the powder dissolves as much as possible. You will have to keep stirring it every fifteen minutes for the next four hours."

She picked up the glass rod, inserted it into the neck of the flask, and swirled the contents until they were thoroughly mixed and mostly dissolved in the water. The flask's contents took on the color of a thick black tea.

"Now we wait. Just make sure you keep mixing it on schedule," he reminded her. He turned over an hourglass.

"So, what do you want to talk about while we wait?" She sat against the table with the heels of her palms pressed against the edge.

How about how bad I want to kiss you right now? "I don't know. What do you want to talk about?"

"Did you see Lord Xornan leave? Do you know where he went?"

"Yes, he used a magical gate at the top of the tower. I don't know where he went or what he was going to do though," he told her, glad to have a topic of conversation. "He took ten guards with him: six human, four minotaur. They had some big packs on their backs. The minotaurs and humans did, not Xornan, of course."

"He must be on one of his expeditions to add a new bauble to his collection. I have heard he travels to many places to add to his hoard of rare and magical items, but I have never been up there to see any of it myself. What do you do up there all day long?"

"He has me organizing everything right now. For things that are so important to him, he does not seem to take very good care of them."

"For him I think it is the getting more than the having. It is all about prestige. He likes to tell others about the rare and valuable things he has. His ability to lord it over them is more important to him than their actual use or worth. It is the same for his slaves too. We are only useful so long as we serve a purpose or benefit his reputation."

"I thought it was the gold he won from betting on me," Azerick said.

"Gold is not that important to him, though he will kill anyone who steals from him or cheats him. Your winning brings the prestige he covets. He will punish you severely if you lose. It's not because of the gold, but because your loss would appear to be a weakness. Any weakness you display he feels others presume to be a failure of his."

"I guess I better not lose then."

She scowled back at him. "No, you had best not. This is neither a joke nor a game of any kind. Most who lose in the arena do not survive. Even if your opponent allows you to live, you will be punished terribly afterwards. I would not like to see that at all."

"You need to stir your potion now," he told her and turned the timer back over. "So what would you like to do with your life some day?"

"What do you mean? I am a slave. I have no life nor hope for any other."

"You will not always be a slave. We will escape him one day. I cannot allow myself to believe this is all my life will ever come to. I have some unfinished tasks I will return to one day," Azerick told her with certainty.

"How will you get away? He binds us with something stronger than chains. We are secured by a lock that has no key and cannot be picked or forced open."

"I will kill him someday, and I will not waste half my life before I do. I will play his game for now, as I must, but one day my chance will come and I will take it."

"No, you cannot even think such a thing! He knows what we think, and if he so much as thinks you can hurt him, he will punish you or kill you. I have tried to defy his orders, but every time I try, my mind refuses to do anything except what he says."

"He knows I want to kill him. My defiance amuses him. I do not know how I will do it, but he will make a mistake, or I will figure something out. Time to stir your potion again."

Delinda turned back to the table and mixed the simmering potion once again then turned back toward Azerick. "I do not see how you can hope to oppose him when you are even afraid of me," she said with a mischievous grin.

"What do you mean? I'm not afraid of you."

"Then why don't you kiss me?"

Azerick's eyes went wide and his heart started pounding in his chest like a drum. "Um, what makes you think I want to kiss you?"

"I think you try very hard to hide your emotions and are usually successful, but in this instance, you have failed miserably. I don't need to have Lord Xornan's mind-reading ability to see something that obvious."

"What makes you think you can read me so well?"

"When you are helpless against those around you, you learn to read them so you know who you can trust and who to avoid. I have been a slave for a while now. It has not been an easy life," she said, trying to hide the pain behind her eyes.

"You mean Lord Xornan…" Azerick hesitantly asked.

Delinda followed his line of reasoning and gave a small laugh. "No, I do not think his likes are to the female persuasion."

"Oh, that's good. Oh by the gods, you don't think he—?"

This time she burst into uncontrollable laughter. "No, I do not think he has any interest in humans of any sort. I am sorry for what has happened to me, but I have never been kissed by anyone I actually wanted to kiss me. Please understand."

Azerick cut off her words by taking her into his arms and kissing her ardently for several long moments, moments he never wanted to end, except they both needed to breathe eventually.

"Well, perhaps you are not such a coward after all," she said playfully.

"I'm afraid I burned up most of my fear a long time ago. At least I thought I had until today. Now that that is taken care of, I cannot imagine what else there is left to be afraid of."

"You could die in the Games."

"Death does not frighten me. The only remorse I would have is that I could not be with you."

"You would not have to wait long. If you were to die, I am certain I would soon follow you to the afterlife," she promised as she looked deep into his eyes.

Azerick held her even closer and kissed her once again. They nearly ruined their potion when the timer ran out while they were preoccupied. Fortunately, Delinda remembered before it was too late and stirred the black liquid on time for the duration of its cooking cycle.

Once the potion was finished simmering, Azerick showed her how to strain it through several cloth filters of increasing fineness then instructed her to allow it to cure for seven days in a sealed and completely opaque bottle. Once it was stored away from any light source, they stumbled up the stairs in each other's arms and into Azerick's chambers.

CHAPTER 4

Azerick awoke early the next morning. A weight across his chest startled him, but he smiled when he realized it was just Delinda's arm. He was elated to find her next to him. He was afraid last night had just been a dream. If it was only a dream, he hoped it never ended. Delinda's eyes opened and she smiled back at him and held him tighter.

"Good morning," she greeted him warmly, smiled, and closed her eyes again.

"And a great night."

"Men," she sighed and dug her knuckles into his ribs. "Come on, get up. We both have work to do. Besides, I'm hungry."

"But it is cold out there and so warm in here," Azerick groaned as he tried half-heartedly to fend off her tickling.

"Get up, lazybones, before Lord Xornan comes back."

"He just left yesterday. I'm sure he won't be back this soon."

Delinda rolled out of bed. "Fine, stay in bed all day, but you can lie here by yourself," she told him as she slipped her dress on over her head.

"Fine, I'm coming."

He shivered as his bare feet touched the cold floor and stepped onto the thick rug next to the bed where his discarded clothes lay in a pile.

"I'm going to go brush my hair and wash up. I'll meet you in the kitchen." She kissed him once then bounced out of the room and went downstairs.

Azerick refreshed himself in the cold water of the washbasin sitting on a small table before dressing. He descended the stairs a few minutes later and made his way to the kitchen. Cook was already up, and the kitchen was invitingly warm. The smell of cinnamon-spiced oats, bacon, and fried eggs filled the air.

"Good morning, Cook. Has Delinda been in here this morning?" he asked the former ship's cook who now prepared the meals for Lord Xornan's household.

"No, Azerick, can't say as I've seen her since yesterday. What's got you grinning like a fox in a henhouse? Ah, I think I see," he said as Delinda walked into the kitchen and hugged Azerick's arm.

"Good morning, Cook. Do you mind if we help ourselves to a plate?" she asked in a chipper voice.

"Good morn to you, lass. Of course not, have at it."

Azerick and Delinda each filled a bowl with oatmeal while Cook fried a couple of eggs on the stove. He slid them onto plates, piled on several strips of bacon, and served the young couple with a flourishing bow. Azerick and his new love, first love actually, sat at a plain wooden table set against the far wall of the kitchen. Cook gave Azerick a wink then found something he had to do somewhere else.

"So what are you going to do today?" Azerick asked as he poured honey onto his oats then did the same for Delinda.

"Weed the garden as usual. The cold is making many of the plants lose their leaves, and Lord Xornan gets very angry if he sees them on the ground. I also need to tend the spices in the hothouse. Will you be going back to the vault?"

"I suppose I had better. I don't know how long Xornan expects me to take, but I had best show measurable progress, or he may find me something less enjoyable to do."

"I cannot imagine there are too many less enjoyable tasks than organizing a bunch of dusty books, scrolls, and trinkets," she said, wrinkling her nose.

"I actually enjoy it. Not the organizing so much, although it's not so bad, but I also get to research the artifacts and scrolls. Most of it can be rather dull, I will agree, but you can also find useful knowledge in some of those books and scrolls."

"I guess I would think differently if I were a powerful wizard. Let me know if you find anything that rakes the leaves or waters the plants."

"I'm a sorcerer, not a wizard, and I am not that powerful," Azerick corrected her.

"I'm afraid I don't know the difference. Enlighten me, oh-not-so-powerful sorcerer."

"An invisible energy exists that wizards and sorcerers tap into and shape to create their spells. They call it the Source. It is the source of all arcane magic. If you could see it, it would look like a river of liquid silver," he explained.

"If it is invisible, how do you know what it would look like if you could see it?"

"I saw it once when I first tapped into the Source as a sorcerer. It was kind of an accident. Another student at the school I was at said some things that got me really angry. I accidentally connected to the Source, drew too much power, and I passed out. I was very lucky I did not kill myself and everyone around me."

He paused for a moment and took a deep breath. "A wizard must follow very specific weaves to make a connection to the Source by shaping the energy with gestures and words of magic. Their spells are mostly predefined, sort of like keys to gain access to the Source. A sorcerer is said to have a natural connection with the Source. We can touch it and harness its power with weaves solely of our own creation. Once a wizard figures out a weave to connect with the Source and shape it into a spell, he can write it down for other wizards to copy and learn. But their spell is very specific, and the shape of the weave must be precise or it will unravel. That is why you always find wizards with their noses in their spell books. They have to get the spell exactly right and cast it the exact same way each time. It cannot vary in the slightest. Sorcerers must create their spells on their own through their own study. How we shape our spells is unique to each of us. We do not have to write it down and make sure we cast it the exact same way because we can make it work for us even if it is a little different each time. Since we cannot look at someone else's spell and learn it like wizards can, it takes longer to create new spells, but we can harness more power more efficiently since we have a natural connection to the Source."

She grasped his hand in hers. "What did the other student say to you to make you so angry? Did it have something to do with the pain you try to hide behind your eyes?"

Azerick looked away. "What do you mean?"

"I see it sometimes, when you think no one is looking. I feel it when you tense up for no reason, like you are trying so hard to hold something back."

Azerick took another deep breath and debated whether to tell her everything. Would she think he was a monster? A murderer? He warred with these thoughts for only a moment before deciding he would keep nothing from her. She had a right to know everything about him. He told her what Travis had said about his mother and what had happened to her. He told her about his father and his revenge on the thieves' guild and the man who killed his mother.

She had tears in her eyes as she got up from the table. For a brief moment, he was terrified she was going to run out the door, but she came around the table and held him tightly.

"I'm so sorry for you, for what you have gone through, and what you have lost. And now you are here, forced to serve this vile creature and risk your life fighting in the Games."

He held her to his chest and whispered into her ear. "It's all right. As long as I have you here, I am happy. I learn more every day, and every battle I fight I get stronger. One day, I will be strong enough to get us away from here, I promise. I will take you away, and we will be happy. We can put all this fighting and death behind us. For you, I will even let go of my mourning and forget about this vengeance in my heart."

"I love you, Azerick."

"And I love you, Delinda," he swore and kissed her passionately.

She finally pushed him gently away. "It is getting late, and we need to see to our tasks."

"I suppose you are right. I fear I may not be able to focus on my work with you occupying my mind."

"You better pay attention to your work and make sure Lord Xornan is pleased!" she commanded and thumped his chest smartly with her small fist.

"I'll do my best," he promised and kissed her once more before they parted and sought out their duties.

Azerick stepped into the main hall on his way back to the tower stairway. Zeb, and nearly the entire crew of the *Sea Star*, were enthusiastically polishing the marble and silver planters. They all looked up as Azerick entered the large chamber and Zeb shot him a thumbs up and a wink as he crossed the room.

He now realized where Cook had gone in such a hurry. The former sailors gave him a loud whoop and cheer as he mounted the stairs. Azerick's face burned with embarrassment, but his comrades' good cheer put a smile on his face nonetheless.

Azerick pressed his hand to the silver plate and entered the vault once more. He began skimming through the stacks of books, setting aside those dealing directly with magic and spell casting. These he would read in detail whenever he decided to take a break from sorting the others.

Azerick and Delinda were able to spend four more nights together before the master of the tower returned. Azerick was arranging the last of the books when the gate flared to life early one evening. An exhausted and disheveled-looking Lord Xornan, two humans, and a pair of beaten and battered minotaurs stepped from the barren world on the other side of the gate into the vault. The gateway snapped shut as soon as the last guard crossed through.

Here is another item for you to attend to, the psyling stated and thrust a black, rune-engraved staff into his hands.

Without another word, Lord Xornan and his guards exited the chamber and filed down the stairs. Azerick looked at the dark rod and threw it into the corner of the room. He could feel the malevolence of the awful power it contained, and he wanted nothing to do with it. That particular item would be the last one he studied—if he ever did.

He stayed in the vault late that night to avoid the master of the tower and toiled away at his duties. By the time he decided to quit for the night, or early morning, he had most of the books arranged in a logical order, indexed, and cross-referenced in a catalog he had created. The dozen or so books he had left would require further study to determine the subject matter and author. He retired to his room exhausted and alone. He already missed Delinda's warm body next to his. With a sigh of longing, he crawled into bed and fell asleep.

Azerick awoke all too early as the weak morning sunlight oozed through his narrow window. He was still tired. His night's sleep had been far too short, but he decided he had better rouse himself and get back to his work. Maybe he could find something out about what had happened to Lord Xornan and his guards. He hoped he would see Delinda before he went back to the vault.

Azerick stepped into the warm, fragrant kitchen a few minutes later and was overjoyed to see Delinda already sitting at the small table talking to Cook.

"Good morning, lad," Cook greeted him. "Let me get out of your way and prepare you a plate."

Cook got up, grabbed his plate, dropped it in the sink, and started fixing the young sorcerer some breakfast. Azerick walked over to the table, leaned down, and kissed Delinda good morning before taking a seat across from her.

Delinda looked into Azerick's eyes and found that they mirrored her own exhaustion. "It looks like your night was as late as mine."

"Yeah, I didn't want to bump into Lord Spider-Face, so I worked late. What about you?"

Delinda smiled at him. "You should not say such things, or even think them."

Azerick waved off her admonishment with a flick of his hand.

"I had to tend to Lord Xornan and his guards until just a few hours ago. I have to go check on him again soon. I was waiting here for you or else I would have already seen to him."

"What happened? He had ten guards when he left."

"I guess whoever owned the thing he wanted was reluctant to part with it. It happens sometimes," she answered with a shrug. "So what did he bring back that was so important?"

"A staff with a very evil feel to it. I do not like it. I hope I can avoid having to deal with it, at least for a while."

"Please be careful. I don't know much about magic, but I know some of it can be very dangerous."

"I will, love, I promise."

Cook set a plate of food in front of him and a hot cup of strong tea then he busied himself with the few dishes in the sink.

"I'll leave you to your breakfast. I need to go check on Lord Xornan before he starts calling for me. He does not handle pain well and can be quite difficult when he is convalescent." Delinda got up and kissed Azerick before leaving him to his meal.

Cook took advantage of the recently vacated chair and sat down with his cup of tea. "How are you holding up, Azerick?"

"I'm doing all right, I guess."

"From the looks of it you're doing a bit better than all right," Cook said with a glance at the door through which Delinda had exited and gave him a conspiratorial wink.

"Yeah, I guess I am. She is really great."

"She's a good catch. Best hold onto her, kid. I heard you are going to be fighting again soon."

"Yeah."

"You be careful out there, do you hear me? You got a lot of friends here, and none of us want to see you get hurt."

"I'm glad to hear it. I'll be careful, I always am."

Cook laughed. "You, careful? Hardly, son. We know you better than that!"

"I'll be fine."

"Now, that I'm more inclined to believe."

Azerick finished eating and went back to the vault. He started working on sorting the scrolls next. There were a lot of them, and he realized they were not going to be as easy to identify and catalog as the books had been. It took him two days to figure out a method of organization. Once he was able to determine that, the work went a bit faster. Several scrolls had been penned by wizards or sorcerers in ages past and contained significant power. These he separated as he did the spell books and other tomes directly relating to magic.

It was on the third day after the master's return that he came to see Azerick in the vault chamber. Azerick was studiously reading over several scrolls and noting their context and author, when available, and adding them into his indexing journal when the psyling glided through the door.

I see you have been making satisfactory progress in your task. I was afraid Delinda might have been an unfavorable distraction to you. I am pleased that is not the case. I value her work and would dislike being forced to dispose of her.

Azerick flushed at the mention of Delinda then his face burned with rage at the master's mention of disposing of her. "I am doing my work as best I can. Delinda is not interfering in the least."

It took all his effort not to shout and issue impudent threats at the vile creature for daring to hint that he would send her away or harm her.

Do not be overly concerned, my pet. She shall remain safe so long as you do as I instruct. You will be fighting in the Games in three days. I hope you are prepared.

"I am always prepared," Azerick replied with restrained hostility.

I know your magic is always at the ready. I am referring more to your state of mind. It is even more important for it to be prepared than the power you wield.

"I'm fine. I will be ready, and I will win. I always win, no matter what," Azerick said in a way that was as much assurance as it was a warning.

Good, see that you do.

Azerick was not sure if Lord Xornan had noticed his veiled threat or not. If he had, he gave no indication and left him alone to his studies. Azerick was working on a new spell but was unsure if he would have it mastered by the time he was required to fight his next bout. It did not matter. If this fight was anything like the last, he was unconcerned. As he had told his master, he would win. He always won one way or another.

He knew better than to ignore his master's warning about allowing his relationship to interfere with his duties. He forced himself to focus on becoming stronger, knowing that the only way he and Delinda could ever be happy and truly together was if he could free them from their bondage. They did manage to find some time together when they could, however brief those shared moments might have been.

Azerick was now more desperate than ever to escape Lord Xornan's control and take Delinda away with him. He just wished he knew how. He began to search through the books he had, but so far he had found nothing helpful in that regard. Even if he did find the answer, the compulsion the psyling had placed on him would most likely not allow him to use it.

Lord Xornan summoned Azerick to him early on the morning of his bout. He told his pet sorcerer not to go to the vault. Instead, he was to focus on the fight ahead. Azerick wished he had been able to complete the spell he had been working on, but it was not ready yet. It did not matter. He would win this bout, and his new spell would be ready long before his next fight.

Around what passed for noon in this seemingly sunless land, Lord Xornan conveyed him in his palanquin to the arena once again. Xornan was unusually silent during the short trip there. He invaded Azerick's mind only once with his mind speech to warn him once again that he had better be prepared and not to embarrass him. Azerick did not bother to reply and said nothing the entire way.

The dwarf, Braunlen, met them as soon as they arrived just as he had the last time. Braunlen took his charge in tow and led him down the ramp to the gladiator's area under the arena. Azerick hated the sounds and smells of the stadium as the dwarf took him to the same small training room he had the first time.

"So how are you, boy? Are you ready for your fight?" the stout creature asked.

"I'm fine. I just want to get this over with," Azerick replied, feeling surly at being forced to fight like an animal, to injure or kill someone he did not even know and who had done him no harm.

Braunlen seemed to read Azerick's thoughts. "It's a way of life, boy. You'll get used to it if you live long enough."

Whatever reply Azerick was going to make was cut off as the half-orc, Rangor, stood in the entrance to Braunlen's training room. "Good luck today, kid. You're going to need it. I hope you didn't use up all your luck fighting Gragnoc."

Braunlen spun around. "Get out of here, Rangor, and quit trying to distract my fighter!"

The half-orc curled his lip up at the dwarf's comment. "He's no fighter, and I hope he wins so I can prove it. That's right, kid, I really do wish you luck in this battle, because you'll be pitted against me next. Then I'll show you what a real warrior is." Rangor turned with a snort and stalked off.

Braunlen turned back to Azerick. "Ignore him and stay focused on this fight. You don't need no luck. You'll win because you're good, smart, and fast. You stay smart and fast and you'll go a long way, I promise you."

Azerick grabbed his spear and Braunlen took him into the arena. The shouts and cheering at his entrance were even more powerful this time, with less jeering. People remembered his last fight, and it sounded like many of them were betting on, or at least rooting for, his victory. He cast his armor spell while he waited for his opponent to arrive. He did not have to wait long. The crowd erupted in cheers again as a human entered the opposite gate.

The arena master gave the signal to begin, and the two fighters joined in combat. Azerick was more aware of what he would face this time. If the crowd had come for a good, drawn-out, bloody fight they were to be sorely disappointed.

The human was only slightly more experienced at the Games than Azerick was, and he had no idea how to battle a spellcaster. He tried hurling a dagger as he charged, but Azerick's magical ward easily deflected it. The sorcerer dropped the fighter to the ground with a lightning bolt.

The man writhed, struggling to catch his breath. The crowd seemed undecided whether to cheer or boo Azerick as he walked back to the gate completely unscathed.

You must finish him. He is undeserving of a continued life.

"Go to hell," Azerick responded aloud and kept stalking toward the exit.

Azerick felt the psyling invade his mind more deeply and found himself returning to the fallen fighter. There was not a bit of resistance or struggle he could apply, for the psyling's control was complete.

He watched his hand rise before him and could only look on as the lightning erupted from his fingertips to strike the man twice more. When he once again had control of himself, the man was little more than a charred husk waiting for the arena staff to clean it up.

Azerick refused to speak even to Braunlen. The dwarf seemed to understand and quit trying to engage the young sorcerer in conversation as he took him back to their master.

Your battle was rather disappointing, Lord Xornan commented as he entered the palanquin.

"I won. I thought that is what was important to you," Azerick responded flatly. "The crowd got to see me kill a man for no reason. That should be enough."

You also failed to obey me. Now you understand the level of my control. I can make you kill anyone I choose, even your mate. Think of that next time you choose to pit your will against mine.

"We fought, he's dead. The crowd got to see someone die. That's what matters, isn't it?"

There is more to the Games than simply one killing the other. The people expect a show and to be entertained. If they are not, they will lose interest in the fighter, and the fighter's owner loses prestige. I will not have you diminish my standing within the Games.

"I'll try to be more entertaining next time I kill someone for your pleasure," Azerick replied acerbically.

I am confident your next battle will be enough of a challenge to provide the proper amount of entertainment. In fact, I strongly recommend you do not get overconfident in your abilities.

"You refer to my fight with Rangor."

I see you are aware of your next match. Rangor is the most experienced fighter you will have faced thus far. He is strong, fast, and cunning. It would be of the greatest foolishness to underestimate him. He has nearly a dozen wins to his name and is highly favored even against you. This will also be an augmented match, meaning that certain magical trappings will be allowed. Expect Rangor's owner to outfit him with defenses to offset your magical power. The abilities of such items are limited and will be explained to each fighter's master in the days before the battle.

Azerick gave a noncommittal grunt in reply and said nothing else for the rest of the trip home. Delinda was waiting in the courtyard when the palanquin arrived carrying her master and her love. She stood to the side wringing a handkerchief in her hands until Lord Xornan went inside before rushing into Azerick's arms.

"I was so worried about you. Are you all right?" she cried and buried her face into his chest.

"I'm fine. I did not even get scratched."

Delinda clung to him as they went inside. "When do you have to fight again?"

"I'm not sure, but I do not think it will be long. They already have my next opponent selected."

"Who is it this time?"

"Some big-mouthed half-orc named Rangor."

"Oh no! I hear he is very good and very dangerous! Please be extra careful. I was so worried for you this time. It terrifies me to think about you fighting that killer."

"I will be fine, I promise you."

"You had better, or I will never forgive you," Delinda swore half-heartedly.

After they ate lunch, Azerick disengaged himself from Delinda to work on his new spell. He did not know how long he would have before his next bout, but he was sure it would come sooner than the last one had, and he needed to be certain he was ready. Azerick was under no illusion that Rangor would be an easy battle. He expected it to be the most challenging fight he has faced thus far.

He sat in the middle of the library, let his consciousness flow out of him, and touched the raging silver river representing the Source. He trailed an ethereal finger through the swirling liquid current and pulled a tendril of power into himself. Azerick chanted the words that helped him shape the thread of magic into a purposeful form.

A woven shape of energy that only he could see began to form in the air before him. He drew a finger connecting one node of the weave to another. He was so close now he could feel it! Just one more thread should complete the spell! He gently drew another tendril from his form's node and pulled it to the last one to stabilize the sigil. As he pulled the last strand into place, he felt it begin to unravel.

"Damn it!"

He forced himself to relax and began again. Azerick worked late into the night, so lost in concentration he forwent dinner. He was unable to get the entire spell form to come together, but he knew he would have it soon. Azerick soon realized the extent of his own exhaustion and went to bed so he could get an early start in the morning.

Delinda met him in the kitchen to break their fast, as was their new ritual, before attending to their separate duties. Azerick returned to the library and began concentrating as he had before. Once again, he relished the now familiar feeling of power the Source sent through his body. He had eaten a large breakfast so he could study through lunch without interruption. Delinda would not be happy with it, but she would forgive him. She understood how important his studies were to his success in the Games.

Late that afternoon, Azerick finally achieved success in creating his new spell. Moreover, it was a spell all his own, not based on any he had seen or read about in any book. He needed to test it. It was one thing to create the form, but he also needed to practice its practical application as well. He had to be able to cast any spell he knew until it became second nature, especially when stressed. He bounded down the stairs, excited at the prospect of seeing his creation brought to life.

He exited through a rear door and went to an unfrequented patch of ground behind the tower, which looked to have once been the larger part of a garden. Additions to the central structure and an expanded section of wall had closed it off from the rest of the outside grounds and made an excellent secluded area in which he could practice without fear of interruption.

The young sorcerer drew power from the Source, shaped it into the form he had just learned, and watched in exultation at the effect his spell wrought. He cast it twice more, changing its shape and size before he needed to rest. Pleased with the results, he had just enough time to meet Delinda for dinner.

The next morning, Azerick returned to his duties in the vault chamber, occasionally taking short breaks to practice his new spell form. After his evening meal with Delinda, he returned to his private practice area and cast his new spell as many times as he could before fatigue made it impossible. Azerick repeated this routine for nearly two weeks before Lord Xornan came to him while he toiled in the vault.

The rules for the tournament have been established and agreed to by both parties. Your battle is in three days. Are you prepared?

"I am as ready as I can be," Azerick replied.

I hope for your sake that you are. I have negotiated with many of the more prestigious members of our fair city regarding this battle. Your opponent's master in particular is a long-standing rival of mine. I would be extremely displeased to lose face to him.

"Not to mention my life."

The loss of your life should be the least of your worries. You have never seen me greatly displeased. Let me assure you that you do not wish to do so. I have a few items to give you that will aid you in your battle.

The psyling glided over to a shelf of items arranged in some semblance of order. He selected a ring and a set of wide bracelets off the shelf. The bracelets were made of finely wrought metal, were heavily rune inscribed, and enameled in deep burgundy.

The ring was made of a silver metal but shone with far greater brilliance than simple silver could attain regardless of the level of polishing. It gleamed so brightly it looked to be almost liquid, as if a small piece of the Source itself had been formed into a decorative piece of jewelry. Only the sigils covering the entire surface belied its solid form.

The bracelets will help protect you from physical harm just as I imagine your opponent shall be similarly protected from your magic. The silver ring is forged of the purest arcanum and will allow you to harness the power of the Source more efficiently. You will find your castings less fatiguing whilst you wear it. It would not do for you to run out of your only potent offensive capabilities before the outcome of the battle has been conclusively decided.

Lord Xornan handed the precious items over to Azerick. Azerick took them reverently in his hand and examined them more closely. He had never been in possession of such magical items before and was slightly in awe. His work in the vault put him in proximity to even more potent artifacts, but they were never his to use. He always felt detached, their presence simply academic and impersonal, but these would be his, for a time, to wear and use.

The bracelets opened by way of the most delicate and unobtrusive hinge he had ever seen. There were no clasps or buckles to secure them, but they snapped firmly shut when he closed them over his wrists. A slight tingle encompassed his body for a moment then faded almost entirely.

The arcanum ring he wore on his right hand. As soon as he threaded his finger through the band, he felt a surge of energy course through him, making him feel almost jittery. He let out a sigh as he reached out to touch the Source and felt the energy knife through the ether like the prow of a well-built cutter ship slicing through the water instead of feeling like a simple fishing boat rowing against the current.

Do my gifts meet with your approval? Good. Keep working on your duties here, but do not neglect your training. It is the more paramount of your responsibilities at this time. You fight in three days.

With that last unnecessary reminder, Xornan flowed out of the chamber and left his slave to his own devices. Azerick spent the next half hour examining his new acquisitions in minute detail. He went to his private practice ground and cast his newest spell. He was able to unleash its power half again as many times as he had previously, and for a sorcerer, that number was substantial.

He felt so giddy at his newfound power that he unleashed nearly every spell in his arsenal before retiring for the night and was so exhausted he even skipped dinner with Delinda. He would have to make it up to her tomorrow somehow.

That night, his dreams swirled in torrents of chaotic images. He stood in the arena atop a pile of bodies so high he could see over the walls. The city burned, and the dead littered the streets like refuse. Azerick smiled at the sight of dead psylings and minotaurs, but horror gripped his heart when he spied Braunlen, Zeb, Balor, and the rest of his crew lying amidst the destruction. His heart felt as though it had been torn in two when he found Delinda pinned beneath a collapsed wall, her perfect flesh blistered and blackened by fire.

"Azerick, you said you would protect me. You said you would take me away from here."

Azerick stepped over the wall as if he were a titan and knelt next to his love. "I tried, I swear I tried!"

"But you failed. You failed to protect me just like you always do."

"No!"

Azerick awoke in a cold sweat. His heart pounded and his stomach was heaving. He took a deep breath and tried to relax. He lay back down and stared at the ceiling, desperately trying to convince himself it was just a dream. While he was unable to reconcile the vision, he did manage to fall back asleep.

Delinda was cross with him the next morning for missing their usual dinner date, but he warmed up her frigid peevishness by showing her what Lord Xornan had bestowed on him to help him in his duel. He decided not to tell her about the dream. She would try to console him and convince him it was nothing, but neither of them would truly believe it, and there was no reason to make her worry.

"The bracers act like a set of armor, and the ring lets me harness the power of the Source much more efficiently," Azerick explained to

Delinda. "I think I can actually see how a wizard feels drawing from the Source by comparison. I feel rather bad for them. It must be like wading through waist-deep water whenever they try to cast a spell."

"You just worry about yourself and come back safe. Do that and I'll forgive you for standing me up last night."

Azerick flashed her a smile and leaned in for a quick kiss. "Deal."

Azerick used all his available time to practice until the day of his fight. Lord Xornan came for him early in the afternoon. His was to be the highlight contest of the day. Azerick noticed the psyling was particularly agitated on the ride to the arena. His silent restlessness served to impress the importance of this battle on his slave. To Azerick it was just another fight. It was no more than another animalistic performance put on for the pleasure of these vile creatures.

Braunlen was waiting in his usual spot for his fighter to arrive and ushered him down the ramp to the training room. Several of the gladiators surprised Azerick when they shouted encouragement to him. Azerick gave a curt nod or small wave of appreciation for their good luck wishes. Rangor's gravelly voice cut short this small amount of pleasure a moment later.

"How does it feel to know this is the day you are going to die, boy?"

"You had best check your calendar, orc. My day may be coming, but it is not today."

"We'll see, spellslinger, we'll see."

"Ignore him, kid," Braunlen told him. "He is more than a mite nervous, if you ask me."

"What makes you think that? He seems pretty confident to me."

"I've watched him for a while now. The look in his eyes and the way he moves is different. You got him rattled, no doubt about it, but don't think for a second this is going to be an easy fight. You stay on your toes and be ready for anything."

"I'll do my best."

"It had better be your best, or it will be your last. Now let's get you out there."

Since Azerick was the lower-ranking gladiator, he once again entered the arena first. He noticed the stadium was packed, and a large percentage of those in attendance were richly dressed psylings.

He spotted Lord Xornan sitting in a box seat next to another psyling. Both appeared stiff with an air of artificial or forced cordialness. Rangor entered the arena to a cacophony of applause and cheers rivaling his opponent's. If the ovation was greater than Azerick's, the difference was so minimal it went unnoticed.

Unlike his other bouts, an official of some kind stood in the exact center of the fighting grounds and called the two combatants to him. He or she, Azerick could not tell the difference, signaled to the fighters to take a position in chalked circles about fifty feet apart. The close range put Azerick at a severe disadvantage. He wondered if Xornan had agreed to this in order to drive up the stakes.

He cast his armor spell as he stepped into the circle. The crowd cheered once more as Rangor raised his arms and bellowed loudly. The half-orc wore a full suit of piecemeal plate armor and wielded a wickedly sharp broadsword in his right fist. Strapped on his left forearm was a heavily embossed round shield about two feet across. The shield was made of a silver metal nearly as reflective as the ring Azerick wore on his right hand.

Once the two combatants were in their circles, the official strode purposefully across the arena floor and took his place in one of the box seats through a cleverly hidden section of wall that swung out to allow him passage. As soon as he mounted the raised platform, he lifted a brightly colored swatch of silk and let it fall to the arena floor.

The moment it dropped, Rangor charged with incredible speed, covering more than half the distance before Azerick was able to release his lightning bolt. The big half-orc was ready for the attack and nimbly dodged to the side and rolled back to his feet without breaking stride.

Azerick gaped in astonishment at Rangor's speed and agility and was barely able to duck the lethal sword that whistled over his head. Before he could recover, Rangor slammed his shield into the young sorcerer's side, sending him flying and numbing his left arm so badly he nearly lost his grip on his spear. Only his new bracelets and shield spell saved him from a debilitating injury.

Azerick rolled to his feet and spouted a quick word of magic, and half a dozen duplicates of himself sprang into view. Rangor lunged at him with his inhuman swiftness and cleaved one of the duplicates in half. Instead of charging blindly at his antagonist, Rangor turned his shield toward Azerick and grinned as he looked into the reflection on its shiny surface. Azerick saw himself reflected in its surface but not his illusory images.

Rangor charged at the real Azerick who had to tumble once more to the side to avoid the blow. Fortunately, even though Rangor could see through Azerick's spell using his shield, the awkward sighting threw his aim off enough for the sorcerer to dodge the attack. However, fatigue would sap Azerick's strength if he had to keep running and dodging for the entire battle.

Azerick sprang to his feet and launched a stream of magic dagger-shaped missiles at his foe. He was once again shocked to see the huge half-orc raise his shield and block every one of the magical bolts.

Impossible! Azerick thought to himself as he watched his spell be blocked and Rangor stride toward him laughing triumphantly.

"I know your tricks, wizard! Now what are you going to do without your precious magic to protect you?"

"I guess I will just have to kill you the old-fashioned way," Azerick replied much more calmly than he felt.

The truth was that Azerick was very concerned for his chances in this battle just now. He had his new spell, but if he tried it prematurely, surprise would be lost and Rangor *would* know all his tricks.

Azerick jabbed at him with his spear quick as a striking snake, but a spear was a poor weapon against a well-trained swordsman. Rangor deflected the thrust with his shield and lashed out with his sword, destroying another of Azerick's illusionary copies.

The half-orc cursed the inconvenience and once again used his shield to sight in on his opponent's true position. Azerick spun the butt of his spear like a staff, striking at Rangor's large, tusked head. The half-orc interposed his shield between the shaft and his head and struck out with his sword once more. Azerick ducked under the blade and swung the other end of the spear around low, catching the half-orc on the side of his right knee.

Rangor was more angry at being struck than suffering any real injury and flew into a frenzy, lashing out wildly until none of Azerick's duplicates remained.

"There, now we can fight like real men. At least I can. I don't know what you call yourself, boy."

"At least I'm not a slab of pork just waiting to be sliced and smoked. Tell me, who was the pig and who was the human in your parents' bestial coupling?"

"I'm going to take my time killing you, boy, and I'll enjoy every second of it! I'm going to cut you up, make you bleed, make you—"

"Squeal like your mother?" Azerick finished for him.

Rangor charged forward with a roar of outrage and swung wildly. Azerick ducked and dodged the furious blows and waited for his opening. The sorcerer stooped under the enraged half-orc's wild swing and jabbed his spear deep into Rangor's side just above the hip where the top of the thigh plate and the bottom of his breastplate left a vulnerable opening in the armor.

Rangor slammed his shield into Azerick's chest and face, knocking him to the ground. The half-orc took a step back and surveyed the wound above his hip. Deciding it was not critical, he advanced with renewed caution as Azerick regained his feet. Blood streamed from the sorcerer's nose where the shield had smashed him in the face. He spit out a wad of blood and his teeth were painted red from where they had cut into the inside of his lip.

Azerick dropped back into a guard position as Rangor stalked in, sword swinging in short arcs before him. The sorcerer made three quick thrusts with his spear: two high and one low, but his opponent easily blocked them with his shield and slapped them away with his sword. The half-orc deflected his last thrust wide and darted in before Azerick could bring his spear back around to defend himself.

Rangor's broadsword took him low in the side, piercing all his defenses, and cutting deeply. Azerick retreated as swiftly as he could. He felt the warm blood running down his side, soaking his shirt and breeches. His hand came away covered in blood when he pressed it against the wound. Rangor relished toying with his opponent when he knew he had the upper hand in a barely contested battle.

Azerick rattled off the words to another spell, but the half-orc easily dodged to the side with his impossible swiftness and agility. Azerick realized he must possess a magical item that greatly enhanced his speed. With an evil grin of triumph, Rangor charged back in with a flurry of blows. It took all the skill Azerick possessed to ward off the blows, but the half-orc's strength and his rapid loss of blood were exhausting him.

Azerick spotted an opening, thrust with his spear, and tried to take his opponent low in the gut. Rangor's tusked smirk grew wider as he watched the foolish spellcaster take the bait and fall into his trap. He brought his shield down hard and fast, driving the point of Azerick's spear into the ground between his large, booted feet. He stomped his heavy boot down on the wooden shaft and stripped the weapon from his opponent's hands.

The big half-orc lunged forward at the same instant and plunged his blade deeply into the upper right of the sorcerer's chest. Azerick felt the steel slide between his ribs. He backpedaled furiously as blood filled his mouth from the wound which was far more serious than his split lip. He kept stumbling back, trying to put as much distance between him and the creature that had just inflicted the potentially mortal wound.

Azerick pressed his hand against the hole in his chest and felt the air escaping in a frothing gurgle every time he inhaled. Rangor basked in the cheering adulation, raising his sword and shield to the thundering applause. He pointed his sword at the retreating sorcerer as the crowd chanted for him to kill the human.

"Are you ready to die now, wizard?" Rangor taunted.

Azerick pressed the tip of his nose up with the finger of one hand to give him the impression of having a pig nose and flashed a crude gesture with the other. The half-orc's face burned with rage, and he charged forward with his magically enhanced speed. Azerick pulled together every bit of concentration he possessed and wove what could be the last spell of his life. Rangor brought his shield in front of him to block whatever spell was coming his way.

The half-orc was almost on top of him when Azerick released the pent-up energies within him. Long triangular stone spears four to five feet long erupted from the ground directly in front of the charging half-orc. The stone protrusions looked like long obelisks jutting out of the earth away from the caster and tapered to a point as sharp as any spear. They covered the ground between Azerick and his opponent in a field ten feet wide by ten feet deep.

Unable to react to the unexpected obstacle, Rangor impaled himself on several of the needle-sharp spears. The half-orc looked down at his wounds then back at Azerick in confusion. The crowd stared in silence at the stone spikes piercing the half-orc's chest, stomach, and legs.

Azerick staggered but managed to stand up straight and faced his vanquished foe. He raised his arm and unleashed a lightning bolt straight into Rangor's face, blasting him free of the spears holding him upright. The last of his energy spent, Azerick collapsed into a heap before he could hear the crowd erupt into a cacophony of cheers, clapping, and pounding feet.

General Baneford sat in his command tent, one amongst the three dozen erected in a small clearing miles from any road or town, and warmed himself next to the small iron field stove. General Baneford was a man of unquestioning loyalty, but lately he found he was developing some sincere doubts as to the efficiency and viability of his orders.

He and his men had been chasing rumors of the locations of Dundalor's armor for the past few years without pause. The last piece, a pair of glossy black and gold-filigreed greaves, they located in the midst of a hellish swamp rife with quicksand, sinkholes, mosquitoes, and highly territorial barbarians. He lost a dozen men and seven horses on that mission: five to the barbarians, five to bogs and sinkholes, and two to a basilisk that added two men and one of their mounts to a rather impressive collection of exceedingly lifelike statues of barbarians and other local fauna.

That was over a year ago, and Duke Ulric's missives had been expressing his growing impatience with his general's slow progress more and more. It was enough to drive a man to drink, and his professionalism and sense of duty rarely allowed him to drink while in the field. He was now in the midst of a dense forest following a rumor about some crazy hedge wizard who allegedly knew the location of one of the pieces he sought. He and his men had been scouring these cursed woods with their thick brambles that left burs in the horses' tails and manes for the past two months without a sign of another living soul, unless you counted the orc bands.

Do orcs have souls? The general guessed they must, but he hardly counted them amongst the useful races and disregarded their presence except for increasing the guard roster. So far, they had shown little interest in attacking the well-armed band under his control, for which he was grateful. He had had his fill with the barbarians' hit and run ambushes over the previous year. A tapping on the doorpost alerted him to someone outside his tent.

"Sir, a messenger has arrived from the duke," one of his guards informed him.

"Very well, send him in," General Baneford replied with a sigh that expressed his lack of desire to read whatever the duke had to say.

The tent flap was thrown open, but due to the double, light-disciplined vestibule, he saw only the inside of the outer flap of his tent when the messenger entered. The young rider gave the general a sharp salute before and after handing over the wax-sealed parchment. Out of habit, General Baneford studied the seal and impressed crest for signs of tampering or forgery before breaking the seal and reading the contents.

> *General,*
>
> *Due to the inordinate amount of time you seem to be taking to accomplish the simple acquisition duty I have assigned you, I have taken it upon myself to seek outside help in locating the items of interest to me. My sources, which are costing me a great deal of gold should you be interested in such a triviality, have informed me that one of the items I desperately seek is known to be in a monastery high in the Witch Crag Mountains in a hidden vale between two of the highest summits in the range.*
>
> *Since I do not wish to overtax your limited imagination, I have included a crude map that even you should be able to follow. Since I have done everything but*

have the item placed directly into your hands, I pray you will be able to accomplish this task before I am too old and feeble for it to do me any good. I have sent the courier with a stipend of seven hundred fifty gold crowns so you do not have the excuse of lacking the means to acquire provisions or information. Report to me immediately upon the success of your mission or do not report to me at all. I would consider any further failure as a possible act of subversion or treason.

Subversion, treason; how could Ulric even consider such a thing? He had earned his rank through years of loyal service and commendation during the border wars with Sumara and in largely ridding the kingdom of the cross-border, marauding nomads prowling the southern deserts like packs of jackals.

I need a drink, General Baneford said to himself and rummaged through a trunk where he eventually came up with a small bottle of liquor he often carried to help loosen the tongues of certain guests. He was breaking one of his own cardinal rules, but the way he felt right now more than justified it in his mind. *Treason! Preposterous! As if any other general could have held these men together and accomplished the tasks they had, and without a single desertion or mutiny!*

The general downed the small glass of amber liquid and felt his nerves calm almost immediately as the alcohol burned a path to his stomach and spread warmth throughout his innards. He looked at the still nearly full bottle and, with a shrug, poured himself a second glass. He would sit and relax for the rest of the day before moving out at first light for the frozen reaches of the Witch Crag Mountains.

General Baneford ordered one of his lieutenants to pass along the movement orders to the men. They would be prepared to ride before first light. They were good soldiers, loyal and professional. The general smiled to himself as he thought about the men who followed him, him, not that blowhard duke who did not know how to treat those who were worthy and loyal. He would never treat his men with such contempt. They had earned his respect and admiration just as he had earned theirs. They were good men, and they were his men.

He had never allowed such disrespectful thoughts to enter his head before. They almost bordered on treason. He knew in that instant something had changed inside him. It would definitely be a good time to retire when all this sordid business was finished. General Baneford chuckled at his own thoughts as he sipped at another three fingers of whiskey. A blowhard—that was all Ulric was. He was just a man with money and the power money could buy.

Yes, things were definitely changing. He wondered how much. He decided he would complete his mission; his own sense of duty required it, but this would be the last one. Whether Ulric got his crown or not, once he handed over the armor, he was retiring and that was that.

"What an ass," the general said aloud. He then laughed before stifling his mirth to a chuckle as he sipped at his drink.

CHAPTER 5

Azerick awoke with a gnawing in his stomach, a dry mouth, and a great deal of pain. He turned his head and saw Delinda, apparently asleep, in a chair near his bed. She must have sensed his return to consciousness because her eyes opened as he looked at her.

"Azerick, you're awake!" she cried and nearly fell out of her chair as she rushed to his side. She pressed her small hand against his cheek and kissed his lips. "I was so worried. I gave you the healing potion we made and it closed your wounds, but you had already lost so much blood by the time Lord Xornan brought you back."

Azerick touched the wound on his chest and winced in pain.

"The potion stopped the bleeding and closed the wound, but it didn't come close to completely healing it," she explained. "I've been giving you the fast-heal potion as best I could in the meantime, but it is such a horrible injury. I didn't know if it would be enough."

Azerick reached up and wiped away the tears streaming freely down her cheeks. Delinda took his hand in hers and squeezed it gently.

"I prepared another healing draught, but it will not be ready for at least two more days. You have been asleep for nearly four days now."

Azerick pointed to a pitcher on the small table next to his bed.

"Oh, of course. I'm so sorry." Delinda filled a cup halfway with water from the pitcher.

The water was a welcome relief to his parched throat even though he coughed a large amount of it back up onto his chest. He sipped at it more slowly as his beloved tilted it up to his lips.

"You must be hungry. Do you think you could eat something?"

"Yes, please, I'm starving," Azerick croaked out.

"Let me go to the kitchen. I'll be right back."

Delinda darted out the door and down the stairs. Azerick tried to recall the events of the battle just before he blacked out, as Delinda's footsteps echoed down the stairs. He remembered Rangor had stabbed him deeply in the chest. He recalled a lot of blood and the air bubbling out of the wound. After that, his memories became fuzzy. He was sure he had used his new spell, but he could not remember the exact results. It must have been successful, or he would certainly be dead right now. He was surprised he had even lived through his so-called victory.

Delinda returned a few minutes later with a bowl of honey-sweetened porridge. "Cook was glad to hear you are awake. I imagine Zeb and the others will learn of your recovery soon enough and will wish to give you their regards as well."

Azerick smiled and nodded his head in appreciation of his friends' concerns and well wishes. He gratefully took the bowl Delinda offered and took little bites of the warm, soft food. He had a hard time eating even the small bites, but he forced himself to work through it until the bowl was empty. He leaned back against the pillows once more, his hunger satiated. With the food weighing in his stomach, he felt his eyelids getting heavy and fell back to sleep while Delinda stroked his hair.

He had no idea how much time had passed when he next awoke, but his stomach told him it had been substantial. There was some soft bread and liver paste under a glass dome next to the water pitcher on his side table. Azerick managed to pour himself a cup of water and helped himself to the small repast. He felt stronger this time and was able to eat the simple fare without too much difficulty.

He looked up when he heard the door creak open as Delinda stepped into the room. "Oh, you're up again. I'm sorry I was not here when you woke. I had to attend to my duties."

"That's all right. I just woke up a few minutes ago."

"You seem much stronger today." She sat on the bed next to him. "I'll get you some warm food if you feel up to eating."

"Definitely," Azerick replied gratefully as his stomach let out a loud growl of agreement.

"I'll be right back then."

She returned a short while later with a large, steaming bowl of stew, thick with vegetables and diced chunks of meat. She also carried a silver flask Azerick recognized as the one containing the healing potion.

"I think this is ready now. You can take it after you finish eating."

Azerick felt his strength slowly returning as he devoured the bowl of stew. Once he wiped the bowl clean with a chunk of bread, Delinda unstoppered the flask and handed it to him. He took a short sniff of the pungent liquid before draining the contents in one long pull. He winced at the bitter taste and handed the empty flask back to Delinda. A warm heat spread through his body as the potion worked its way through his bloodstream. His wounds began to tingle and itch as it forced their rapid healing.

"How do you feel?"

"Like getting out of this bed."

"You should not push yourself too soon."

Azerick grinned at her mischievously. "Well, if I can't get out of bed maybe you should get in it," he teased. He grabbed her wrist and pulled her down to him.

"Azerick, stop it! You are recovering from nearly being killed," she chided him but did not resist as he kissed her.

"That's the difference between nearly getting killed and getting killed."

Delinda sprang from the bed with a gasp when the door swung open.

Leave us, girl, Lord Xornan commanded.

Delinda skirted past her master warily with one last fearful glance back at her love before she fled the room.

You have recovered significantly from your grievous wounds, I see.

Azerick did not respond to the statement.

That witless half-orc very nearly killed you. Do you realize how shameful it was for me to have your nearly lifeless carcass hauled out of the arena?

"I won. Isn't that the important thing? I win too easily, it shames you. I win with great difficulty and it shames you. The crowd surely enjoyed it, so what is it I have to do exactly to please you?" Azerick asked caustically.

You were nearly beaten. You, a powerful sorcerer, were nearly beaten by a savage creature swinging a sword. Your weakness in the bout reflects poorly upon me. Your weakness in the Games is construed as my own failure in properly training you. I will not be humiliated like that again!

Azerick was surprised at the psyling's vehemence. It was the first time he had ever heard his master raise his voice in anger. These thoughts were lost as his whole world began to swirl and dissipate like a morning mist blown away by a powerful wind.

Warped wooden planks replaced the mauve stone walls of Azerick's room. The smell of smoke filled his nose and burned his eyes, and he began coughing to clear his lungs of the contamination. He turned his head at the sound of a child crying. He saw Maggy in the corner holding little Beth in her arms as flames climbed up the tinder-dry walls. He looked around the room and saw Jon and the others sitting forlornly near the center of the room.

"Jon, we have to get out of here!" Azerick shouted.

"It won't do no good, boy. We're already dead."

Azerick ran across the room and slammed into the door with his shoulder, but it would not open. Something was blocking the door shut. His shirtsleeve caught fire and he slapped it out with his hand. He heard Beth wail louder and turned to see her dress had caught fire and was burning her small legs. Azerick ran over and tried to smother the flames, but they continued to spread and ignited his shirt.

"No!" he shouted as he felt the searing heat burn his arms, raise blisters, and char his flesh.

The flames disappeared and the room shifted once again. He saw he now stood in the room he once shared with his mother at the inn. As he turned and looked around, he saw a large man looming behind his mother. Azerick tried to scream a warning, but his voice came out as nothing more than a weak croak.

Azerick charged forward and grappled with the big sailor as he tried to grab his mother. Harlow was considerably larger and stronger than the young Azerick was and easily pinned the boy beneath his bulk. His breath reeked of alcohol, and his large hand wrapped around Azerick's throat. In his other hand was a sharp, curved knife that Azerick fought to keep away from him.

He drove a thumb into Harlow's eye. The big sailor reeled back with a roar of pain and released his grip on Azerick's throat. Azerick grabbed the hand holding the knife and twisted it around until he heard bone snap. Harlow dropped the blade with another bellow of agony. Azerick scooped up the fallen blade and stabbed the drunken sailor in the stomach, causing him to fall backward off him.

Azerick rolled to his feet and sprang on top of Harlow, squeezing his eyes shut in rage as he plunged the knife into him repeatedly while shouting a wordless, feral scream. Azerick opened his eyes when the body under him stopped fighting and shouting. He looked down in horror as the face of his mother looked up at him in anguish and then anger.

"You killed me, Azerick. Why did you kill me?" his mother wailed.

He spun toward the source of another voice behind him. Azerick recoiled as he looked at the pale, dead face of his father. His throat was cut and dried blood covered his neck and chest.

"I am disappointed in you, Azerick. You were supposed to be the man of the house while I was gone. You were supposed to protect your mother, but you let her get murdered."

"I tried, Father! I tried to protect her and take care of her! I swear I did! I was just a boy, Father!"

"And what about now?" the shade of his father demanded. "You sat in that school like a high-born prince. Why have you not avenged me? Do I mean nothing to you now? Now that you think you are some powerful sorcerer your family no longer matters to you?"

"I have not forgotten you! Who killed you, Father? Who killed you?" Azerick screamed.

The ghosts of his parents stalked toward him, reaching with desiccated, claw-like fingers. "You did," they chanted in unison. "You did. You did. You did. You did."

His room spun back into view, his throat was raw from screaming, and his body was soaked in cold sweat. Lord Xornan stood at the foot of his bed staring at him with his arms tucked inside his voluminous silk sleeves.

You see how I can punish you when you fail me. If you fail me again, your punishment will be far more severe. I will hurt you in ways you cannot imagine.

"I fought as best I could, and I did win. Does that not count for anything?" Azerick asked in a whisper, fearing his voice would crack if he spoke louder.

Fortunately, you were victorious no matter how hollow that victory was for me. Because of the severity of the wounds you took, others criticized me for being an ineffectual master. Perhaps there is some truth to their accusations. I have made an error in not taking a more direct role in your training.

Azerick shuddered as he listened to the psyling admonish himself. Not because he thought Xornan actually felt any responsibility, but because such self-recrimination could only mean something unpleasant was in store for him.

These last several days I have researched ways in which I may speed your learning, and I am confident I have discovered a method that has a nearly equal chance of being successful.

"A nearly equal chance of being successful or what?" Azerick asked.

Of destroying your mind of course. It is a rash action, but a necessary one in my view. Fortunately, my view is the only one that matters.

In a blink, Lord Xornan closed the few feet separating him from his slave and clasped a cold, long-fingered hand over the top of Azerick's head. The convalescent sorcerer tried to pull away, but he was unable to move a single muscle. He moaned loudly, his attempt to scream coming out as a strained whimper. It felt as though the psyling's fingers were piercing his skull and digging into his brain.

Strange lights and images of such complexity he could barely make sense of them whirled through his mind. Sigils and arcane runes burned in his vision like the floating spots the sun left when you stared into it too long. Unfamiliar words of power echoed deafeningly in his head like temple bells. Azerick had no idea how long it lasted, but it seemed an eternity.

The sights, sounds, and at least some of the pain left as quickly as they had come. Total blackness replaced the chaotic images and noise. Azerick was certain he had not slipped into unconsciousness, at least not like any form of slumber or trauma-inflicted blackouts he had experienced before. His body floated in an ethereal oblivion, but he was aware. He could think, but he could not feel, hear, or see anything.

Where was he? Was he still on his bed in his room? Was his mind shattered? Did his body live on as a mindless shell? Would he exist until he starved to death, or would his consciousness wander in this endless void even then, floating through this nothingness for all eternity?

Azerick found that by concentrating he could move his body. At least he thought he was moving. There was no sense of motion since there was no object on which to judge his movement.

As he slowly turned, he thought he spied a thin line in the distance only slightly brighter than the blackness around him. Azerick blinked, unsure if he had seen anything at all. He slowly turned his head from left to right and picked up the line in the very periphery of his vision. He imagined himself moving toward it at an oblique angle so he would not lose sight of it again. As he drew nearer, the line grew brighter until he could look at it straight on without losing it.

Azerick stared confusingly at the jagged line hanging in the empty void, unsure of what it was. It appeared to be a hair-thin crack in fine crystal, if crystal were made of perfect blackness and had no substance. He pondered this enigma for an indeterminate amount of time. Time simply had no meaning here, wherever here was. Azerick concentrated and circled around it. He felt a sudden sense of unease, almost panic, when the mystical fissure disappeared. Azerick was relieved when it reappeared as he came full circle and floated before it once again.

It appeared that whatever it was existed only in two dimensions, much like Magus Allister's gate spell. On a whim, he pressed his eye against the faint line, wondering if he could see anything beyond it. Through the fracture, he could see Delinda weeping over his prostrate form on the bed. His view shifted, and he could see himself lying on his bed through her eyes. Azerick looked closer and saw a golden aura wreathing his body.

He was certain Delinda could not see this aura, but he could not say how he knew. He looked at his floating body within the void and saw it was limned in a sickly green instead of gold. Azerick peered back through the fissure and studied Delinda. She too was outlined in the same sickly green aura he had in this place.

Why did he have two different auras? He was floating in an endless void he was certain was not a physical place. It possessed a flaw that allowed him to see the physical world, but his body had a different aura there. Delinda had the same aura in the physical world that he had in this one.

The flaw is in my psyche! The green aura is the taint of the psyling's mental control. The fissure is a crack in the mental domination Lord Xornan has over me.

Through that tiny breach, he saw himself free of his master's mental shackles. Azerick began shouting, kicking, and clawing savagely at the flaw in an attempt to widen it. If he could get his spirit through it, he would be free.

He knew what he would do if he could free himself. He prayed he would have the luxury of time to inflict the amount of pain he desired on the psyling. He threw his mind at it with all his will. He imagined a mental wedge jammed into the crack and forced the fissure to expand.

There, at the end; it split just a fraction! He redoubled his kicking and mental pounding and watched as the crack expanded millimeter by millimeter. Azerick began to notice the blackness was growing lighter. Black turned to grey and grey slowly turned to white. The white began resolving itself into colors that became shapes. He realized the shapes were the objects in his room and Delinda sitting next to his bed.

Delinda threw herself onto him and held him tightly. "Azerick, oh Azerick, I thought he had killed you!"

Azerick tried to shove her away. "No! No, I have to go back! I was almost out! I was almost free!"

Delinda sat up with tears in her eyes and a look of shock on her face. "What do you mean you were almost free? What's wrong with you? Are you hurt?"

"I was almost free of Xornan's domination! I could see myself through a weakness in his control. I don't know how it got there, but I think it has something to do with whatever he did to me. I think he caused a small breach in whatever compels us."

"I'm not sure what you mean. I'm just glad you are all right now. Are you okay?"

"My head hurts terribly, but I think I'm all right. At least as all right as I was before."

Azerick reached out with his mind to touch the Source and found it there to do his bidding just as it had been before. He touched his wounds and found they were still tender, but not debilitating. He got out of bed and washed up with the fresh water in his washbasin then got dressed, eager to move about once more. His muscles felt weak and clumsy, and he tired quickly. He sat back down on the edge of his bed and held Delinda's hand.

"How long was I out this time?" he asked, feeling a bit ashamed for neglecting Delinda's concern for him.

"Three more days. I heard you screaming and ran up the stairs, but I dared not enter the room. I wanted to rush in and claw that beast's eyes out with my bare hands for whatever he was doing to you, but I could not. I don't see any wounds on you. How did he hurt you?" she asked as she stroked his shoulder.

"He brought back my most horrible memories and twisted them to make them even worse. Then he did something to me. I don't know what he did, but it hurt badly. When I came back to my senses, I was floating in a lightless void bereft of all sensation. Then I saw the crack or breach in my mind. I tried to break through and was starting to succeed before I woke and was pulled away from it."

Delinda looked at Azerick quizzically. "Can't you find it again? If you found it before you can find it again and free yourself."

Azerick shook his head. "I don't know. I just don't know. I don't know how I got to wherever I was or how I could possibly get back there."

"Maybe you can enter a trance or through meditation of some kind. If it can be done, I know you can do it. You will find a way."

Azerick hugged her tightly and kissed her, grateful for her confidence in him. "Let's go for a walk. I need some fresh air."

"Are you sure you're strong enough?"

"My head is still a little loopy, but I really need to get out. Walk with me through the garden."

Delinda helped him stand and slipped her shoulder under his arm. "All right, but let me help you, at least on the stairs."

"Gladly," he replied.

Azerick was able to cross the room without trouble, but he was grateful for Delinda's steadying hand traversing the stairs. She helped guide him through the glass-paned double doors leading into the garden. Azerick relished the cool air even though the smells of city life tainted it. Negotiating the stairs had taken a considerable amount of energy out of him, and he was ready to take a rest on the first marble bench they came to.

"I wonder how long it will take our spider-faced master to find out he didn't kill or cripple me," Azerick said to Delinda as they sat down on a bench under a red-leafed tree bearing a resemblance to a maple tree.

Not long at all, my pet, came Lord Xornan's immediate reply.

Azerick jumped despite himself and looked furtively around. The psyling had silently walked up on them and was standing just a few yards down the path Azerick and Delinda had just come down. Delinda gasped in surprise, and Azerick could feel her shiver in fear.

Do not be terribly alarmed. I have grown accustomed to your impertinence and find your feeble attempts at resistance amusing, on occasion. Do not presume to construe my tolerance as license to act inappropriately. It would be unpleasant for you if you should overstep your bounds or try my good humor.

"You seem to be in a better mood than when you last saw me." Azerick scowled.

It was necessary. I am pleased you survived. I have too much invested in you to have you easily replaced. Have you discovered the gift I gave you yet?

"If you mean the splitting headache and horrible nightmares, then yes."

I expect you will return to your studies tomorrow or the next day. Search your mind, and you will find I have paved a path to new potent spells. It is beyond even my extraordinary power to imbue you with the ability to know them outright. It will require study and training, but I have laid out the groundwork for you. It will still take a great deal of work on your part, so do not procrastinate.

The psyling stared at Delinda for several uncomfortable seconds, turned around, and padded off the way he had come. Delinda and Azerick both knew he had allowed her to hear his instructions to Azerick as a warning not to distract him.

"Do you know what he meant by that?" Delinda asked after the vile lord glided away.

"I think so, in a vague sort of way. I'll find out more the next time I study."

Azerick's greatest fear was that the psyling would discover the flaw in his control and close it. The sorcerer did not know if he could do anything to prevent its discovery if the creature purposefully searched his mind, but he would do his best to avoid any errant thoughts of it to surface and pray it was sufficient.

The couple resumed their walk before Azerick decided he needed to return to his room and sleep. Whatever limbo he had been in had not afforded much, if any, real rest. He awoke early enough the next morning to break his fast with Delinda before going to the library to study.

He sat in the center of the room, relaxed, and slipped into a meditative trance. Normally he would connect with the Source while in this condition, but this time he decided to see if he could delve deeper into his mind, into the same void Lord Xornan's mental assault had sent him.

He was able to reach a state of extreme relaxation and introspection, but it was nowhere near the level he needed to achieve total sensory deprivation. Azerick did discover something odd, however. He searched his mind and found several partial patterns as well as casting techniques that had not existed before. He studied the sigils intently and recognized them as weavings for new spells, but they were incomplete.

Even in their unfinished form, he was able to deduce their meaning and effect through detailed study. They were potent spells indeed. Two were earth related and were based on similar properties to the spell he had created himself which he had used to defeat Rangor in his last battle.

Lord Xornan must have examined his mind for what he already knew and used that information, along with his own understanding of magic, to forge the basis of the spell within his mind. The other spell was a more powerful version of the incantation that helped shield him from magical attacks. If he should ever fight another spellcaster, it would prove to be invaluable.

The other bits of knowledge the psyling literally rammed into his brain involved two separate casting techniques. One allowed him to cast spells without verbal commands, the other without the need for somatic gestures. Both required a great deal more energy and focus to accomplish such a feat. Azerick was ecstatic at his new discoveries but he would still kill his master most painfully the first chance he got.

As Azerick studied the new spell weavings, he also realized he needed to find a way to move about the arena more rapidly. Rangor's magically enhanced speed had taken him by surprise, and Azerick could not disengage himself from melee combat to make effective use of his magical powers. He thought about the magical doorway Allister had used the day the old mage had entered his former home. That would work. He just hoped he had the time to research it before his next battle. For now, he would focus his energy on the new weavings and casting techniques.

That evening, he and Delinda sat in his room, and he told her about what he had learned. She was excited for him but her anxiety over how he had attained the knowledge worried her.

"But what about being unconscious? What about that crack, or whatever it was you saw? What if it is some kind of damage he did inside your brain?"

Azerick shrugged knowing there was little he could do about it if that were the case. "I seem to be all right, all things considered."

"Just be careful, please," she begged. "The gods only know what he did to you."

"I will, love. Don't worry about me."

"Impossible. I always worry about you."

Thus far, Lord Xornan had left Azerick to his studies without interference, nor had Azerick been forced to fight in any more arena battles. Even with splitting his time between his studies and his cataloging duties, he managed to hone his new spells and abilities to an acceptable level of proficiency within a month. Such progression, as far as he knew, was unheard of. He was discovering that Xornan had done far more than simply carve knowledge into his brain. Azerick's efficiency in gathering and shaping the Source and his understanding of sorcery in general was noticeably greater. He had always been a good student, but his focus was sharper now.

Lord Xornan occasionally checked on his progress to ensure his pet was advancing as he should. Satisfied that Azerick was not neglecting his responsibilities, he left the sorcerer mostly to himself. It was toward the end of the month after he had recovered that the psyling appeared in the vault with a full score of minotaur and human guards, all equipped for conflict and an extended expedition.

I will be gone for a time. Continue to study and work with due diligence on your other duties. Expect your next tournament shortly after I return.

The psyling paused and looked at the foul, black staff still resting untouched in the far corner of the chamber. After a few moments of contemplation, he crossed the room and took possession of the sinister artifact before opening the gate and stepping through with his entourage. The scene beyond the portal was a barren land of reddish stone and blowing dust. Lord Xornan and his soldiers stepped through the arch and into the wasteland beyond.

Azerick paid close attention to the operation of the portal as he always did, knowing that if he were ever able to free himself and Delinda, this was the best hope for their escape.

With their master away, he and Delinda were able to spend more time together, particularly the nights. The time he spent with her was the greatest joy he had experienced for as long as he could remember. He prayed fervently to any god who would listen that one day they would be able to be together without the dark cloud of fear always hanging over them as slaves to an evil and capricious master.

A second week passed before Lord Xornan unexpectedly returned late one night. Delinda awoke and jumped from the bed she shared with Azerick, her husband in her mind. She and Azerick had pledged their vows to one another and considered themselves a married couple even if there were no priests or governing lords to officiate their union.

"What is it?" Azerick asked, fully alert the moment he felt Delinda spring up from the bed.

"The master has returned. He summons me. I have to go tend to him," she told him hurriedly as she threw a long shift over herself and pulled on her slippers.

Azerick threw on a robe, donned his own slippers, and followed her out of the room with a sigh. He had to run to keep up with her as she bolted up the steps, not wanting to keep the master waiting. They met Lord Xornan partway up the stairs with his guards in tow. He had managed to return with a higher percentage of his guards this time, though still fewer than when he had left. The psyling's robes were scorched and tattered, and all of his guards showed signs of combat as well.

Delinda, attend to my guards and me downstairs. Pet, you know what to do with this, he said as he shoved a thick leather and wood-bound tome into Azerick's hands. *Be very careful with it. It is by far the most valuable object I have ever collected.*

Delinda followed the group downstairs while Azerick continued the ascent to the vault chamber with his master's newest acquisition. He was going to just stuff the book on a shelf and deal with it in the morning, but he was awake now, and his curiosity won out over his desire to return to his bed.

The book was written in a familiar language, but with a very old-style grammar and syntax as if written in centuries past. As he delved deeper into the pages, he began to find historical references to people and events that occurred in his own kingdom's past. He soon realized this book must have come from his own world! He tried to recall the exact sequence Lord Xornan had used to open the gate. When he was certain he remembered everything correctly, he wrote it down in the ledger of his catalog so he could duplicate the process if he ever got the chance.

Not only did the book come from his world, there was a fantastic amount of information regarding ancient forms of magic. Azerick had only been able to study at the Academy a couple of years, but he was certain much of what he read had been lost over the centuries. There was a treatise written in great detail by a wizard of obviously extraordinary power. It detailed magical concepts and spell mastery unheard of today by any wizard or in any writings he knew of. Much of this writing was far beyond Azerick's understanding, but years or even decades of study would change that.

Azerick was so absorbed in his readings he lost track of time. His stomach told him it was probably past time to break his fast with Delinda, but he walked briskly down the stairs in hopes of catching her still in the kitchen. He felt a bit of disappointment when he strode through the kitchen door to be greeted only by Cook and the smell of fried ham, eggs, and oatmeal.

"Morning, Cook. Have you seen Delinda yet?" Azerick asked as he resigned himself to the small, empty table against the kitchen wall.

"Aye, lad. She's been shuttling plates of food to Lord Xornan's men and tending their hurts all morning. Ah, I think I hear her coming now," he replied just before the door swung open.

Azerick looked into Delinda's tired eyes, which brightened when she saw him sitting in the kitchen waiting for her. "Oh, I'm glad you made it. Did you stay up also, or did you go back to bed?"

"I stayed up. The book he brought back was too fascinating for me to go back to bed—at least alone."

"Good. I was getting peevish with jealousy thinking of you sleeping away the morning while I was up working."

"I'm glad to know you appreciate my suffering."

Delinda was forced to eat a hurried breakfast before returning to her duties. Azerick took the time to drink a second cup of tea before bidding Cook farewell and resuming his studies and tasks. As much as he wanted to delve back into the new tome, he needed to continue his proper studying. He had not yet mastered the portal spell, and he wanted to have it ready before his next battle.

As luck would have it, Azerick managed to squeeze in another week of study before Lord Xornan found him in the library to inform him that his next bout would be in two weeks. Good fortune and hard work paid off for him once again as he completed the gate spell the very next week.

He spent the remainder of the week honing it and the other spells he had learned to battlefield effectiveness. It took endless long nights and early mornings to accomplish, but by the time the day of his battle arrived, he had perfected his spells to the highest degree of proficiency he could expect given the time he had available.

A couple of the gladiators looked at him with increased hostility, but the vast amount of fighters showed him increased respect and acceptance as Braunlen got him prepared. Azerick was now in a higher fighting bracket, so he was able to retain the magical items he used in the last fight and would do so until a loss moved him back down—assuming he survived a loss, which few did.

The only thing he knew about this fight was that his opponent was a creature and not a fighter. Gladiators were pitted against powerful and dangerous animals nearly as often as they were against more intelligent humanoid opponents. In fact, as a fighter gained in popularity they increasingly fought against creatures to improve the likelihood of their continued survival while still providing a good show for the crowd.

The spectators cheered when Azerick entered the arena, chanting his name, and stomping their feet. Despite his disgust at being forced to fight and kill for someone else's pleasure, his pride, and perhaps even a small part of his ego, could not help but find a little bit of satisfaction in the recognition he received. The adulations went on for several long minutes before subsiding. The clinking and rattling of chains drew his and the audience's attention to the other gate as it slowly opened.

One of the strangest creatures Azerick had ever seen cautiously emerged from the dark portal. It was a huge beast nearly twice the length and height of a large bull. It sported six squat but powerfully thick legs. Its hide was the color of stone and covered with large fish-like scales the size of serving trays. It had a long, flat face ending in a short, boney muzzle. Its wide head sported horns, each as long as Azerick's arm, sticking straight out above its small, beady eyes. It snuffled loudly as it swung its armor-plated head back and forth.

Azerick cast his duplicate spell, and his illusory clones sprang out around him, shifting positions every few seconds to help confuse his enemy. Given the way the creature was casting its head about, Azerick assumed the creature probably had rather poor eyesight, but it tensed when it apparently picked up his scent. The creature seemed to stare straight at the sorcerer as its small round ears twitched toward him and it took another deep breath through its nostrils.

It sounded a long, loud trumpeting challenge and charged directly at him, not falling for his magical trick. Despite the creature's great mass, those thick legs propelled it across the arena at a fantastic speed. It would likely not win any endurance runs, but its sprinting ability was incredible.

Azerick released a lightning bolt straight at its broad head. Twin bright white bolts limned in crackling blue energy forked out at the rushing monster and scored black burns across its thick scaly plates. The creature let out a bugle of either pain or anger, but it did not slow or deviate from its course in the least.

Azerick threw himself aside to avoid being trampled under several tons of charging flesh and bone. He evaded the pounding flat feet, but two of his images were less fortunate. The great ivory horns and the creature's own girth tore through them, rending them to mist. He rolled to his feet and launched a stream of magical bolts into the armored, grey side as it wheeled about for another charge.

Despite the enormous size and inertia of the creature, it managed to twist around and reverse its charge with startling rapidity. Azerick tried to dodge again, but the little space it had was still sufficient for the animal to get a full head of steam. It clipped his hip and spun him painfully to the ground. It whirled around for a third pass as Azerick picked himself up, trying to ignore his throbbing bruised thigh. He barely had enough time to cast his dimensional gate and jump through before the beast trampled the ground where he had just been standing a second before.

The portal deposited him close to the wall at the far side of the arena. The beast cast its head around and charged as soon as it picked up his scent once again. Azerick launched a bright, fiery arrow and struck the creature directly in its broad chest, but its only reaction was a trumpet of rage, and it lowered its horns in another attempt to skewer its antagonist.

Azerick opened up another gate and leapt through, once again just in time to avoid the lethal rush, and found himself near the distant end of the arena. He shook off the disorienting effects of traveling through the dimensional doorway as the massive beast charged across the arena after him. Azerick raised his arms and uttered a string of arcane words. Stone spikes erupted from the ground directly in the charging animal's path.

The beast tore through the deadly obstacle without slowing and shattered the granite-hard spears with little more than some deep scoring on its armor-plated hide.

Azerick was forced to escape the beast's wrath once more by way of his gate spell. He was becoming truly alarmed at the ineffectiveness of his spells to cause any significant damage to the six-legged juggernaut. He wracked his mind for a solution to his dilemma as the monster bore down on him once more.

An idea finally formulated in his mind. As the beast neared, intent on killing the small, annoying creature in front of it, he cast his dimensional portal once again; however, instead of fleeing through it, he dove to the side at the last moment. The raging beast plowed straight through the magical doorway where it emerged on the other side of the arena a scant number of feet from the magically reinforced rock wall.

Unable to arrest its charge, the creature slammed into the immobile barrier at a dead sprint. With all of its considerable mass behind it, the long ivory horns broke against the stone and a sickening crack echoed above the sound of the bone-jarring impact.

Several spectators jumped from their seats the instant they saw the beast heading straight at them despite the protection of the wall before them. They sat back down with nervous laughs at their own reaction as the beast sank down to the ground.

Azerick edged toward the doomed creature and saw blood streaming out of its nose and spattering the wall as it huffed in short, panting breaths. The victorious sorcerer looked sympathetically into the beast's small black eyes as they slowly glazed over and it breathed out its last rattling breath.

He felt disgusted at the senseless loss and his own feeling of pride for the cheers of the people around him, people he saw as more animal or monster than the unfortunate creature lying dead before him.

He walked slowly back toward the gate that would allow him to leave the arena and the cheers of the audience behind him. He no longer cared for their adulations and remained silent all the way back to the tower. Even when his master commented on his performance and cleverness in defeating the creature in such an unorthodox manner, he merely grunted and shrugged in reply. Lord Xornan did not let on that he sensed his fighter's dismay, but Azerick was certain the psyling knew exactly how he felt and why, just as he knew his evil master took pleasure in his consternation.

Delinda met him in the courtyard as she always did and blissfully threw herself into his arms when she saw he had returned unharmed. Azerick returned her embrace but not her joy, and she clearly felt it in his touch. She did not say anything then, instead choosing to follow him as he plodded up the stairs and retreated to his room.

"You seem unhurt. What troubles you so much?" she asked as soon as the door closed behind them.

"I fought a creature today, not a man or anything close to the intelligence of a man," he replied softly.

"Why does that bother you so? I know you don't like fighting for their amusement, but never have I seen you this upset by doing what you must."

Azerick's face darkened with renewed anger. "A man or anything close to such knows why he is in the arena and what he must do whether he is a willing participant or not. That beast knew no such thing. It was taken from its home and put into the arena to be slaughtered. It was not evil. It had no particular hate or desire to kill me personally. It saw me as a threat or perhaps an interloper into its territory and defended itself as its nature dictated. It may not even have had those primal instincts directing it. The gods know what these bug-faced monsters did to its mind to make it fight. It was an innocent! It was even more of a slave than I am. I swear I will make these creatures pay for what they do to us."

Delinda held him tightly and rocked him in her arms in an attempt to console him. "I'm sorry, my love. I'm sorry you have to kill to survive, but I would be sorrier if you had not come back to me."

His rage eventually turned into exhaustion, and he fell into a fitful slumber in her arms. He awoke sometime after the sun had set. Delinda was lying beside him, sleeping contentedly, so he simply wrapped her in an embrace and fell back to a more restful sleep.

Azerick returned to his regular duties of organizing and cataloging the assortment of items in his master's vault. He spent far more time reading than actually delving into the secrets of many of the artifacts, but he made certain to spend enough time each day doing the latter so as not to appear neglectful of his tasks. The peace he found by losing himself in the books around him was short-lived.

You will fight in the arena in two weeks. This will likely be the most difficult battle you have faced thus far, and the most important one to me.

Azerick looked up from the ancient book he was studying and saw the psyling standing in the now open doorway. Azerick wondered how the creature could move so quietly. Maybe he used his abilities to block his presence from Azerick's mind. He discarded these ponderings as unimportant as his master continued to address him.

One of my archrivals has issued a personal challenge, and the wagers are exceptionally high. As it is a private contest, his fighter has not advanced through the rankings. I do not know the strength or capabilities of his champion, but he must have gained possession of a gladiator of exceptional power to be so confident of his success. Need I remind you of the consequences of disappointing me?

"No, you don't," Azerick replied tersely.

Do not fail me.

He did not bother to reply. He was always ready, and whether or not he was had no bearing on what was going to happen anyway. His pathetic resistance seemed childish now and needlessly exhausting. He would get his moment or he wouldn't. There was no sense in wasting energy or even words until the time actually arrived.

Azerick found Delinda and told her of his upcoming battle.

"I have been distilling another healing potion since before your last battle in order to make it as potent as I could. I'll start another one now. It will not be as strong as the first one, but it will help," she said, her trembling voice betraying her fear for Azerick's safety.

"You do not seem to have much confidence in me if you think I will be injured so badly."

"I know of this other creature who has challenged Lord Xornan. They are bitter rivals, and he would not have made such a public challenge unless he was supremely confident of his chances to win. I am sure you will be victorious; my mind will not allow me to think otherwise, but it is sure to be a most difficult battle. We both must face the fact that it is unlikely you will emerge unscathed, so it is best we be prepared for it."

Azerick hugged her closely, grateful for her support. "I am lucky to have you by my side."

Azerick spent the time he had practicing his spells. He experimented with using different combinations and tried to imagine every possible scenario ahead of time so he could react quickly and properly. When the day of his fight came, Azerick stepped out into the courtyard to accompany his master to the Games. He was surprised to see Delinda standing next to Lord Xornan and the palanquin. She was standing resolutely with a canvas satchel hung over one shoulder, prepared for an argument.

"Delinda, what are you doing here?" Azerick asked.

"Lord Xornan has agreed to allow me to go with you to the arena. I brought the potions with me. The sooner they are administered the more effective they will be."

Azerick was going to argue, but the determined look in her eyes showed he could not dissuade her. "Will you be watching the battle?"

"No, I will stay with Braunlen in the trainer's room."

"Good, this is not something I wish you to see."

"Nor would I," she said quietly.

The two humans and the psyling loaded themselves into the palanquin and were borne on the wide shoulders of the minotaurs to the arena. Delinda squeezed Azerick's hand the entire way and did not let go until they were in Braunlen's training room.

"I think you got a hard fight on your hands this time, lad," Braunlen told him gravely.

"Can you tell me anything about him?"

"It's a she, and an abyssal elf. Rumor has it she is a wizard too."

"I have to fight a woman?"

Delinda's face darkened. "You're damn right you have to fight a woman, and you will hit her with everything you have! You had better not take it easy on her just because she's a girl. You can be sure she won't do the same for you."

"She's right, kid. Don't go soft just because she's a she. She's an abyssal elf to boot. Abyssal elves are a mean bunch and masters of magic. They look down on surface races as being inferior in every way. They are fast and smart, so you better be on your toes."

"All right, I'll do my best."

Azerick prepared himself as he entered the arena by casting a ward to protect him from magical attacks. Azerick was a crowd favorite by now, and they cheered loudly for him when he entered the fighting pit.

The crowd fell silent as the abyssal elf entered through the other gate. She was shorter than he was, but not by much. She strode with the grace and surety of a queen. Her skin was stark white like freshly fallen snow, and it contrasted eerily with her large black eyes. Her silver hair hung in a tight braid down her back, reaching past her waist.

She wore a pair of tight-fitting black breeches and a tunic. A short black cape or cloak trailed down her back, split down the center by her braided hair. She would have been startlingly beautiful were it not for the aura of menace radiating from her.

The official dropped the kerchief and both casters broke into the chanting and hand waving of spellcasting. Azerick's spell was a minor one and quick to cast. His illusory duplicates sprung out around him to confuse his enemy as to his true location. The elf formed a familiar weave. Azerick deduced the intent of the spell and bolted to the left as the wizard flung her hand forward. A massive ball of fire erupted a scant second later where he had just been standing. He felt the searing heat wash over his back, but his quick thinking and spell shield saved him from serious burns.

He retaliated with a lightning bolt the instant he leapt to his feet. He saw the telltale flicker of it meeting the spell shield of the abyssal elf. What little energy got through seemed to inflict little, if any, harm on the alabaster-skinned wizard.

Frustrated, he began another incantation as the abyssal elf completed her follow-up spell. Azerick did not notice any immediate effects, nor did he recognize the spell she cast. He threw his hand forward and launched a heavy arrow of fire straight at his opponent.

He stared in shock when the wizard disappeared. He spun around and found her several yards off to his right. Bolts of arcane power slammed into him before he could ready himself. His shield absorbed most of them, but two managed to penetrate and sting him smartly.

Azerick was holding his spell at the ready when the abyssal elf blinked away once more. He turned in a circle, casting his eyes all around the arena as he waited for her to reappear. Azerick launched another lightning bolt at her as soon as she popped into existence. The electrical charge caught her squarely and sent her staggering several steps backward.

She cursed something in a language resembling elven, but it sounded darker and more sinister in tone. Azerick made out the words man, human, and what he assumed was a powerful expletive before she blinked away again. Azerick tried to spot her before she could retaliate, but he was too slow in discovering her new location. She appeared only a score of yards away and brought her palms together in front of her with her fingers splayed outward at an angle forming a V lying on its side.

A swirling vortex of skin-numbing frost erupted from her delicate white hands. The icy blast caught Azerick full on despite his best attempt to dodge the attack. He felt his clothes stiffen and his skin burn from the sub-zero assault. He forced his frozen fingers to obey and hastily cast his portal spell to get away from the current kill zone. He escaped just in time as another fireball burst directly over the area he had just vacated.

It was the abyssal elf's turn to scan the arena for him before he got the jump on her. Her own dislocation spell now worked against her as she tried to search the grounds while her position changed every few seconds. Azerick released his spell the moment his opponent blinked back into view. Stone spikes erupted from the earth and covered a large patch of ground with their deadly, sharp tips.

The elf amazingly spun away, somehow avoiding the stabbing stone spears enough to keep from being impaled. One of the tips did manage to tear a deep gouge in her left hip and thigh. Instead of cursing him in anger or outrage, she actually smiled and nodded in appreciation at the human's clever spell.

The abyssal elf mage waved her slender hands in a complex pattern. Azerick sent a barrage of magic darts streaming at her in hopes of interrupting her spell, but her shield negated all but one missile, which did not appear to faze her.

She shouted her spell's execution command, and Azerick felt the earth rumble beneath his feet. He dove to the side as a column of stone erupted beneath him and shot forty feet in the air, taking barely a second to reach its apex. He tried to regain his feet, but another colossal stone pillar burst directly under him. He splayed himself out across its five-foot-wide surface as it launched him above the arena floor. The column reached its apex in the blink of an eye, and the sheer velocity of it catapulted him another thirty feet into the air.

Azerick forced himself to remain calm despite the terrifying situation in which he found himself. He controlled his falling flight and carefully but rapidly drew the magical weaving he hoped would save his life. The portal flared open directly below him a fraction of a second before the hard, unyielding ground abruptly and lethally arrested his fall. Azerick's body flew out of the gateway's exit point in a low arc before hitting the sandy floor and rolling to a stop in a cloud of dust.

Azerick's quick thinking and clever spell use had saved his life for the moment, but his uncontrolled slide and tumble across the arena floor introduced his body to a world of pain. He was certain one arm was broken as he opened his dirt-encrusted eyes and saw it bent at an unnatural angle. The sharp pain accompanying every shallow breath attested to several broken ribs. As he struggled to his feet, another sharp pain lanced up his right leg, which refused to support him.

He managed to stand, bearing most of his weight on his left leg as the abyssal elf seductively sashayed toward him. She came to a stop and seemed to study him for a moment before speaking.

"You are clever for a human, and you fought well," she said in a surprisingly deep but soft and melodious voice. "It is a shame one with your talents at such a young age must meet his end in this place. But look on the bright side. At least you will no longer be a prisoner of these vile creatures." She looked forlorn for a moment. "I look forward to the day I can say the same. I just pray I can take some of them with me when I go."

She began chanting the words to another spell, and Azerick knew there was nothing he could do to prevent her from destroying him now. His body was too battered to attempt to dodge, flee, or cast a counterspell. All he could do was brace himself as an invisible force slammed into him with the weight of a runaway carriage. His already broken body was blasted backward, and he landed in a heap several yards away.

The abyssal elf stalked forward when the human sorcerer refused to submit to death. She stared down at his battered and broken form, summoning the energy for a simple spell to extinguish what little spark of life still flickered inside him. She had never known the emotion called remorse, but the feeling she had at being forced to kill such a rare spellcaster for no reason except for a master's entertainment came as close as she likely ever would. She would have been delighted to be able to dissect the young human's mind and abilities at her leisure.

"What a waste," the elf said as she prepared to unleash her spell.

CHAPTER 6

General Baneford rode at the head of the column of riders. Only the four scouts ranging three hundred yards ahead preceded him. The breath of men and horses formed a pervasive fog in the thin and frigid air. He turned in his saddle and caught his men gazing up at the towering, snow-covered peaks seeming to reach up to pierce the sky itself. The general was certain his men were all sharing his same fear, that the massive peaks would suddenly disgorge their shells of ice and snow to bury the intruders in a great frozen tomb.

As cold as it was, it was still better than that wretched swamp. The cold only became truly unbearable when they stopped to rest. General Baneford decided that when he retired, and soon he hoped, he would go south where it was dry and warm. He figured he could put up with the occasional sandstorm if it meant his fingers and toes would never ache from the cold and his feet would stay dry enough that they would not grow more fungus than a decaying pile of horse dung.

Despite the mountains' seeming desolation, the pass they followed appeared to have a definite purpose. Six miserable days of arduous climbing later, one of General Baneford's scouts came riding toward him, evidently with news of some kind.

"Sir, the pass opens up just half a mile ahead into a small plateau of some sort. There are a few stone buildings and halls at the far end of the vale and people walking about."

"Excellent, it's about damned time we got out of this forsaken cold," the general replied bitterly.

One of Baneford's officers turned to him. "How do you want us to proceed?"

"Did you spy any walls or armed men?" he asked the scout.

"No, sir, although the buildings look strong and well-constructed. Several of the men looked to be carrying some kind of long implements, but we did not approach close enough to tell if they were weapons or simply tools."

"Tools can be weapons in the right hands, but in this case I think not. These are supposed to be priests of some kind. We will proceed openly but cautiously. No one is to draw weapons unless they are overtly threatened. If we can get in and out with what we seek without resorting to a bloodbath, all the better."

General Baneford led his men after the scout and came upon the plateau entirely ringed by steep-sided, impassible mountains. If these priests had been soldiers, it would have been an easy task for a few men to hold it against ten times their numbers, although if an enemy ever were to break through, the defenders had nowhere to run.

As they drew near the small town with its large stone cathedral and smaller outbuildings, General Baneford saw that defense was the furthest thing from these men's minds. Dozens of men wielded shovels and rakes against the snow covering the flagstone courtyards and pathways. They all wore heavy brown robes of wool and simply paused in their work to watch the armored men approaching on horseback.

One of the men handed his shovel to another and walked toward the group with a pleasant smile splitting his trimmed grey beard. He was not ancient, but a significant sense of wisdom shown on his age-lined visage.

"Good day to you, gentlemen. I am Brother Paul," the man said in introduction. "It is very rare we get visitors to our isolated redoubt. What brings you on such a long and arduous journey, may I ask?"

"Are you in charge here?" General Baneford asked shortly.

"I was elected to be this year's senior brother four months ago, so I suppose you could say I am in charge, although we are primarily communal in most all matters of importance."

"Good, then you can tell me where to find the piece of Dundalor's armor you keep within your abbey." Baneford chose not to give the brother a chance to deny its existence by posing it as a question.

The smile dropped from Brother Paul's face. "No, I am sorry to say I cannot help you with that, but you and your men are welcome to share the warmth of our fire and food before you depart."

"You did not deny having the artifact, so it is here. It is not that you cannot help me, but instead choose not to."

Brother Paul smiled benignly into the aggravated face of the man astride the big horse. "Our order was sworn to protect the artifact so its evil would not be loosed upon the world once more."

"Bah! It is a tool and no different from that shovel you were wielding. Evil is in the intent of the man, not the tool."

"And what is your master's intent?" Brother Paul asked shrewdly.

General Baneford's argument was stopped in its tracks. He could not honestly say Ulric's possession of Dundalor's armor was for the greater good of the realm regardless of what the duke told him. Then another thought occurred to him.

"What makes you think I have not come for the armor on my own behalf? Surely you recognize the breastplate, greaves, and gauntlets I wear," General Baneford countered, displaying the infinitely black pieces of armor chased in gold.

"It is my opinion that you wear the armor to achieve an end. You are not the kind of man to abuse its power and commit evil for the sake of personal gain."

"Maybe you misjudge me, Priest."

"Perhaps you misjudge yourself, warrior," Brother Paul countered serenely.

"Enough of this talk! You will show me where the armor is, or I will order my men to make you talk!"

"That would not be possible. We have all taken the vows and will not betray the secret with which we were entrusted."

"Damn you, man! Don't you realize I have a hundred men with swords who will cut down every last one of you unless you tell me what I want to know?"

Brother Paul bowed his head. "We do not fear death. Such threats will achieve nothing but blood that may be washed from your blades, but will stain your souls forever."

"I will find what I came for. I will tear down your precious abbey and every building here brick by brick. Save yourselves such needless destruction and just tell me."

Brother Paul simply smiled up at the general. "They are only stones. We will rebuild."

"Damn your stubborn hide, man!" He turned to his men. "Search this place from top to bottom. If you do not find what we came here for then we will tear the place apart!"

His men spurred their mounts toward the waiting buildings, half of them heading toward the large abbey in the distance. Baneford's men entered the smaller buildings and began a very thorough search. The sounds of shattering pottery and overturned furniture reached General Baneford's ears.

"You could save yourself and your brothers a great deal of grief if you would simply tell me where it is."

"The next bell is the call for supper. I invite you and your men to dine with us in the abbey's dining hall. It is simple fare, but quite good. Goat stew, I believe; one of our better stews. You arrived at a fortuitous time. Most often it is only rice and vegetables."

General Baneford ground his teeth in frustration at the insufferably kind abbot. Rage made him want to backhand the priest in his smiling face, but it was an empty fantasy. The general had to content himself with spurring his horse forward and riding toward the abbey. He was certain the armor would be found somewhere within those walls, if it was here at all. Brother Paul had not actually said it was here on the grounds much less in one of the buildings. For all he knew, some monk hundreds of years ago carted the thing to the top of one of these peaks where he still held it in his frozen hands. No, it was here; he was certain of it.

General Baneford entered the abbey and heard a similar ruckus going on within its vast halls and cathedral ceilings to that he heard in the smaller domiciles outside. Although there was little to break within the abbey since the monks lived a rather austere sort of life, his men managed to create a significant amount of havoc.

He walked into what was obviously the chapel or prayer room from a side door. A massive sun made of what must have been gold-plated iron or bronze, given its size, was suspended high above a white marble altar at the front of the large hall. There were no benches, but the floor held scores of thick wool mats lined up in rows where the monks knelt and prayed.

A huge stained-glass window occupied an enormous section of the eastern wall opposite the large golden sun. General Baneford surmised that when the sun rose and shone through the window, the polished golden disc glimmered with the radiance of a small living sun itself.

"Stop!" the general shouted at one of his men who was about to throw a brazier through the stained-glass window. "We are here to find the armor, not cause unnecessary damage."

"Yes, sir; sorry," the soldier replied sheepishly.

"Go and spread the word. I don't want any more damage done than necessary, especially to things that may be irreplaceable."

The soldier snapped a salute and sped off to pass on the general's orders.

"That was most kind of you, General. We would have all mourned the loss of Solarian's eye," Brother Paul's voice came from behind him.

General Baneford spun on his heel. "If he had destroyed it, it would have been because of your obstinacy!"

The small brother shrugged his bony shoulders. "One man's obstinacy is another man's duty."

Baneford strode past the aggravating brother with a growl and helped direct his men in the search. After three fruitless hours, a loud bell tolled from the tall tower above the chapel.

"Ah, supper time at last," Brother Paul said with a smile. "You and your men need only follow one of the brothers to find the dining hall. I hope you will join us, General."

Brother Paul bounded down the hall with as much haste as his priestly decorum allowed. General Baneford watched several more of the brown-robed monks pass by the open door of the room he was in, presumably on their way to the dining hall. He was going to continue searching the abbey, but the thought of eating actual food instead of dry trail rations changed his mind.

"Lieutenant, tell the men to fall in behind the next monk they see and follow him to the dining hall for chow."

"Yes, sir!" his subordinate replied gleefully, also anxious to have some warm food for a change.

There's plenty of time to search this place. No one is trying to kill us, and it's warm. Besides, the men deserve it, the general thought as he followed the slapping sound of a monk's sandals down the hall.

The general entered a large room where several long tables were set up with backless bench seats to sit on. A cauldron was suspended over a low fire in a huge fireplace at the front of the chamber. General Baneford saw Brother Paul waving him over to a table set nearest the fire and the cauldron of stew.

"I took the liberty of ladling up a bowl for you," the monk said as General Baneford took a seat next to him. "The meat tends to sink to the bottom, and the first bowls usually get the best pieces," Brother Paul said with a smile and pushed the clay bowl with a wooden spoon over to the general.

General Baneford eyed the stew warily. He saw that everyone took from the same pot, so it was unlikely it was poisoned. Then again, he did not see his pulled from the communal pot.

"Would you rather have my bowl, General?"

General Baneford scowled at the smiling monk, snatched the offered bowl, and ate heartily. The stew was so good that at that moment he did not even care if it was poisoned. At least he would die with a full stomach.

Just as she was about to put this wretched human out of his misery, the dark wizard felt the power she had gathered slip away. Her master's voice sounded in her head and ordered her to stop. She looked toward the special box seats where her master and the human's sat together. Lying in the dirt, much like the human at her feet, was a crumpled silk kerchief. Knowing the kind of punishment her foe was likely to receive for not only losing but also for his master conceding the bout to spare his life, she considered granting him mercy by crushing his windpipe with the heel of her boot.

Nevertheless, she obeyed her master's command and let the sorcerer live. She hoped they would meet in the arena once again when he recovered and grew in experience and power.

Delinda heard her master's furious voice fill her head as she sat worriedly next to Braunlen inside the trainer's room fearfully awaiting the end of the match. Every time the crowd cheered, her heart raced and her stomach twisted, not knowing if they were cheering for her beloved or his opponent.

Then Lord Xornan told her that Azerick had been defeated and needed aid immediately. Terror gripped her heart as she raced up the ramp toward the open gate at the top leading into the arena.

The first thing she saw when she burst through the gate was the form of a lithe, impossibly white-skinned woman standing over her husband. She ran to him as fast as her legs would carry her, for a moment thinking to tear this creature to shreds with her fingernails. She discarded the idea knowing Azerick needed her right now and that such an action would likely result in both of their deaths.

The abyssal elf took a step back as Delinda pulled out the silver flask filled with the potent healing potion she had been distilling for over a month. She cradled Azerick's limp head in her lap and gently placed the flask's stem between his lips. She dribbled the contents down his throat as quickly as she dared. It seemed to take an eternity to empty the entire flask's contents.

Delinda prayed fervently to every god she could name for her love's life. She wept openly as she rocked Azerick's head in her lap and waited to see if the potion was strong enough to overcome such terrible injuries. Her heart soared and she cried even harder when Azerick's eyelids fluttered open.

"He is a talented sorcerer. I am glad you were able to save him," the abyssal elf's sultry voice said from behind her.

Delinda ignored the woman's words and took out another metal vial. "Here, drink this, my love," she told Azerick as she raised another healing potion to his lips.

Azerick did as Delinda bade him and felt the effects of the potions as they ran their course through his body. His muscles burned and his bones ached where the elixir forced them to heal at an unnaturally rapid pace. Delinda was gladdened to see Braunlen running toward her with his short, bow-legged gait.

"I am Teraneshala. Remember that name, human, so you may warn the denizens of the abyss of my eventual coming should you see them before I do," the abyssal elf called out as Azerick was half-carried out of the arena to Lord Xornan's waiting transport.

Lord Xornan was furious beyond anything Delinda had ever seen. Azerick sat half-dazed, gritting his teeth against the lingering pain of his partially healed wounds.

I should make you walk back to my manor for your utter failure even if it takes you all night to drag yourself across the city! the psyling raged.

The tension inside the palanquin was palpable the entire way back to the tower. The bearers gently set the palanquin down when they finally arrived. Lord Xornan hurriedly stepped outside and ordered his retinue away, an order with which they were glad to comply. The psyling glared at the exhausted young sorcerer standing before him.

Do you have any idea what you have cost me? The price for saving your miserably useless life in treasure and dignity alone is likely beyond your comprehension! I warned you that the price for your next failure would be severe. You have left me no other choice.

Azerick braced himself as best he could for the expected mental onslaught. However, instead of a barrage of torturous mental images, he felt Delinda stiffen as she held tightly to his arm. He looked over at her and held her as her eyes rolled back until only the whites showed and let out a small grunt of pain. Azerick gently guided her to the ground as her legs buckled beneath her.

"No, stop! Do to me whatever you wish, but leave her alone!" he begged.

Thin rivulets of blood ran from her nose and ears as she shuddered and let out a last gasp of air. Azerick pressed his ear against her breast but heard no heartbeat or sign of breathing.

"No, no, you would not kill her," he denied in anguish. "She was useful to you. This is just another of your sick mental games to punish me," he said more to himself than to his master.

I assure you, this is all quite real. Unlike my previous lessons from which you were able to recover once the images ceased, this lesson you will remember and feel for a very long time. You will continue to feel the pain and loss of your loved one, and the little bastard whelp growing within her!

Azerick felt as if he had been dealt a mortal blow at the revelation that his beloved had been pregnant. He was cradling her head against his chest and stroking her hair but froze at the words of his vile master and let out a deep groan.

Do not let your emotions for your loss distract you from your training. I have invested a great deal of time in you, and I still have enough confidence in your ability to grow in power to redeem yourself. If you please me, I will get you a new female, a prettier one even.

Azerick heard none of these words as the world around him vanished. An unending expanse of intense whiteness replaced the mauve stone of the courtyard and tower. He was once again floating in the void of nothingness. The only difference was that this void was one of pure white rage instead of the blackness of pain. He frantically searched for the fracture he had discovered the last time he was lost inside the recesses of his own consciousness and found it. He saw it as a black, jagged slash out of the corner of his eye. Azerick willed himself to fly to it as fast as his mind would allow.

He slammed into the weak spot with as much force as he could muster. When that failed, he began kicking, pounding, and clawing at its edges in fury, but it refused to yield to his assault. The grief-maddened sorcerer stood back from the fissure as rage and loss suffused his soul. The death of Delinda and his unborn child burned in his heart with the intensity of every loss he had ever suffered—his parents, Jon Locke and his extended family, his flight from the Academy, his slavery, and all the senseless deaths in the arena all combined and then magnified tenfold.

He released all the grief and emotional torment in an ear-shattering scream of fury and anguish. From his mouth erupted a roar that carried every ounce of love, hate, fear, and pain raging within him, augmented by the raw power of the Source. He pulled and pulled from the Source as he never had before and used all these emotions to shape and direct it in this one massive assault.

The fracture quavered under his emotional charge then shattered under its intensity. Azerick's world returned with a flood of light, color, and sound. Lord Xornan took a step back in shock as his former slave stood up and looked balefully into his liquid black eyes. The psyling tried frantically to regain control of his servant, but Azerick was far beyond his power. An impenetrable mental fortress now blocked the psyling's every attempt to reassert his dominance.

Azerick drank in the Source like a man dying of thirst gulps down water. Crackling arcs of excess power swirled around the sorcerer, giving him the appearance of some terrifying, vengeful god. He pointed an accusing finger at the psyling and released an awesome bolt of lightning that struck with such intensity it burned a hole clean through his former master's chest large enough to shove his arm through without any of the gore touching his sleeve.

Lord Xornan's lifeless corpse flew backward and landed on the flagstone courtyard. Azerick leapt atop the body with a feral roar and began pummeling the bulbous head of the psyling with his fists. Gore soon covered his hands and spattered his body and face as his former master's head split open like an overripe melon. The enraged sorcerer barely heard the shrill cry of brass horns blaring across the courtyard.

Breathing heavily, Azerick looked up from his assault and spotted several minotaur, human, and orc guardsmen running at him through the open gates. With another bestial roar, he raked a stream of lightning across the line of charging guardsmen. The smaller humans and orcs were thrown back into smoking piles while the heavier minotaurs were brought tumbling down onto the flagstone avenue.

More clarions were ringing in the distance and were drawing nearer. Azerick knelt beside his beloved Delinda and stroked her hair. He took the small knife Delinda always wore for trimming plants and chopping herbs and cut off a lock of her long dark hair. He then lifted the satchel she carried and looped it over his shoulder. He turned and saw more guards nearing the gates. With a few words and gestures, stone spikes erupted across a large expanse of the courtyard, impaling several of the guardsmen and effectively keeping the rest from gaining the inner grounds.

Azerick knew he only had a few minutes at best before the guardsmen negotiated their way past the obstacle and psylings were sent to deal with the deadly rogue sorcerer. He stepped back a few paces and said a short prayer and farewell to his wife and child. He then raised both of his hands and drew deeply from the Source once more.

A jet of intense flame erupted from his outstretched hands and engulfed Delinda's small body in a magical pyre. Azerick poured more power into the relatively simple flame spell than was normally possible. His rage fueled the engulfing flames by drawing an unsafe amount of magical energy into himself, but he would not leave their bodies in this world. He would send their ashes to Solarian borne upon the winds.

In less than a minute, only ash covered the heat-cracked stones where Delinda's body had lain. Azerick looked up at the sound of the shouting guardsmen who were slowly picking their way past his stone spikes. With a last look at the vaguely human-shaped burn mark on the ground, he ran into the manor.

"What's going on out there, son?" Zeb asked as Azerick burst into the foyer and dropped a heavy crossbar across the thick wooden doors.

Azerick turned and saw Zeb and several of his former crew looking at him from the large gallery beyond the foyer. "He killed Delinda, and I killed him."

"Killed who, lad? Who did ya kill?" the old captain asked, his voice laced with sorrow at the news of Delinda's death.

"Lord Xornan. We are free now, but we need to get out of here. There are guards and psylings coming. Go round up as many of our people as you can, and get them to the top of the main tower. I will meet you all up there. Grab what you can, but do not delay."

"They'll have us trapped up there, lad. It's suicide. We need to escape out one of the side doors and try to vanish into the city, or maybe take one of their boats and sail out of here," Zeb argued.

"No, the only way out is at the top of the tower. Trust me, Zeb, and get moving."

Zeb looked into the young man's eyes and nodded his head. "All right, you scallywags, you heard him. Drop your mops and grab your socks, we're getting outta here! Move it! Round up everyone you can find and get 'em to the top of the tower!"

Azerick ran down to the laboratory, taking three stairs at a time in his headlong rush. He selected several herbs and a few small vials of finished healing draughts before sprinting back up the steps. He saw several of the human slaves running about in their haste to inform the others, grabbing whatever possessions they had. Azerick rushed up the stairs to his room and stuffed a couple of his most important books in a canvas pack before heading to the library. Loud booming echoed through the mansion as something heavy repeatedly slammed into the main door.

Zeb ran straight to the kitchen with several of his men to get Cook. "Cook, pack it up, we're getting out of here."

Zeb looked at another form sitting at the small table in the kitchen eating a haunch of mutton. Toron was one of Lord Xornan's old gladiators. He was one of the few to survive long enough to retire. He was a big brute of a minotaur, greying around his muzzle and one horn had about six inches of the tip lopped off. A thumb and two fingers were all that remained of his left hand. He worked around the manor these days doing a bit of menial labor and acting as a house guard.

"What's going on, Zeb?" Cook asked as he slid several large, sharp kitchen knives out of a rack and pressed them into Zeb's and a few of his crewmate's' hands.

Zeb kept his eyes on the old minotaur as he told Cook what had transpired. "Toron, you always seemed a reasonable sort, if not much on conversation. I don't want to have to fight you, but you got two choices here. Lord Xornan is dead and we're leaving. You can fight us, or let us go, but we won't be stopped."

Toron set his food down on the plate and stood to his imposing height of seven feet, just over eight if you added the horns—the one on the right anyway.

"I believe I shall take a third option if you please and depart with you, if you will allow me to accompany you," he rumbled in a deep, gravelly voice.

Zeb considered the request for just a second before answering. He was glad the old minotaur was not going to fight them. Even past his prime, it would have been a brutal and costly battle.

"Suits me fine, I guess. I don't know where we're going, but a powerful fighter like you would be most welcome so long as you never give us reason to doubt your loyalty. Grab what you need and make for the top of the big tower. Azerick's got us a way out."

Cook and crew grabbed large sacks and stuffed them full with food from the pantry and smoke room. They filled bladders and jugs with water and slung them over their shoulders with leather and rope cords. Every man slipped a kitchen knife into his belt before hurrying upstairs to the top of the tower. They met Toron near the top of the stairs, dressed in a thick leather kilt reinforced with steel plates, a chain hauberk, and with a large double-bladed battle-axe strapped to his back. Zeb gave him a nod, and they made their way to the meeting point.

The door at the top of the stairs was open and they all scrambled inside. Azerick was standing near a bookshelf stuffing scrolls into hard leather tubes as nearly a score of men and a few women from Lord Xornan's household staff piled into the room.

Azerick paused and looked at the big minotaur standing amongst them, his horns nearly scraping the ceiling.

"He's coming with us, lad, if you'll have him," Zeb informed Azerick.

"Any who wish to flee this horrible place are welcome to come. I need everyone to pack away and carry everything on that table." He pointed to a stack of books, scrolls, and baubles.

A loud crash resounded from down below as the heavy doors gave under a tremendous force. Booted steps pounded up the stairs and throughout the rooms below as guards searched for the rebels.

Azerick stepped over to the multicolored gemstones and activated the portal. It was not the same sequence Lord Xornan had used on his first expedition. Azerick had learned the book had not come from his world, but he had discovered the way there within its pages. The portal snapped open and revealed a wall of darkness beyond.

"Everyone step through quickly now. I'll follow in a moment and provide light," Azerick instructed his group of refugees.

Azerick made his way through the stream of humans and closed the vault door. Brackets were bolted on each side of the doorframe, and a thick crossbar rested in a corner, its surface covered in dust. He started to reach for the oak beam but got another idea. He grabbed the black, evil-tainted staff leaning against a bookcase and dropped it into the slot instead.

"C'mon, lad, everyone is through but us," Zeb called to him.

"Just a moment, Zeb. I have to do something first. No one will ever run slaves or gladiators out of this house again," he swore and cast his sunder spell on the artifact.

More hard thumps sounded against the door as guards threw themselves against the magically reinforced barrier. The artifact was extremely powerful and resisted Azerick's attempts to tamper with it. It felt almost like a living thing and it tried to return Azerick's endeavors to destroy it with the black energies it contained.

Azerick's determination finally won out, and the spell weakened the physical structure of the ebony rod. He followed Zeb through the gateway as even more powerful blows shook the entire chamber. As soon as he passed through, Azerick closed the portal behind him.

A score of guards stood waiting for battle as five psylings launched their powerful psionic attacks against the barred door.

"The door and chamber beyond are protected by powerful magic," one of the evil creatures told its kindred. "We will have to join our powers together to overcome it."

"So be it," the others answered.

The psylings clasped hands and stood in a half-circle before the door. They all concentrated and sent their psychic energies to their brother who stood in the center, gathering and focusing their combined strength. As the power built to a crescendo, he released it all against the resilient door in one massive burst. The stubborn wood and steel yielded under the titanic assault and split asunder.

When the door and the ebony staff barring it were destroyed, all the pent-up power in the black rod detonated with such force it caused an instant chain reaction of destruction. Every magical staff, ring, gem, necklace, piece of armor, and scroll containing magical power, as well as the dimensional gate and the powerful enchantments protecting the chamber, detonated as well.

A colossal blast erupted in a bright white light so intense it seared the eyes of anyone who had been looking in that direction seconds before the explosion washed over them. In that same instant, the massive eruption sent a shockwave of destruction through the city, killing everyone and reducing every building to rubble in a miles-wide radius. Thousands, perhaps even tens of thousands perished in an instant. The great psyling city was wiped out of existence.

Teraneshala, the powerful abyssal elf wizard, felt the blast and the mental control her psyling master had over her slip for just a brief instant. However, that instant was enough to enact the spell she had prepared the moment of her capture. She saw the wall bow under the intense force of the blast at the same instant her spell whisked her across the planes and back to her deep subterranean home.

The elf staggered away from the rune-inscribed circle carved into the floor of a secret chamber, one which only she knew of its existence. She paused to consider what had just transpired. The wizard replayed the event in her mind and examined the "smell, taste, and feel" of the magic that had surely destroyed that warren of evil.

Teraneshala threw back her head and laughed deeply, her melodic voice echoing off the cavern walls. "Oh, very nicely done, little human. Well done indeed."

The elf was certain the human had played a hand in whatever it was that had just happened, though she could not know what exactly that was. She hoped he had somehow escaped the destruction.

Far beyond even the abyssal elf's home, across planes of existence few could, and even fewer would want to, reach, another creature shared in the elf's laughter.

Yes, my hand, send me more souls, the goddess of death cried out in exultation as thousands of new souls flooded into her dark afterlife.

On the other side of the dimensional gate, a mass of humans huddled in darkness and muttered in fear. Azerick scooped up several plum-sized stones from the cave floor and cast an enchantment upon them. Bright light flared from the stones resting in his cupped hand. He passed them around to a few select people along with a scroll tube each.

"Carry this light. If we call for the lights to be extinguished, drop them in the tube and cap them," he instructed the light bearers.

"What do we do now, Azerick?" Zeb asked.

Azerick looked at the huddled refugees and the cavernous chamber around him. He studied the wall of stone behind him, using his light to illuminate its hard grey surface. The anger and adrenaline that had been fueling his body left him in a rush. Spots swam before his eyes and vertigo overcame his balance. His knees buckled beneath him, and he slowly slid down the wall to a sitting position.

"Azerick, are you all right, lad?" Zeb asked worriedly.

"I'm fine, Zeb. Do not worry about me. I just overdid it today. I need to rest right now, is all. We can figure everything else out later. Just have everyone relax for now."

Unable to keep them open any longer, Azerick's eyes closed and he fell into a deep, fitful sleep. When he next opened his eyes, he found himself staring into Lord Xornan's soulless black orbs.

Did you really think you could defeat me and escape so easily? The psyling gurgled in his mind, mockingly.

"No, this isn't real! You are not real!" Azerick shouted. He rubbed his eyes.

Reality is what I make it, my pet. Have you not learned that by now?

"I killed you! I killed you for real this time!"

Just like you killed me the first time and escaped? Just like you killed your mother? You are mine until I decide otherwise, pet. You will serve me for the rest of your life. I will not let you escape, and I will never let you die.

Azerick trembled in horror, looked down at the ground, and saw Delinda still lying dead on the flagstones by his feet.

"No!" Azerick cried out as the guards grabbed him roughly and dragged him toward the tower.

CHAPTER 7

Despite the monks' apparent pacifism, general Baneford ordered a small group of guards to stand watch over the men sleeping in the dining hall upon their bedrolls. He had wanted to continue the search, but he and his men were exhausted.

The continued hospitality of the men whose homes they invaded, and were essentially robbing, perplexed the general to the point of hostility. This was not how people were supposed to act! He almost hoped the monks would try to sneak in and attempt to drive them out by force. At least he understood that kind of mentality. Despite his exhaustion, sleep refused to come.

Damn Brother Paul and his tolerance and hospitality, and damn his goat stew too!

Unable to find peace, General Baneford got up, strapped his sword around his wool-clad waist, and stomped out of the dining hall with no purpose or intent other than to try to clear his head. He stalked down the silent corridors where only the tiniest flame flickered in every third oil lamp to guide him. He felt a draught to his left and found the door leading to the outside.

Maybe some fresh air will clear my head, he thought.

The general stepped out into the cool night air and almost returned to his bed when his body shivered involuntarily at the sudden drop in temperature. He chose instead to cross beyond the door's threshold and gazed up into the night sky. The view was amazing. Not a single cloud marred the black, sparkling mosaic, and no moon shone in an attempt to compete with the luminescence of the stars. The surrounding peaks made it look as though he were gazing into the very depths of the heavens from the bottom of a colossal well. A rainbow of wavering lights swam in the currents of invisible ether just above the peaks to the north.

"One of the first things our few visitors ask when they come to this remote place is how we can live in such isolation. The lucky ones see this, and they never ask again," Brother Paul said, his voice preceding him out of the darkness.

General Baneford flinched inwardly at the unexpected noise but passed it off as a shiver born of the chill wind. "Do you always wander about in the middle of the night, or only when you have uninvited guests?"

Brother Paul's teeth flashed in the faint starlight. "I seem to recall inviting you and your men to sup with us and to enjoy the warmth of our fire."

General Baneford snorted. "We would have been here regardless."

"Then it is fortunate I extended our hospitality before any further rudeness occurred that could have caused some embarrassment for either of us."

"What are you really doing out here?"

Brother Paul stared up at the humbling night sky. "Much the same as you, I imagine. I feel a restlessness born of duty and a feeling of unease at the wrongness you and your men are committing."

"I am a soldier, and I follow orders as I am supposed to do. I do not question them, and I feel no shame for it," the big commander snapped, almost believing his lie.

"We had a goat die a few years back just after giving birth to a kid. One of our herding dogs had a litter of pups and adopted the baby goat as one of her own. As the kid grew, it acted just like its littermates. It would romp and play, fetch sticks, and try to herd the other goats. It would even defend its herd against any perceived intruder, but no matter how hard it tried to bark at them, it always came out as the bleating of a goat. Do you know why that is, General?"

"Because it was a goat not a dog, of course."

"Yes, because it was a goat. Despite growing up amongst dogs, and doing everything as dogs do, it was still a goat, and nothing could change that. We could tell it to sit, it would sit; tell it to lie down, it would do it just as its adopted brothers and sisters did. But no one could teach it to bark because in its heart it knew it was a goat."

The general looked darkly at the small monk. "So what are you saying? That I'm a goat?"

Brother Paul looked at the general with a wide smile and replied, "Naaaah," with a goat-like bleat and walked back toward the abbey.

General Baneford scowled at the retreating monk until he heard the door of the abbey close behind him before he allowed the laughter he was holding back to break the tranquility of the starry night. With a final deep breath of fresh air, the general returned to his bedroll in the dining hall and fell fast asleep.

The ringing of the bell signifying morning ablutions woke the sleeping men early the next morning. Soon after the soldiers had their bedrolls stowed away, the monks of the abbey began gathering in the dining hall to break their fast with cooked oats, bread, and cheese before going about their daily routines of prayer, tending the animals, and grounds maintenance.

Once the general's men finished eating, they renewed their search of the monastery. There were several small anterooms, but their austere furnishings made for very quick searches. The library was another matter entirely. Thousands of books and scrolls filled the shelves and cubbies of several chambers. It was in searching these rooms that his men received the first protests and resistance from the monks. Many of the books were so old that improper handling easily damaged them. Several monks ran about in a state of great agitation as soldiers pulled books out of the shelves and looked behind the bookcases.

Brother Paul walked briskly into the library with General Baneford in tow. "Please, General! Many of these tomes and scrolls are irreplaceable."

"I told you I would tear this place apart to find what I came for. It is your stubbornness doing this. Tell me where the armor is and we will leave."

The monk resolutely cast his eyes at the floor. General Baneford looked at the monk and saw the sorrow in his determination not to reveal the location of that which he was entrusted to protect.

The big soldier let out a sigh of resignation. "Is the armor within any of these rooms or behind the bookcases? Are there any hidden doors or passages concealed within the walls?"

Brother Paul looked the general in the eye. "No, there is nothing here that will lead to or help you find the artifact. Not even written words in any of the books or scrolls."

General Baneford studied the man's face and found no hint of guile just as he expected he would not. "Pack it up, gentlemen. There's nothing here."

The soldiers paused but marched out and began searching elsewhere.

"I must thank you once more for your sufferance, General."

Baneford turned toward Brother Paul. "You had best pray I find the armor soon, or so help me I will burn every book and scroll in this place if I even think for one second you have deceived me."

Brother Paul bowed his head and smiled. General Baneford stormed out of the abbey and found himself walking the grounds and wracking his brain for answers. He saw the herds of goats and sheep munching on bales of hay which must have been quite a chore to have had delivered to the isolated monastery.

The general wondered how the monks received the things they could not craft or grow themselves. The nearest trees were three days' ride through the steep, narrow passage, and it was a week to the closest town. If he were in charge, he would probably send two or three men into town once or twice a year to commission a caravan to deliver wood, hay, and whatever other supplies they needed to survive the harsh winters.

Thinking along these lines as he walked, a sudden realization sprang to mind. With one last look around, General Baneford strode with a determined purpose for the first time since he and his men had arrived. After asking a few of the other monks, the general found Brother Paul kneeling in the chapel below the big golden sun that was still catching and reflecting the last of the morning's sunlight.

"Where are they, Brother Paul?"

"Where are who, General?" the monk asked hollowly without looking up.

General Baneford smiled humorlessly. "You know damn well who—your dead. There are no grave markers anywhere in the vale. I imagine digging graves in the frozen ground in the winter would be quite a chore." The general watched Brother Paul's shoulders sag and knew he had hit the mark.

The monk whispered a final, quiet prayer and rose to his feet. "It is unwise to disturb the rest of the dearly departed, General."

"I'll take that chance. Now take me to the tombs."

"As you wish, General."

General Baneford ordered a few of his soldiers to follow him as Brother Paul led them toward the lesser-used wings of the monastery. The monk's sandals seemed to drag a bit, and for once, a smile failed to find its way onto his face.

The small group stopped at a blank wall where Brother Paul pulled out a large iron key from within his robes, slipped it into a slot that looked like nothing more than a spot of broken mortar, and gave the key a twist. There was the heavy clack of a bolt drawing back, and a large section of the wall swung in on well-balanced and oiled hinges.

Behind the wall was a small landing atop the head of a narrow set of steps carved into the natural bedrock upon which the abbey was built. An oiled torch rested in an iron sconce from which a piece of flint and steel were suspended by pieces of twine. The abbot struck the rough metal against the flint and sent a shower of sparks to ignite the oil-impregnated cloth of the torch.

Brother Paul lit several more torches as they descended before reaching a long hall with a series of corridors leading off in both directions. The monk stopped at the foot of the stairs and turned to face the general.

"This is where we inter our brothers who have been received into Solarian's warm embrace. I can take you no further."

General Baneford nodded his acceptance at the abbot's words. He no longer needed him to reveal the armor's location. He knew it was here. He could almost feel the pieces he now wore calling to it. He turned to the men who followed him down.

"Two of you go back and grab a couple of those torches from the stairs and start looking around."

The soldiers returned with light in hand and split up to search the tomb. Several more torches flared to life when the men found them as they proceeded down the hall. There were soon enough torches lit that

General Baneford could nearly see the entire corridor they were standing in from the foot of the steps.

Wall niches held the linen-wrapped remains of the dead. Stone statues of monks, carved in exacting detail, stood near some of the larger interments. Brother Paul followed the general as he walked over to one of the nearer statues and examined it.

"These are very well done, Abbot. I assume they were carved by some of your fellow monks?"

"Yes, we have a few brothers who are quite gifted, though all the ones you see here were done by brothers long since departed. Those brothers who carve now make smaller statuettes and figurines that we sell or trade to augment the small stipend we receive from the church. We do not lack for quality stone here."

General Baneford continued down the hall, gazing at each of the statues with an interested eye. He crossed all the way to the end of the passageway past several life-sized statues of pious-looking men in robes, appreciating the monks' excellent artisanship. As he turned to walk back, his men began assembling in the main corridor.

"Sir, we have looked down every hall and into each chamber with no sign of the armor. Unless you wish us to move the remains, we see no more areas to search down here. We have even looked for hidden doors and passageways, but if there are any down here we cannot locate them."

"What say you, Brother Paul? Will you tell me where it is, or shall I have my men pull your brothers' bones from the walls?" General Baneford asked nonchalantly.

The monk's face reddened in his greatest show of emotion yet at the threatened sacrilege. "If you feel it is necessary then I shall not stop you, but I will not help you in your quest."

The general smiled at the abbot then looked back to the soldiers. "That's all right, Lieutenant. I already know where it is."

The soldier looked at his commander in surprise. "You do, sir? Where is it? How did you find it?"

"It is right in front of us, isn't it, Abbot?"

Brother Paul did not bother to respond.

"As to how I found it, I guess you could say the armor told me. You see, it wants to be complete so it can fulfill the purpose for which it was created. It just needed to get close enough to its kindred pieces to hear their call."

General Baneford stopped in front of one of the older, dust-covered statues and drew his sword. With one last look at Brother Paul, the general brought the heavy pommel down on the outstretched statue's arms. After a few sharp strikes, the stone-like material making up the draping sleeves of the statue's robes crumbled away to reveal a set of vambraces, edged in gold, buckled around the solid stone forearms.

General Baneford unbuckled the vambraces and tucked them under one arm. Despite his brutal hammering, the armor was unmarred and gleamed like the blackness between last night's stars.

"I appreciate the hospitality you have shown me and my men, but I believe it is time for us to be going."

"I will show you out, General," Brother Paul said as he morosely led the way back up the stairs.

General Baneford and his men soon remounted their horses and made ready to leave the monks to their normally serene monastery. "You do not look quite as pensive as you did when we first arrived, Brother Paul."

"Although I have failed in my duty, I do not believe all is as lost as I once feared," Brother Paul replied, his smile fixed back upon his face.

"One of us was destined to fail in our duty, and the odds were always in my favor."

"I just hope you do not live to regret your success, General."

"I imagine I will live to regret many things I have done. If this is one of them, then that's just one more on what is becoming a rather long list." General Baneford handed him a small leather pouch containing a good bit of gold. "For the stew. Maybe you can buy some better furniture too."

"May you find your bark, General."

General Baneford laughed heartily and led his men away from the monks with his newest prize.

"Azerick, wake up, lad," Zeb's gruff voice called to him from the depths of his unconsciousness.

Azerick sat bolt upright and looked at the cave and people around him. Zeb was shaking his shoulder and looking at him with concern in his eyes.

"Zeb, is that you?" Azerick asked, desperate for confirmation.

"Aye, lad, of course it is. You were moaning then started shouting in your sleep."

"Are you sure it's you? Are we really here in a cave?"

Zeb looked at him curiously. "Of course we're here. Where else would we be?"

"Never mind," Azerick said as he ground the heels of his palms into his eyes. "How is everyone else doing?"

"They're a little scared and unsure of where they are, but they're glad to be gone from that place. Why don't you eat something before we move on? You've been asleep for some time."

Azerick had absolutely no appetite, but he knew his body needed the sustenance the food would provide. If it had just been him, he may have simply resigned himself to curling up on the cold cavern floor until he joined Delinda and his child. Nevertheless, he had rescued these people, and now he was responsible for them. He ate purely by rote and then stood to address those around him.

Azerick winced in pain as his body protested and demanded that he lie back down. His partially healed wounds caused him the most pain, but every muscle seemed to be on fire and resisted any kind of movement. He had channeled far too much power, and his body was making sure he was well aware of the fact. Despite it all, he knew they needed to press on.

"I am sure you are all wondering where we are. The truth is I am not sure. We are obviously underground, but how far I have no idea. I do have reason to believe we are under or near the kingdom of Valeria, which is where most of us are from. I see that Zeb and his crew brought food, water, and a few weapons, for which we should all be grateful. As soon as you are all ready, we will start to make our way to the surface."

Azerick moved toward the front of the group under the stare of frightened eyes. Once everyone was on his or her feet and ready to move, he began leading them down the dark passageway. The light from the stones he had made preceded them down the tunnel and chased away the darkness. The tunnel constantly changed shape, growing wider, narrower, taller, and shorter as they went, but fortunately not so much they could not easily negotiate the passage.

The caves were cold and the travelers were poorly dressed. Using his magic, Azerick was able to provide the group with a small measure of warmth when they stopped to rest and fatigue declared it was nighttime. It was at such a rest point on the fourth day of their journey toward the surface that Zeb and Toron sat next to him and revealed some problems.

"Water is getting short. If we don't find a water source down here in the next couple of days we're really going to be in trouble," Zeb informed him.

"There may be a more immediate concern at hand," the big minotaur rumbled. "I used to work in the mines back in my kingdom, and I can tell that these passages have been worked, and recently. Even more disconcerting is the fact that we are being followed."

Azerick's eyes widened in alarm. "How long have they been following us, and who are they?"

Toron shook his big horned head. "I noticed them about an hour ago. Who they are, I have no clue. Dwarves, abyssal elves, and many other races live under the surface. Some, like the abyssal elves, can be extremely unpleasant. Others are more benign, but those are few. The underworld is a harsh place, and its inhabitants have to be tough to survive. If it is dwarves or another of the less hostile races, they are likely just keeping an eye on us until we are beyond their territory. If they are abyssal elves, then we are in a great deal of danger. They are either waiting for a good ambush site, or their numbers are not great enough to risk an attack and they are waiting for more of their kind to reinforce them."

Zeb asked, "What should we do? I'm a ship's captain and a decent fighter, but underground battle tactics are not my forte. Should we just go back and ask them what they want, or create an ambush site of our own and try to parlay there?"

Azerick took charge once more and directed his people. "No, I think we should avoid whoever it is no matter what their intentions. If we confront them, it may cause them to attack out of alarm. Divide whatever weapons we have amongst those best suited to use them. Myself, Toron, and a third of the armed men will take up the rear. Zeb, you and the rest of the men guard our front, but leave a couple in the center with those who are unarmed. I have a sneaking suspicion if they are going to attack us they will have a group hit our front or flank in an attempt to block us or divide our party in two."

Toron nodded his horned head at the young sorcerer's wisdom. "The larger party will likely be the one to our rear. Any attack to the front will be to slow us down, and if the fight goes badly for them they would want their path of retreat to be in the opposite direction of wherever we are going."

Azerick looked around the cavernous chamber where they had decided to stop to rest. "We'll sleep here. If they are going to attack us, we need to get as much rest now as we can. The two passages leading into here are narrow, and that gives us a defensive advantage. Double the guard, tell everyone what you know, but reassure them as best you can and tell them to sleep with one hand on their weapons."

Fortune seemed to smile on them, and their rest went undisturbed. Their hidden watchers, lacking in interest or courage, chose not to attack them that night. Their luck did not hold for long, however. Just a little over an hour after the refugees resumed their trek to the surface, their pursuers decided to confront them.

"They are drawing nearer," Toron informed Azerick in a low voice.

Azerick nodded and dropped his light stone onto the cave floor. A minute later, he saw the creatures following them as they stepped cautiously into the circle of light fifty yards behind them. Whoever they were, they were short: about four feet tall with long, slender arms and grayish skin. Azerick could see they were a well-armed party, wielding crossbows and picks that looked as effective against flesh and armor as they did stone.

Azerick raised his empty hands in a gesture of peace. "We mean you no harm and do not wish to trespass on your territory. We have recently escaped a city of evil creatures and just wish to return to the surface. We could be gone from your tunnels more quickly with your help, which would be greatly appreciated."

The cavern gnomes answered Azerick's request by raising and loosing their crossbows. The sorcerer spoke a command and raised a ward in front of him just before the steel-headed quarrels could tear into his flesh. The bolts' flight halted just a foot from his heart and clattered to the ground when they met the spellcaster's invisible shield. Azerick called for peace once more, but the cavern gnomes raised their pickaxes and charged.

He let a lightning bolt rip from his hand and dropped several of the wiry creatures in their tracks. He heard the clamor of battle behind him as another contingent of gnomes attacked the head of the party. Furious shouts from the humans and the foreign battle cries of the gnomes reached his ears as he let loose another lightning bolt, killing several and driving back the rest of the cavern gnome forces harrying their rear.

"You men, go search those bodies for weapons. Toron, go help Zeb at the front of our party while I guard our rear," Azerick ordered.

He followed just behind the remaining men to where the cavern gnome casualties lay. Azerick erected a long field of stone spikes along the passage to slow any pursuit as the men stripped the fallen cavern gnomes of picks, daggers, crossbows, and small shields.

"Half of you guard our rear, the rest come with me," Azerick ordered.

Azerick and four of the men raced to the front of the small column of former slaves while the remaining four men fired their pilfered crossbows at any enemy coming within view.

Toron charged into battle swinging his battle-axe in huge, sweeping arcs. His arrival was welcome relief to the unarmored humans who were trying desperately to fight off numerous enemies with nothing more than kitchen utensils. The gnomes had wounded several of the sailors, but the humans were acquitting themselves well despite their meager weapons. Sailors were often accustomed to fighting with various makeshift weapons, from gaffs to belaying pins, and their advantage in reach had left two of the gnomes dead on the ground before Toron made his appearance.

Azerick and his relief force arrived to see the huge minotaur wading into a knot of vicious gnomes and cleaving two them nearly in half with one powerful swing. The gnomes were quick and wily though, darting around and under Toron's thick hairy legs and delivering painful wounds of their own.

Azerick sent a stream of energy bolts into two of the gnomes, knocking them away from the harassed minotaur. Toron swept his great axe down at the off-balance gnomes, taking the head from one and the weapon arm from the other.

The armless cavern gnome stumbled back, spraying his kin with bright arterial blood from his stump. Azerick sent another barrage of magical bolts into the gnomes and turned their fighting withdrawal into a rout. Toron was about to chase after them until Azerick called him back.

"Let them go, Toron. Help us with the wounded and let's get out of here."

Toron looked at the fleeing gnomes with a hunger in his eyes then turned back toward his comrades with a sigh of regret. "It has been a long time since I last felt the stirrings of battle lust in my blood. It felt good."

"I have a feeling you will get another chance at them. For now, we need your strength to help carry our wounded." Azerick looked down at the minotaur's blood-soaked legs. "Make sure you get those bandaged up too. I shudder at the thought of having to carry you."

"These little scratches? They are nothing, but I will do as you ask."

The few women in the group tore any extra clothing they had brought into strips for bandages. Azerick took one of the precious healing draughts from his satchel and gave a measured dose to those most in need. Unfortunately, two of the men were beyond the potion's ability to help.

"I'm sorry, Zeb," Azerick told his captain. "We will have to leave them here. We need to be able to move swiftly, and I doubt it will take long for the gnomes to regroup and hit us again."

"Aye, lad, you're right. They died free men, and none of us can ask for more than that. Their spirits are grateful to you, don't you let that worry you none," the old sailor assured his young friend.

The men salvaged what weapons and armor they could from the bodies of their enemies and moved out with haste. None of the armor fit any of the men, but many of them now had metal helms and small shields as well as weapons that were more formidable than kitchen knives. One of the smaller women slipped a hard leather cuirass over her head and gripped a kitchen knife in her hand.

Humans and a huge horned beast were in their caves. This was intolerable. Particularly after the creature with the spider's face and his soldiers had caused so much trouble a few months ago. The human who threw lightning had spoken some words and made gestures hinting at peaceful intent, but that was irrelevant. A stone master was coming with more soldiers. He would take care of that one. This was their territory, and they would tolerate no trespassers.

Azerick and the refugees moved as fast as they could, helping the wounded walk as swiftly as they dared. He would treat their injuries more thoroughly when they stopped. He wished Delinda were here. She was a better herbalist and healer than he was, and she would know how to care for the wounded under these conditions. She had mastered the few tricks he had shown her in regards to brewing healing potions. Given time and practice, she would have become a master herbalist and healer.

His thoughts brought a wave of fresh grief crashing against his heart, threatening to rip it from its moorings and shatter it upon the rocks of his pain. Azerick suppressed his sorrow as best he could and focused on getting these people to safety. He did not have the luxury of time to mourn. He would do that later.

Fear energized their steps, and they put a great deal of distance between them and the site of the ambush. No signs of pursuit were apparent, but Azerick and Toron both agreed it was very unlikely the cavern gnomes would simply let them go. They continued their exodus until fatigue and the pain of their wounds forced them to rest.

Azerick treated the debilitating wounds with his scant supply of healing potions. For the others, he used raw ground herbs to make a poultice to deaden the pain, prevent infection, and speed healing. They posted guards at the three tunnel entrances leading into this particular chamber. They could not afford to rest long, but continuing without it was impossible.

Zeb sidled up to the young sorcerer sitting with his back against the clammy cavern wall. "How long do you think they're going to let us rest before they hit us again?"

Azerick answered without opening his eyes. "To be honest, I'm surprised they have waited this long. If we get a full rotation of sleep it will be a miracle."

Azerick knew better than to believe in miracles and rightfully so. Barely three hours passed before the twang of crossbows and the shouts of men and gnomes woke him. He jumped to his feet with everyone else as the clanging of metal on metal resounded throughout the cavern.

"Toron, take most of the men and defend the forward tunnel. I'll handle the rear," the sorcerer instructed.

Azerick followed the sounds of battle to the tunnel they had traveled down a few hours before. One man was down with a quarrel through his chest while four others showed bloody wounds but were still battling furiously against twice their numbers in gnomes. Azerick sent missile after brilliant missile streaking into the ranks of cavern gnomes until his spells forced them back or killed them.

"You men fall back and do not pursue them," Azerick ordered.

As the wounded humans slowly retreated, the tenacious cavern gnomes regrouped and renewed their assault. As the short, sinewy creatures charged forth with a cry of anger, Azerick wove another spell. Being in a world surrounded by stone had its advantages. He directed his stone spikes to sprout from not only the floor but the walls as well. Stone spears slammed into the forward ranks of the attacking gnomes, skewering several of them and completely blocking the passage for the ones behind.

Azerick watched as a solitary gnome stepped forward and raised a fist-sized gem over his head. Balor came running up behind him as the gnome glared at the sorcerer and spoke an incomprehensible stream of words. The gem flared brightly, and the stone spikes Azerick raised crumbled to dust.

"Azerick, the gnomes have retreated up front. One man is dead and another has a bolt in his gut. Zeb wants to know what you want to do now," Balor reported hurriedly.

"Get the bolt out of the man and have him drink this," Azerick said and handed the sailor a small metal vial. "Then get everyone moving as fast as you can. I do not like the looks of this."

Azerick expected the cavern gnomes to charge the instant the magic-wielding gnome cleared his spikes from the passage, but they stayed back as the gnome raised his gem once more. He uttered another stream of strange but obviously magical words, and the ground began to tremble beneath Azerick's feet.

"Go! Tell them to run as fast as they can!"

Balor and the others ran back to the rest of the group with one last look at the sorcerer and yelled for everyone to get moving. Balor reached the wounded man and saw a blood-soaked wad of cloth had replaced the bolt in his stomach. He popped the cork and emptied the contents into the stricken man's mouth. The potion stopped his bleeding almost immediately. His shipmates then helped him to his feet and carried him along.

The gnome's gem flared, the rock trembled, and three mounds of earth started rising in front of Azerick. The heaps began to take shape. The tops of the mounds formed a rough approximation of a human-like head, thick arms sprouted from the sides, and legs formed beneath them. The creatures were so large they had to stoop to fit into the passageway, but Azerick doubted that would hinder their ability to crush him to a pulp.

He released a powerful bolt of lightning into the earth elementals. Chips of sharp stone flew off the creatures, and black scorch marks seared across their wide chests. The stone juggernauts ignored the trifling damage and rumbled toward him, causing the ground to vibrate under his feet with each step. The sorcerer sent a flight of arcane missiles into the lead elemental followed by a jet of intense flame. More stone flecks sprayed off the granite titan and blackened its surface, but his assault failed to slow it down in the slightest.

Azerick made one last desperate attempt to slow the creatures' advance. He erected another barrier of stone spikes extending directly in front of him and several yards down the hall. The sharp monolithic shards scored tracks along the elementals' stone bodies, but they caused negligible damage. With single-minded determination, they swung their huge fists and feet, snapping and battering their way through the granite spears as if they were no more than dry corn stalks.

Azerick ducked when the lead elemental swung its maul-like fist at his head. Sharp stone flecks peppered the side of his face and neck when the elemental's massive fist crashed into the cavern wall. He heard whistling and caught a glimpse of steel as it whisked past the top of his head. With a roar of defiance, Toron cleaved a huge gouge of stone out of the elemental where its shoulder and neck joined.

If the massive attack bothered the extraplanar creature in the least, it did not show. It silently swung its other huge fist at the big minotaur who had dared to interrupt its assigned task. Toron brought his axe back around in another powerful blow in the opposite direction. Metal met stone in a colossal impact setting Azerick's ears to ringing. Finely honed steel won out against the unnatural stone and severed the arm of the elemental just below the elbow.

Azerick was forced to roll out of the way to avoid being pummeled by the hundred-pound chunk of arm that narrowly missed crushing his head. "Toron, let's go! We need to catch the others."

The big, stubborn minotaur was loath to flee combat, but he knew there was discretion in valor and followed the sorcerer's instructions. He leapt back as the elemental swung its remaining arm at him, intent on killing these weak creatures of flesh. Azerick and Toron ran back in the direction in which the rest of their band had fled.

"How far ahead are they?" Azerick asked the minotaur who puffed in deep breaths behind him.

"A few hundred yards at best given the speed they were moving. They have some wounded who will force them to a slower pace."

Within minutes, Azerick and Toron spotted the light of the group's rear element just ahead of them. Azerick shouted out a greeting before the guards filled them with crossbow bolts in a case of mistaken identity.

"Where is Zeb?" Azerick asked one of the rear guardsmen.

"He's leading the column up front," one of them answered with a jerk of his thumb.

"Go find him," Toron rumbled. "I will stay back here and help guard our rear."

Azerick had a hard time reading the expression set in Toron's non-human face, but the glint in his eyes spoke volumes. "Don't do anything foolish, Toron. We still have need of you."

The old minotaur's grey muzzle curled into a grin revealing a row of sharp teeth. "It is only foolishness when a brave act fails."

Azerick could not order him to do anything, but he hoped that Toron would not sacrifice himself needlessly. He had grown somewhat fond of the big creature in the short amount of time he had known him. Azerick raced up to the front of the column of fleeing humans and found Zeb breathing heavily but pressing steadily onward.

"Glad to see you made it back, lad. What the boys told me they saw before you ordered them off had me a bit worried."

"What I saw before I left still has me worried," Azerick replied in all seriousness.

Zeb grimaced. "So what's our situation look like now?"

"Not good. The gnomes brought in some kind of spellcaster who has rather potent earth magic. He summoned three earth elementals, which is a feat I could not hope to achieve. Worse yet, I have nothing in my spell inventory I can think of that will cause them any serious harm."

"So are they indestructible or what?"

"No, not quite. I think Toron could chip one into rubble with that axe of his, maybe two in his prime, but not all three."

"Can we outrun them?"

"For a time. They do not seem that fast, but they are tireless. I think the gnomes will be content to let the elementals hound us until we exhaust ourselves, and then sweep in when we are at our weakest."

"Do you have a plan?"

"Not at the moment. Just keep moving and hope something presents itself."

Now that Azerick and Toron had caught back up to them, they increased their pace for as long as they could, but fatigue and their own wounded men soon forced them to slow down. Azerick made his way to the back of the column to check on the rearguard and to see if their enemies were catching up to them.

"Where is Toron?" Azerick asked Balor when he failed to see the minotaur.

"He keeps stopping whenever the tunnel gets narrower. Doesn't say why, just tells us not to worry about him and to keep going."

Azerick had started to head down the tunnel after Toron when he heard footsteps and heavy breathing coming at him. Azerick readied a spell but let the energy dissipate when he saw the dark shape of the asymmetrical horns on top of the large, shadowy figure. Toron grinned brightly when he saw Azerick standing in the circle of light his enchanted stone threw off.

"Toron, what are you doing back here?"

The grey muzzle grinned even wider. "Slowing those giant dirt clods down a bit to buy you all more time. Whenever the tunnel narrows enough to allow only one of those creatures through and restrict its movement, I wait and chip a few more chunks off it. I left one of them crawling on the ground after I took its leg off. Same one that lost its arm to my axe earlier. I think we can call that one out of the fight unless that gnome can put it back together."

Azerick saw Toron try to stifle a gasp of pain when he breathed in. "Are you injured?"

"The downed creature's friend wasn't too happy and paid me back a bit, is all. Caught me squarely in the ribs. I've lived through worse."

Azerick wondered how old he had been when he received those wounds, but he pushed the thought out of his head. "How much time do you think you have bought us?"

"We were gaining ground on them for a while, and I managed to increase our lead with my harrying, but we've been slowing down for a while now. I would say we are only slightly farther ahead of them than we were when we first fought them. I give us an hour at best if we do not slow down any further."

Azerick doubted the group's ability to maintain even this somewhat sedate pace for much longer. If something did not present itself soon to give them some sort of relief, they were in serious trouble.

"Save your energy for a last stand. Your axe will serve us a lot better in a concerted fight than your slowing actions are likely to bring us at this point."

"Yes, you're probably right," Toron sighed as he ran a thumb over the notched and blunted edge of his axe.

"If we get out of this, we all owe you our lives, Toron. I'm glad you came with us."

"It is I who owe you for giving me the chance to live and die like a true warrior. I thought I was going to die a feeble old man."

"You may yet still get the chance," Azerick replied.

Toron glared down at the sorcerer. "That's a hell of a thing to say!"

Azerick threw the old minotaur a wink, clapped him on his broad, hairy shoulder, and ran back to the front of the group.

"Any changes up here, Zeb?"

"It looks like we're coming up to another large chamber. Just pray nobody is waiting for us inside."

Azerick and the men looked around intently as they entered the large chamber, but they saw no sign of ambush. Several tunnels branched off from the large domed cavern. Their magical lights were just able to illuminate the tips of the stalactites clinging to the ceiling lost in inky blackness farther above. Stalagmites jutted up from the floor in a parody of Azerick's stone spike spell. Some were over ten feet tall with bases that would take three men linking arms to surround them. The humans scouted the room and found four new tunnels, presenting them with a decision to make.

"Which way do you think, lad?" Zeb asked him.

"I don't know, Zeb. I just don't know. Damn it all!" Azerick swore in frustration and knuckled his forehead, thumping it rhythmically trying to induce it to produce an answer.

Whether it was luck, divine intervention, or just thumping his head to jar his brain into action, he had a flash of inspiration. He held out his hand and produced a small flame. It hovered just above his palm, flickering like a tiny will-o'-the-wisp.

Zeb hushed and held back his men as Azerick paced around the chamber near the wall, pausing in front of each tunnel. After he had made nearly a complete circuit, he returned to the second tunnel on the left from the one they had entered.

The tiny flame flickered and danced upon the sorcerer's outstretched hand. "This one, Zeb. There is a breeze coming from this passageway. Get everyone moving, quickly."

"You heard him, folks! Let's get a move on," Zeb called back to the people trying to catch their breath.

Azerick paused by the tunnel entrance and made sure no one was left behind, particularly Toron. The old minotaur flashed him a grin as he brought up the rear guard. Satisfied all were accounted for, he jogged back up to the front of the troop column. The tunnel twisted and turned its way through the solid rock. In less than an hour, the group found the source of the breeze wafting through the tunnel and came to a halt. It was not a surface exit as Azerick had hoped, but a massive chasm, its depth and width lost in darkness.

"This doesn't look good, son," Zeb remarked with concern.

"Hand me a crossbow bolt," Azerick commanded.

One of the sailors plucked a quarrel from a short quiver at his hip and passed it over. Azerick chanted a word of magic, and the bolt lit up with the same bright light as the stones he had made.

"Fire it across the gulch. Try to hit the far wall near the same level we are at," he told the sailor as he returned the bolt.

"If there is a far wall," the sailor muttered.

The man made a guess as to the distance and fired his crossbow. The magical, makeshift flare sped across the dark expanse before clattering against the stone side about fifteen feet up from their position on the far side. The illuminating bolt looked little more than a bright star surrounded by an expanse of darkness when it finally came to a rest at the bottom of the chasm.

"Did you all see the tunnel on the other side?" Azerick asked the men standing around him. Several of them affirmed they had. "All of you give me a bolt, but do not take your eyes off where you saw the tunnel."

Azerick repeated his spell over the half-dozen quarrels and returned them to the men holding the crossbows. "Try to get your bolts to land inside the cave on the other side. One of you shoot first to get a second look, then the rest of you aim for the cave."

They all raised their crossbows and waited for the lead man to loose his shot. The bolt sped away across the dark expanse like a shooting star. It struck surprisingly near the entrance, just a few feet above it. The twang of the crossbows hurling their projectiles echoed through the cavern the moment the first one revealed the cave entrance. Three of them landed just on the outside of the distant cave and joined the previous two at the bottom of the deep gulch, but two made it inside and illuminated the passage.

"Good shot, men."

"Shoot, weren't nothin'. Try it from the top of a rocking ship's mast at sea," one of the grizzled sailors replied.

"Stand back, everyone," Azerick instructed and began another enchantment.

Azerick deftly wove a spell, and the air began to shimmer before him. Light appeared in a thin line as if someone had just taken a knife and made a long cut in the air revealing the sunlit surface. The thread of light widened until it was six feet wide and eight feet tall. Through the magical doorway, the men could see the cave with the illuminated crossbow bolts lying on the ground, but it now looked only a few feet away.

"Zeb, get everyone through. I don't think we have very much time."

Azerick slapped his head in rebuke as the rest of the party ran through the portal. "I am such an idiot!" Azerick pulled a scroll tube out of his pack and began shuffling through the pages.

"What's the matter, boy? Why are you smacking yourself about?" Zeb asked.

"I have a veritable treasure trove of magical spells at my fingertips, and I completely forgot about them!" he snarled as he set a couple of the scrolls aside before rolling up the rest and dropping them into the leather tube.

"Everyone else is through, little wizard. Time to go," Toron rumbled.

"Not just yet. They may know a way past this. I want to convince them it is not worth their effort or lives."

"Whatever you are going to do, make it quick, lad," Zeb cautioned.

"I will wait here and guard you," Toron insisted.

Azerick was going to argue, but the look in the minotaur's eyes made it obvious that it was a statement and not a request. He jogged down the tunnel with Toron close on his heels. A minute later he stopped, handed Toron his light stone, and unrolled one of the scrolls. He read the spidery runes of magic, each one flaring out of existence with a tiny flash of flame as soon as he read them aloud. When he came to the end of the scroll and the last rune had burned away, Azerick let the charred vellum drop to the ground.

"I do not see any effect," Toron stated.

"Not yet, but the gnomes will. Let's go. We are not done yet."

The pair ran back up the tunnel toward the magical doorway and stopped about halfway back. Azerick unrolled the second scroll and cast the spell it contained with similar invisible effects.

"That takes care of that. I'll follow you through the doorway," Azerick told Toron.

"I do not care much for a wizard's chicanery. I hope you appreciate the level of trust I show you by stepping through such a thing."

"Your trust in me is greatly appreciated. Now get your big hairy butt through the portal."

Azerick dropped his light stone before he followed Toron through. The magical gate snapped shut as soon as Azerick stepped through the doorway. He walked to the ledge and cast his gate spell on the far side of the chasm. The portal's exit he placed several feet away from the distant wall over a hundred feet above the chasm floor. He then unrolled a third scroll and prepared his last surprise and waited for the enemy's arrival.

The two earth elementals lumbered into the rune field Azerick had cast from the first scroll with the gnomes following close behind them. The elementals strode through the field without setting off the magical traps, their stone forms lacking the flesh and blood the spell required to trigger its effect. The unfortunate cavern gnomes had no such protection.

Several gnomes made it nearly halfway across before the first trap erupted in a bright burst of energy, searing the flesh of the individual who stepped on it. Several more bursts followed as more of the gnomes marched into the trapped field.

The elementals continued their pursuit of the fleeing humans, oblivious to the attacks on the gnomes. Less than a minute later, the lead elemental reached Azerick's second trap. A sphere of pent-up energy floated invisibly over the center of the passageway, waiting for anyone or anything to pass near it.

When the first stone behemoth came within a few feet of it, it became visible and exploded. The force of the blast shattered the lead elemental's entire upper torso. It took two more steps then fell forward and lay still. The remaining elemental lost its left hand, and a web of cracks ran through its chest. The gnomes had wisely chosen not to follow quite so close behind their summoned creatures, but flying bits of stone still caused several deep lacerations in those nearest.

The stone caller was furious at the destruction of another of his creatures and shouted in rage at the remaining elemental's back. He was familiar with the chasm ahead, and he knew the humans could not be far unless they could fly. He urged the earth elemental onward, desperate to destroy these interlopers once and for all.

The stone caller saw a pale light ahead and knew the humans must be just around the bend. The remaining earth elemental rounded the corner, took three more steps, and unwittingly stepped through the dimensional gate, which deposited it a hundred feet over the great black abyss of the chasm. It fell soundlessly until its hulking body shattered on the stones below.

The spell expired just as the stone caller rounded the bend. He glared at the sorcerer who had somehow managed to get his people across the deep gorge.

Azerick called across the chasm as more gnomes appeared on the other side. "I will tell you one more time. We have no interest in fighting you or encroaching on your territory. We are merely refugees trying to get home, but we will defend ourselves. How many more of you are willing to sacrifice your lives in this pointless pursuit? Cut your losses, and allow us to leave unmolested."

"Human, I am named the stone caller. All around you is stone, and I am its master. You and your people are doomed. Your petty tricks are no match for the power within the rock!" he shouted and raised his gem once more.

It felt as though the entire world began shaking beneath Azerick's feet. Stalactites began falling from the cavern ceiling all around him. The gorge echoed with the sharp crack of rock splitting apart.

"You have made a very poor decision, stone caller," Azerick yelled and read the last word remaining on the scroll he held in his hands.

The instant the remaining rune burned away from the paper, a massive fireball erupted behind the ranks of cavern gnomes standing on the far side of the gorge. The blast sent a dozen of the short figures hurling out over the black abyss as if flung from a catapult. Another half-dozen or more of the gnomes gathered near its epicenter perished under the intense heat of the inferno. Those who were able raced back in the direction from which they had come, deciding that these humans were not worth more of their lives.

The earth shaking subsided when Azerick's spell blasted the stone caller through the air, along with many of his kin, and dashed them upon the rocks below. Azerick turned from the needless destruction and walked back to his people.

"I do not think they will be bothering us any longer," Azerick told Zeb when he returned to the front of the group.

"I would think not." Zeb recognized the despondent look on Azerick's face. "Don't let it get you down, son. Life is hard all by itself, but some people insist on making it harder than it needs to be. Don't let it make you hard on yourself."

"You're right, Zeb. I know. I'm just getting so tired of all the death that seems to happen around me. Just once I would like to be an agent for good—for life."

The old captain scowled at the young man. "Look around you, boy! That is exactly what you are to these people! If it weren't for you, they would be living and dying as slaves right now. They know you are good, and they know you have given them a chance at a real future. You have made good things happen, and you have the power and character to make a lot more good things happen for a lot of people. I see the greatness in you, lad, and so do they."

Azerick looked into the faces of the dirty, exhausted people around him. Several men nodded and the women smiled as he looked at them.

"Thanks, Zeb, I'll do my best to remember that. Let's find a place to rest a while. I'm beat."

The tattered and weary company plodded on for another hour before finding a suitably large yet defensible cavern in which to rest. Azerick channeled much of his remaining energy into a large stalagmite, warming it until it glowed bright orange and started to crack under the intense heat. The spire put out enough heat to keep the group of humans warm for several hours as they rested. Toron woke him some time later. Azerick saw that almost everyone was up and preparing to move once more.

"Toron, I completely forgot about your injury. How are you doing?" Azerick asked the big minotaur.

"I will survive, though it does pain me a small amount," Toron replied.

Azerick knew that for Toron to admit to any pain it must be quite severe. "Let me take a look at it before we move out. I may be able to make a compress to dull the pain and quicken the healing."

"If you think it is necessary I will submit myself to your ministrations," Toron acquiesced, secretly grateful for any help in relieving the discomfort. His pride insisted it was only because it might hinder his fighting ability.

Azerick held a light up close and gently smoothed the coarse hair away from the wound to see it better. Even this gentle touch made the stout creature flinch. The damage was evident, and Azerick was amazed that even a hardy creature like Toron had been able to endure such injury without complaint for so long. An area the size of a small dinner plate was swollen and purple. He could feel the sharp edges of at least three fractured ribs that must have been grinding together and causing an extreme amount of pain.

Azerick winced internally at the sight of the injury. "I need to bandage these ribs. That should help keep them from moving about as much. I can also make a poultice to numb the tissue and take down the swelling."

Toron simply nodded while Azerick used the last of his water to make a paste out of some of the herbs he carried. He then tore several shirts, almost the last of the spare clothing any of them possessed, into long strips. He applied the paste in a thick glob over the injury then wrapped the linen strips tightly over it and around the minotaur's broad chest.

Azerick paused in tying off the bandage as his breath caught. His mind recalled the time he had met Delinda after his first fight and how she had treated a similar injury of his. With great effort, Azerick pushed this memory down where he collected and stored the other traumatic experiences of his life. The young sorcerer still had a duty to perform. His mourning would have to wait a bit longer.

"I wish I could do more for you, but that's the best I can do for now," Azerick told him.

"I thank you for your help. It feels better already."

"Just try to avoid any fighting for a few weeks," Azerick advised sarcastically.

"Only if fighting avoids us," Toron rumbled without a hint of mirth.

Azerick walked next to Zeb as they negotiated their way through the underground labyrinth of tunnels. His people were exhausted and scared, and their rations were almost gone. Everyone was looking to him for all the answers, but he did not have any.

"I had to use the last of my water making a poultice for Toron. How is everyone else doing?"

"Not good. Even drinking sparingly, this will be the last day any of us will have so much as a drop to drink."

Toron's deep voice came from behind them. "As we near the surface we should find water as it seeps through the ground above and feeds the natural aquifers below. Every stalagmite and stalactite you see was formed by dripping water and minerals."

Azerick added, "All we can do is keep going and hope we find an underground spring or pool."

At the next short rest break Azerick, Zeb, and Balor collected every skin and jug containing any amount of water, consolidated it before passing it around, and gave an equal amount to each person. When the last person drank their mouthful, the last of the water was completely depleted. Unless they found water soon, their exodus may well come to an ignoble end.

The small company marched until the weakest amongst them became too exhausted to continue before stopping for another long rest. Everyone's throat was parched, and people were becoming irritable and despondent, but their common cause helped keep them together. Another obstacle presented itself about three hours into the day's march when the tunnel they were following came to an abrupt end.

"Damn all the dark luck to the abyss!" Zeb cursed. "The last time the tunnel forked was where we started this morning!"

A young man by the name of Derran stepped toward the wall, craning his neck up to try and glimpse the top of the cavern hidden in darkness. As a lad of only sixteen, Derran was the youngest sailor and former slave amongst them. He was known for his keen eyesight and was often put on watch duty in the crow's nest when they were at sea.

"I think the tunnel might continue up there. It looks a little darker toward the top than the surrounding rock," he said. "This wall don't look too hard to climb. I'll scramble up there and take a closer look."

Derran found some suitable handgrips and hiked one leg up, pushing off with it as soon as he found a secure foothold. He brought his other leg up and began to scale the rough rock face. The young sailor let out a yelp of surprise and appeared to levitate up the wall.

Without hesitating to think, Azerick ran forward, leapt as high as he could, grabbed ahold of the belt strapped around Derran's waist, and pulled himself up, climbing the lad's back like it was cargo netting. Whatever had ahold of Derran was reeling both young men up the side of the wall like an angler landing a fish.

"When we get to the top, grab the ledge as tightly as you can," Azerick spoke into his ear as he climbed higher up Derran's back.

The two humans were nearly twenty feet above the cave floor when they reached the edge of the tunnel high above the humans gathered at the base of the wall. Azerick's head appeared over the ledge first, and he stared into the black, bulbous eyes of some strange chitin-covered creature.

A long, black, ropey, tongue-like appendage extended between two large mandibles had attached itself to Derran and was reeling them both in. Not wanting to wait until they came within reach of the pair of massive claws the creature wielded, Azerick let loose a powerful blast of lightning right at the creature's open mouth. Both humans dropped as the creature released its hold on its prey with a loud screech of pain. Fortunately, Derran had the presence of mind to grasp the ledge before they both fell painfully to the floor below.

"Do you have a good grip?" Azerick asked the struggling young man under him.

"Not good enough if you don't get off my back in the next few seconds," he grunted.

Azerick clawed at the rough floor of the cave and pushed off Derran's shoulders until he was able to get his center of gravity over the ledge and safely onto the cave floor. He spun around on his stomach, grabbed Derran's wrists, and helped pull him up over the ledge. The two young men sat on the ledge a moment to catch their breath.

"Hey, you two all right up there?" Zeb called up from below.

Azerick poked his head over the edge and answered. "Yeah, we're fine. Derran was right. The passage continues up here."

"Well, if you're done foolin' around with the local wildlife, maybe you can help get the rest of us up."

Azerick could see Zeb's teeth shining in the light he carried and knew the old coot was teasing him. He would get everyone else up in a moment, but first he wanted to make sure there were no more surprises waiting for them up here. Derran drew one of the gnome picks from his belt as Azerick stepped toward the creature now lying dead on its back.

"Oh, man, that thing stinks," Derran complained, drawing his arm over his nose.

He looked it over as Azerick conjured up another light to get a better look at what lay behind it. The tunnel continued for as far as the sorcerer's light could illuminate. Azerick turned around and walked back toward the edge with the intention of bringing everyone else up. He saw Derran digging his fingers into a large crack his lightning bolt had rent in the creature's hard carapace. Before Azerick could say anything, the lad drew out a large piece of white flesh cooked by the intense heat of his lightning bolt, and stuffed it into his mouth.

"Hey, it tastes kind of like crab! Needs butter though."

"Great, if you don't die from poisoning we can eat some fresh meat tonight."

He stopped chewing. "You think it's poisonous?" he asked, his words muffled by the meat stuffed in his cheeks.

Azerick grinned. "Probably not, but I think the rest of us will wait a bit before joining you for dinner."

Derran shrugged his shoulders and began chewing again, figuring if the meat was poisonous it was too late to spit it out now. At least he would die with a full stomach. Azerick stepped near the edge of the cave and cast his magical doorway to get the rest of the group up to the top.

Further exploration revealed a small pool of water about a hundred feet farther back down the tunnel. It was more of a puddle than a pool.

Dripping water had formed a bowl in the floor of the cave about three feet across and three inches deep. By the time everyone drank their fill and refilled everything that could hold water, the basin was nearly dry. The water had a strong taste of minerals, but it was cool and refreshing, and no one was about to complain. Derran did not yet feel any ill effects from eating the cave creature, so Azerick used his magic to cook the meat the sailors and women cut from the carcass.

They had only been marching a few hours today, but they decided this would be a good place to rest and recuperate from their long ordeal before continuing their journey. Since there was no night or day in this subterranean abyss, the group did not need to wait for the sun to rise before marching on. After several hours of rest, they were ready to resume their quest to the surface.

Mile after mile the group trudged through the cold, dank cavern, wondering if they would ever find their way out. All Azerick could do was encourage them to push on and try to ease the fearful mutterings of those who were rapidly losing all hope.

Near the end of the next day, excited whispering began to circulate amongst the refugees as a faint draught became evident within the tunnel. The whispers broke into wild cheering when one of the lead men shouted back that there was light up ahead. Azerick, Zeb, Toron, and the rest of the weary runaway slaves raced toward the orange glow and fresh air streaming into the tunnel from a large cleft partway up the side of a mountain range.

The sun was just setting, so they decided to spend one last night sheltered in the confines of the cave, but with jubilation not felt since they had escaped their captors. Azerick sat with his back to the fire made from wood foraged from the forest below, and stared out at the clear, star-filled night.

Zeb took a seat next to the young sorcerer. "You did it, lad. You gave these people hope, and you gave them their freedom."

"Maybe there is something else waiting for me other than a life of anger and vengeance. What are you going to do now, Zeb?"

"Find a port and a ship, I guess. That's all I really know. I imagine some of the other lads will follow me. Some may be done with sailing, not as I could blame them."

"I guess we will see soon enough."

"Yep."

CHAPTER 8

Everyone awoke early to watch what they all considered to be the most glorious sunrise of their lives. Men, women, and minotaur stared at the glowing horizon and watched in hushed anticipation as the ultimate symbol of freedom crested over the distant hills. Some wept, some hugged those next to them, and all felt their spirits brighten as the soft, golden rays of the great fiery orb burned away the darkness and destroyed the oppressive bleakness from their souls.

Azerick turned to his captain. "I would appreciate any advice you could offer on just what we do from here."

Zeb gave him a half-smile and a soft grunt. "I'm not much of a landlubber, but I know everything ends up in the ocean eventually. I say we find the nearest river or stream and follow the flow. We'll either find a settlement of some kind or the sea. I've been up and down Valeria's coast a thousand times since I was a cabin boy, and I reckon I'd be able to tell ya pretty much where we are from the look of the coastline. Assuming we're in Valeria, that is."

Azerick nodded in agreement. "I have a good knowledge of geography, but without a reference point it's useless. I imagine we will find a town along the river. I guess our first step is to find a waterway, follow it down, and see where it leads us."

"That's the way I figure it," Zeb agreed.

Shortly after the sun cleared the top of the distant hills, the group headed west in hopes of finding civilization. Game was scarce and skittish, but they managed to bring down enough rabbits and squirrels to keep the group fed. A few wild roots and spices also made for a palatable stew. On the third day, two of the sailors killed a small doe drinking at the edge of a river.

The river was narrow, but fast and deep. They followed it downstream for the first three days, and it never expanded to more than a hundred yards wide. Frothing whitewater rapids and waterfalls were common. Most of the falls were only a few feet in height, but one cascaded over a cliff and crashed into a deep pool a hundred feet below. The roar of thousands of gallons of water continuously striking the pool sounded like the charging of a thousand warhorses.

The majestic cascade began its plunge at the top of a rocky cliff. The group was forced to follow a steep ridgeline for nearly half a day before the slope gentled enough for them to make their way back down to the river. After two more exhausting days of travel, they found the landscape slowly transforming from rough mountains to rolling hills.

The hills eventually flattened out until the river opened up into a large valley. As the land smoothed out, the river grew wider and wider until a fired crossbow bolt would fall well short of reaching the distant bank.

Upon entering the valley, tilled fields and small farmhouses began dotting the countryside. Azerick let Zeb talk to the farmers, as he did not consider himself a very sociable person. The farmers stared warily at Toron and held flails, hoes, or pitchforks in a white-knuckled grip, but they were polite enough.

The farmers told Zeb they had a small town called Riverdale of maybe two thousand souls counting all the folks from the outlying farms and woodsmen. Riverdale was perhaps another three days on foot, but there were several farms that might allow them to take shelter in their barns and purchase food if they had something to trade for it.

Most of the farmers treated them much like the first ones had. They were initially cautious of such a large number of strangers, especially the intimidating minotaur, but they were polite and allowed them all to rest in their barns to get out of the elements. After weeks of sleeping on the hard ground of the mountains and even harder stone of the caverns, the soft hay in the barn's loft felt like a bed fit for royalty.

Many of the gnomes had carried small lumps of raw gold and uncut gems that the humans were able to trade for milk, cheese, bread, and cooked oats. Such common fare tasted like a banquet after eating nothing but game meat and wild roots.

Only one farmer gave them any trouble. A surly old codger who tilled a small patch of ground by himself was ready to fight the entire group of humans single-handedly if they did not clear out immediately. Even Toron was unable to impress the truculent farmer.

The group slept outside that night, but they still had the food they had purchased along the way to keep them fed. The party spied a quaint community in the distance just past noon the next day. A wooden wall and palisade jutted up a dozen feet from ten-foot-high earthworks encircling the town. Wide wooden gates were propped open to admit those entering or leaving the town.

Two men, town militia from the looks of them, maintained a relaxed guard at the gates. One man leaned on a spear just in front of the gates while the other stood watch from the catwalk near the top of the inside of the wall.

Azerick noted that the man on the ground had a crossbow slung over his back while the guard on the catwalk kept his resting between the pointed tips of the wall. The men did not seem overly surprised at their appearance. Azerick knew they had probably been watching them approach the town for the last hour.

As they drew nearer, he also noticed over a score of armed men gathered just inside the gates. These were probably a group of militiamen hastily assembled in case the strangers proved to be troublesome.

When Azerick and his band of refugees approached to within fifty feet of the gates, the guardsman on the ground called out to them. "Stop right there, if you please."

Zeb and his party complied with the man's request. "Hail, guardsman. My name's Zeb, ship's captain and trader. My friends and I would like entrance to your fair town."

"Unless you brought a river barge upstream, you're a long way from any boats, Captain. What is it you want in Riverdale?" the guard asked.

"We are poor travelers trying to get home. We would like some lodging and to trade for some food and traveling supplies. On my oath, none of us wish your town or people any harm. We will abide by your laws and cause no trouble while we're here," Zeb assured the guard.

"Mayor Remkin has been told of your approach and will be here shortly. He's the one to decide whether you come in or go around and be on your way. Normally, we don't bother travelers, but you're a big bunch and more than a bit haggard-looking. No offense. Moreover, we don't get many of your big friend's type around here. Never in fact." The guard looked back toward the town beyond the open gates. "Here comes the mayor now. He'll get it all straightened out."

A short, overweight man with a jovial face and wearing a well-made suit, which was at least ten years out of fashion, waddled through the press of militia and gawking citizens to present himself to the travelers waiting outside his beloved town. Zeb stood slightly forward of the group, so the mayor addressed him as the spokesman for them all.

"Good day, travelers! I am Mayor Remkin. Please allow me to welcome you to our fair town."

"Oh, so we are welcome after all. I was getting worried we weren't wanted here," Zeb said sourly.

The mayor's plump face reddened at Zeb's bitter comment and replied in a conciliatory voice. "Please forgive us for our cautious greeting. We are far from any major city and must rely on our own for most of our defense. It is rare to have so many travelers approach our gates at once, particularly with such a formidable-looking, ah, gentleman in their midst. What brings you all to Riverdale, if I may inquire?"

Zeb gave a shortened version of their capture, escape, and travails through the caverns. "We only wish to rest, get some good warm food, and purchase or trade for some traveling supplies."

Mayor Remkin remained silent throughout Zeb's tale of woe, and the guard nearly fell over as he leaned on his spear trying to eavesdrop. The mayor's face went from flushed to pale then flushed again as he listened to the party's tribulations.

"By the good gods above what an incredible ordeal you all went through! On behalf of the people of Riverdale, I bid you welcome. Follow me to our inn where you will drink and dine on my town's hospitality. Perhaps if you are willing, you can regale the evening crowd with your story. We get so few tales of adventure or news of the kingdom out here, and we are all eager to hear of happenings outside our valley."

"I suppose that would be more than fair compensation for your generosity," Zeb replied, brightening at the prospect of some proper food.

"Follow me then and I'll see that you poor folks are taken care of properly," the mayor invited. He turned and preceded them down the packed dirt avenue.

Zeb led the group through the throng of citizens who stood around talking in hushed tones about the strangers, especially the big minotaur. Azerick noticed the gate guard run off to spread their tale as soon as they passed. It took only a few minutes for them to reach the inn located near the center of town.

At three stories, it was the tallest building around with the exception of two tall grain silos. The first two stories were rough stone, mortared in place. The third story was made of wood and had likely been built sometime after the original two floors. The rest of the town was built primarily of wood logged from the abundance of trees growing in the nearby hills and mountains. Most buildings were single-storied, but a few rose as high as two.

The owner kept the inside of the inn even better than the immaculate outside. Wagon wheels suspended from the rafters supported six oil lamps, each providing warm light to the interior of the common room. Two dozen tables, each surrounded by four chairs, and four long tables with benches, provided seating for a large number of patrons.

A long, well-polished bar ran nearly the entire length of the back of the inn. Through a swinging door wafted the scents of the entrees being prepared for the evening's meals. A wide staircase with an ornately carved banister rose up to the second floor where several doors were visible behind an open balcony protected by a rail crafted in the same fashion as the banister stretched above the bar overlooking the common room below.

The man standing behind the bar bore a striking resemblance to the mayor, albeit he was considerably thinner, which still put him just over the line of heavy. He looked up as they all strode in and Mayor Remkin hailed him.

"Belkin, these are visitors to the town and my personal guests. Let's get them washed up, fed, and bunked down for a couple nights until I can figure out what else we can do for them."

The innkeeper did a double take when he watched Toron duck his head to keep his horns from striking the wagon wheel chandelier then gave the mayor his attention.

"I can put the ladies in one room and divide the gentlemen up between a few others. It'll be a bit cramped, but I can get some extra mattresses stuffed with straw and laid out for them." Belkin called back to the kitchen where a plump woman with greying black hair promptly burst through the swinging door. "Sofia, we'll be putting these folks up for a couple days. Rustle up some help and get washtubs taken up to rooms two, three, five, six, and eight. We'll also need mattresses stuffed and brought up for each of them."

Sofia made a quick count and disappeared back into the kitchen where they could hear her issuing orders to more of the staff.

"You folks look like you could use a drink. Food will be ready in about two hours if you can hold off a bit longer and make yourselves comfortable."

Belkin filled mugs of ale for the men and watered wine for the women. The innkeeper set the cups on the bar as soon as he poured them and they were promptly passed around with many words of thanks. When the last glass was served, he waved the mayor over to him while his guests took up seats around several of the tables.

As Azerick, Zeb, and the rest of their motley band sat sipping what to them was the finest drinks they had ever tasted, several men, women, and boys carted washtubs, buckets of water, and mattresses up the stairs. The mayor and the innkeeper were having a hushed discussion at the end of the long bar.

"Now, brother, maybe you can tell me what is going on. Who are these people, and where did they come from, and what in the world is that massive bloke with the horns on his head?" Belkin asked his brother, the mayor.

"They say most of them were sailors who were captured by some foul creatures and made slaves somewhere far off. They escaped, though they didn't really say how, crawled days through tunnels under the Witch Crag Mountains from the sound of it, and found their way here," Mayor Remkin told his younger brother. "I figured to put them up for a time. Their stories alone will have your inn packed for several nights and will more than make up for the cost of housing them."

"Not to cast aspersions on your good nature, but I find it hard to believe you would go through this much trouble to accommodate a gang of bedraggled strangers. What is it you are looking to get out of this?" Belkin asked, narrowing his eyes at his rotund brother.

"I have not asked nor demanded anything in return, but I hope I might convince them to stay on awhile and help us out. You know as well as I do we need as many hands as we can get."

"I'm glad to hear you have some ulterior motive. For a moment there, I thought you had gone completely angelic. What about you know who?"

The smile dropped from the mayor's face at the reference to the name not mentioned. "I imagine they'll all be gone by the time he shows up. If for some reason they aren't, I seriously doubt they will cause any trouble. Who would dare?"

Belkin shook his head. "I don't know, that big hairy fellow with the horns looks like one not to be pushed around, and have you spoken to the young man with the eyes that seem to look right through you?" he asked with a nod toward Azerick.

"No, he hasn't said much of anything since I met them at the gate. He's just a young sailor. What harm could he cause?"

"Remkin, I've run inns for a long time, and I've met a lot of folks. I may not be as worldly and knowledgeable as some big city gossipmonger, but I can read people with the best of them. Mark my words, that lad is no mere sailor. They ever tell you how they all managed to escape from where they were held, or what happened to the ones who held them?"

"No, they never really gave me any details."

"I'll bet my inn the lad played a big part in it, and whoever held them is no longer in any condition to ever try it again," Belkin replied ominously.

"What makes you say that?"

"Look how he carries himself. You see how everyone is enjoying themselves, talking, and laughing? Everyone but him. He keeps looking around the room, making sure no one surprises them, as if he alone is responsible for their safety."

"Maybe he's just paranoid. If half of what they say is true, that would be enough to make any man wary."

The mayor's brother shook his head. "Nope, that's the look of a predator, not prey. Anyone who runs an inn learns how to spot trouble quick if they want to stay in business for long. All the others in that band keep looking at him, not the captain, and not that big fellow. Push comes to shove, he'll push back; mark my words."

Zeb and Balor both spoke freely, trying several times to get Azerick to join in on the conversation. Toron was his usual quiet self, offering little more than a grunt or a shrug of his big hairy shoulders in answer to any question posed to him. Azerick was too busy staring over his cup, watching the discourse between the innkeeper and the mayor, to pay any heed to his friends.

"I have to tell you, lad," Zeb turned to Azerick, trying to engage him once more, "I've set anchor in many ports and been to many places, but this is by far one of the friendliest. What do you think?"

"They are gracious to be sure, but why? Why are they putting themselves out like this for a bunch of tattered strangers who look like they were pulled straight out of a gutter?" Azerick asked almost rhetorically.

"They're small-town folk, eager to hear of adventures and news beyond their secluded valley. It's not so much to give a bit of food and a roof over our heads in exchange for some tales."

"I suppose not. Do me a favor though. Do not say anything about me other than I am an herbalist, and spread the word to the others," Azerick insisted.

"Sure, lad, I can do that. Do you really think there is something wrong here? Are we in trouble?"

"Something is not right, but I can't say what. Just something I feel. It may not even be from them, but be careful. Guard yourselves and your tongues around them."

"Sure, lad, I'll go tell the boys." Zeb picked up his tankard and made his rounds to all the tables occupied by his men.

Mayor Remkin finished his chat with his brother and waddled over to Azerick's table. He glanced in Toron's direction and saw that the minotaur was paying him no attention and sat down.

"I hope you men are comfortable. Is there anything else I can do for you?" Remkin asked kindly.

"No, Mr. Mayor, you have been most generous to us all," Balor replied, giving him a salute with his mug.

The mayor turned to Azerick. "What about you, young sir? You don't look to be enjoying yourself as much as the others. Is there something I can do to make your stay more pleasing?"

"Forgive me, Mayor Remkin, I am just lost in thought, I guess. You have shown us every kindness, far more than anyone could ask," Azerick responded flatly.

"That is good to hear, good indeed. Tell me, I'm sorry I did not seem to catch your name."

"Azerick."

"Tell me, Azerick, you do not appear to be a sailor like the others. You strike me more as an educated and contemplative sort. What is it you do if, I may be so nosy?" the mayor prodded.

"I'm an herbalist."

"Excellent! I should introduce you to Margaret Thistledown. She is our town healer. She's getting on in age and is teaching her herb lore to Anna Tanner. You three should have a lot to talk about."

"Perhaps, if we are here long enough."

The mayor clapped his hands together one time and stood up. "Well, I believe my brother Belkin has your rooms ready. Several washtubs have been filled, and there is a large communal bath with warm water through that door," he told them, indicating a door near the kitchen entrance. "I will leave you all to get settled and relax before dinner is served."

The three former slaves looked at each other as the plump mayor walked out of the inn. Balor was the first to break the silence as Zeb sat back down with them.

"He seems sincere. Do you still think there is danger here?" Balor asked Azerick.

"I don't know. I wish I did, but I just do not know," Azerick replied shaking his head.

"He is hiding something, keeping something from us, but I do not think he means us harm," Toron said, adding his deep voice to the conversation for the first time.

"What do you think he is hiding? We have nothing to steal or swindle." Zeb said.

"So what should we do?" Balor asked.

Azerick stood up from the table. "I for one am going to take a warm bath and eat every bit of food they will give me."

"And drink all the ale!" Toron joined in.

The three men, the minotaur, and Cook took advantage of the large communal bath while the rest of the men and women were shown to their rooms and cleaned up in the provided washtubs. The communal bath was far nicer than any of them had expected. It was simply tiled, but it was six feet on each side and three feet deep. Wisps of steam rose above the water, promising a deeply relaxing soak.

"Now this is what I needed," Azerick sighed, feeling relaxed for the first time in as long as he could remember.

The water rose to just under his chin as he sat on a small stone step running along the entire bottom of the bath. The heat soaked deep into his muscles, unraveling knots that had been tense for so long he thought the pain was a normal part of his existence.

"It is grand," Zeb agreed. "However, I'm afraid I'm going to end up with more hair on me than Toron by the time we're done," he remarked as he pinched a wad of coarse reddish-brown fur between his fingers and flung it onto the floor.

"You should be so lucky," rumbled Toron, not even bothering to open his eyes.

"I feel like a clam being boiled for supper. Mm, steamed clams," Cook mumbled sleepily.

Nearly an hour later, their skin as wrinkled as prunes, the men finally pried themselves away from the luxurious bath. Azerick noticed that the water never cooled, and the bottom seemed to radiate heat.

"They must have pipes running just under the bottom tiles with heat fed by a furnace or the kitchen stoves. It is a clever idea, whoever thought of it," Azerick remarked.

They had started to put their old, filthy clothes back on when the innkeeper stepped in carrying a stuffed burlap sack. "The mayor organized a collection, and folks from the town donated a bunch of clothes. It's nothing you would want to wear to a ball, but it's clean and in decent shape. I would offer to get your own things washed, but I think they would all unravel if we tried."

Zeb took the bag from the innkeeper and thanked him for his and the townsfolk's continued generosity. Belkin nodded in appreciation and left them to get dressed. Zeb dumped the bag out and picked through the various articles of clothing, sizing everyone as best he could. There was plenty to choose from, so it was not hard to find something for everyone. They even found a large pair of overalls and a heavy sleeveless shirt that almost fit Toron.

When they finally walked out of the bath chamber, they found most of their band seated at the tables drinking wine, beer, and ale. In front of them were plates laden with slabs of beef, cooked vegetables, and fried potatoes. Loaves of bread so fresh they were still warm filled baskets on the tables. Many of the men broke out in cheers and applause when Zeb and Azerick stepped into the common room.

They took a seat at an empty table and were promptly served. Everyone's mouth began watering even before the plates were set down. The food was as delicious as it was plentiful. It was an effort, but Azerick managed to finish his plate, even going so far as to wipe it clean with a chunk of bread. When he looked over at Toron, he was surprised to see the minotaur was only half-finished with his meal. Then he noticed the two empty plates beneath the one from which he was eating.

Azerick and Zeb were both leaning back in their chairs to take some of the pressure off their stomachs and sipping at ale when the mayor entered the common room. He gazed around the room until his eyes settled on Zeb and Azerick. He gave them a friendly wave, which only Zeb returned, and strode over to their table.

"Gentlemen, I trust you and your people are feeling better after a good bath and a fine meal," he said cordially.

"And clean clothes," Zeb added with a smile. "We owe you and your townspeople a great deal for your generosity and kindness."

Azerick shot the captain a hard look of caution. "It would not be called generosity if one expected something in return, only payment."

"Please, think nothing of it, we are all glad to help," Remkin replied, waving off Zeb's feeling of indebtedness. "However, if you would like to return a kindness with a kindness I do have a small request. I have kept the locals away from here, at great difficulty I might add, so you and your friends could refresh yourselves and eat in peace, but soon Belkin will have to open his doors to his regular customers and likely a great deal of infrequent ones. Everyone in town is going to want to meet you all, buy you drinks, and hear of your arduous journey. If you would be kind enough to indulge a bit of their curiosity then please consider any debt you feel you may be beholden to paid in kind."

"I'm sure my people would be glad to entertain yours with tales of their adventures and travels. It's the least we could do," Zeb responded and gripped the mayor's soft, meaty hand in his own, once again missing Azerick's glare.

"I have passed the word that we mustn't pry too hard. If any of your folk feel as though anyone is overly nosy, please do not be afraid to politely tell them so."

"I'm sure we'll be just fine, Mayor," Zeb assured him.

With a polite nod, Mayor Remkin excused himself and left. Within minutes, local townsfolk started filtering into the inn, ordering drinks and food. They slowly began striking up conversations and buying drinks for the newcomers, hoping to elicit a few stories from them. It was not hard to do. Most of the former sailors enjoyed spinning yarns and chatting with new faces.

Three young women from the town surrounded Derran. He regaled them with his daring exploit with the cave creature that had roped him in and nearly made a meal of him. Except in his version, it was Azerick who had been caught, he who had jumped onto his back, and plunged his pick through the creature's brain. The girls let out a squeak of shock then broke into fits of laughter when Derran told them of how he had reached into the creature's cracked shell, plucked out a chunk of meat, and popped it into his mouth. Azerick did not mind the young man's spin on the event since it left his sorcery unmentioned.

After several rounds of drinks, people even gathered the courage to talk to the taciturn Toron. A loud, angry bellow and the sound of toppling chairs broke the congenial atmosphere and ended every conversation.

Azerick looked toward the commotion and saw that Toron had a local man pressed against the wall with one huge hand wrapped around his throat and was holding the man a foot above the floor so the angry minotaur could look him in the eyes. Azerick sprinted across the room and laid a hand on Toron's muscular arm.

"Toron, let him go! What's the matter?"

"This fool asked if my eating the beef tonight was something akin to cannibalism!" Toron growled. "Do I look like some grass-eating, cud-chewing, simple-minded bovine?" the minotaur roared.

The terrified man tried to shake his head, but Toron's powerful grip held it fast. The man's face was turning purple, and Azerick knew he had to defuse the situation before something bad happened.

"To be honest with you, Toron, there is a striking resemblance from the neck up. A most powerful and impressive bull to be sure, but the similarity is quite uncanny." Azerick said with a grin. "Please, Toron, these are isolated people who know very little outside their valley. I doubt many of them have ever even heard of your kind and they meant no offense."

Toron looked at the terrified man he held then smiled widely, revealing his sharp, prominent teeth. "Forgive my abruptness and prickly nature. I have shown myself to be a poor guest." Toron set the man gently back on his feet and released his grip on the man's throat.

"Think nothing of it, sir. I should have known better."

Toron clapped the man on the back amidst the strained laughter of the onlookers.

Azerick took a seat in a shadowy corner of the common room and hoped he would be able to pass the rest of the night in peace. The drinks kept flowing and laughter and revelry grew louder as the night progressed. He spotted the mayor several times making his rounds through the common room, stopping to visit each table. Mayor Remkin spotted the quiet young man in the corner, but the look on Azerick's face convinced him he was in no mood for conversation or joining the festivities.

"What is your game, Mayor? What is it you want from us, and when are you going to tell us what it is?" Azerick wondered aloud.

Azerick soon tired of sulking in his dark corner and decided to go to his room and read a bit of the ancient tome he had escaped with before going to sleep. Before ascending the stairs, he glanced over once at Toron's table to reassure himself that the big minotaur was not apt to cause any more trouble.

Toron was currently arm-wrestling a big farmer who must have been the one who donated the clothes that came close to fitting him. The minotaur put the farmer down easily. Azerick felt it safe to leave him alone as Toron squared off against two men at once and was seconds away from pressing both opponents' hands to the tabletop.

Zeb and the rest of the men Azerick currently shared accommodations with staggered into the room with the usual amount of excessive noise intoxicated men usually do at various hours of the early morning. Azerick awoke for the final time just as the sun rose, to the smell of alcohol fumes expelled by his friends' loud snoring. He got dressed and quietly descended the stairs even though he could have ridden a horse down them without waking the occupants.

The first thing Azerick saw when he came down the stairs was a large number of his men had not made it back to their rooms and lay scattered about the common room, with an equal number of locals sleeping off the effects of their revelry in chairs, sprawled across tables, or lying under them. The second thing he noticed was the smell of cooking coming from the kitchen. Azerick decided to poke his head through the swinging door and spotted the middle-aged woman named Sofia busily preparing the morning meals. She turned and found him looking through the door at her.

"Good morning to you. I'm surprised to see anyone up this early," Sofia greeted him warmly.

"Sorry, I did not mean to distract you from your duties. I am sure I will be about the only one up for quite some time."

"It's no bother. Would you like a bite of something to eat? I just pulled out some small loaves stuffed with cheese and sausage from the oven. It's my personal specialty. You won't find them anywhere else."

"If it's no trouble it sounds like just the thing to accompany me. I thought I would walk around the town and enjoy the quiet morning and cool air."

"Here, take two then in case you work up an appetite while you're out." Sofia smiled and wrapped the small loaves in a clean linen towel.

Azerick thanked her for her kindness and stepped out of the inn into the brisk early morning air. Fall was well upon the quiet valley. It would not be long until snow blanketed the entire vale and covered the mountains. He strode about the town, almost eerie in its stillness. The usual smells of city living were still evident but subdued. The odor of the tannery, horse stables, and emptied chamber pots would always carry on the air, but this early in the morning, it was more than tolerable.

It did not take Azerick long to cross from one end of the town to the other, and he decided to walk along the river for a while. He noticed the gates were closed and was disappointed at the thought he may not be able to get out until they were opened. A few guards walked the walls, and one stood next to the large, closed portal.

"Good morn to ya! Out and about early, I see," the guard next to the gate hailed him as he approachehd.

"Good morning to you too. I was hoping to take a walk along the river before the sun rose overmuch," Azerick replied as he drew up next to the guard. "I see the gates are closed. Does this mean folks are not allowed to leave the town yet?"

The guard gave a small laugh and shook his head. "Not at all. We keep the main gates closed for security, is all."

"Do you see so much trouble out here to need such security?"

The guard seemed to shuffle his feet and glance down at the ground. "No, not so much. We used to have an occasional raid by orcs or sneak thief goblins, but it has been quite some time since the last trouble arose."

He stepped over to a small postern gate Azerick had not noticed until now, lifted a heavy crossbeam out of its socket, and then opened it for him. "You're more than free to come and go as you please."

"Ah, good, thank you." Azerick stepped through the open door and wondered about the guard's discomfort at his question.

A low fog rolled over the ground as the rising sun slowly burned off the morning dew. He walked toward the river and followed along its bank, tossing rocks into the water, and letting his thoughts drift to nothing in particular. The sound of a rock turning underfoot close behind him snapped him out of his reverie.

He spun, tracing a sigil in the air as he pulled power from the Source, ready to unleash arcane energies against any threat. A young woman let out a squeal of surprise when Azerick faced her with dark intent evident in his eyes.

"I'm sorry! I didn't mean to startle you!" Anna said.

"Then you should not sneak up on people," Azerick replied crossly. He let the energy he had gathered drain back into the ether.

"I'm sorry. I was looking for plants and herbs along the ground. When I looked up you were right there. You looked distracted, and I thought I may startle you more if I called out."

Azerick grunted in reply and skipped another stone across the river's dark surface. Anna warily stepped closer and stood a few feet to Azerick's side. She was comely, perhaps a year or two younger than he was. She had soft brown hair plaited in a typical rural fashion. She wore a simple homespun linen dress with a light jacket and shawl to ward off the chilly morning air. A canvas satchel was slung over her shoulder from which the green tops of various plants stuck out of the opening.

"You are the herbalist the mayor mentioned, are you not? You fit his description, especially in the eyes."

"And what exactly did the good mayor say about my eyes that makes me so apparent?" Azerick asked sourly.

"That they are distant, unfriendly, and seem to look right through you," Anna stated with a lift of her chin.

"I guess the mayor has me figured out pretty well then." Azerick skipped another rock across the water.

"I don't think he does at all. I see a great deal of hurt in your eyes, and that your unfriendliness is deliberate to armor yourself against further pain."

Azerick turned and faced her once more. "What do you know of hurt and pain, living here in your nice, quiet, safe valley? Neither you nor your precious mayor know anything about me, or what I hide behind my eyes—or fail to obviously."

"I see you are in no mood for company. Forgive me for intruding. I shan't bother you any longer," Anna said and stalked away.

With a grunt of anger and embarrassment, Azerick flung the stone he had in his hand out across the water as hard as he could. He needed an outlet, a way to let go of the anger, rage, and pain still boiling up within him. He almost wished he were back in the arena so he could unleash it all through his magic, hoping each lightning bolt or destructive spell would take away part of the fury and anguish seeming to infuse every part of his body.

He forced himself to calm down, taking several deep breaths and letting himself sink into a trance-like state. Once he felt reasonably calm, he continued his walk along the river, trying to burn off some of the excess energy running through him. The sun's height showed it was approaching late morning, so he decided it was time to head back to the inn and see if Zeb and the others were up yet. The main gates were open now, and people milled about the streets. He spotted Zeb sitting at a table with the mayor as soon as he walked in. Zeb and the mayor both waved him over the moment he entered.

"Azerick, my boy, I see you decided to wake early and go sightseeing. Tell me, what do you think of our fair town and countryside?" the mayor asked in his usual cheery voice.

Azerick felt all the anger he had worked at suppressing come to a boil once more. He leaned onto the tabletop and glared at the fat man smiling up at him.

"Enough of your pleasantries, Remkin! What is your game, and what do you want from us?"

The morning crowd of guests and locals went dead silent at the young man's outburst. All eyes in the room turned toward the source of the confrontation.

Zeb watched the mayor's face go from fear to indignation at the young man's effrontery. "Azerick, what are you doing? This man is our host and has been most gracious in accommodating us."

"He's hiding something, and I damn well want to know what it is. People are not this selfless. Well, Mayor, what is it? Why are you trying to keep us here?"

Mayor Remkin sighed and cut off Zeb's continued apologies for Azerick's rudeness. "The young man is right. I do want something from you. I was trying to delay your departure and hoped to convince you to stay a while longer."

"Why? Why would you go to so much effort to burden yourselves with a bunch of homeless refugees?" Zeb asked. "Most towns would be pushing us out as quickly as possible."

"It has become apparent that winter is going to come early this year, and it will be especially harsh. We do not have enough hands to bring in our late summer crops before the first frost comes. I was hoping I could convince your people to stay long enough to help us bring in the harvest before the frosts destroyed them in exchange for putting you all up in the interim. Several of the farmers have agreed to make room for you all to stay with them through the winter if you would agree to help."

Azerick looked at the mayor quizzically. "Why did you not just come out and ask us? Why the charade to try and keep us here?"

"It was not a charade, although I suppose I laid it on a bit thick. We really are a good town, full of nice people and good intentions. It's just that with your story about escaping your captivity, I thought you would be too eager to return to your homes and would decline my request for help. If I could have convinced you to stay here for another week, snows would likely have closed the pass out of the valley, and you would have had no choice but to stay." The mayor looked abashed at his own duplicity. "I know it was wrong of me to attempt such a thing, but as the mayor it is my responsibility to ensure the continued success of my town. The harvest is very important to all of us, and it caused me to act with poor judgment. Please forgive me."

"Are you saying we are stuck here, that we cannot get through the pass?" Azerick asked a bit more calmly.

"I give you better than an even chance if you leave within the next day or two. Another week at most and the upper pass will be blocked by snow. Even if it is not, the threat of avalanche is too great to risk. If it is not too presumptuous of me, I still have to ask if you would consider staying on and helping us."

Azerick allowed himself to relax and sat down at the table. "That's it? That is what you were hiding from us? All you wanted was some manual labor in exchange for providing for us through the winter?"

Mayor Remkin lifted his hands, palms up. "That is all. Would you do it, or at least talk it over with your men?"

Azerick felt all his anger and suspicion drain from him. "Mayor Remkin, please forgive me. Any duplicity on your part pales in comparison to my rudeness and suspicion. I think an extended stay in your town is exactly what we may need. I also have no desire to walk home in the dead of winter."

Zeb concurred and promised to talk it over with his people today. Mayor Remkin returned to his usual jolly self at Azerick and Zeb's promise to discuss his proposal with the others. By the time lunch came around, Zeb had spoken to nearly everyone who had fled through the portal with him.

When the mayor returned to the inn, Zeb was able to give him the answer he wanted. Although several people had families they eagerly wished to return to, they realized the dangerous and harsh journey ahead made waiting until after the cold season a wiser decision.

Everyone supported the plan with varying levels of enthusiasm. That day, most of the men and women left to stay at the homes of outlying farms. A few remained in town to work at the silos and receive the crops the farmers brought in.

Azerick elected to reside at the inn and was introduced to the town's healer, Margaret Thistledown. Margaret was an ancient woman, but she was still fiery and full of life. It appeared even death respected her wishes and left her to decide on her own when her time was up.

"Anna is out collecting roots and plants with medicinal properties. I know I have waited too long to take on an apprentice to take over when I'm gone," she admitted. "Now my eyes are bad and my hands are too stiffened with arthritis. I need someone with a good knowledge of herb lore to show Anna firsthand the kinds of plants and roots she needs to collect."

"I suppose I could do that. I doubt I have nearly the experience you have accumulated, but I can take her out and find the plants you need," Azerick assured the old woman.

"I would have taken on an apprentice long before, but every girl who came to me was a bubble-headed little twit without the sense of a mentally deficient turkey."

The wizened herbalist began quizzing Azerick extensively on his knowledge of plants, herbs, roots, and healing. After more than two hours of interrogation, she concluded the young man was fit to assist her in educating her apprentice.

Azerick was impressed with the old woman's knowledge and was certain she contained a great deal more within that wrinkled, thinly grey-haired head of hers. Anna walked in just as Margaret finished grilling the young sorcerer.

"Anna, this is the young man the mayor sent to assist me in your education."

"Yes, we met briefly the other day," Anna replied formally.

"Please make us some tea before you hang your plants to dry," the old healer told Anna. She turned back to Azerick when Anna left the room. "She did not sound pleased to meet you."

"I am afraid I was a bit abrupt with her earlier."

Margaret let out a rough cackle. "Don't let it bother you overmuch. The girl's gotten a thick skin since she came to work for me. She'll be fine."

Azerick noticed several books upon a shelf, chose one at random, and began flipping through the pages. It was a handwritten journal detailing the properties and uses of various plants and roots accompanied by detailed color drawings. He replaced it and pulled out another. This one was entirely about mushrooms and fungi. Drawings, their benefits or toxicity, along with each variety's spore count accompanied every entry.

"Did you write all of these?" Azerick asked as he selected a third book from the shelf.

"Oh yes, back before my vision went. I wrote those over the last fifty or sixty years."

"They are spectacular. The drawings and descriptions are some of the best I have ever seen. Anna is fortunate to have such material at her disposal."

Margaret waved off the compliment with a snort. "There are many things a person must learn that simply cannot be put in books. Healing takes as much intuition as education, and you can't get intuition from a book. That is why she needs someone to go out with her and give her firsthand knowledge of such things. If healing and herb lore could be done out of a cookbook then everyone could do it."

"I had a teacher who told me very much the same thing," Azerick replied quietly.

Anna returned with three cups of tea and a small crock of honey to sweeten it. The conversation was light and subdued. When they finished with their tea, Margaret told Anna to go and hang her gatherings in the drying room and recommended that Azerick help her.

He followed the young woman through a door and was surprised to find the room beyond was even larger than the main room where they had sat and drunk tea. There was a large fireplace with a warm fire burning. Azerick knew it was more to dry out the air than to provide comfort.

Plants, roots, herbs, and fungi of all sorts hung from wires strung across the room. Anna went about using clothespins to clip the plants she had gathered this morning to the lines to dry. It did not take long for Azerick to decipher the organization she used. Like plants hung with like and were organized by their uses and properties.

"Anna, I would like to apologize for my rudeness the other day. I have not been myself for quite some time," Azerick explained.

Anna's face softened at his words. "It's all right. I imagine you are under quite a lot of stress from your ordeals. Margaret is not one to work for if your feelings are easily hurt."

Azerick grinned. "So she told me."

The rest of the day went much more smoothly. Azerick spent time discovering what Anna already knew so he could decide where best to start her training. The old healer had done quite well with her tutelage thus far, but Azerick found a few gaps in her education that he could start working on.

He returned to the inn that evening, found Zeb and Toron sitting at a table enjoying a meal and ale, and took a seat between the two. Both man and minotaur worked in town, so Azerick was not surprised to see them. Zeb's experience as a ship's captain made him an excellent foreman, and Toron's incredible strength allowed him to do the work of two men.

"How's the work going so far, Zeb?" Azerick asked as he took a seat.

"Well enough, I guess. It lacks the excitement of sailing, but it beats the heck out of polishing marble floors and brass all day. There's not much work to be done just now, but we'll be pulling some long nights when the crops start coming in."

"I for one will be glad to be finished with this farm labor," Toron rumbled. "I am eager to swing an axe again, even if it is only at trees."

Zeb answered Azerick's questioning look. "You see, I figure if we're going to be here for several months, the boys and I could build a ship and take it down the river by midsummer at the latest. It would make for much easier and faster traveling. I've asked around, and as far as anyone knows there are no falls or shallows to keep us from reaching the sea. Each man would have a stake in the boat and a share of any profit we might make with it."

Zeb got more and more excited as he continued to talk about his plan. "This place is ripe with timber, and not only for building the ship. The river runs right through the Habberback Plains. Great farming land, but not a piece of wood bigger than a broom handle for hundreds of miles or any iron ore to be mined. These folks mine much of their own ore from the nearby mountains. We load up the ship with timber and as much smelted or raw ore as we can, trade it for grain and produce at one of the Habberback towns on the river, then sell that load to one of the large coastal cities for a huge profit!"

"Sounds like you have it all figured out, Zeb. Do you think you can make a decent ship with what you have to work with here?" Azerick asked.

"No doubt about it. The boys and me know all there is to ship construction, and the locals have some excellent woodworkers and a waterwheel-driven saw to make the timbers. The hardest part is going to be getting enough tar to seal her up, but the locals told me there's a supply a few days southeast of here where the river drains into some lowlands making a marsh that has a couple natural tar pits. It'll be a chore getting it, but we'll manage."

"Let me know if there is anything I can do to help. It sounds like a grand idea, Zeb."

"You'll be going with us won't you, lad?"

"I imagine so, but who knows what will happen by then. I may grow to like the peaceful life here and stick around a while."

"Well, whatever you decide, I wish you luck, but I sure hope you go with us."

"Like I said, I haven't made my mind up one way or the other. We will see what happens when the time comes. I may find the quiet life is not for me."

"That's an understatement!" Zeb laughed.

Within days, wagonloads of crops began coming in to be stored in the silos and grain bins. Most of the women in the town were busy boiling water for canning fruits and vegetables into sealed glass jars to preserve them through the winter.

Azerick and Anna got the opportunity to treat the inevitable injuries that sprang up during such times of intense labor. One man broke his arm and injured his back when he fell from a grain elevator, and another got a nasty gash in his leg when he slipped from a piece of farm equipment and got it hung up on a sharp piece of metal. Two women had to be treated for burns they received from the boiling water used to seal the jars during the canning process.

Azerick and Anna continued to get along well. He even began to enjoy their walks in search of poultice and medicinal ingredients. The crops had been harvested with no more than three days to spare when the first heavy frost coated the ground and froze the earth solid. Within days of the frost, the first light snows carpeted the lower hills, and soon after the valley itself. Zeb, Toron, and Zeb's men along with a few local woodsmen worked through the snows, chopping down trees and pulling heavy logs on sledges with a team of mules to the mill next to the river.

Azerick walked into the inn one cold night after leaving Margaret's home and found Zeb sitting with Mayor Remkin. From the look on Zeb's face, he must have been talking about his ship. The mayor's face did not show Zeb's enthusiasm. Azerick picked up their conversation as he strode toward the table.

"How long do you think it will take you to complete this ship of yours, Zeb?" the mayor asked.

"I reckon we'll have her finished by the end of spring or early summer. If I just wanted a boat to get us home I could probably have her done before the snows melted, but I figured I'd make a good working ship, one I can use along the coasts as well as the river if I choose to."

"I just thought you would want to be gone as soon as the passes cleared and the river was navigable. You know the river is much more negotiable early or mid-spring, maybe you should think about a smaller ship." The mayor wiped beads of sweat from his brow.

"What's the matter, Remkin, are you trying to get rid of us already?" Zeb asked with a laugh.

"No, no of course not, I just want to be sure your travels go as smoothly as possible, is all. You let me know if you need any more assistance. I'm sure the townsfolk will be more than happy to return the favor of help."

"Thanks for the offer, Mayor, but we got about as many hands as we can use right now. The logs are coming into the warehouse faster than we can cut them, and my men already have a passable dry dock built and the keel laid out. Any more hands and they would just get in the way and slow us down."

"All right then, let me know if there is anything you need. I'll leave you two gentlemen alone." With a nod of acknowledgement to Azerick, the mayor stood and left the inn.

"The mayor seemed anxious to see us leave, don't you think?" Azerick asked Zeb.

"Naw, I'm sure he's just trying to be helpful, is all. So how are things working out for you?"

"Well enough, I suppose. I have actually learned at least as much as I have taught. Ms. Thistledown is extraordinarily knowledgeable, although she is more thistle than down."

Zeb gave Azerick's attempt at humor a chuckle. "That Anna seems a nice young lady though, attractive too, and smart."

"She's nice enough and capable, I suppose," Azerick admitted.

"Capable, huh?" Zeb grunted and shook his head.

Azerick changed the subject, not wanting to be drawn into any kind of personal discussions. They talked about Zeb's ship and his plans to sail out of here. They ate a good meal and shared a couple of mugs of beer before Zeb retired for the night.

CHAPTER 9

The weather gradually warmed, the snows retreated to the upper reaches of the mountains, and wildflowers bloomed to announce the arrival of spring. It also heralded the coming of planting season. Zeb's ship should have been near to completion, but the work was going so well that the original plans got more elaborate.

Once the planting was completed and he and his crew could return to working on it, Zeb figured the ship would be ready to launch within two months. It would then need to float for at least a couple of weeks while the wood adjusted and they patched any leaks that might spring up before they could load it with cargo.

The mayor seemed edgy that they would not complete the ship at the more optimistic estimation of time Zeb had given him. However, the mayor was excited at the prospect of having his own boats, claiming it would be a great symbol of pride for him to have the first cargo ship delivering trade goods this far up the river come from his own town.

He even thought it might open up another complete industry and business opportunity if his people could build their own barges and create a viable river trade between Riverdale and towns along the river in the Habberback Plains.

Zeb thought it a great idea and drew up plans for a flat-bottomed riverboat that was optimal for river travel. He and his men spent weeks training a few volunteers who were interested in how to care for and handle a ship. There was not enough canvas to equip Zeb's vessel with the sails it was capable of flying, but they were not necessary along the river, and he could pick them up once they arrived in a larger city.

The days and weeks continued to roll by. Azerick found he enjoyed the peaceful life in Riverdale and the sense of purpose teaching Anna brought him. It was a summer's day, just past the cusp of mid-season, and Azerick and Anna were out collecting the plants they needed in order to practice their craft.

"So, your friend's ship is finished and ready to be loaded I hear. Will you be going with him?" Anna asked warily.

Azerick let out a sigh and shook his head. "I just don't know. I don't think I have ever been so torn between two decisions in my life."

Anna stepped in front of Azerick and placed her hand on his chest to bring him to a stop. "I would like it very much if you would stay. Perhaps I can help sway your decision to remain."

Before Azerick could ask what she meant, Anna stretched up onto her tiptoes and kissed him full on the mouth. When Azerick closed his eyes, he saw Delinda and passionately returned her kiss. It took his brain only a moment to remind him he was not kissing Delinda. He opened his eyes, and his face turned red with anger and shame. His heart pounded, his flesh burned, and he pushed Anna sharply away from him.

"What do you think you are doing?" he shouted.

"I thought you wanted me to. I thought you liked me!"

"Well I don't!"

"I'm sorry!" she shouted back and ran toward the town, her face buried in her hands and her eyes streaming with tears.

Azerick fought and lost the battle to control his emotions at the renewed memory of his beloved Delinda. In anguished rage, he tore at the Source and demanded that it serve him. He released the arcane energy in the form of a massive lightning bolt into the nearest tree. The air resounded with the peal of thunder and the cracking of wood as the heat of his bolt split the big oak down the middle.

He launched bolt after bolt into the old tree until nothing remained but a charred stump. His magical outburst did little to release the anguish and rage still in him, so he began pounding the earth with his fists until he bruised and bloodied his knuckles and his hands ached.

The sorcerer thought he had moved past his grief, but he realized he had only ignored it. He had distracted himself with work and teaching Anna what he knew of herbalism, but he had not truly faced and dealt with his grief. Azerick wondered if he ever could. Should he even bother? The moment he let go of his torment, a new source of heartache would emerge and start the cycle all over again.

He spent some time composing himself before walking back to town. Zeb was sitting at a table seemingly waiting for him when he entered the inn. When he motioned for Azerick to take a seat, he knew Zeb had heard what happened. With a sigh, Azerick sat down and waited for the rebuke that was sure to come.

"I'm not going to ask what's wrong, lad. I have a good idea what it is. I miss her too, son," Zeb said quietly. "I think I knew Delinda well enough to know she loved you so much that she would want you to be happy, even if that meant finding happiness with someone else."

"So what do you want me to do, Zeb?" Tears overflowed the banks of his eyelids and raced down his face. "Do you want me to grab on to the first girl who throws herself at me?"

"I don't want you to do anything, son. All I am saying is that Delinda would want to see you happy. Whether it means being happy alone or with someone else is for you to decide. Just don't push everyone away who tries to get near you because you think you are being faithful to Delinda's memory. I've been a sailor a long time, and in that time I have met many widows. Whatever you do, however you live, do it for yourself and how you know would make Delinda happy, and not because of some misguided notion of loyalty."

Zeb got up from the table and gave Azerick's shoulder a squeeze before leaving him alone to his thoughts. Zeb's words made sense, but it was hard for him to let go of his memories of Delinda. He was afraid that if he moved on he would be leaving her behind, and the thought terrified him. He could never forget her, *would* never forget her. He declined dinner that night and went straight to his room to think in silence and without distraction.

By the time the sun started to show, Azerick was little closer to finding the answers he sought. He thought maybe the fresh morning air would aid in his deliberations, so he draped a light cloak over his shoulders and headed out of town. The sun was just rising, so the main gates were still closed as he approached. He waved to the guard on duty, picked a direction at random, and began walking with a purpose in his feet if not in his mind.

He stared at the ground ahead of him as he wracked his brain for answers. It did not take long for him to come to the decision that he owed Anna an apology, but the other answers he sought were not so quick in coming. When he finally looked up, he saw that the sun had risen much higher in the sky than he had anticipated, and he had walked all the way to the base of the foothills on the northern side of the valley.

As he took refuge from the sun beneath the boughs of a massive evergreen tree, a huge shadow flew across the ground, prompting the young sorcerer to look up. Expecting to see a large hawk or eagle, Azerick froze in place at what he beheld. A massive scarlet, black, and deep amethyst-scaled reptilian behemoth was flying just a few hundred feet above him. A dragon! If he ran, it would almost certainly see him, but it seemed intent on looking in the direction it was traveling and not at the small human who would have made little more than a snack to such a huge monster.

Azerick finally regained control of his body when he realized the direction in which it was headed. He pumped his legs furiously and ran as fast as he could back toward the town. He drew in the Source and fed his starving muscles. Even with the aid of his magic, Azerick knew there was no way he could possibly get back in time to do anything to help, but such knowledge did not slow him down.

Such a beast could easily reduce the town to splinters long before he arrived to do anything about it. Could he even do anything about it? Was his magic powerful enough to faze such a creature? He did not think so, but he had never let such concerns stop him from defending himself or those he cared about before, and he would not do so now.

By the time Azerick neared the town his legs ached and his lungs burned from running the several miles back. He saw that the gates and a large section of the palisade had been smashed and lay in pieces upon the ground. The fact he saw no smoke, and that there were people milling about, greatly reduced his fear of coming upon a slaughter.

Azerick saw Toron's large horns and grey-muzzled face rising above the crowd. He ran toward him, suspecting that Zeb would be close by. His assumption proved correct when he drew near and saw Zeb talking with the mayor, next to Toron. Zeb seemed angry and

Toron held his big double-bladed battle-axe tightly in his fist and wore his heavy leather battle kilt.

"What happened?" Azerick yelled as he drew near the small group.

"Seems you were right, lad. The good mayor here was keeping something from us all along. I assume you saw the dragon. It seems that the dragon shows up every year a bit after the spring harvest and demands tribute as some kind of tax. It took me and three of my men to keep Toron from trying to lop its big ugly head off and getting himself, and probably a lot of us, killed in the process."

"It's not our fault!" the mayor cried. "We do not have the weapons or fighters to even try and defend ourselves against the creature, and we are too far away from any vassal to expect help from them."

"You should have let me go," Toron growled. "Better to die as warriors defending yourselves and what is yours than living as cowards to be preyed upon by another!"

"I agree with you, Toron, but it is their town and their way of life to live as they choose. I say we get the ship loaded with whatever goods you plan to take, I'll get my things and my books, and we will leave them to their own problems as soon as you are ready to set sail," Azerick said with undisguised contempt.

Zeb looked a bit squeamish. "I'm sorry, lad, but the mayor gave most of your things to the dragon."

Azerick spun on the squat little mayor. "You did what?" Blue arcs of power began jumping across the knuckles of his clenched fists.

Mayor Remkin backed away with his hands raised before him, realizing for the first time exactly what made this young man so intimidating. "It wasn't my fault! The dragon could sense some of the things in your room and demanded we bring them to him or he would peel the roof off the inn and dig them out himself. I have never seen him so insistent. Besides, you were all supposed to be gone by now."

Azerick paced, gnashing his teeth and clenching his fists in frustration. He spun toward the mayor's quaint yet opulent home and struck it with a lightning bolt powerful enough to shatter a large section of the front wall. Lacking the supporting base, an equally large section of its roof followed the wall down to lie atop the pile of smoldering rubble.

He then spun about and faced Zeb. "Zeb, load up the ship with whatever you plan to trade, get the men on board, and get out of here."

"Aren't you coming with us?"

"No."

"I will stay here with you," Toron proclaimed.

"So will the rest of us, lad."

"No, Zeb. If I cannot take care of this myself, then you and your men will not be able to provide much help. There is no sense in you all dying for nothing. Toron, there is no one I would want more by my side and watching my back in a situation like this than you, but if it actually comes down to a fight, I don't think even your great strength and battle prowess will get me out alive. I need you to take whatever books I have left and keep them safe. Just get them to North Haven. Deposit them in a strongbox under my name. I will retrieve them there if I am able."

"Very well, I will guard them with my life. They will be there for you when you come for them," Toron swore.

Azerick stalked up to his room and filled his pack with essential supplies. He stopped by the kitchen and stuffed some food into his bag. When he re-emerged from the inn, Zeb and a few others were still standing near to where he had left them. The mayor and several locals were surveying the damage to his house.

"Which way did it go?" Azerick demanded.

Several locals pointed to the north and slightly west of the town.

"What are you going to do, son?" Zeb called after him as Azerick headed for the ruined gates.

"I'm going to get my things!"

"Do you really think your magic is powerful enough to destroy a dragon?"

"No!"

"Then how are you going to get your things back?"

"I don't know!" Azerick shouted over his shoulder.

"Do you think getting yourself killed is going to make Delinda happy?" Zeb shouted back.

Azerick spun around to face him. "All of my life people have taken from me! They took my father, home, mother, and friends. They took my freedom and my wife. They took my child, Zeb! They took everything because they were strong and I was too weak to protect them, but no more! I have power now, and I will kill or die to protect what is mine."

Azerick turned and stalked out of the ruined gates, snatched a spear from the hand of a surprised guard, and headed out of the town toward the mountains.

Mayor Remkin sidled up to Zeb. "That is a troubled young man. I will pray for his safe return."

Zeb turned and looked at the fat mayor. "You better pray he finds his things if he does return here." Zeb turned away and started issuing orders to his men.

Azerick put the town to his back and walked in the direction of his stolen property. He was sick and tired of someone always taking from him the things that were most important to him. Murderers had taken his parents, Travis' foolish actions had taken away his school, Xornan had taken away his love, and now this dragon dared to take away his books and his chance at living a peaceful life in this valley. He stopped and turned at the sound of someone calling his name. Anna ran up to him, breathing hard from the exertion of catching up to him.

"Anna, I'm sorry. I completely forgot about you. I want to apologize for my behavior once again."

"No, Azerick, it is I who must apologize. Zeb told me what happened to you, and I am so sorry. If I had known of your loss, I would not have thrown myself at you. I'm not sorry for liking you, but I understand this was a bad time for you."

Azerick's words were heavy, and his eyes filled with remorse. "Please don't think it had anything to do with you. You are lovely, kind, and smart, much like Delinda was, and it confused me. I still should not have reacted as I did. If things were different, if I were not so messed up in my head, I would never have pushed you away."

"I understand. Please be careful." she stretched up onto her toes and kissed him once again. "For luck."

She turned away and ran back toward the town before he could think of anything to say. Azerick watched her for several minutes, then resumed walking in the direction of his stolen property.

CHAPTER 10

O ne of the first things Azerick had learned about magic was that a mage was capable of imbuing his more valuable possessions with trace magic to allow him or her to know precisely where it was once they got close enough. Magus Allister had taught him a rather painful lesson when he was still nothing more than a street rat. A clever street rat, but a street rat nonetheless.

After three days of hiking, Azerick knew he was getting close. He could feel the effusion of his trace magic, albeit very faintly. He climbed the foothills and followed the base of the mountains westward. At the rate he could sense the magical emanations increasing, he estimated that he would find their location shortly before sundown.

The terrain became increasingly arduous as rocks and boulders replaced trees, and the normal forest detritus turned from leaves and branches to scattered skeletal remains. Most of the bones were scoured clean, but a few still showed stains of dried and rotted flesh. As he climbed the treacherous rock-strewn slope, he prayed the dragon would not be home, and he could simply walk in and take back his things lest he become just another addition to the grisly rubbish littering the slope.

As usual, his prayers went unanswered, and a deep voice rumbled out of the cave mouth with the force of an avalanche. "You are either very foolish or very stupid, little sorcerer."

"I'm a sorcerer not a—oh, never mind," Azerick responded, cutting short his habitual clarification.

"So which is it that brings you to seek your death on my mountain?"

"No one has ever called me stupid before, quite the opposite really. So if I had to choose, I guess I would have to go with foolishness."

"You are fortunate. I have just finished a rather large meal, and I am in no mood to exert even the minimal amount of effort it would take to crush you. Now, go away lest I find room in my belly for dessert."

Azerick surveyed his surroundings, looking for anything that might provide him with any kind of advantage. He stood next to a huge boulder the size of a carriage that must have fallen from the high cliff face rising above the dragon's cave some centuries back.

"I'm afraid I cannot do that."

"And why is that?"

"You took some things from the town of Riverdale that belong to me. I would like to have them back."

A deep rumbling reverberated from the cave opening. "Anything within my cave belongs to me, just as anything that comes into my valley. I will allow you to leave since you have thus far provided me with amusement, but you amuse me no longer."

"I will make you a deal. I do not care one whit about the things you have taken from the town, its people, or whatever else you may have collected. Just let me have my things back, and I will not trouble you any longer."

"So you will *allow* me to keep the things I have taken if I return what was once yours? What arrogance, what presumption! The only thing being allowed here is my allowing you to live, and that gift I now choose to revoke. I will show you what you have the power to *allow*!"

Azerick heard the scraping of claws and scales on stone. A slight wind picked up as the dragon filled its huge lungs full of air. The sorcerer stepped behind the large boulder just as the dragon stretched its long neck out and breathed a massive jet of flame. Azerick could feel the incredible heat of the blast as it splashed against the boulder. He could feel the rock heating up and cracking under the awesome, fiery assault.

Azerick prepared a spell he had been practicing since his arrival in the valley. It was one that he had studied the description of in the great tome he was so desperate to get back. He called out to the dragon once more from the short-term safety of the massive boulder.

"Last chance, dragon. Just give me back my stuff. There is no need for us to do battle!"

He heard the dragon drawing another great breath and jumped out from behind his stone barrier. He released his spell just as the dragon's head stretched out of the cave and began spewing another burst of stone-melting flames.

Azerick's spell did not appear to have any visible effect. The crashing of stone and sickening crunch of bone echoed across the mountainside, and the jet of fire abruptly cut off, giving testament that the sorcerer's magic had wrought the desired effect.

A massive boulder, only slightly smaller than the one Azerick was hiding behind, fell from the towering face of the mountain. It plummeted silently as if dropped by the gods and struck the dragon before rolling and crashing down the slope. A dense stand of hardy trees finally arrested the runaway juggernaut's flight a hundred yards down the face of the slope. Once the dust began to settle, Azerick stepped out from behind his stone barrier, which was still radiating a great deal of heat, and went to examine the destruction his spell had wrought.

The massive horned head of the dragon lay still upon the rocky ground. A large rent in its hard, glittering scales oozed blood near the back of the huge wedge-shaped head. A glint of white showed the cusp of one of the creature's great vertebrae protruding from the ghastly wound. Azerick's eyes traveled up the cliff face and examined the smooth indentation marking the spot where his spell had undermined the stone holding the big boulder in place and which had ultimately proved to be the dragon's demise.

"I take no pleasure in your death, great dragon. Despite your greed and arrogance, I find you to be a magnificent creature."

It was not until Azerick squeezed past its massive bulk that he realized how impressive the dragon truly was. From his studies, he estimated it, much like him, to be just at the transition point of being considered an adult by its kind. The tunnel leading to its lair was long, and the dragon's body blocked most of the waning outside light from reaching very far into the cavern, so Azerick conjured up his own magical illumination.

From the looks of the huge claw marks, the dragon had widened much of the long passage in order to accommodate its ever-expanding girth. Large patches of stone had been worn smooth, most likely by the continual scraping of the dragon's hard scales. It took several minutes of walking before the tunnel opened into a huge central cavern. Azerick circled the vast chamber and saw that much of its walls had been scraped smooth by the dragon just as the tunnel leading in had been.

The chamber looked like a giant stone bowl turned upside down with Azerick trapped beneath it. He ran his hand along the smooth, almost glassy walls where the dragon must have used magic or the heat of its powerful, flaming breath to melt the stone smooth.

The most impressive feature of the dragon's lair was the massive glittering mound of treasure piled near the back wall of the cavern. A great mound of gold, jewels and numerous other items of value lay in a heap as tall as the sorcerer and twice his height in width at its base.

Azerick doubted that even the king's treasury contained so much wealth. In fact, only the church could likely match or exceed this hoard's value in all of Valeria. Azerick cautiously approached the immense source of riches, and an ominous rumbling filled the chamber. A loud crack sounded from the direction of the cave entrance followed by the deafening thunder of thousands of tons of stone crashing down and spewing a choking, blinding cloud of dust into the cavern.

Azerick hunkered down and covered his nose and mouth with his sleeve. Even that bit of protection could not prevent his lungs from getting a thick coating of the fine grey powder. As the rumbling ceased and the dust began to settle, Azerick's lungs violently tried to expel the contaminants. His coughing brought up mouthfuls of grey, gritty phlegm, but it finally abated as the dust settled enough for him to see and breathe.

A fine grey powder coated everything in the cavern including the sorcerer. Azerick looked like an animated statue while the pile of treasure appeared to be an oddly shaped boulder. Azerick crossed the cavern to examine the passageway to the outside. His findings were not optimistic. Several feet in, rubble blocked the entire tunnel. From the amount of dust and the force of the cave-in, Azerick surmised that thousands of tons of stone, if not more, now choked off the entire passage.

Azerick cast the spell he had used to bring the boulder perched above the cave entrance down onto the dragon's neck. Several square yards of stone turned to little more than dust in an instant. A second rumbling sounded and more stone fell into the opened passage, blocking it off once more and sending another cloud of dust into Azerick's face. He sighed in exasperation at his failure.

"I probably would have died of thirst before I could tunnel all the way out anyway," he muttered to himself.

He circled the large chamber and examined the walls in search of another way out. Fortune smiled upon him for once. He found a small crevice from which he could feel a faint breeze. Azerick cast his excavation spell once more. As he had hoped, the crevice opened into a tunnel large enough through which to crawl.

Azerick returned to the main chamber and examined the treasures piled high near the back wall. He found his books, including the large, ancient tome, and his scrolls near the golden hill's summit. He dropped the scrolls, still safely rolled into their tubes, into his pack. He picked up the large tome, blew off the thick layer of dust, and began flipping through its yellowed pages for a particular passage he had studied before. He sat upon a dust-covered pile of coins and began studying the pages before him.

After two hours of careful research, he picked up his short spear and channeled raw magical power into its steel head. The metal glowed orange, and a faint nimbus of eldritch energy limned its shape. Azerick began drawing a series of runes in the stone floor all around the pile of treasure as easily as if it were wet clay. Once he felt his work was complete, he compared his work to that shown in the book and felt confident it would do. He cast another spell, and the magical sigils glowed faintly for a moment then subsided.

Careful not to step on his work, Azerick filled a pouch with gold and silver coins and several cut gems. He packed the precious tome into his pack and crawled through the exit he had created, leaving behind the large chamber and its treasure. Once he gained the natural cave beyond the magically carved exit, he cast his excavation spell once more and caused the small passage to collapse, sealing off the treasure chamber once more.

"Great, I'm in a tunnel again," he muttered to himself, something he was doing more and more frequently.

Azerick was confident it would not take him nearly as long to find the surface as it had when he and the others had escaped from their captivity and forced servitude. He knew he was only a few hundred feet from the outside—laterally. As the floor of the cave continued to slope down, guiding him deeper beneath the mountain and farther from the surface, his confidence began to wane.

When the second day of his spelunking came and passed, he began to feel downright nervous. His water was nearly gone, and his food was running short. To make matters worse, the tunnel he was traversing was growing smaller and smaller until he was forced to crawl on his hands and knees. It did not take long before the knees of his trousers were rubbed through and the skin beneath was worn raw.

Azerick pulled a heavy shirt out of his pack and tore it into strips he then wound around his hands and knees to protect them from the coarse, flesh-scouring rock. The tunnel became so narrow he was forced to remove his pack and push it along ahead of him.

"How in the abyss dwarves can stand living like this day in and day out all their long lives without going stark raving mad is beyond me," he said to the surrounding grey stone.

"Oh, we get used to it pretty quick and rather enjoy it. Then again, maybe we're all just stark raving mad," answered a gruff voice to what was supposed to have been a rhetorical question.

Azerick wriggled around until he was on his back and looked up at several short, wide bodies with prominent potato noses and thick, scruffy beards. The one who had answered grinned down at him. Through his thick beard and mustache, his white teeth shone in Azerick's magical light. Azerick returned the grin, but before he could form a greeting, the dwarf's heavy boot came down on his head and sent stars blazing across a field of blackness.

Two of the stout dwarves reached down and dragged the human intruder the rest of the way out of the small tunnel from which his head had emerged rather unexpectedly. The mining crew had just arrived at the cavern to begin their day of chipping away at the rock walls in search of a new vein of ore or minerals when they noticed Azerick's light glinting out of the small chute at the end.

Azerick had a peculiar feeling of weightlessness as he swung slightly from side to side. The next thing he noticed was that his wrists burned and his ankles felt constricted. He tried to mutter a curse and realized that a thick braid of cloth had been tied around his head and ran between his jaws like a horse's bit. Azerick opened his eyes and found his wrists and ankles bound together and looped around a long timber being carried on the broad shoulders of two of the stout dwarves.

I really need to stop getting hit on the head before I end up with brain damage, Azerick thought to himself.

"Looks like our young trespasser is wakin' up, Togar," one of the dwarves called out to the dwarf leading the small group.

Azerick looked around and saw there were four of the short, burly creatures. One was several yards ahead, two carried him like a fresh kill from a hunt, and one followed a few yards behind. The one they called Togar wheeled about and strode toward Azerick's hog-tied form.

"As ye can see, wizard, we dwarves don't take too kindly to trespassers," the dwarf said with the same wide grin he wore just before he had kicked Azerick in the head.

Azerick tried to protest that he was not a wizard and he did not intend to trespass, but all that came out was a stream of unintelligible mumblings.

"That's right, we know what ye are, though ye don't look much like a wizard." Togar waved Azerick's scroll case in front of his face. "I thought all you wizards wore those big fluffy dresses. I never seen one carrying a spear neither. Of course, who can say? All you wizards are half mad anyhow."

Azerick rolled his eyes and tried to protest once again.

"What are we goin' to do with ye?" Togar interpreted. "Hard to say just yet, but I can tell ye I'm mighty hungry. Can't raise cattle under a mountain ye know, and I need my meat."

Azerick's eyes went round for a second, but fortunately, the other dwarves sniggered at what must have been an attempt at a joke. Togar flashed Azerick another bright, big-toothed grin and resumed his lead as the dwarves moved out once more.

Azerick's wrists seriously chafed and ached from bearing much of his weight. He tried to shift his body to relieve some of the pressure on his wrists and restore at least a moment of circulation to them.

"Stop your squirming, or we'll drop you on your head."

Just as his bearers seemed to be getting ready to make good on their threat, a sharp crack was followed by the crashing of stone and a large cloud of dust erupting from just ahead. When the dust cleared, Togar was nowhere to be seen. In his place was a mound of rubble completely blocking the passage ahead. The dwarves bearing Azerick dropped the unfortunate sorcerer painfully to the ground and raced forward, calling out to their lost comrade.

"Togar!" a dwarf called Roran shouted at the pile of rock blocking the passage.

The dwarves took their picks to the stone with wild abandon in an effort to rescue Togar. Strong stubby fingers pulled out stones the size of a dwarf's head and cast them carelessly behind them.

Azerick was forced to roll around to avoid being struck by some of the wildly tossed stones. Some of the rocks blocking the passage were the size of boulders and weighed several tons or more. Sharp flecks of stone flew in all directions as the dwarf-forged steel rang against the resilient barrier like the pealing of bells.

Azerick tried unsuccessfully to spit the wad of cloth out of his mouth. He closed his eyes and turned his focus toward the Source with all his will. The sorcerer found and channeled the Source easily enough, but lacking the use of his hands and mouth, forming the magical energies into a useful form was arduous.

He had practiced shaping the Source without the verbal or somatic hand gestures but never both at the same time. In fact, he was not at all certain it was even possible. He bent his considerable will to the task and was amazed at the amount of effort it took to form what should have been an extraordinarily simple casting. The slightest distraction or errant thought flashing through his mind tore the weave apart like a spiderweb in a windstorm and forced him to start all over again.

Sweat beaded on his brow, and his breathing grew labored as he bent the Source to his will. Azerick was ready to give up the task as hopeless when he felt the cloth loosen in his mouth. He redoubled his efforts and gritted his teeth until spots began forming before his eyes from the strain, and the binding holding the wadded cloth in his mouth finally came free.

Azerick forced the gag from his mouth with his tongue. "Untie me and I can get to your friend!" Azerick shouted over the ringing of steel hammering against stone.

One of the dwarves stomped toward him with his pick raised menacingly. "Shut up, wizard!" he snarled. "We have enough trouble on our hands without ye casting any of your foul sorceries about!"

"I can get your friend out a lot faster than you can. Are you going to let him die because of your distrust and stubbornness?"

The dwarf looked uneasy at the prospect of releasing a magic user, the most distrusted and disliked members of any race, but he knew it would take hours to reach Togar with the tools they had.

"I give you my word, on the soul of my dead wife, I will not cast any magic or take any actions against you or any dwarf who does not intend to do me harm."

The dwarf dropped his pick, pulled a knife from his belt, and cut the cords binding Azerick's ankles and wrists to the pole. "Ye had better not betray us, wizard, or there will be no magic nor gods that will keep ye safe from our wrath."

Azerick stood and promptly fell down again as blood raced back into his starved extremities. The sorcerer propped himself up on his knees, not trusting his near-lifeless feet to support him, and began casting his spell. His hands rebelled against his casting nearly as much as his feet thwarted his attempt to stand, but he concentrated and took his time to form the invisible sigil properly.

"I don't know anything about mining, so tell me which stones to remove. The last time I tried this, I nearly buried myself," Azerick told the dwarf.

Roran grunted at the mage. "Typical. Start with that big one on top."

The moment he uttered the spell's command word, the passage became clouded in grey dust. The dwarf continued instructing Azerick as to which rocks to pulverize.

"Togar, are ye there?" Roran called out and walked slowly forward, trying to wave away the dust to clear his vision.

"Aye, I'm here," Togar's voice sounded from the darkness.

"Damn, Togar, I thought ye was squished into paste for sure when ye didn't answer!"

"Yeah, I heard ye, Roran, but I had a rock on my back. And it had me scrunched so tight I could hardly breathe much less holler."

"Are ye all right then?"

"Yeah, I'm fine. I got lucky that the boulders around me propped up the one pinning me to the ground. I guess I got hit with the family curse."

Roran raised a bushy eyebrow. "What curse is that?"

"Had a cousin o' mine named Borik Deepstone. He got caught under a cave-in years back. It took us three days to dig him out. When we finally got to him, he was half-mad. Said he heard and seen the ghosts of dwarves who had been killed in the tunnels from ages past. A few days later, he said he couldn't take living here no more and left. Ain't seen nor heard of him since."

"You ain't gonna run off now too, are ye?"

"Nah, I'm made of sterner stuff than that. Besides, Borik always was a bit of an odd one. I see the wizard's loose. What happened?"

"It was him who got ya out. He gave me his word he wouldn't do nothin' but get ya out so long as none tries to do for him," Roran informed Togar.

Togar turned to face Azerick and looked him up and down. "I guess I owe ye my life, wizard. I suppose I can let ye walk the rest of the way like a man, so long as you keep to your word."

"I am not a wizard, I'm a sorcerer. What happens to me when we get to wherever we are going?"

"Sorcerer, wizard, what's the difference? Never mind, it probably won't make no sense to me anyhow. As far as what happens to ye, I guess that'll be up to Duncan to decide. He'll know what to do with your type. Worst comes to worst we'll put ye out at some distant gate and let ye go wherever it is ye want to go, so long as it's away from our tunnels."

"I guess I cannot ask for more than that. It's certainly better than being eaten."

"So what's a wizard doin' down in our tunnels anyway?" Togar asked.

Azerick was hesitant to tell the dwarves about the dragon, and even more so about the treasure hoard. "I was seeking refuge in a cave when the entrance collapsed. I was too far in, and the cave was too unstable for me to try to burrow my way out magically. I found a small cleft at the rear of the cavern and hoped it would lead me out."

The dwarves nodded their heads. "This mountain range is very old, and this section in particular is notoriously unstable, and it just gets worse the farther you go in the direction you came from. I guess I should go ahead and make introductions seeing as how you saved my life and all. That there is Dornan Bournegre, Roran Ironarm, and Kragnar Stonebiter," Togar said, pointing at each dwarf in turn.

"Let me guess, you are Togar Skullcrusher." Azerick rubbed his head where the dwarf had kicked him.

Togar and the other dwarves laughed loudly. "Deepstone, but hey, maybe I'll change my name!"

The previously taciturn dwarves, although not talkative, were far more jovial than they had been earlier. It took Azerick very little prodding to get Togar talking about the mountains and mining, but he was very tight-lipped regarding the dwarves or their home. After what seemed like two days of traveling, although Togar said it had been only a few hours, Azerick spied a soft azure glow up ahead. The human's jaw dropped in wonderment when they stepped out of the tunnel onto a high ledge.

The tunnel ended in a cavern of enormous proportions. It was at least half a mile wide and several times that in length. The starry night sky showed through an oval opening at about two hundred yards across and hundreds of feet over their heads. The upper reaches of the walls were lost in darkness, but Azerick could imagine the aperture resting atop the conical walls of an ancient, hopefully extinct, volcano.

Along both sides of the walls for as far as he could see were numerous terraced levels with open arched doorways carved into the sides of the cavern from which more soft-glowing light emanated. Through many of the doorways, a warmer orange glow from candles or lamps radiated out into the expansive cavern. Far below him, directly under the distant opening to the sky was what appeared to be a small mountain peak over two hundred feet tall and three times as wide at its base. It was a mountain inside a mountain. More stone archways were carved all along its surface, some were illuminated while others were visible only by the deeper blackness of unlit chambers.

The sound of hammers ringing on steel and numerous rough, deep voices echoed throughout the vast expanse. Azerick watched in fascination as short, dark silhouettes scurried about like bipedal ants performing their daily tasks.

As the small group descended to the cavern floor by way of a long ramp carved into the side of the cavern, Azerick saw that the blue glow providing much of the subterranean illumination was created by glass globes filled with a blue liquid. These globes were hung throughout the cavern like oil lamps.

Most dwarves stopped and looked as Azerick and his escorts made their way toward the conical monolith. They entered one of the stone archways at the base of the massive conical structure and walked up a spiraling stairway circling the entire structure on its inexorable rise to the top. The trek was long and arduous.

"These stairs must be terrible if there is ever an emergency or a need to get to the bottom quickly," Azerick said.

"Naw, if we ever need to move with a sense of urgency, like in the case of defense or some such, we have faster ways of getting down." Togar pointed out the steel poles Azerick had mistaken for some kind of structural support. "In times of emergency, or just expediency, we slide down the poles. They run through openings in the floors and ceilings for five levels, then you take another pole down until you reach the floor.

"What if you want to go up?" Azerick asked.

"There's an elevating platform we use for heavy freight, or if we just don't feel like walking."

"If you have a lift, why in the abyss did we walk up miles of stairs?"

"I thought ye might care for the scenic route." Togar grinned mischievously. "Besides, it don't bother me none, and I get a kick outta watchin' ye sweat 'cause of a little work."

Azerick rolled his eyes at the dwarf's peculiar sense of humor, but he kept his mouth shut and continued climbing the stairs without further complaint. By the time they arrived at their destination near the top of the spire, Azerick was winded and soaked in sweat.

"Hey, Duncan! I brought ye a present from one o' the mines," Togar called through the open doorway.

Azerick noticed that this doorway was different from the multitude of others they had passed. Numerous runes and carvings were scrawled in relief all along the doorframe, and a brighter, whiter light emanated through its open passageway.

Another stout dwarf, though not as brawny as Togar and his crew, stepped through the door. He tucked his beard into a wide leather tool belt carrying a vast assortment of chisels and hammers. His long, braided, salt and pepper hair ran down between his shoulder blades and ended in a bright silver ring near the small of his back.

The two dwarves began conversing in their own tongue, often glancing over at the human standing quietly in their midst. Togar handed over Azerick's scroll case along with the rest of his belongings to Duncan. Duncan slipped the scrolls out of the case and glanced at the writings upon them.

Azerick busied himself with examining the runes carved along the doorway and realized that they were far more than mere ornamentation. An unknown magic radiated from the carvings, but he could tell they gained their power from the Source, even if in an indirect way.

Duncan's curt voice interrupted Azerick's contemplations. "Once you're done gawking at my door, grab your bag and follow me inside."

Azerick looked away from the engraved symbols and saw that Togar had left him and the new dwarf alone. He picked up his pack lying on the ground a few feet away and followed the dwarf through the doorway. Inside was a stone table surrounded by stone benches. Nooks carved into the walls held books, tools, stones, and crystals.

"The name's Duncan, Duncan Runecarver, in case you didn't catch it before." The dwarf set the scroll case and Azerick's small leather pouch containing the coins and gems he had taken from the dragon's lair onto the workbench.

"My name is Azerick."

Duncan's only reply was a grunt as he looked over the scrolls he had spread out before him. He then pressed a small cylinder with thick glass lenses onto his eye and studied each of the jewels he poured out of the leather pouch. Once he was finished examining them, he scooped them up along with the coins, dropped them back into the bag, and casually tossed it off to one side of his workbench. The old dwarf then dug through Azerick's pack and pulled out the few books he could not bear to leave behind with Zeb and Toron as well as the ancient tome on magic.

Duncan set the books in a stack on one side of his desk, picked one from the top, and began flipping through its pages. Azerick winced when the dwarf tossed the first one to the side of the bench and grabbed another. Duncan showed no reaction at the books' contents until he came to the ancient tome Azerick prized so highly. The dwarf's thick bushy eyebrows rose as he scanned the pages with interest. He set it aside with considerably more deference than he had shown the others and selected another book.

Azerick stood back with as much patience as he could muster while the dwarf ransacked his belongings. He contented himself with looking around the dwarf's workshop, studying the myriad tools and engravings littering the place. Not quite littering, Azerick thought as he adjusted his first impression. Everything was clearly organized, and not a fleck of stone or speck of dust gathered on the floor or tables.

Duncan finished looking at the last book and turned his attention to Azerick. "Where's your spell book? All these books are on magical theory and such. Where's the book you record your spells in?"

"I don't have one. I'm a sorcerer not a wizard," Azerick said, preparing himself to answer the inevitable question.

He was almost disappointed when the dwarf merely grunted instead of asking what the difference was like almost everyone else always did. Instead, he waved to Azerick to take a seat on the bench next to the table as he pulled out a stool from under the workbench and sat across from him.

"So what were you doing in our mines?"

Azerick had to look up at the dwarf since the bench was set at a height for a dwarf where Duncan's stool was built to allow him to work over his workbench. "I was taking shelter in a cave when the entrance collapsed. I found a small passage farther back I hoped would lead me out."

"Why didn't you use the spell you used to free Togar to clear away the blockage?"

"I was too far back, and the cave was unstable." Azerick replied.

Duncan raised one of his bushy eyebrows at Azerick's answer. "Why were you so far back? Most humans would only go back far enough to get out of the wind or weather."

Azerick scoured his brain for a plausible explanation, but he realized the wily dwarf had cornered him.

"Stop yanking my beard and tell me what you were really doing in that cave."

Azerick took a deep breath before answering. "A dragon came to the town I was staying in and stole some of my books and scrolls. I went to get them back."

"What happened to the dragon?"

"I was forced to kill it when it refused to return my things and tried to roast me."

Duncan's eyebrows rose until they nearly reached his hairline. "You're that accomplished a sorcerer to kill a dragon just like that?"

Azerick shook his head. "I got lucky. I was able to dislodge a large boulder above the cave's entrance and crush its neck."

"Bah, luck," the dwarf waved off with his calloused hand. "We make our own luck in this world. It ain't some random force pulled out of the ether at the whim of some god."

Duncan hopped off his high stool and pulled a carved stone disc about as wide as his hand out of a cubbyhole built into the wall. He stepped in front of Azerick, spoke a word, and waved his free hand over the top of the disc. Azerick was surprised to see several of the runes carved in its surface glow with varying intensity.

"You have an affinity for earth and air magic. That's an unusual combination, especially for a human wizard, or even sorcerer, I'd wager. Most of your kind tends to lean toward fire and air for the big flashy spells that scare the heck outta the common folks."

Azerick shrugged his shoulders. "I have always felt drawn more toward the earth and stone than fire."

"Why do think that is?" Duncan asked in a knowing voice.

"Stone is eternal. It does not bend or yield. It does not flare up in a spectacular sight then fade away."

"It may not bend, but it can be shattered if it is struck hard enough."

Azerick stared back stone-faced. "You cannot shatter a mountain."

The old dwarf nodded and replaced the stone disc in its cubbyhole. "You know what a volcano is?"

Azerick nodded.

"Then you know that a mountain can destroy itself under its own pressure, annihilating not just itself, but everyone and everything around it." Duncan sat back down on his stool.

"I thought all dwarves disliked magic and did not use it themselves."

"Yes and no. It will probably come as a surprise to know there are many forms of magic and many different sources as well. Dwarves make some of the best weapons and armor ever crafted, and occasionally we imbue them with powerful enchantments. We couldn't do that if we didn't have some kind of access to magic."

Azerick listened intently as the dwarf explained.

"You wizards and such power your spells by drawing energy from what you call the Source, but that is a bit of a misnomer. That is merely *a* source of magic, not *the* source of magic. Dwarves and other races use magic that comes from the very earth and stone around us, and rune carvers store that energy in carved sigils. Druids power their spells from both the divine energies provided by their god or goddess as well as the natural energies found in plants, trees, and all living things in nature," Duncan explained as if Azerick were his newest pupil.

"Can all dwarves use rune magic?" Azerick asked.

"Can all humans cast wizard spells?"

Azerick's face flushed.

"No, it takes a special talent and affinity for the elements to be able to draw on its energies and store them in a rune."

"So the rune you carve is a spell form much like wizards and sorcerers shape with the Source," Azerick stated as he began to understand the principal.

"Precisely. Stone is most often used as the medium to hold the runic energy, but most anything that can hold the shape can be used."

"So is the magic permanent then as long as the rune holds its shape?"

Duncan shook his head. "Not necessarily. The energy bleeds out of the rune at a rate dependent upon the power of the rune caster, with a few exceptions. When a weapon, tool, or some such is created to carry a permanent enchantment, a special rune is created to hold the magic in place, but it is a difficult process and limited in its use. I've carved runes to strengthen the doors and gates leading into our territory, but even those I have to replenish from time to time."

"So what are you going to do with me now?" Azerick asked.

"Well, normally we would put you out the nearest surface exit with a swift kick to the arse." Duncan grinned at his guest. "But I've developed an interest in that big book you brought with you. If you're willing to accept, I would like to show you a bit of dwarven hospitality for a while so I can study it further. The snows are coming soon, and unless you planned on returning to Riverdale, you would have a tough time getting through the pass to the next human settlement."

"I thought I had already experienced dwarven hospitality," Azerick replied and rubbed his head where Togar had struck him.

"Naw, our hospitality involves a bit less kicking and a whole lot more drinking, but I gotta warn you about dwarven alcohol. It kicks harder than Togar's boot!" Duncan said and laughed loudly.

"You say the snows are coming. Surely there are several weeks before the snows hit, even up here in the mountains."

The dwarf shook his head with a look of concern. "The snows have been coming earlier and staying longer these last couple years. It's a strange thing, and a bad omen."

"What kind of omen?"

"Can't really say for sure. All I know is the animals are spooked and there's something wrong in the air. Maybe it's nothing, maybe it's something. Whatever it is, we'll keep down here to ourselves as we always have and let it pass over us."

"If you are willing to teach me something of rune carving, I would be willing to share what I have," Azerick agreed.

"All right then, let's drink on it!"

The dwarf sprang from his stool and disappeared into another room and reappeared with two jugs and two cups. He uncorked one of the jugs and poured a mouthful of a clear liquid into the bottom of both cups.

"This is how we dwarves seal a contract," he explained and lifted his cup.

Azerick did the same, and at a nod from Duncan, they both downed the cup's' contents. Duncan slammed his cup down on the tabletop. Azerick squeezed his until he thought it would shatter in his grip as the liquid burned down his throat and brought tears to his clamped shut eyes. It felt as though his throat and stomach had been set on fire.

"You didn't cough it up! I'm impressed!" Duncan crowed and poured an amber liquid from the second jug into both their cups.

Azerick desperately downed the beverage. The warm, heady beer slid down his throat and helped cool the fire the dwarf spirits had ignited.

"That is good beer," Azerick told Duncan in a raspy voice.

"'Course it is. The only thing dwarves do better than beat metal is brew beer and ale. Let me show you to a place you can bunk down while you're my guest."

Azerick's head swam when he stood up and followed the dwarf through one set of rooms to another. A stuffed straw mattress lay on a stone slab carved into one wall. Thankfully, it was just long enough to accommodate Azerick's size, but if he had been two or three inches taller, his feet would have been hanging over the edge. Duncan set his belongings on a table built into the other wall. A round hole had been bored through another wall allowing an impressive view of the city below and around him. Since there were not elements like strong wind or rain inside the mountain, windows were unnecessary.

"You go on and rest up here and we can talk more tomorrow," Duncan offered as he pulled out a couple of wool blankets from a large cedar trunk and tossed them onto the stone pallet.

"Thanks," Azerick replied. He lay down, feeling the full effects of both the powerful liquor and his own exhaustion.

Duncan left his human guest to get some rest, sat down at his workbench, and began reading the ancient tome. The rune carver was amazed at the breadth of subject matter and history involving several of the races of the land.

As one of the few scholarly dwarves, Duncan wanted to study the book in its entirety, but that would take years to do properly, so he contented himself with skipping to the sections involving dwarven history, earth magic, and rune carving. The rune carver eventually closed the book with a grunt and pried himself away so he could get some sleep before the coming day.

A tapping sound woke Azerick from his slumber. He followed the sound and found Duncan seated at his workbench tapping a fine chisel with a small wooden mallet. Azerick peered over the dwarf's shoulder and saw that he was carving a complex rune into a flat piece of stone. He was impressed at the deftness and assuredness of the rune carver's strikes. The lines, swirls, and patterns he carved into the stone were every bit as smooth and elaborate as if he were penning a scroll with quill and ink.

Duncan blew away the stone flecks and set aside the hammer and chisel. He picked up the stone disc, held it at eye level, and examined every stroke. Seemingly satisfied, he set the carving down and spun around on his stool.

"You're up! Hungry?" Duncan asked his guest.

"Famished," Azerick replied.

"Good, let's go get something to eat."

Azerick followed Duncan out of his home and through another doorway. Duncan stopped at the edge of a large circular hole cut through the stone floor with a steel pipe running directly through the center of it. Azerick stepped to the edge, looked up and saw that the pole extended two floors up and three more down before terminating at another landing.

"Think you can handle a little slide?" the dwarf asked. "If not, we can take the stairs."

Azerick shook his head. "I would rather risk the pole than walk all those stairs again."

"That's the spirit!" Duncan laughed gleefully before leaping out over the opening, wrapping his thick arms and short legs around the pipe, and zipping down at a speed that would have left Azerick's stomach lodged firmly in his throat.

With a deep breath, Azerick leaned out and grabbed the pole, swung his legs around it, and slid down. He found the rune carver standing patiently three floors down where another hole and pole waited several feet away to take passengers down the next five levels. After three slides down the poles, Azerick felt comfortable enough to begin to enjoy it. When they reached the ground floor a few slides later, Azerick had to ask Duncan more about it.

"What happens if someone hops on as someone else is coming down? How do you avoid accidents?"

"It's the responsibility of the one on the lower portion to look up before jumping on," Duncan explained. "Still, there's been many a fight over dwarves getting knocked off their pole and falling a few floors."

"Don't they get hurt?"

Duncan shook his head. "Naw, not very often. Dwarves are made of pretty strong stuff, like the rock around them."

Azerick took a closer look at the structure of the massive cone's base as the pair stepped into the enormous cavern. He saw that the base was not uniform and smooth with the cavern floor like other stalagmites he had seen and asked Duncan about it.

"This is not a natural stalagmite, is it?"

"Nope. It used to be the peak of the mountain we're in now before it caved in. This entire mountain was once an active volcano. It's calmed down and been dormant for at least a thousand years, but before it did, the whole top fell in and made a nice place to carve out our homes. That's why we got that big skylight way up yonder," Duncan said and pointed up toward the large iris glowing with the pale morning sunlight.

As they walked down the worn paths acting as the dwarven city's streets, Azerick noticed that he drew a glance from most of the dwarves they passed, but none stared openly or for more than a brief second before continuing with their own business.

The pair finally arrived at an arched doorway and stepped inside. The room beyond was full of dwarves sitting around stone tables and on stone benches eating, drinking, and carrying on a multitude of conversations in their rough and grumbling language. Most of the talking paused in a momentary lull then regained their previous clamor as Duncan and Azerick found a small open table and sat down.

"Do you get many human visitors?" Azerick asked as he looked around the room. "It does not seem that anyone takes much notice of me."

"No, we don't get many at all. We're not what you would generally consider hospitable, nor do we invite topsiders into our warrens much.

Word travels fast down here, and just about everyone has likely already heard about you and why you're here. We dwarves aren't a curious bunch like humans and elves. A dragon could come and roost here, and so long as it didn't cause any trouble, we would go about our own business rather quickly and not pay it any further heed."

"How do you make the light in those globes?" Azerick asked as he looked at the round, glowing, blue orbs hung throughout the bar and cavern beyond.

The dwarf shook his head and grinned. "Human curiosity," he mumbled. "Centuries ago, we found a phosphorescent lichen growing in one of the caves. We found a way to cultivate and distill it to make the glowing liquid inside of it. Now are you gonna badger me with questions all day, or are we gonna put our mouths to good use and get something to eat?"

Duncan waved to a passing serving woman and said something to her in his coarse tongue. She soon reappeared with two large platters covered in meat, sausages, eggs, and bread along with two tankards of beer. Azerick looked at his food with a bit of trepidation.

"Something the matter?" Duncan glanced up and asked.

"Where do you get your meat? You can't raise much livestock underground can you?"

Duncan roared with laughter. "Did Togar say something to you? No, we don't raise animals in the caves. We have a few hidden little valleys between the peaks of the mountains where we grow grass, grains, vegetables, and raise our livestock. The only thing on that plate is goat, beef, and pork."

Azerick grinned, shook his head at his groundless fears, and gratefully dug into his breakfast. He was surprised to find that despite the dwarf's compact size, Duncan ate as much as a large human, even going as far as to finish Azerick's plate when he could eat no more. The pair sat back and sipped at their beer, letting their meals settle as they talked.

"That's quite a book you brought. I can see why you were so determined to retrieve it," Duncan told the young sorcerer. "How exactly did you come about obtaining it?"

"What happened to dwarves not being a curious bunch?"

"I'm a bit different from most dwarves."

Azerick nodded. "I was on a ship to North Haven by way of a roundabout course when a very large and unnatural storm hit us. That was just a few days after two pirate ships tried to plunder us. When the storm broke, a ship full of minotaurs and a creature called a psyling appeared. They took us captive and sold us into slavery. I was forced to fight in an arena for about two years—I think. It was hard to keep track of time there. One day, the psyling's control over me wavered. It did not end well for him."

"From what you said about that dragon, I imagine not."

"I grabbed the book, and we fled through a magical portal that deposited us in some very deep caves. It took at least a couple weeks for us to find the surface. When we did, we wintered in Riverdale. That is when the dragon took my things."

The dwarf shook his head in amazement at the young human's experiences. "Psylings, cavern gnomes, and you killed a dragon. Well, I won't try to keep you here against your will. It just doesn't seem healthy! I am glad you decided to stay a spell and let me study that book of yours. It's going to be winter soon, and even though we can take you under most of the passes to wherever you have a mind to go, it's still no fun traveling in the bitter cold. Like I said, the snows have been coming earlier and earlier these last couple of years and dropping more snow than usual."

"Do you think I can learn some of your rune magic?"

"I can try to teach you, but I can't guarantee you can learn more than the theory of it."

Azerick was in no particular hurry to go anywhere at the moment, and staying with the dwarves would give him a chance to learn something few would ever have a chance to know. Even if he was unable to learn to use rune magic, he could learn of it and of the secretive dwarves as well.

He thought about Zeb and how he might be concerned about Azerick's whereabouts, but he would just have to deal with that himself. Right now, being ensconced under millions of tons of rock and away from the rest of the world sounded like a good place to stay and plan his future.

Duncan queried Azerick about his discoveries from the book's contents, and Azerick in turn inquired more into what was required to create magical runes. Azerick sipped at his mug of beer while Duncan downed far more than Azerick thought appropriate given the early hour, but he put it down to dwarven customs. After a tour of the forges, smithies, potteries, and other various shops filling many of the caves, the pair returned to Duncan's home and shop where they each sat and exchanged knowledge.

The first week of Azerick's stay consisted mostly of learning the history of the dwarves and their rune carving art. Duncan explained how all runes were comprised of representations of a natural element, and how these elements were often combined to create the desired effect. Other than that, there were few rules to rune carving. Azerick saw that it was very similar to his sorcery in that the rune carver's imagination and interpretation decided the shape of the runes and they were not fixed in any set form. There existed a multitude of runic combinations that would cause the same effect, the shape of which was left strictly to the carver.

At the start of the second week, Duncan gave Azerick some shallow glass discs filled with a hard wax, several small chisels, and a list of runes. The dwarf had Azerick practice carving various runes in the wax until he mastered the form. Each time he carved a rune in the wax vessels, Duncan would inspect them before holding them over a candle and melting the wax smooth again so Azerick could start all over. Azerick found he had deft hands, possibly a side effect of his spellcasting experience and requirements.

While the sorcerer was busy carving his wax runes, Duncan identified several areas of interesting text that he marked by sliding a slip of vellum between the pages. Once the rune carver had identified the passages of interest, he began studying them in earnest.

Duncan began to think that the tome itself was magical in that it seemingly contained more knowledge than even its numerous pages should allow. There were entire treatises on dwarven history and lore that had been lost ages ago and were no longer found in the libraries or even the memories of the short-statured but long-lived race.

Glancing up from the tome, Duncan looked at the human meticulously carving the small wax disc. He was impressed at the young man's diligence and attention. His focus was quite remarkable for one of such an impatient and impetuous race. It made the rune carver realize it was about time he took on an apprentice and passed on his knowledge to ensure that the next generation kept his craft alive.

Azerick raised his head, examined his work against the drawing, and found it nearly identical in detail. He looked over and saw Duncan watching him. With a mix of pride and trepidation, he handed the wax carving over to the rune master. The dwarf studied the width, depth, and quality of lines making up the rune for fire.

"Not bad for a clumsy-handed human," Duncan's prickly reply came. "I think you are ready to move on to stone."

Azerick smiled at the dwarf's approximation of a compliment. Duncan passed him three soapstone discs and a finer set of chisels wrapped in a soft square of leather. Taking up one of the chisels and a small wooden mallet, Azerick began inscribing a rune upon the soft, mottled stone chit. He discovered that carving into the steatite disc was significantly more difficult and less forgiving than the wax had been.

It took over two weeks for the young sorcerer to graduate from the soapstone to harder types of stone. The hard grey rock before him frustrated Azerick to no end, as it seemed determined to fight his every attempt to create smooth, sharp lines with his chisels. It was thus that Azerick found himself hunched over the workbench, blowing away the tiny flecks of stone from his most recent attempt at carving the resilient rock, when a dwarf burst excitedly into the room.

Duncan looked up from the tome when the dwarf entered the room and began shouting. "Master Runecarver, a group of miners have been attacked by a huge beast in one of the caverns, and it has them trapped!"

Duncan hopped down from his stool, grabbed a wide belt adorned with several pouches, and buckled it around his thick waist. "C'mon, lad, I might need your help."

Azerick jumped up and followed the two dwarves down the series of slide poles. Despite their short legs, Azerick had a hard time keeping up with the dwarves as they sprinted through the streets and out to the mining tunnels beyond. Several more dwarves, wielding axes, hammers, and shields, fell in behind the running rune carver and his human guest. Most had found the time to slip a chain or heavy leather hauberk over their shoulders before rushing out to join the rescue party.

Azerick was the only one breathing hard by the time they arrived at a tunnel where empty ore carts sat lined up on steel rails. Azerick followed closely behind Duncan as he vaulted over the side and into the mining cart. A few of the dwarves pushed the carts together and connected their couplers with steel pins before cramming themselves into the four-cart train.

Duncan reached into one of the pouches on his belt and pulled out a palm-sized stone disc with the runes of air and iron engraved on its surface. He closed his eyes in concentration for a brief moment and uttered the words in the rough dwarven language that would release the runes' energy.

Azerick grabbed the sides of the cart tightly when it lurched forward, propelled by an unseen force. Duncan leaned forward with his head just above the front wall of the cart, his beard flapping in the wind. Azerick's eyes widened and his grip tightened on the sides of the cart as it continued to pick up speed.

Within moments, the train of carts was hurtling down the steel tracks with a velocity that would make a racing charger appear about as swift as a plow mule. Azerick's stomach fluttered and his eyes widened so far the whites showed all around as the carts rounded a sharp bend in the tracks.

Azerick let out a scream despite himself as the invisible centripetal forces shoved him against the outside wall of the cart. He was certain the dwarf-laden cars would be hurled off the narrow tracks and their living cargo thrown to their deaths.

The dwarves leaned into the curve, and Azerick felt the inside wheels regain contact with the iron rail before continuing their terrifying dash down the dark tunnel. Azerick saw that Duncan had the rune-carved stone in his hand once again and was calling forth its power. The cart began slowing nearly as quickly as it had taken off, and it soon came to a halt just short of a stout wooden barrier at the end of the tracks.

Azerick tried to follow the dwarves as they leapt out of the cart, but when his feet touched the ground his legs felt as though someone had removed the bones. Duncan grabbed him by the elbow and forced him to hobble along as the rescue party ran down a side tunnel.

Azerick soon heard the crashing of stone, the shouting of dwarves, and the hissing of some large beast coming from up ahead. Several of the dwarves' glowing orbs lit up a large cavern at the end of the tunnel with their pale blue light.

Near the back wall of the chamber, a massive creature, looking a great deal like a forty-foot-long centipede, was hurling itself at a narrow cleft in the wall and furiously trying to burrow through the stone.

Curses streamed out from inside the fissure in dwarven, followed by a hurled pickaxe that struck the cave crawler in the middle of its eyeless head. The cave crawler hissed in anger and pain, trying to dislodge the pickaxe as it lunged forward once more, tearing a large chunk of stone out of the wall with its massive, diamond-hard mandibles.

Azerick conjured forth a palisade of stone spikes between the fearsome beast and the dwarves trapped in the crevice. Several of the sharp stone tips burst up from the ground and struck the cave crawler in its soft underbelly, wounding the beast and forcing it to back away from its trapped prey. The multi-legged creature swung its huge head toward the dwarves running at it and shouting a loud battle cry that rang off the cavern walls.

Azerick let loose a barrage of arcane darts that flared brightly in the gloomy cave and struck the beast in its head. Duncan retrieved another rune stone from his pouch-laden belt. The earth and air runes engraved upon the stone glowed as he chanted under his breath. Several rocks the size of a large man's fist rose from the cavern floor then flew across the open space as if hurled from a ballista. The projectiles hit with such force that the impact echoed throughout the chamber and cracked the beast's hard chitinous shell.

The cave crawler turned its glare away from the charging dwarves and locked its eyeless gaze on the magic-wielding human and the few dwarves remaining near it.

Azerick saw the thick, caustic liquid dripping from its mouth as it drew back its head. The sorcerer had a gut feeling of what was about to happen and raised a ward just as the creature whipped its head forward like a striking viper. A stream of venomous acid sprayed from its mouth, easily covering the tens of yards between them. Azerick bent his concentration into his ward and was just able to deflect the stream away from him and the dwarves. Where it struck, the stone hissed and bubbled like the mud around a hot spring.

The attacking dwarves reached the cave crawler and scurried about like ants attacking an intruder, hacking at its many legs and underside. One of the dwarves went flying across the cavern when the segmented creature whipped its hind end around and struck the dwarf solidly in his back.

The cave crawler snapped up a second unfortunate dwarf in its powerful mandibles and lifted him high above the ground. Even as the sharp pincers pierced the dwarf's armor, the valiant warrior raised his hammer high over his head and brought it down onto the monster's forehead between the space where its eyes should have been. The powerful blow cracked the hard carapace near the area where the pickaxe was still lodged. A stream of gore flew out from the wound when the cave crawler whipped its head to the side and tossed the dead dwarf away to lie lifelessly in a heap against the cavern wall.

"Azerick, keep that thing from charging us as soon as my dwarves fall back," Duncan ordered.

Azerick nodded and the rune carver yelled for the harassing dwarves to fall back to him. The attacking dwarves retreated to the cavern entrance with military precision. As soon as they gained a few feet of space between themselves and the colossal creature, Azerick brought forth another field of stone spikes. The cave crawler tore at the spikes, tearing the sharp tips off with its mandibles and shattering others with its huge body.

Duncan raised a rune of water and earth, and the stone beneath the numerous feet of the cave crawler turned soft. Its own incredible weight forced it down into several feet of mud. When Duncan turned over the stone disc, Azerick noticed the runes of earth and fire engraved upon it. The runes glowed as Duncan fed power into them and caused the mud to return to its solid form once again. The cave crawler shrieked its rage at finding most of its legs trapped in solid stone. It thrashed about and began tearing at the rock with its powerful jaws.

"Stay back, ya thick-headed louts!" Duncan shouted as his dwarves, along with the miners hiding in the crevice, started to charge the restricted cave crawler.

Duncan retrieved another rune carving, this one of earth and spirit, from his belt. The floor trembled slightly as the magical runes worked their power upon the surrounding stone. Sharp snapping noises were all the warning the cave crawler got before several large, sharply-pointed stalactites lost their hold on the tall ceiling overhead. The heavy stone spears, hurled down by the force of gravity, struck the creature along its hard carapace, cracking and piercing it in several places.

Dwarves rushed forward swinging their axes, hammers, and pickaxes at the restrained and severely wounded behemoth. Though hindered, the cave crawler was far from helpless. When the rescuers and miners charged the beast, it whipped its head around, snapping angrily at any dwarf drawing near it. One dwarf was barely able to dodge the lethal mandibles, but he still got himself butted by the creature's enormous head, sending the hapless attacker rolling halfway across the cavern floor.

The cave crawler reared back to launch another stream of caustic acid, but Azerick distracted it with a salvo of magical bolts straight at its head. The dwarves drove their hammers and axes into the rents caused by the fallen stalactites, hacking and prying large chunks of the chitinous armor from its body and chopping at the soft tissue beneath.

Azerick poured lightning into the cave crawler and was heartened to see the creature shudder under the assault. A second blast brought the creature down, and dwarves scurried up its hard back and drove their weapons into the creature's skull.

Duncan ran and attended to the injured using rune stones marked with the glyphs of flesh and spirit. Azerick saw that one of the dwarves trapped in the cleft was Togar. He watched the dwarf walk over to the front of the cave crawler's head, grab the handle of the pickaxe lodged there, and pry it loose before striding over to where Azerick stood watching the dwarves tend to their wounded and recover the one unfortunate dwarf who had perished.

"Looks like I owe my life to ye again, wizard!" Togar yelled as he approached.

"You have Duncan and the courage of the other dwarves to thank just as much," Azerick replied, grasping forearms with the dwarf.

"Aye, that be for sure, but there'd be a lot more injuries, and no less than a few more deaths, without your help and I'll thank ye for that."

"I'm glad I was able to help."

Togar walked back to the other dwarves and clasped wrists with Duncan after the rune caster finished tending to the injured. His ministrations finished, Duncan returned to where Azerick was standing out of the way. The unwounded dwarves were helping those who had sustained injuries that made walking difficult or impossible. Four other dwarves, using a blanket as a makeshift litter, carried the warrior who had given his life in defense of his comrades.

"It's been a long time since a human has fought beside dwarves. I want to tell you that we all appreciate your help. You likely saved a lot of lives today," Duncan said.

"I was glad to help, as any guest should be. I'm sorry one of your people fell to that beast."

"He died a warrior's death, and many tankards will be lifted in his name tonight. Living under the earth is a hard life, and it has made us a hard folk. We'll mourn his death and cheer his life and his return to the great forge where he will be made anew. So, you ready to go now?"

"Depends, can we take the mine cart?" Azerick asked with a grin.

CHAPTER II

The young page ran through the marble-floored halls of Castle North Haven in search of Duchess Mellina. The young boy in russet velvet page's livery came to a halt in front of the large wooden doors just outside of Her Grace's sitting room. The page paused to catch his breath and straighten his doublet before rapping sharply on the door exactly three times. He opened and passed through the large, ornately carved hardwood door as soon as the lady beckoned him to enter.

Sitting in one of a pair of padded, high-backed chairs was Duchess Mellina embroidering a cloth. Lady Mellina was the duchess of North Haven and its ruler since the death of her husband nearly ten years ago. At forty-six years of age, she was still a startlingly beautiful woman with only a trace of crow's feet at the corners of her dark blue eyes to hint at her age. Her face and hands still maintained the smoothness of youth, and many considered her one of the most beautiful noblewomen in the kingdom. About the only thing preventing her from being mistaken for her daughter's older sister was her constant stern expression.

Her unwavering poise and always serious demeanor had earned her the nickname of the ice queen by her subjects and those who were familiar with her. Though she was often stern, she was deeply devoted to her people and their nickname for her was always spoken with the warmest of regards, for her citizens returned her devotion in equal measure.

Her daughter, Lady Miranda, was much more like her sire. Her dark auburn mane and jade green eyes were nearly the mirror of her father's. She was outgoing, outspoken, and loved to live life to its fullest. She was often found riding about the forests in leather leggings, jumping fallen logs and low walls, laughing all the while as her entourage tried valiantly to keep up.

Miranda was much beloved by the people of North Haven and often conversed and danced with the locals in some of the nicer inns whenever she was able to sneak away from her handmaidens and guards. Not that she really needed any guards within the walls of North Haven. With the exception of perhaps the most dangerous and poverty-stricken areas of the city, every man and woman in the city would thrash anyone who so much as raised a hand, or even a voice, to their beloved lady.

The young page strode forward with the cadence of the most highly trained soldier in the army, a silver tray resting lightly on his upturned palms. He stopped precisely two paces from the duchess, his heels together, toes splayed at exactly a forty-five-degree angle, and bowed slightly at the waist. He dipped his head nearly parallel with the floor, all the while never letting the tray he bore move so much as an inch in any direction.

"Milady, there is a letter for you," the page said as his blond, shoulder-length hair swayed lightly next to his face.

"Thank you, Jonathan," Duchess Mellina replied formally and retrieved the folded, wax-sealed paper from the silver tray. "You may go."

Lady Miranda caught Jonathan's eye as he bowed to each of the women and beckoned him over with a crook of her finger. Jonathan stepped smartly to stand before his lady as she reached into a pocket of her dress and, with a warm smile that reached her eyes, handed him a piece of hard candy wrapped in wax paper.

Despite his best effort at maintaining his professional countenance, the page could not help but smile back at her. Miranda shooed him away with a brush of her fingers. Jonathan marched back through the doors and closed them behind him before popping the treat into his mouth and running back through the lavish corridors with a large smile on his face.

"What is it, Mother?" Miranda asked, looking up from the book she was reading.

"It is an invitation for the two of us to be Duke Ulric's guests at his winter festival ball," the duchess replied as she read the fine script written upon the expensive paper.

Miranda's face became cross. "You know as well as I that he is fully aware your responsibilities would not allow you to travel during winter festival. That snake is just using you to try to get me to attend. I will not have it. The man is a troll."

"He is not a troll. He is quite handsome and very charming when he wants to be. You should be more receptive toward him."

"The man is a pig and traitor to the crown! He subverts King Jarvin's authority every chance he gets!"

"Do not speak thusly, daughter. The duke has done nothing overtly subversive toward our monarch, and such talk will only sow discord."

"Not overtly subversive? What must he do before his actions are considered overtly subversive, wave a bloody sword in one hand whilst swinging Jarvin's head about in the other?" Miranda demanded.

Duchess Mellina set down her embroidery and glared daggers at her daughter. "Many of the nobles disagree with King Jarvin's edicts. I have even debated the merits of more than one of his proclamations myself, yet I consider myself loyal to His Majesty."

"Mother, you know how important winter festival is to me and how involved I am with setting it up. I could not possibly attend Duke Ulric's ball. I have a responsibility to my people."

"That is as you say. Very well. I will decline Duke Ulric's invitation for the both of us. However, I must insist that you be his guest at spring festival, and I will inform him of such in my reply," the duchess said in compromise. "It would do well for you to attend Duke Ulric's ball if for nothing else than to strengthen the ties between our two cities. Perhaps you may even find he is not as boorish as you imagine. It has been several years since you met him in person and opinions change. A marriage could have enormous benefits for both our people, and our own treasury, which I need not remind you, is growing more meager with each passing season."

"If it is so important to you to join our houses then you should have married him yourself when he sought to suit you!" Miranda shouted waspishly.

"Lower your voice, child, and conduct yourself as a lady. Shouting is crude and unseemly. You know perfectly well I swore I would never marry after your father died, and I do not intend to break that vow. Besides, I am well past the age of begetting an heir to the duke anyhow."

"I suppose it is better to whore off your only daughter, your only child, to improve our standing, for that is what it is! No matter the amount of jewels, titles, and riches you would trade me for, it still makes me no more than a high-priced harlot!" Miranda screamed in rage. She wrenched the doors open and prepared to storm out of the room.

"Miranda you will not speak with the tongue of a common tavern wench."

Though Duchess Mellina never raised her voice, the fire in her eyes was clearly evident, and Miranda could feel them burning into her back as she fled the room.

"That was a clever spell you used to raise those spikes from the ground," Duncan said while the two sat in the rune caster's workshop enjoying a well-earned mug of beer.

Azerick nodded his appreciation at the dwarf's compliment. "I particularly liked the way you turned the stone into mud then reversed it to trap such a large creature. I will have to study that and find a way to mimic the effect with my sorcery."

"That is one of my better ones!" Duncan crowed.

It did not take the rune carver long to duplicate Azerick's stone spike spell, far less time than it took the sorcerer to develop his own earth transmutation spell. Azerick continued to practice the art of rune carving, diligently scratching sigils into stone day after day until he achieved perfection. When Duncan decided Azerick's carving skills were sufficiently honed, he began trying to teach him how to draw energy from the earth to empower his runes so they would serve a purpose beyond mere decoration.

Azerick found that this was far more difficult than learning the carving process itself. His own natural instinct to seek out the Source to power all things magical always leapt to the fore in an attempt to complete the task, which frustrated both student and master.

"You must get it through your head that there are more sources of power and magic than the one you use to channel your sorcery," Duncan told him for perhaps the hundredth time.

"I know, but it is like trying to force myself to walk on my hands. I know I'm supposed to, but my feet always want to take over the task."

"I think what you need to do is learn how to talk to the stone first."

Azerick furrowed his brow. "How am I supposed to talk to stone?"

"I'm talking about communing with the primal forces that imbue all natural things like stone, fire, water, and air. Of course, as a dwarf, I'm most familiar with and have the easiest time with earth and stone. I can hardly get them to shut up. Do you remember the first time you intentionally reached out and touched your Source?"

Azerick nodded.

"You need to sit down and focus your mind on the elements and find the energy locked inside. They all have a spirit, just as you do, if a bit different."

Azerick spent the next several days sitting and meditating upon the problem, locking himself away in a room devoid of all light, sound, and anything else that could cause distraction. He was near giving it up as futile after spending so many hours a day repeating the same processes when one morning he felt a tiny surge of energy in the stone around him. Instead of trying to grab on to it and force his will upon it, he relaxed even further and let himself slowly drift toward it as if he were trying to catch a soap bubble in his hands.

As he gently touched the tiny spark, he blew upon it with his consciousness and was astounded at the amount of power radiating around him. The energy of the earth was subtle, unlike the raging torrent of the Source, but it was vast! The power of the earth and air stretched out from horizon to horizon in a soft, constant glow. If the Source was a raging river, these elemental energies were an ocean.

Much farther down, he could sense the burning energy of the molten hot fires deep within the ground. He could see and feel the rivers of lava coursing through the rock like blood through his veins and arteries.

Azerick reached out, pinched a small measure of the ethereal energy with his mind, and attempted to guide it into one of his rune carvings. The energy felt slick and insubstantial, slipping between his fingers like so much smoke. When he came out of his trance, he looked upon the stone chit resting on his crossed legs where he sat on the floor. The sorcerer traced a finger over the rune and felt the slight tingle of energy it contained. Elated at his discovery, he rushed out of his dark room and into Duncan's workshop.

"Aye, I think you're finally getting it, boy," Duncan rumbled as he studied the rune Azerick handed him. "It's faint, but it's there. Ha, I'll make a rune carver outta you yet!"

Over the next several weeks, Azerick continued to practice, but with only minor improvements. He was able to touch the energy trapped within the elements almost easily, although not with the natural affinity he could tap into the Source; however, getting it to work his will was another matter entirely. Earth was stubborn and was loath to do anything except what it wanted to do, which was to do nothing at all. Air was flighty and raced away like a startled bird the moment Azerick tried to catch it. Fire was openly hostile and fought him for control. Water was probably the most confusing and contentious of them all and displayed the characteristics of all three depending upon its mood.

Duncan judged most of his efforts passable, but he finally had to confess that Azerick would likely never become a true rune carver, at least not by dwarven standards, but he had a small talent and there was no such thing as a useless skill no matter how minor his ability.

"Well, I'll tell you, lad, you've done well. Better than I expected from a human, and a young one at that. I told you I'd put you up through the winter. I thought I'd let you know that the snows are clearing out of the passes, and traveling ought not be too difficult in the coming days, but you're a likable sort and you're welcome to stick around a bit longer if you've a mind to."

"I appreciate the offer, and I have enjoyed my stay here. I have really learned a lot from you, but it is time for me to move on."

Duncan nodded his understanding. "I'll help you get a bag packed that will see you well enough through your travels. Where will you be heading to if you don't mind me asking?"

"I think I'll go to North Haven. It was where I was heading before we got lost at sea. From there, who knows? I have some friends sailing around up there that I need to get in touch with."

Duncan spent the next two days gathering the supplies he thought Azerick would need to make a comfortable trip. His pack was heavy, which made Azerick glad he had stayed in decent physical shape while he was with the dwarves. It promised to be a long walk and something best not taken by the ill-prepared.

Duncan and several other dwarves offered to take him a couple of days closer to North Haven through their tunnels, which he gladly accepted. Although he was anxious to return to the surface and feel the sun on his skin, he knew he would cover far more distance in less time underground than he would crossing the several leagues of rough terrain above ground until he found a road of some sort. While the small party was gathering at the entrance of one of the main tunnels heading westward, Azerick heard someone call his name.

He turned toward the source of the call and saw Togar running toward him with a staff in his hands. "Hold up there, lad! I'm glad I caught ye. I told ye that I owed ye for my life, twice, and I settle my debts."

"I was glad to help. You don't owe me anything, Togar," Azerick assured him.

The dwarf turned serious. "It be a poor thing to refuse a gift, boy. Now I made this for ye outta my appreciation for what ya done. Now ya can take it in yer hand, or ya can take it upside yer head and that's all there be to that!"

"In that case, Togar, I will gladly accept your gift, and with great pleasure."

"Good, that's more like it!" Togar shouted, a smile leaping back to his bearded face. "I just happened to find a nice vein o' arcanum when that big cave bug jumped out at us, and I used a goodly portion of it on this here staff."

Azerick took the staff from Togar and marveled at its craftsmanship. It was just over six feet long, the bottom two feet capped in arcanum, while the top sported an arcanum sphere the size of an apple. The wooden shaft was made of a burgundy wood so dark it was almost black. It was surprisingly light, but he could tell by the feel of it, as well as a certain intuition, that the staff possessed extraordinary strength. By far the most impressive features were the vast assortment of runes carved throughout its length and the brilliant ball of arcanum topping the end.

"Togar, this is incredible. I don't know what to say," Azerick said as he stared in awe at the weapon. There was no doubt in his mind that the staff was far more than a mere decorative walking stick.

"Of course it's amazing! It has to be to cover the debt I owe ye since I'm pretty damn amazing myself!" Togar roared with laughter along with the assembled dwarves.

Azerick studied the runes adorning the staff. "Duncan, did you carve these runes?"

"Aye, boy, I did at that. You saved more lives than just Togar's, and when he told me about the staff he was making, I figured I would add my own touch on account of everyone you helped. I know I got more from that big book of yours than you probably got from my rune teachings, so I figured I'd pitch in."

"Thank you, Duncan. You have all been most hospitable."

"Well, if we're all done lollygagging and getting all weepy over a stick, let's get on our way," Togar bellowed and led the procession down the tunnel.

It was an uneventful three days of tunnel crawling. The large, well-sculpted tunnel soon turned into a smaller passage with much rougher walls and support beams. The entire journey was easy going if incredibly boring. As much as Azerick enjoyed the dwarves' company, he was eager to be outside again beyond the few trips he had made to the surface with Duncan during his stay to see their highland pastures. When they came to the end of the tunnel, one of the dwarves ran up and jabbed the handle of his pickaxe up through a small hole in the cave ceiling.

His prodding brought down dust and clumps of earth followed by a warm beam of sunlight shining down through the hole. The dwarf then pulled a metal pipe about three feet long off his shoulder and stuck one end up through the hole he had cleared. He turned left and right while peering through an eyepiece set into the end of the pipe and announced that the way was clear.

Three more dwarves raced up, turned a handle, and pulled. Azerick was amazed to see a four-foot section of the cave wall swing in on concealed hinges. He thrust his hand before his eyes as bright sunlight washed over him.

"This is where we part ways, Azerick. I'm sure I don't have to tell you that we don't want any gossip floated around about our home, or this doorway here," Duncan said.

"No, of course not. I won't tell a soul about it. Not that I could likely find it again if I wanted to."

Duncan looked at the staff Azerick carried in his hand. "That staff is more than just a stick, as I'm sure you know. Those runes I carved and enchanted it with can help you out in a fix. You just concentrate and that arcanum ball will assume just about any shape you can imagine. It'll make a fine spear point if the need arises. It'll also come to you on command no matter where you are or how far away you be from it. It'll do more, but how much even I don't rightly know. That'll be up to you to learn. A tool is only as good as its wielder, no matter how well-made."

The dwarves all shook Azerick's hand, bid him farewell, and sealed the cave door behind him. Azerick looked at the wall of stone before him, but he could not see any lines, no matter how faint, that would lead one to presume there was anything here other than a huge outcropping of stone.

He pulled out a map Duncan had given him that was rendered in magnificent detail on a large, thin square of soft leather. He saw that all he needed to do was head due west until he found the coastal trade road between Southport and North Haven then follow the road north. It was going to be a long journey on foot, but he was well prepared and eager to walk amongst the trees and fresh air once more.

After a week of travel, Azerick's feet were aching and his blisters had blisters yet he felt as though he had barely made any progress.

Fortunately, he was in no real hurry and simply enjoyed the tedium of putting one foot in front of the other. He just wished he could do it with less discomfort. He sat near the small fire he had created, keeping his back to it in order to protect his night vision while he once more studied the staff in his hands. He ran his fingers lightly over the engraved runes embossed in arcanum and let his mind delve deeper into the magic of the staff. He had already learned a great deal about the abilities with which the weapon was imbued, but there was still so much more to it.

One of the first things he had learned was that he could store a vast amount of energy in the staff by channeling arcane power into it each night and replenish his own magical stores while he rested. The staff already held nearly as much power as he could, which was considerable. Tapping the power of the staff was far less taxing than coaxing and shaping the Source from across the ether.

He practiced shaping the gleaming silver globe on the top into various forms: some artistic, some martial like a spear point over a foot in length. He also practiced setting it down, walking away, then calling it to him. The first few times it had felt strange when the staff appeared in his outstretched hand, causing him to drop it more than once.

While making his arduous trek home, he thankfully ran across a couple of small settlements where he was able to replenish his supplies. Taking down a deer or rabbit with a spell was rather easy, but game had been uncommonly scarce. The few animals he did see bolted the instant they so much as heard a twig snap under his feet. He had been born and raised in the city, and he was not accustomed to wilderness survival, but the animals seemed especially skittish to him.

These observations were supported by reports from a few of the villagers he had spoken to. They claimed that evil walked the land, and no one would step outside their homes after dark. Villages posted guards and kept torches and lamps burning throughout the night.

Azerick dismissed it as small town superstitions. Besides, he was far from helpless, but he could not shake the feeling something was wrong in the world. Camping just a day out from the last small settlement, he caught a flicker of movement out of the corner of his right eye. Azerick turned and stared into the darkness, but he could see nothing out of place. He wrote it off as a shadow created by the flickering of his fire.

He focused back on his staff when another movement just outside his line of sight snapped his head around. Again, there was nothing there except the shadows created by his campfire. He listened intently, but he could hear nothing but the crackling of the warm fire against his back. Azerick was about to return to his studies when it dawned on him that the *only* sound he heard was his campfire: no owls, crickets, or other nocturnal noises that normally pervaded the night.

As he stared intently into the black forest, one of the shadows separated from the surrounding darkness and glided toward him. Several more shadows drifted out of the blackness before the sound of twigs snapping and leaves and pine needles crunching underfoot shattered the eerie silence.

The sorcerer sprang to his feet and launched a stream of magical darts into the nearest shadow creature. Three struck and caused the shadow to pause in its advance, but the other two streaking orbs passed harmlessly through its incorporeal body. The shadows advanced without the least sign of fear as more substantial undead in the form of zombies and skeletons appeared within the glowing boundaries of his campfire.

"All right, you want a fight?" Azerick shouted at the mindless creatures. "You got it!"

The sorcerer raised his arm and unleashed a brilliant bolt of lightning into the swift-moving shadows. The white-hot bolt ripped two of the insubstantial creatures to shreds, their mouths elongating in a silent curse before their forms lost all cohesion, spread out in every direction, and dissipated into nothingness.

The bolt blasted apart several of the zombies and skeletons shambling behind the wraiths, but a third shadow was unaffected. Azerick brought his staff up to parry the swing the shadow launched at his face, but the undead creature's arm passed right through the stout wood.

The sorcerer felt as though his blood had turned to ice when the shadowy, clawed hand tore through his chest. The overwhelming sense of pure cold and evil almost caused him to lose his grip on his weapon and crumple to the ground, but knowing that to do so would result in his death kept him upright.

Azerick ducked and rolled to his left as the shadow took a swipe with its other arm. He felt an icy chill pass over his back as he dodged under the blow and rolled back to his feet. Azerick released a flow of magical energy into the staff, causing the entire length to glow with a brilliant azure aura.

The shadow advanced relentlessly, intent on devouring the human's rich life force. Azerick brought his staff around in a swift horizontal arc as soon as the fell creature came within range. The enchanted weapon passed right through the insubstantial shadow just as his spells had.

He ducked another swipe from the shadow and brought the staff down through the center of the shade's spectral head. Azerick felt resistance press against his staff as if he had struck water. A brilliant flash of light erupted from his weapon with a resounding crack as it passed through the shadow's body and blew it apart.

He felt a sharp burning pain when a skeleton's claw-like fingers raked across his back, gouging deep furrows in his flesh. Without even turning to look at his assailants, Azerick gripped his staff in both hands, raised it vertically over his head, and brought it down with a shout. His magical command released a powerful burst of energy in a ring of expanding force, blasting over a dozen undead creatures and sending them hurtling away from him.

Fury burned in the sorcerer's eyes as he glared at the tide of undead closing in on him. Azerick savagely shouted out another spell and conjured forth a semicircular wall of stone spikes that impaled dozens of the undead abominations on their sharp tips.

The sight of the animated skeletons and zombies writhing and trying to pull themselves off the spikes holding them in stasis was almost more disturbing than seeing them bent on trying to kill him. Azerick called forth a shimmering gate and promptly stepped through. The magical doorway snapped shut as soon as it deposited him nearly a hundred yards away from where he had been standing. He turned to face the now distant horde as he shook off the dizzying effects of gate travel.

Azerick had never been as comfortable with fire-based magic as he was with earth and air, but it was far from beyond his ability to use it. As the monstrous undead creatures detoured around and picked their way through the spike field, Azerick used the campfire as a focus for his spell and unleashed a massive explosion.

The incendiary burst blasted apart a large swath of the advancing undead, sending those trapped upon the stone spike flying apart as burning bits of bone and charred flesh. Azerick unleashed his wrath in a fiery hellstorm of pure destruction.

Screaming like a ferocious, demented demon, he loosed his rage in scorching balls of fire that lit up the forest like miniature suns, destroying masses of undead. Any living creature facing such an unparalleled hellish assault would have fled in terror in the face of such wrathful destruction. But most undead were mindless creatures that knew no fear nor bore any sense of self-preservation. Oblivious to their losses, the skeletons and zombies pressed on with their attack, intent on killing the creature who dared to live whilst they anguished in this mockery of life.

When the remaining undead closed in upon him, Azerick incinerated them with cones of fire from his staff and blew them apart with magical bolts of pure energy. When the zombies and skeletons got dangerously close, Azerick raised another densely packed palisade of spikes and forced the undead abominations to split up and negotiate the obstacle.

With the time he gained for himself, Azerick was able to pick off the smaller groups before they could reach him. He leaned on his staff in exhaustion, his strength sapped from expending so much energy, not only from himself but from the power stored within his staff as well.

Azerick scanned what was now a large clearing lit up by several trees still burning and smoldering from the fiery onslaught he had wrought in his determination to destroy the undead menace. Bones and bits of blackened flesh littered the charred, scorched ground, but nothing moved other than windblown ash and a few burning leaves floating gently down from trees that had the misfortune to have been within the sorcerer's range of destruction. As much as he just wanted to lie down and sleep away his exhaustion, Azerick forced himself to walk away from the scene of the battle, leaning on his staff for support.

CHAPTER 12

Settlements were few and far between this far north, but fortunately the spring rains were also fewer in number. Azerick's magic kept the rain from reaching his skin and clothing, but it was still cold, particularly in the early mornings and evenings. He decided that a horse would prove a wise investment. His right foot throbbed in agreement.

As the miles ground slowly by, he became increasingly aware of the weight on his back and the distance involved. As a youth, any traveling he had done was aboard one of his father's ships. Until he had made his escape from the psyling city, the furthest he had ever traveled on foot was from one end of Southport to the other, all within the confines of the city walls.

Just as the sun was setting, Azerick spied a small hamlet nestled next to a bend in the river. It was a quaint, quiet, and friendly place where several people gave him a nod or a wave of welcome as he strode through the charming village.

Azerick spent the night at what passed for an inn and enjoyed a delicious home-cooked meal. He bought a gelding from a man who ran a small stable. As far as he could tell, it was a sturdy horse and appeared to have a great deal of patience even for riders as inexperienced as Azerick was.

It was a basic riding horse of mellow temperament that did not mind being burdened by a rider as long as it was fed and treated well. Azerick led the horse for several miles before attempting to mount. He had never ridden a horse in his life, and he was not about to embarrass himself in front of anyone by falling off. He placed his foot in the stirrup and lifted himself into the saddle.

The horse stood patiently, flicking its ears while the human scooted around in the saddle trying to find a comfortable and secure perch upon its broad back. If this particular saddle had either of those two things, Azerick was unable to find it.

Now that Azerick was finally seated in the saddle as securely and comfortably as he was likely to get, the horse seemed twice as tall to him compared to when he was safely on foot standing next to it. The sensation of being so far off the ground was slightly disconcerting.

With a deep breath to steady his nerves, Azerick gave the horse a small tap in its flanks with his heels. The horse bobbed its head forward and began walking at a sedate pace while its rider maintained a white-knuckled grip on the reins with one hand and the saddle horn with the other.

Azerick became increasingly more confident in his riding ability and the horse's tolerant temperament the farther he traveled. After they enjoyed a short lunch, dried beef and biscuits for Azerick and oats for the horse, it was time to mount back up and continue their westward journey. He nudged the horse to a walk and then to a loping canter that ate up the miles at an impressive rate without overtiring his mount.

Azerick became fond of his steed and spent much of the day trying to come up with a name for it, but having failed to come up with one, he simply settled on calling him Horse. Apparently naming animals was not one of his better skills. He set aside the issue for a later date figuring it was unlikely that the horse cared one whit what he called it. Despite there being at least an hour of good daylight left, Azerick and Horse stopped at a small clearing just off the narrow path which was the closest thing to a road in these little-traveled parts.

The wood and leaves were still wet from the light drizzle that had persisted throughout most of the day and would be impossible to ignite with flint and steel. Azerick left the tinder kit in his saddlebag and cast a jet of scorching magical fire onto the pile of logs and kindling. The wood burst into flames, unable to resist the extreme heat no matter how sodden it was, and burned with a merry orange glow.

Azerick spread the legs of a folding metal tripod and suspended an iron pot filled with water beneath it. He then took a small knife to three potatoes, several carrots, turnips, and barley, cut them each into bite-sized cubes and let them boil in the pot. He then pulled out a decent-sized smoked ham and added a gratuitous amount of the meat to the soup. The sun had just dipped below the horizon by the time the soup was ready.

Azerick looked out over the fire and called to the individual who had been watching him since he and Horse made camp. "You may as well join me for dinner if you are going to sit out there all night anyway."

For a moment, the sorcerer thought the stranger was going to turn down his invitation and he was going to be eating alone.

"Who are you?" a young boy's voice demanded to know.

"My name is Azerick. I have plenty of food, and I am willing to share."

"Are you a slaver? Because if you are, I'll kill you if you try anything." His voyeur's voice sounded from a different direction.

"I am no slaver, I promise you. I have been a slave in fact and would probably kill one on sight myself."

Azerick waited while the boy apparently tried to make up his mind. His stomach must have won the internal debate, and a small, filthy form separated itself from the shadows and hunched down directly across the fire from Azerick.

The boy was dressed in buckskin leggings and a dark green leather shirt. His feet were shod in crudely made shoes of soft leather. In his hands, he carried a small hunter's bow with an arrow nocked and ready to fly at the first sign of danger. A hunting knife hung from the somewhat crude leather belt encircling his narrow waist.

"I saw how you started the fire, so I know you are a wizard. Don't try to use your magic on me, and speak only in the common tongue, unless you can speak elven, otherwise I will assume you are casting magic on me and I will put an arrow in you."

Azerick was certain it was no bluff. The boy crouching before him had a feral look to him and carried himself with assuredness. He wondered at the comment about speaking elven, but then he noticed the pointed ears just poking out of the long brown hair pulled loosely back into a ponytail and secured with a leather thong.

"You're an elf?" Azerick asked his young guest.

The boy narrowed his dark almond-shaped eyes. "My name is Nanarin, and I am a half-elf. Is that going to be a problem for you?" he asked coldly.

"None at all. I've just never met an elf, or a half-elf, before. I did meet an abyssal elf once, although that was an extremely unpleasant situation. Do you live near here?"

"I live wherever I please. The forest is my home."

"Do you live by yourself? Isn't that kind of dangerous?"

"The woods are dangerous only to those who are weak or not clever enough to take care of themselves. I could have started that fire without magic," the half-elf proclaimed.

"Really? Then you can probably hunt and feed yourself too," Azerick replied in a half jest.

The boy looked at the stew pot and nearly lost his confident demeanor. "I can, usually, but all the game seems to have disappeared lately. I wouldn't mind sharing your food with you, even though you had to buy it from a human town."

Azerick laughed to himself at the young half-elf's confidence. He could see that the boy was positively famished, but he would never beg from anyone. He looked across the fire at the half-elf eyeing the simmering contents of the pot and saw a reflection of himself several years ago.

"Why don't you go wash up in the river, and I'll pour us a bowl of soup."

"A bath you mean? Why should I need a bath?" the half-elf demanded indignantly.

"Because you are filthy, and you smell worse than Horse over there. How do you think I knew you were watching me?"

Nanarin glared at Azerick for a moment, and he thought the half-elf was going to refuse and run off. Then he burst out laughing and sprinted for the water. The half-elf dove in head first, clothes and all, and scrubbed himself liberally with his hands.

He untied the thong binding his hair back and shook it free, scrubbing away the gods only knew how many weeks' worth of grime. Nanarin disappeared under the water for over a minute then came back up, tossing his clothes onto the rocky shore.

A few minutes later, the boy got out of the water, wrung out his leathers, and hung them near the fire to dry. Azerick got him a blanket he could cover himself with while his clothes dried before filling two bowls to the rim with the thick soup. Azerick did not bother the half-elf with questions while he ate, but he noticed that the boy was pushing aside the slices of meat with his spoon.

"Do you not eat meat, Nanarin?"

Nanarin looked up at Azerick and hesitated before answering. "Nanarin is my elf name. My friends call me Wolf."

"Okay, Wolf. Why are you setting aside the meat?"

"I'm just saving it for later, that's all."

"There is plenty here. You can eat that and get more if you like. Is there someone else with you? They are welcome to join us as well. I have plenty of food," Azerick assured the lad.

Wolf looked unsure how to answer. "You will feed my friend too?"

"Of course. As long as they're peaceful."

"Okay, but you gave your word." Wolf let out a low whistle.

Azerick felt warm breath on the back of his neck and turned to stare directly into the bright golden eyes of an enormous black wolf. The wolf's coat was so dark that for a moment Azerick thought the golden eyes were hovering bodiless just over his shoulder. It was not until the animal walked forward, circled around the fire, and sat next to Wolf that he was fully able to appreciate the animal's size.

"His name is Ghost. He's my friend," Wolf said, introducing his four-legged companion.

The human and the wolf, the one that was really a wolf, stared at each other for a moment through the fire. Azerick stood, walked over to his saddlebags, and carried them back to where he was sitting. He pulled out the haunch of smoked venison he had bought in the last hamlet he passed through and offered it to Ghost. The wolf stepped lightly over, and after giving the meat a good sniff, gently took it from Azerick's grasp with its long black muzzle.

Ghost lay back down next to Wolf, held the haunch down with his forelegs, and tore long strips of meat off the bone with his powerful jaws and sharp teeth. Azerick watched Ghost for a moment then motioned for Wolf to hand him his empty bowl. The sorcerer refilled the boy's bowl and decided it was now proper to ask more questions.

"How old are you, Wolf?"

The half-elf shrugged his bony shoulders. "Twelve, I think."

"How long have you been on your own? You are on your own, aren't you?"

Wolf shook his head while he chewed and swallowed a chunk of ham. "This is my second spring living in the forest, but I'm not alone. I have Ghost."

The huge wolf raised his head and looked questioningly at his half-elven companion then went back to gnawing on his cleanly-stripped leg bone.

Azerick wondered what could have happened that a ten-year-old-boy would be left to fend for himself in the middle of a forest. "Are you orphaned? Where is your family?"

"My family did not want me. No one wants a half-breed around." Wolf almost succeeded in covering the bitterness in his voice.

"Do you mean the elves? Did the elves make you leave because of your parentage?"

Wolf shrugged his shoulders again. "They tolerated me after my mother died and took care of me, but there is a big difference between being tolerated and being loved." The half-elf's answer was a wise one for someone of his age. "I left on my own after I got in a fight with some boys who tolerated me even less than the rest of the snobby elves did."

"What happened?"

"We fought, they lost, and I got in trouble. The same thing that had happened many times before, but this time I decided it would be the last time. Ghost and I whipped them really good. We both left them with scars that will remind them not to pick on us, even though we were both smaller at the time." Wolf patted Ghost between his large, wedge-shaped ears.

"I think I know a little about what you went through."

Wolf looked back to where Horse snuffled nervously at Ghost's scent. "So what's your horse's name?"

"I don't really have a name for him. I just call him Horse."

"You're not very imaginative for a wizard, are you?"

"I am a sorcerer, not a wizard," Azerick corrected.

Wolf shrugged his bony shoulders. "Sorcerer, wizard, same thing; either way it's a terrible name for a horse."

"I suppose you could do better on the spur of the moment," Azerick challenged, glad to let someone else pick a name.

"Sure I could. See that white diamond on his forehead? You could have named him Starfire. If you don't like that, there's Thunder, because of the sound his hooves make when he runs, or Zephyr because he runs like a wild wind, or Goblinstomper, Big Red, Will-o'-the-wisp, Lightning, Dasher…"

"All right, I get it. I'll think about a different name."

"If you want. I sort of like Horse though."

Azerick shook his head and felt a laugh wanting to burst from his gut for the first time in quite a while. The boy and the young man exchanged stories for several hours. Wolf told Azerick how during hard times he had filched eggs and even a chicken or two from the small towns and outlying farms. He did not trust any of the humans enough to ask for help or shelter. He did not need their help anyway.

Azerick told the half-elf about how his parents had died and how he had been alone for a few years on the streets of Southport. Wolf pulled his leathers off his makeshift drying rack near the fire, stretched the shrunken leather back out, beat them against a tree to soften them, and put them back on before falling asleep. Azerick left him the blanket to sleep on and spread out his bedroll.

Azerick woke just as the sun cleared the horizon enough to shine a reddish glow through his closed eyelids. The sorcerer sat up and saw that Wolf and Ghost had already gone, taking the blanket and a small sack of food with them. He had almost hoped the young half-elf would have stuck around, having felt something of a kindred spirit in the boy. Azerick did not allow himself to dwell on it. The boy seemed at home in the woods, and if he chose to make his home here then so be it. He wished the boy and his wolf well, mounted Horse, and resumed his westward journey.

CHAPTER 13

Lady Miranda suffered through dance after dance with Duke Ulric. It took all of her will and court etiquette to maintain the polite smile required of her when socializing with the powerful leader of Southport even though she despised the man. She recalled meeting him when she was younger, back when her father was still alive, and she and her parents had attended a social event hosted by the Duke of Southport. She met him once a few years after that at another function, and now having met the man on a more social level, her dislike turned to disgust.

Duke Ulric complained and openly criticized King Jarvin, but he always made sure to stay just inside the line of outright ridicule. Miranda had met the king several years ago during his coronation when her father and the other dukes and barons swore their oath of fealty to their new monarch. She had found him to be a decent and honest man. He did not wrap himself in deceit and hide behind false faces like most of the nobles she knew. She had just finished telling Duke Ulric her opinion as the two of them stood alone in the duke's study.

"Really, Miranda, how can you support a man as your king who is not only the product of a bastard's union, but lived as a peasant himself until taking the throne?"

Miranda fought to maintain her composure as she answered the duke's question. "Your Grace, King Jarvin's mother may not have been married to his father, and no, she was not a noble, but she came from a decent family and did quite well for herself. King Harlan loved her dearly. Although King Harlan could not bring his son to live as the heir to his throne for propriety's sake, he still ensured that Jarvin received the best education he could provide."

Ulric gave Miranda one of his condescending smiles. "Miranda, no amount of education can compensate for a proper bloodline, especially if one is to be king. Otherwise, we would have every scholar in the kingdom making a claim for the throne."

"King Jarvin has every bit of his father's blood running through his veins, just as much as he would if King Harlan's wife had been capable of producing his heir."

"Ah, but you see," Ulric said meaningfully, pointing at Miranda with his wine glass, "Jarvin would also have House of Bagguette's lineage in him as well, but now Harlan's blood has been diluted, tainted if I dare say so, with that of his commoner mistress."

Miranda breathed in deeply then let it out slowly. "Your Grace, it is late and these talks of politics do make me quite weary. With your leave, I shall retire for the evening."

"Of course, Lady Miranda. Please forgive me for not noticing the strain I have put on you. Politics is one of those things best suited to men. I look forward to the morning when we can perhaps speak of more delicate things better suited to a lady."

Miranda forced a polite smile. "I am so sorry, Your Grace. I am afraid I must depart for home in the morning, and it is best if I begin my journey early. I left many matters unattended at home in order to endure—enjoy—your hospitality, but I really must not neglect them any longer."

Duke Ulric knew a brush-off when he heard one. The fact was that he could tell quite early on that the duchess of North Haven's daughter was even less open to a partnership than the duchess had been. It was a shame; such a union would have considerably bolstered his power base.

He plastered on his most gracious smile, pretending to accept her departure at face value, and raised his hand to bid her goodnight. "It has been my utmost joy to have been gifted with your visit. I hope you sleep soundly and have a smooth journey home."

Miranda ignored the proffered hand, curtsied, and fled the duke's presence for the relative safety of the room she shared with her handmaiden, Sarah.

Duke Ulric sat in his plush, high-backed chair and sipped the remnants of his glass of wine. An oaken panel opened near the fireplace and his chamberlain stepped into the room by way of the secret passageway hidden behind it.

"Your courting did not go as well as you planned, Your Grace?" Alton asked even though the answer was clear on the duke's face.

"No, she is far too much like her father. If only that frigid mother of hers had been more receptive after her husband died. It was nearly a waste of my time to have had the oaf killed. At least it got rid of one more fool who supported the embarrassment sitting the throne."

"What are we to do with her, Your Grace?"

Ulric drummed his fingers on the arm of his chair while he pondered the very question he had asked himself several minutes ago. He would like to have North Haven as an ally when he made his bid for the throne. He knew that Duke William of Brightridge openly supported Jarvin, and that provided the bastard king with a very powerful ally. William's was the only city rivaling his own in both wealth and soldiers.

"I think North Haven would be far more cordial to me if I were to rescue their precious lady from the bandits who are holding her for ransom," Ulric said slyly.

"I see, Your Grace. I will make the appropriate contacts at once."

"Alton."

"Yes, Your Grace?" The chamberlain turned back to face the duke.

"Ensure you make it abundantly clear that Miranda is not to be harmed or sullied in any way—until I say so."

"Of course, Your Grace."

Lady Miranda stewed as she and her handmaiden rode in the swaying, bumping carriage, enduring the rough ride as she had urged her driver to put as much distance between them and Southport as quickly as possible.

"The man is a swine and a traitor!" Miranda fumed once more.

"Yes, milady, you told me that. You have told me that every day for the past three days," Sarah reminded her lady.

"That is because it is still true. Gods, I will have to burn the dress I wore to the ball. I will never be able to wear it again without feeling his lecherous hands on it. It is a shame; it was a lovely dress, and it cost enough to feed a common family for a year."

"Perhaps you could sell it and give the money to a charity," Sarah suggested without looking up from her knitting.

"That is a fantastic idea! You are very clever, Sarah. It is why I put up with you," Miranda teased.

"You put up with me? Have you forgotten all the trouble you have got me in over the years? Sneaking out to listen to tavern musicians and pinching food from the kitchens to feed those filthy children who will cut your purse strings if you are not careful. And let us not forget the incident involving that lord's white horse and the raspberry stain."

"I thought the horse looked lovely in pink. Besides, the man was rude to Father."

"All nobles are rude. You should not need me to remind you of that."

"Father was not rude, nor is His Majesty."

Sarah was about to comment on how rare both men were when the coach jerked forcefully with a loud crash, sending both women sprawling to the floor.

Azerick and Horse stepped off the narrow dirt path constituting the road heading east into the more remote towns and onto the broad, cobbled northerly trade road. The unexpected transition took him by surprise, and once again, Azerick was pleased with his decision to purchase Horse. Together they had covered a distance in one week that would have taken him at least three or four on foot. He gently guided Horse toward the last leg of their journey to North Haven.

The weather was pleasant, which was a nice change from the constant grey drizzle of the past several days. His body had finally adjusted to Horse's broad back, and it took only an hour or so to assume a somewhat normal walk after dismounting, unlike the early days requiring the entire night and more.

The northern trade road was a busy route, and barely half the day had passed when Azerick heard the clatter of multiple, steel-shod hooves thundering up from behind him. He guided Horse off the road and onto the earthen shoulder. Preceding a large cloud of dust, he saw a handful of armored men on horseback obviously in a state of great haste. He brought Horse to a halt well out of the way of the mounted men-at-arms escorting a carriage he could now see barreling down the highway toward him.

When the carriage drew closer, Azerick saw that it was an opulent affair of black enameled wood with gold detailing along all of the joints and seams. A team of six white horses pulled the carriage along at a steady gallop. Azerick imagined the fat, pompous lord riding comfortably inside the plush, velvet-lined interior, sipping wine and eating dates while the horses worked themselves into a lather pulling the extravagant, heavy coach and his pasty, bloated body down the road.

Just as the coach and its armed escorts raced past in a cloud of choking dust, ropes with grapnels attached to them flew out of the woods on both sides of the road. The large steel hooks caught the gold-painted spokes and, as the ropes reached their full length and went taut, ripped the rear axle completely off the carriage.

The driver shouted fearfully as he tried to get his panicked team under control. The sudden weight and noise terrified the horses, and it was all the driver could do to keep the powerful animals from bolting and dragging the wrecked coach behind them.

At least a score of men burst from the woodline about fifty yards from where Azerick waited and watched the bizarre scene unfold. Crossbows fired and pierced the heavy breastplates of three of the guardsmen. The remaining bandits charged the surprised guards who wheeled their horses around to defend the carriage and its occupants. The bandits, Azerick was sure that was who they were, wielded swords, spears, and catchpoles they used to unseat the mounted soldiers.

The guard captain, distinguished as much by his command voice as his blue-plumed steel helm, ordered the remainder of his men to surround the coach and protect it with their lives. Even though most of the guards remained mounted and the bandits were on foot, the odds were not with the defenders. The guard captain and three of his men charged into the ranks of bandits, hewing at them with their swords and running them down with their chargers.

The remaining guards were heavily engaged against several times their numbers and were being pressed against the side of the coach, severely limiting their effectiveness. The bandits with the catchpoles put them to expert use and unseated the mounted soldiers, stripping away what little advantage they had.

Although Azerick did not condone such brutal criminal activity, he was impressed with the planning that had gone into the task and its near-flawless execution. It was obvious that this was a well-planned raid and not just a target of opportunity.

It took just minutes before only the captain and two of his men were left to defend the coach with its precious occupant or occupants. Another guard fell to a spear to the stomach, and the bandits laughed at the men's futile show of resistance. As the captain and his last loyal soldier stood back to back against over a dozen remaining bandits, one stepped forward and spoke to the valiant soldiers.

"Further resistance is unnecessary and futile," the bandit, most likely the leader of the group, told the captain. "Put down your weapons and go home. You cannot keep us from taking the lady."

Azerick had to strain his ears and was barely able to make out that the bandit leader had referred to a lady.

So what if some fat nobleman's even fatter wife is kidnapped. He would pay a ransom and most likely get her back. That is how these kinds of things worked, Azerick thought to himself.

Besides, it was no business of his. He was a sorcerer, not a paladin charging in to save every fool not able to save themselves.

"I will die before I allow her to fall into the hands of the likes of you!" the captain shouted at the bandits.

"What of you, soldier? Are you willing to die for some rich lady? You're hardly more than a boy yourself. Are you willing to die needlessly before experiencing all that life has to offer?"

Even at this distance, and with the soldier wearing a pot helm, Azerick could see that the young guard did not have to shave more than about once every couple of weeks, so much was he still in his youth.

"I stand with my captain and my lady," the lad responded nervously as he clutched his sword tightly in both hands.

"So be it."

A bolt pierced the young soldier's armor, and he fell to the ground to join the rest of his comrades in death. It was at that moment that Horse must have gotten a whiff of the blood now coloring a large patch of the highway around the coach and nickered his dislike of the scent. All eyes turned, and everyone took notice of the young man on his horse just a few dozen yards away who had so far gone unnoticed.

"Hey, boss, what do we do about him?" one of the bandits asked, pointing his shortsword in Azerick's direction.

Azerick's shoulders slumped in resignation, and he slipped off Horse and stretched his sore legs. "This business is none of my affair. Do not waste any effort on me."

The bandit leader looked at Azerick before making up his mind. "Kill him; we don't need no witnesses."

The guard captain put his back to the coach and raised his shield in preparation of the renewed attack. Half of the bandits broke away from the lone soldier and charged the travel-worn stranger. Azerick sighed in annoyance and slapped Horse on his broad rump in an effort to get him clear of the fighting.

Azerick leaned on his staff and called out to the dozen men advancing on him with their weapons drawn. "This is not my business, gentlemen. You do not want to make it so."

Half the bandits fired their crossbows in reply at the young man who calmly stared death in the face while the others charged with swords and spears. Azerick let out his breath and shook his head. The bolts stopped an arm's length from his heart and dropped harmlessly to the ground.

"Bad choice." Azerick glared into the wide-eyed faces of the closest bandits who saw the quarrels stop in midair and clatter to the cobblestones.

Azerick slammed the butt of his staff onto the road with a shout of power. Arcane energy burst out around him, caught several of the bandits in its powerful blast, and sent them flying backward through the air. Those few bandits who were several paces back felt as though they had been kicked in the stomach. Some stumbled, but the others ignored the pain and renewed their charge.

Azerick ducked under the blade of a bandit who tried to take his head off in one powerful but clumsy blow. The sorcerer bent a small amount of his focus into his staff and shaped the arcanum ball at the end into a wicked spear point. Azerick ducked under the thug's awkward slash, lunged forward, and impaled one of his companions just behind him.

The sorcerer spun to his left, caught the first bandit behind his right heel before he could recover from his failed attack, and flipped the rogue onto his back before stabbing him through the heart.

Another quick word and a flick of the wrist sent five blazing daggers of magical energy streaking into the chest of a third brigand, killing him instantly.

The guard captain wasted no time in taking advantage of the distraction the sorcerer had created and lashed out with his longsword, felling two of the outlaws before they were able to turn back and engage him.

However, now that the Captain had recovered their attention, he was once again fighting for his life against more than half a dozen armed bandits. He used the side of the ruined carriage to keep any brigands from slipping behind him. So far, that tactic was about the only thing keeping him alive.

Three more bandits faced Azerick and spread out so the wizard could not target them all with one spell from his dark sorceries, or so they prayed. They were hesitant to be the first one to try to engage him directly and stayed back, pointing their weapons at Azerick. They continually looked between themselves and the wizard to see which of them would be the first to attack—and likely die.

Azerick decided for them. He took advantage of their vacillation and raked a blast of lightning through the bandit in front of him. The powerful electrical arc passed through and struck several of the crossbowmen who were taking aim once more. Azerick spun to his left, figuring the remaining two bandits behind him would make their move as soon as he cast a spell, and they did not disappoint.

The sorcerer stabbed forward with his short spear, but the bandit managed to turn it to the side with his buckler. Azerick realized his attack had overextended him and left him extremely vulnerable to a counterattack. He watched as the second bandit raised his blade and prepared to bring it down on the back of Azerick's exposed neck. Azerick tried to dive forward and use his momentum to roll under and beyond the attack, but he knew he was not going to make it. In the blink of an eye, a long, goose feather-fletched shaft sprouted from the bandit's neck, felling him instantly.

Azerick's roll carried him beyond the bandit who had blocked his thrust. He sprang to his feet and spun around, ready to cross weapons once more with the outlaw. When he turned and brought his spear up into the defensive position, the bandit was already clutching at an arrow in his chest and falling to the ground.

Azerick looked around as the guard captain felled the last bandit facing him. The bandit leader and another of the rogues darted into the tree line where the thundering of hooves announced their retreat.

The sorcerer searched for his hidden rescuer but failed to see any sign of him, although he had a good idea who it might have been. With a tip of his head, he showed his thanks and went to retrieve Horse who was about a hundred yards away busily chomping on tufts of green grass, oblivious to the mortal peril his master had just been in. Azerick led Horse by the bridle toward the wrecked coach as the driver was extricating himself from some dense, thorny shrubbery he had dove into out of terror and the carriage door was opening.

"My Lady, stay in the coach." The guard captain stalked toward Azerick with his bloody blade drawn and his face set in a mask of rage.

"I should gut you where you stand, wizard!" the captain screamed.

"The likelihood of your accomplishing such an act is about as probable as you holding the rear of that coach up the rest of the way to North Haven. It is also not a very nice thing to say to the man who just saved your life, as well as whoever is in that coach."

The soldier stopped a little over an arm's length from the sorcerer. "You could have intervened sooner! Those men are dead because of you!" He whipped his sword around to point at the fallen soldiers behind him, which sent droplets of blood flying off the gore-covered blade.

Azerick was in no mood to listen to the soldier's verbal abuse and accusations. Where was he when his mother was murdered? Where were the guards to come to his rescue when Hugo and his thugs were beating him and chasing him through the streets of Southport? Of course, only nobles warranted the protection of soldiers.

"Let me remind you once more that it is also because of me that you and your passengers are not dead as well! It was none of my affair nor was I honor-bound to risk my life in their defense. That was you and your men's job, one at which I say you performed exceedingly poorly seeing as how were it not for me you would have failed utterly!"

The captain's face went from red to a blotchy purple. Spittle flew from his lips as he forced his words through strained vocal cords. "What do you know of duty or honor? That boy who died at my back had a greater sense of duty and honor in his hairless chin than you have in your entire useless body! You, *sir*, are nothing but a coward and a petty charlatan! I would run you through right now, but it would be an insult to my blade to sully it with your yellow blood!"

Azerick was about to respond with a scathing comment of his own when the carriage door burst open and two women stepped out. One woman was taller, just a few inches shorter than Azerick was, with long, full, wavy auburn hair. She wore a dress of expensive material in white and light blue. The woman following close on her heels was comely in a plain sort of way, wore her soft brown hair braided and coiled upon her head, and was dressed in an emerald green dress snug fitting in the body but flaring out in softer green and billowing white lace at the legs and shoulders.

The auburn-haired woman spoke as she stepped toward the two men who were seconds from trading blows. "Stop this! Stop this right now! Captain Brague, you will put away your sword this instant and not say another harsh word to this man!"

"My Lady, this—" He paused to find a word to describe the sorcerer, "*person*, did nothing to assist me and my men, nor did he come to your aid until his own miserable life was threatened."

"I understand your anger, Captain, and I grieve for the men who gave their lives in my defense. Their families will receive due reward and pension for their sacrifice. However, this man is not duty-bound to risk his life in my defense even if he was aware of who was in the coach, which I assume he was not." She turned to face Azerick who stood silently listening to the guard captain's chastisement. "As much as I wish you had intervened sooner so that more lives may have been saved, I do offer my thanks on behalf of myself, my people, and my mother, Duchess Mellina of North Haven. I am Lady Miranda, this is my handmaiden and friend Sarah, and you met the good Captain Brague. It is a pleasure to make your acquaintance." Lady Miranda extended her right hand, fingertips down for Azerick to give his due courtesy.

"I am Azerick," he replied simply. He clasped Miranda's proffered hand between his thumb and forefinger and gave it an informal shake.

Miranda gave the sorcerer a look of amusement at his awkward introduction. "Not exactly the most gallant are you, Magus Azerick?"

Azerick could not help but lose a small bit of his hostility at Miranda's open and friendly smile. "I am afraid not. Truth be known, my etiquette teacher struck me more often than my weapons trainer."

Miranda stifled a laugh out of respect for her fallen soldiers. "I can well imagine, Magus Azerick."

"Just Azerick please, milady. I do not know if I qualify for such an honorific."

"And I am Miranda to my friends."

Captain Brague decided to interrupt the friendly conversation before he threw up his lunch. "My Lady, I need to attend to the men before we must depart with great haste. We do not know if this is part of a larger bandit force. I did observe their leader and another escaping into the woods."

"Of course, Captain, please see to it. I am sure the good magus will stay to protect us, at least until we are ready to depart. Won't you, Azerick?" she asked with her pleading, green eyes.

"Of course I will. It would be my pleasure."

Miranda's open and carefree sprit softened even his hard heart a bit. Captain Brague doffed his heavy armor, grabbed a pickaxe and shovel from the toolbox at the back of the coach, and along with the coach driver, began breaking up the hard soil.

"I'm sure the good magus will protect us," the soldier seethed as his anger fueled his heavy swings. "It would be my pleasure. Oh, are those bandits plunging their blades into you? Let me help you as soon as I'm finished with my lunch. It's not my job to risk my life for my lords and ladies. No, that job goes to big dumb soldiers who are actually stupid enough to believe in honor!"

"Did you say something, Captain?" Miranda called over to him.

Captain Brague ground his teeth until he was sure they were nothing more than white little nubs just poking above his gums. "No, My Lady."

Despite the early spring, the sun beat down upon the group and made the day rather sultry. The heat was particularly merciless to Captain Brague and the driver, Otis, as they continued to hammer away at the stubborn soil while Azerick kept the two women company.

Miranda turned back to the sorcerer. "Azerick, is there anything you could do to help the good captain and our driver with the graves?"

"Of course, let me go see what aid I can offer."

Azerick excused himself from the women's company and walked up to the captain and the driver who were both sweating profusely from the strenuous work. "Miranda beseeched me to offer you my assistance—again."

"Why on earth would you do that?" Captain Brague asked sardonically. "I thought you only offered help when the job was nearly finished. Besides, I wouldn't want you to get any dirt under your fingernails."

Azerick ignored the captain's sarcasm. It was much more aggravating to be polite than to let himself be baited into another argument.

"I assure you, Captain, I have no intention of dirtying my nails."

Reciting the words of an incantation, Azerick created a large hole between the guard and the driver. He repeated the spell three more times, creating enough grave space to bury all of the fallen soldiers. The bandits they simply threw off the side of the road.

"Why couldn't you have done that an hour ago?" Captain Brague demanded.

Azerick put on the most disdainful and arrogant look he could muster, one fit for a nobleman. "I found your earlier efforts amusing, but then they became tedious."

Captain Brague had never wanted to stab a man in the back as badly as he did the moment the sorcerer walked away. The soldiers' horses were easy to recover, being trained not to spook at the sound of battle. They also found nine more horses, which must have belonged to the bandits, saddled and picketed about a hundred yards from the ambush site.

"It looks as though we are going to have to ride the rest of the way to North Haven," Miranda announced once the fallen soldiers were buried and words of condolences and farewell were spoken. "Come, Sarah, we will have to change into something more appropriate for riding."

Azerick's eyes followed the two women as they disappeared back into the coach to change clothes.

"You had best watch your eyes, boy, or I'll cut them out," Brague promised. "It is my duty to protect Lady Miranda with my life, and I will do so from *every* threat."

"Given the level of competence you have displayed thus far, I am surprised she is not already heavy with child from any number of men, myself included, being I have been under your watchful eye for the better part of an hour."

The captain reached for his sword and Azerick took a step back, smiling at his ability to provoke the soldier. Miranda and her maid stepped from the coach just as Brague unsheathed his weapon.

"Captain, put away that blade this instant! Can I not turn my back for a moment without you two going at each other's throats?"

"My Lady, this scoundrel made some very obscene remarks. I was defending your honor!"

"Actually, it was the very act of you turning your back that got him so concerned. It seems the captain thinks that should he let his vigilance slip but for a moment, every man within eyesight will attempt to mount you as if you were a mare in heat."

Captain Brague's eyes bulged and his face turned violet once more. "Lies, I never said any such thing!"

"Stop it, both of you," Miranda pleaded and stepped between the two men. "I need both of you to respect each other, at least for the duration of the trip to North Haven, assuming Azerick would be willing to accompany us. Would you provide us such protection, Azerick? My mother will certainly wish to bestow her thanks to you for saving our lives."

"I was going to North Haven anyway, so I suppose I can play bodyguard for a while."

"Good, now no more fighting or bickering between you two. Let us mount up and be away from this dreadful place."

Miranda had changed into riding pants and was wearing a leather vest over a white silk shirt. She had exchanged her elegant shoes for tall riding boots reaching just below the knee. Her handmaiden had changed into a similar but more feminine and flowing garb. Captain Brague and the driver, Otis, tethered the horses behind their own. The riderless horses had a variety of packs, bundles, and chests strapped to their backs constituting the majority of the coach's salvaged contents as well as the shields, swords, and personal effects of the fallen soldiers so they could return them to their families.

Captain Brague tried his best to keep himself and his horse between the obnoxious mage and Lady Miranda without appearing too obvious about it. But every time he did, Miranda would work her way right back to Azerick's side.

"So tell me, Azerick, where are you coming from?" Miranda asked him.

"East, but I used to live in Southport."

"Did you study at the Academy?"

"For a while, but I left."

"That must have been very exciting!"

"It was...memorable," Azerick conceded.

Miranda continued to ask questions while Azerick evaded most of them and Captain Brague kept trying to split them apart. Otis interrupted Azerick and Miranda's mostly one-sided conversation about two hours into the ride.

"I think I see my beauties up ahead!" the driver called over his shoulder.

True enough, as they drew closer the white shapes far ahead resolved into the spooked team of horses the driver had been able to free before they destroyed the coach or injured themselves in their panic. Otis rode ahead, calling out to them with soft words to avoid frightening them again.

He slipped off the side of the horse he had commandeered and walked toward the magnificent team that was still trailing their traces and which was attached to the long tongue of the coach he had freed by pulling the linchpin.

Otis slowly approached the team, calling out to each of the horses by name in a soft voice. The horses flicked their ears and looked around warily but did not bolt. The driver went about pulling the pins attaching the heavy piece of lumber to the horses' harnesses while constantly talking to them and stroking their broad, powerful backs. Once he freed them from the long wooden tongue, he led them away and back toward the rest of the party where he attached the lead ropes to the other trailing horses.

Handling so many horses proved to be a rather difficult task even when dealing with animals trained to obey a driver's commands such as these. Fortunately, the party found themselves entering a small town about an hour before sunset. Otis and Captain Brague saw to stabling the horses while Azerick and the two women went inside a quaint but clean inn to find rooms for the night.

The innkeeper recognized Lady Miranda and tried to refuse payment on the grounds that it was enough simply to have the honor of having her stay at his inn, but Miranda insisted that they all pay for their rooms and meals just like everyone else. She knew times were hard for most people and would not deny any of them their due. Otis and Captain Brague entered the inn just as the others sat down at a large table where a barmaid was already serving drinks.

"I paid the stableman to board all the horses except the ones we are riding and using as baggage carriers until Otis and a team of men can come back and retrieve them," Brague informed Lady Miranda, and Otis bobbed his head in agreement.

More patrons began arriving just as the barmaid served their meals. The inn created such a warm and friendly environment even Azerick allowed himself to enjoy the evening. Lady Miranda continued to badger him with questions, questions that continued to hammer away at the emotional defenses he had built up, and he found himself answering more and more of them.

Years of dangerous living and deadly encounters had taught Azerick to maintain a high level of awareness at all times. It was because of this that he found his grip tightening on his staff and a spell coming to mind as a pair of burly townsmen stalked toward their table.

Azerick had seen that smile on men before, and he knew it could indicate trouble. He saw Captain Brague also stiffen at the strangers' approach.

"Excuse me, folks, but my friends and I have a wager between us we needs ya ta settle, iff'n you would be so kind," the biggest of the bunch addressed Miranda directly.

Miranda flashed one of her dazzlingly friendly smiles. "I will help if I can. What is it you gentlemen need from us?"

Azerick was surprised, not only that a noblewoman had deigned to speak to the rugged common men, but that she actually treated them with courtesy and respect.

The speaker of the group swiped the knit hat from his head, began wringing it in his huge hands, and cleared his throat to talk. "Are you Lady Miranda of North Haven?"

"Why, yes I am. How do you do, gentlemen?"

The big farmer turned to his friends. "Ya see, I told ya! I seen her last winter fair lookin' like the goddess o' winter herself!" The excited man turned back to face Miranda. "Milady, may I touch yer hand, like a gentleman, don't ya know?"

Miranda laughed loudly, got up from her chair, stood on her tiptoes, and gave the man a peck on the cheek. For a moment, Azerick thought the man was going to faint and fall atop their table, but he locked his knees before they gave way completely and stuttered his sincerest thanks before he and his friends returned to their table, talking excitedly about the encounter.

Azerick was stunned. Never had he seen a person of wealth, much less nobility, treat someone of such low status so kindly. The friendliest thing a nobleman had every done for him was to aim for the legs instead of the head when he had tried to whip him for being in the way.

"You seem to be very popular amongst your people," Azerick said as Miranda took her seat once more.

"It is easy to be gracious when you have such wonderful people around you." The earnestness of her words earned her several smiles from nearby tables.

"I am afraid growing up in Southport did not leave me with a very good impression of the nobility. I am glad to see not all are greedy, maligned scum who care only about their own ambitions and nothing for the people who they are supposed to protect and serve."

"Is that your impression of all nobles, or are there some in particular you personally detest, such as Southport's duke?"

"Nearly all nobles I have encountered fit rather well into that mold. It would probably be best for me not to speak out openly against the duke. I understand that you have a certain political decorum to maintain."

"Perhaps more than I show, but my mother certainly does. I personally think Duke Ulric is a selfish, treasonous pig of a man who will either one day be king or find his head on a pike. I personally hope for the latter," Miranda stated unequivocally.

Azerick's opinion for this noble-born woman increased even further while the other three at their table gave her imploring looks not to speak so openly. The inn's door opened and another local customer came in. Before the man pushed the door shut, Azerick heard the unmistakable cry of a wolf.

"Was that a wolf I heard?" Miranda asked with more excitement than concern.

"I'm sure it was, but it is highly unusual for wolves to be this near the coastal villages," Otis answered.

"I hope it is not a large pack, or the ranchers and farmers could be severely hurt by their predation," Miranda said with concern for both the wolves and the welfare of the livestock owners.

Just one wolf—make that two, Azerick thought to himself.

The two women bid everyone a good night, retired for the evening, and Captain Brague escorted them upstairs. Azerick got up from the table after the captain and the women left him alone with Otis and made his way to the kitchen. He paid the kitchen staff for a heavy plate of food and any bone scraps they might have.

He took the sack of discarded bones, wrapped the plate of food in a towel, and ducked out the back door. He waited several minutes before he heard Ghost's howl, which was followed by the higher pitched wail of Wolf.

Azerick walked out into the night in the direction of the calls. He crossed the road running through the center of town and into the woods. The trees had been cut back decades ago for building materials and the forest began about two hundred yards from the edge of town.

Azerick walked only a few paces into the woods before setting the plate of food on a stump and leaving the sack of bones and discarded cuts of meat and fat next to it. He looked around for a moment and thought he saw the brief glint of golden eyes in the pale moonlight. Satisfied, he turned around and walked back to the inn.

Otis was gone from the table by the time he stepped back into the inn and went upstairs. He entered the only other room the innkeeper had available and saw Otis sitting on a narrow bunk set against one wall. Azerick's eyes settled on Captain Brague as the man took two steps across the floor, stopped directly in front of him, and jabbed a finger into his chest.

"I don't know what kind of game you are playing, wizard, nor do I see why someone like Lady Miranda treats the likes of you as if you were even close to being an equal. But do not mistake her friendliness and good nature as anything other than being polite. Do not encourage her or pursue her. I guarantee you that once we reach North Haven you will have enjoyed the last of her company. I know a miscreant when I see one. Despite your little conjuror's tricks, that is what you are, and lowlife peasants do not mix with nobility!" The captain emphasized each of his last words by poking Azerick in the chest.

If Azerick had been the least bit offended or outraged at the captain's behavior, not a trace of it showed on his face or in his reaction. Anyone with any ability to read a dangerous man would know that was when they were the closest to lashing out.

"You should know, Captain, that I killed the last person who called me a peasant," Azerick replied emotionlessly.

"Are you threatening me?" Captain Brague asked, pushing his thick-jawed face to within inches of Azerick's.

A malign grin spread across the sorcerer's young face. "I am just letting you know that the largest piece remaining of him would have fit inside that metal brain bucket you call a helmet with plenty of room to spare. Now, if you are quite finished trying to see who has the bigger *sword*, I am going to get some sleep."

Azerick cast a glance at the terrified driver who was certain he was about to be caught up in the middle of a vicious battle between two men who each held a great deal of power in their own right. Otis let out a deep breath when the sorcerer and the warrior both stripped down to their small clothes and crawled into their beds, not once taking their hate-filled eyes off each other.

The night passed and the morning came with neither man attempting to kill the other in their sleep. After a warm breakfast, the party saddled up and resumed their journey north. Captain Brague had offered to commandeer a coach for Miranda and her maid, but the noblewoman refused and insisted that she would rather ride. They made better time by leaving all but the three horses used to carry baggage and provisions back in the small town.

Miranda continued to make small talk while Azerick provided even shorter answers. Azerick avoided Miranda's questions about himself. He deflected her seemingly endless queries with vague answers as a master fencer parries the blade of an opponent. Captain Brague tried to burn holes through the sorcerer's back and out his chest with his eyes the entire ride.

They spent a second night at another inn at what was little more than a way station for travelers. The few patrons who were there also knew Lady Miranda and treated her with fondness. To Miranda's credit, she never refused to shake hands or speak with anyone, and she always treated everyone with a courtesy rarely displayed between noble and commoner.

Azerick was relieved when it became apparent the captain felt no need to renew any of his previous threats and settled for ignoring the sorcerer's presence for the most part. Otis rarely spoke to Azerick, although he felt that was more a matter of the stigma associated with spellcasters and not due to dislike or unfriendliness.

Lady Miranda was even more cheerful and chatty than she had been before as they rode farther north. So warm and welcoming was her personality that even Azerick was having a hard time not opening up to her and divulging some of the personal memories he kept locked up tightly inside him.

"Azerick, tell me about your family. You said you were from Southport. Are they still there?" Miranda asked, once again trying to elicit even a small shred of information from the taciturn sorcerer.

"I do not have a family," Azerick replied shortly.

"Nonsense. Everyone has a family."

"Not when men of power decide they are a threat or have something they want. I have had several families, and each of them was murdered by just such people."

Miranda blushed deeply. "I am sorry. I had no idea. What about the Academy? Surely you have some wonderful stories of your stay there?"

Azerick looked up at the sky and then back at the road ahead of them. "Another person of power sought to take what was not his and I stopped him. For this, he tried to kill me."

"What happened?"

"He failed; I did not. But since his family had wealth and power, my guilt and punishment were unquestionable, so I fled. Another person of power enslaved me and later murdered my wife and unborn child. Is there anything else you desperately need to know about the reality facing those who are not born into privilege?"

The look of pain and loss she saw in Azerick's eyes made Miranda lose her desire for further conversation. She spent the next two hours studying the countryside and occasionally pointing out areas of interest to Azerick, but not once did she resume asking him about his past, for which he was extremely grateful.

Just after noon, the small party crested a long slow hill and gazed down upon the city of North Haven nestled in its protective bay in the distance far below them. Azerick thought it was one of the most beautiful sights he had ever seen. The cobbled road descended into a small valley where the city lay at one end and spread outward from the crescent of the bay's shoreline. Ships with their white sails bobbed peacefully in the calm waters of the bay. Some were tied to long floating docks while others lay anchored hundreds of yards offshore.

Beyond the protective waters of the harbor, the sails of fishing vessels and larger cargo carriers dotted the open ocean. For a moment, Azerick let himself think of his father aboard one of his ships sailing into North Haven to sell his rare cargo from Lazuul. He imagined himself at the helm, guiding the large, four-masted ship into the bay under his proud father's tutelage. Azerick wiped the pleasant fantasy from his mind knowing it could never be. Instead, he wondered if any of the ships he could see belonged to Zeb.

Miranda caught the smile creeping onto Azerick's face. "It is a lovely city, don't you think?" She grinned at the dour sorcerer's obvious enjoyment of the view.

"It is. You must be very proud of it."

"We are. My mother and I both work very hard to keep North Haven the polished jewel my father helped to create."

"How did your father die?" Azerick asked, taking the offensive in the question-asking for once.

Miranda's eye's took on a distant, lonely look at mention of the painful subject. "The healers say it was a heart attack, and Father did enjoy his drink more than some, but he was always very healthy. He could ride, fight, and hunt with any man. It is hard for me to accept that there was any such weakness inside him that could bring him down so quickly."

"Was he a good ruler? Did the people like and respect him like they seem to do you?"

Her smile lit up her face once more. "Oh yes. The people loved my father a great deal. I said he liked to drink, and he did much of it at the various inns throughout the city. He always told me that if I wanted to know how people truly felt about their lords and their troubles, just to go to an inn or a tavern, have a drink, and listen to them. He said that if the people were happy, then their lord was doing a good job. If they were not, then it was likely that the lord was not providing for his people and needed to amend his rule or be replaced."

"He certainly sounds like a rare man. I have met few if any nobles who would share his view."

"He learned that from his father who learned it from his father who was the one that turned North Haven from a small trading port into the wonderful city it is now."

"What about your mother? Does she rule in much the same way?"

Miranda sighed and thought about the question before answering. "Mother loves her people and the city. She rules justly, but even before Father died, she was not as open as he was. After father died, she walled up her emotions. She sort of reminds me of a certain wizard I know," she said mischievously.

"I am a sorcerer, not a wizard," came Azerick's usual, quick correction.

"Who said I was talking about you?" Miranda asked coyly. "It is funny how one picks up on the negative and associates it with themselves. I find people who do so wear their negativity as a façade to conceal their true nature and to avoid more pain."

Azerick's face flushed. Fortunately, he spied a large ruin where a tall tower and crumbled walls and outbuildings still stood on a hilltop about two miles out of town.

"What are those ruins on the hill?" Azerick asked, changing the subject.

Miranda shielded her eyes from the sun with her hand and looked at what her aloof companion was pointing at despite knowing precisely to what he was referring. Everyone in North Haven knew about the ruins, and knew well enough to stay far away from them.

"That was once the keep from where the lord of North Haven ruled with his family before it became a major port of commerce. That was back when it was just a small trading town and a stopover for ships sailing the northern sea on their way to Southport. The keep was the first attempt at bringing legitimacy to North Haven, as well as bringing it into the kingdom as a serious city worthy of having its own duke. However, those were very tough times, and hard people roamed the land and the seas. Pirates controlled everything north of Southport and resisted any attempt from the kingdom to expand its influence into what they considered their territory."

Miranda took a shuddering breath as she recounted the tale. "One night, several shiploads of pirates landed down on the beach and made their way on foot to the walls of the keep. Over the previous months, they had been able to instill several of their own men in the keep as guards. Those men left a sally port open, and the pirates rushed unimpeded onto the keep's grounds. The pirates attacked the guards and overwhelmed them. The lord of the keep was said to have stood in front of his barred bedchamber where his wife and five children hid. Wave after wave of pirates charged up the stairs only to be hurled back by the lord of the keep.

"Finally, the leader of the pirate band ascended the stairs himself and challenged the lord to single combat, promising that if he won the pirates would leave him and his family alone for now. The lord accepted, and even though he was exhausted from defending the door to where his family hid, the pirate captain knew that while this man fought for the lives of his family he could not best him in a fair fight. So the pirate captain maneuvered the lord so that his back was to the stairs, and on his signal, one of the pirates threw a dagger at the lord's back. The lord stumbled from the injury, and the pirate captain ran him through the heart, killing him instantly.

"The pirates broke the door down and gained entry to the room where the lord's wife and children huddled in the corner begging for mercy. The pirate captain was so furious at the number of men the lord had killed, and at the fact he had very nearly defeated him as well, that he ordered the children thrown from the top of the tower. The lady of the keep was forced to watch, as one by one, her children were thrown from the balcony, their cries echoing all the way down until they abruptly ceased when they struck the courtyard. The pirate captain then forced the lady to the same spot where his men had thrown her children to their deaths and offered her a chance at life. The lady was still a very beautiful woman, and the pirate captain promised her that she would live in comfort for the rest of her life if she agreed to be his.

"When she stopped wailing and smiled, he thought the lady was going to agree, but her smile turned into hideous, manic laughter. She dug her fingers deep into the pirate's flesh with inhuman strength and threw them both over the edge, cursing him all the way down. It was after that time that my great-grandfather tried to claim the keep and build North Haven into what it is today, but the lady still haunts the tower. Ever since, any living person who dares to go near the tower is killed, driven mad, or forced to flee in terror. So my great-grandfather built a new keep that eventually became the Castle of North Haven."

"Interesting," Azerick mused.

Miranda looked incredulously at the sorcerer. "Interesting? I tell you a horrific tale of murder, deceit, and eternal haunting and all you can say is interesting? I would hate to see what you would actually find terrible."

"You certainly would. You seem to know an awful lot of detail about the event."

Miranda smiled at the wizard's skepticism. "The pirates loved to talk. The story was recounted many times in inns, bars, and on ships for years. I'll admit, the bards and scribes who took up the tale likely romanticized it, but the outcome is the same. Pirates stormed the keep, murdered the lord, lady, and children, and she haunts the tower and its grounds to this day."

"Interesting," Azerick repeated with a smile.

When they drew near the gates of North Haven, a large contingent of armored men rode out to intercept them. The riders brought their thundering mounts to a halt a few paces away, the leaders rendering a sharp salute to Captain Brague and Lady Miranda.

"Captain, Lady Miranda, thank the gods you have arrived! The duchess sent us out to find you when your carriage did not arrive yesterday. What happened to your coach and the rest of your guards?" the soldier asked the captain.

"We were waylaid by bandits just three days north of Southport. The coach was ruined, and though we slew and drove off the villains, we were the only ones to make it," Captain Brague told his subordinate.

Lady Miranda saw the sergeant cast a glance at Azerick. "This is Magus Azerick. It is because of him that any of us survived the attack."

Azerick could hear Captain Brague grind his teeth as the sergeant replied, "Then we all owe you an enormous debt, My Lord Magus. I am certain Her Grace will wish to see you all as soon as possible."

"Of course, Sergeant," Miranda responded. "Escort us home, if you would be so kind."

The other mounted soldiers had caught up to them and parted to let the distinguished party take the lead before following in behind. Captain Brague and the sergeant headed the vanguard as they passed through the heavy gates and into the city of North Haven.

The castle was spectacular with four large towers and numerous minarets all topped with blue clay tiles. Nearly everyone on the street waved joyously to Lady Miranda and her passing party with many more rushing out of homes and businesses to welcome her return.

As much as Azerick disliked attention, he found the spectacle heartwarming and allowed himself to believe that he may finally be able to call somewhere home. First, he needed to secure an actual home, and he already had a plan for that. He just hoped what he had planned would work. If it did not, it might just kill him.

CHAPTER 14

Lord Beaumonte paced restlessly across the carpeted floor of his study like a caged animal. He was expecting someone, but it was already after midnight, and the longer he waited the more restless he became. He became weary of his constant pacing, so he sat down and poured another glass of amber liquor. Lord Beaumonte brought the glass to his lips and nearly spilled its entire contents down the front of his silk smoking jacket when a voice spoke from behind him.

"You requested my services."

Liquor sloshed onto his chest as he bolted up out of his seat and spun around to face the intruder.

"Who are you?" he gasped at the dark-garbed, hooded figure standing barely an arm's length behind the chair he had just forcefully vacated.

"You know precisely who I am. You sent for me. Now gain control of yourself so that we may conclude our business transaction without wasting any more of my precious time with stupid and pointless questions," the Rook said.

Lord Beaumonte tried to regain his composure, but the ice-blue eyes practically glowing beneath the cavernous darkness inside the cloak's hood unnerved him.

"How did you get in here past my guards?" the nervous lord stammered.

The Rook sighed as if forced to explain the most rudimentary of concepts to an imbecile. "If I could not get past your pathetic guards unchallenged then I would hardly be worth the exorbitant sum you are going to pay me."

Lord Beaumonte forced a calm façade. "Ah yes, of course not. Very well then, let us get down to business."

For all of his bluster and arrogance, Lord Beaumonte had never hired an assassin or had any dealings with the criminal element beyond simple tax evasion and trading of illegal goods. If the assassin standing before him was typical of his kind, he never would again. It was like standing in the same room with the goddess of death herself.

"I wish to hire you to kill somebody."

"That would be obvious. Had you sent for me for anything less I would have been greatly disappointed, and much like having my time wasted, I do detest being disappointed."

Lord Beaumonte swallowed hard as he imagined what happened to those who disappointed this man, if a man was what he really was. "My son was murdered and I want his murderer to face justice."

Lord Beaumonte retreated when the Rook unexpectedly stepped toward him. "I am not a constable or watchman to administer *justice*. I kill people, and not just anyone. There are lesser assassins who will perform your task for a fraction of what I charge. You had best pray you have not wasted my time coming here."

"My son was killed by another wizard while attending the Academy two years ago," Lord Beaumonte hastily explained. "For two years I have paid various men to find out where his murderer has been hiding, but to no avail. I want him found, and I want him dead no matter the cost!"

"Your son's killer was a teacher?"

"No, another student, but do not underestimate him. He is exceedingly clever, or so I am told. When he killed my son, there were pieces of him scattered about for yards in every direction. I do not think we ever found all of him."

"Very well, I will find this wizardling for you and kill him. You have my fee?"

"Of course, it is right here."

Lord Beaumonte crossed the room and pulled a carved wooden box the size of a small loaf of bread from a wall safe hidden behind a portrait. The small chest's contents gave off a metallic clink as he handed over the small fortune to the assassin.

The Rook took the chest and had started to walk backward toward a shadowy corner of the room when all of the oil lamps began flickering as if being assaulted by a strong wind. The room was cast in harsh, wavering light and dancing shadows for only a moment before the lamps once again burned brightly. In that half-second of flickering light, the Rook had disappeared.

Lord Beaumonte glanced around the room, but as far as he could tell, he was once again alone. The lord wondered if he had just made a deal with a demon and prayed it would not cost him more than the gold he had just handed over.

One thing was for certain, he would have to move his study into another room. The Rook had left such a powerful presence that never again would he feel safe or alone in this chamber. He knew his fears were ridiculous. There was no room in the entire kingdom a person could be safe in if the Rook wanted them dead.

Azerick followed Lady Miranda and Captain Brague down the marbled halls of Castle North Haven. The ringing of the captain's boot heels was the only thing breaking the tranquility of the place. They stopped before a pair of ornate double doors guarded by two pikemen in brilliantly gleaming full plate armor.

The two sentries came to attention and opened the doors wide to permit the trio into the room beyond without challenge. A waiting room for those who sought an audience with Her Grace lay between them and the throne room with another set of double doors replete with halberdiers. Felt-covered benches sat against the two walls between large planters from which small bushes and plants grew and filled the room with the fragrance of their blossoms.

The party was not required to wait, of course, and the guardsmen swung open the doors to permit the privileged group access to Lady Mellina without delay.

Azerick tried to conceal the look of awe on his face when he entered the vast hall. Blue marble sheathed the walls, and multiple glass skylights let in the afternoon sun, while magnificent tapestries, brilliantly polished swords and shields, and masterwork paintings adorned the walls. A long, emerald green carpet accented with gold trim ran from the door to the very steps of the dais upon which sat the thrones.

Azerick stifled a gasp when he espied the woman sitting in the right-hand seat of power atop a seven-stepped dais. The woman was beautiful just like her daughter, but there the similarity ended. Her hair was black and straight where Miranda's was a deep auburn and wavy. Miranda's face was open, kind, and affable where her mother's was stern, strictly composed, and shrewd. Azerick could tell this was a woman who commanded respect through sheer presence alone.

When they reached the foot of the marble steps below the thrones, Captain Brague knelt with his head bowed while Miranda bounded up the steps and wrapped her arms around her mother.

For a moment, Azerick thought the frigid woman would not break decorum to return her daughter's display of affection in front of guests, but after a moment's hesitation, she embraced her only child. For just a second, Azerick saw the motherly adoration the woman hid behind the steely mask of propriety. Miranda whispered something into her mother's ear while casting a glance to where Azerick and Captain Brague waited to be addressed.

Captain Brague turned his head to look up at Azerick and shot him a fierce glare indicating he should kneel before Her Grace, but Azerick refused to take the hint and simply bent at the waist when Lady Mellina made eye contact with him.

The duchess extracted herself from her daughter's embrace and sat back down upon her throne. "Captain Brague, it has come to my understanding that you and your men ran into some trouble on the way back from Southport."

The captain swallowed with difficulty before answering. "Yes, Your Grace. Approximately three days ride to the south, bandits set upon us. We were surprised, the coach was disabled, and we were vastly outnumbered. Several of my men fell to crossbows before we were even able to engage. The rest gave their lives to my lady's defense."

"I mourn the loss of your men and my loyal citizens, and they will each be hailed as heroes. Submit their names to my seneschal so we may compensate their families for their loss and pass on their medals of valor. Please take your place," the duchess commanded.

She turned her falcon-like gaze toward Azerick once more. "I understand it is you whom I have to thank for my daughter and captain's timely rescue. Had it not been for you, my loyal captain would also have given his life in my daughter's defense, and she would likely be strapped to the back of a horse riding to some filthy bandit camp where she would stay until I met the cowardly scum's ransom demand. Is that about the truth of it, Magus Azerick?"

Before he could answer, Captain Brague interrupted. "Your Grace, you should know that this man did not intervene until the bandits threatened him. Had he acted sooner, more of my men would likely be alive, and had the bandits not made the critical error of attacking him, the results would have been precisely as you just stated."

"You are certain of this, Captain?" Lady Mellina asked coldly.

"Yes, Your Grace. He sat upon his horse watching the disaster unfold before his very eyes. It was not until the bandit leader told his men to kill him that he got off his horse and used his sorceries to slay several of the bandits attacking us." Captain Brague's voice was thick with scorn.

"You say he was mounted some distance away from the attack then *dismounted* when he heard the bandit's order to kill him. Am I correct?"

"That is precisely how it happened, Your Grace. The man is an opportunist at best, and a coward at the least," the captain replied smugly, flashing Azerick a condescending sneer of disdain and triumph.

"Were any of the bandits mounted?"

"No, Your Grace. They burst out from the tree line on foot."

Duchess Mellina crooked one well-manicured eyebrow at her captain. "So this man, an accused coward, got off his horse to fight a large group of bandits afoot instead of simply wheeling his mount around and fleeing the battle. Is my understanding correct, Captain?"

Captain Brague hummed and hawed for a moment, but he realized where the duchess was going with this line of questioning and knew he had been cornered. "Yes, Your Grace."

"Captain Brague, you are a loyal and valuable member of my domain." The soldier stood straighter, if it were possible, under his lady's praise. "However, diminishing the accomplishments or heroics of another is unseemly and ill becomes you. Men often require leadership and encouragement to act with honor and courage. If they did not, we would have little requirement for outstanding leaders like yourself. You should be grateful to the magus, for he has not only saved our beloved Lady Miranda, but also given you the opportunity to continue to serve us. I hope you take advantage of the chance he has provided you with to learn and grow."

Captain Brague fumed and wilted under his lady's admonishments, but he still managed to force out a reply. "Yes, Your Grace."

"Magus Azerick, despite the splendor you see about you, we are not a wealthy city, but anything I am able to give you as a reward for the safe return of my daughter is yours for the asking."

"Your Grace, I left Southport for North Haven some time ago in search of a new home. Even though events beyond my control delayed my arrival by some time, it would seem that such delays, though accidental, were fortunate or perhaps even destined to occur," Azerick submitted. "I saw the ruined keep upon the hill a few miles from the city. I would be most grateful if you would grant me ownership of it and its accompanying land."

Lady Miranda gasped and even her mother's impeccable calm cracked briefly at the request. Captain Brague looked surprised for a moment then smiled to himself hoping that maybe the upstart sorcerer would be killed, or at least driven off by the very real ghosts haunting the place.

The duchess composed herself with practiced grace. "Magus, I promised to reward you with anything that is in my power to give, and I will honor my pledge, but I would ask you to reconsider your request. There are several fine homes and manors within the city, of which I would gladly give you your pick."

"That is very gracious of you, Your Grace, but it is the keep I wish to possess," Azerick stated adamantly.

"Are you aware of the keep's history?"

"Yes, Your Grace."

"The tales of the haunting and lives lost are quite real and are not some fictitious folklore of superstitious commoners. The lucky ones who have braved the ruins of the keep returned half mad, and many did not return at all."

"I am aware of that, Your Grace, but that is still my request."

The duchess allowed a small frown to show on her stoic face. "Very well, Magus. I will have my seneschal draw up the title. May Solarian bless you and watch over you."

Azerick bowed at the waist once more as the duchess stood and departed the chamber through a smaller door hidden behind the thick folds of a curtain to the rear of the dais. Lady Miranda glided gracefully down the steps and slipped an arm through Azerick's before he had time to react.

"May I escort you out, Azerick?" she asked kindly but in a tone implying his answer would be yes whether he wanted it or not.

"I suppose you would be better company than the captain," Azerick replied.

Miranda guided Azerick down the marble halls of the castle by a different route than they had taken coming in and took nearly twice as long to reach the entrance. Miranda made a good tour guide, pointing out the portraits of her ancestors, who had built which halls and rooms, and when they were constructed. For some reason Azerick could not fathom, Miranda's presence made him slightly nervous. It came as a relief when they finally arrived at the doors leading out.

"Do you know where you will be staying?" Miranda asked.

"No, this is my first time in North Haven. I will find an inn somewhere until I deal with the keep."

"Why did you choose such a dreadful reward? My mother would gladly give you a beautiful chateau or mansion here in the city."

Azerick shook his head. "I want something I can truly call my own. Somewhere set apart from everyone else. The keep will be what I make it, not what someone else has given me."

"Do you truly wish to be apart from everyone else so badly?"

Azerick thought about the question for a moment and shrugged. "It is safer that way, and less painful."

"Safe, yes, but also dull. You must take some risks to find happiness, or it is really not much of a life at all. You may survive, but you will never truly live. Fare thee well, Magus. I look forward to speaking with you again."

Azerick gave her a nod and descended the broad granite steps leading down to the courtyard where a groom stood waiting with Horse. Azerick put his foot in the stirrup and lifted himself into the saddle.

"Do you know a good inn to stay at?" Azerick asked, looking down at the lad.

"The Golden Glade is as nice an inn as you will find in the city, milord," the young groom replied respectfully.

Azerick thanked the young man and flipped him a silver piece for his help.

"Thank you, milord!" the groom replied with a deep bow and scampered away.

Azerick guided Horse through the heavy gates set in the secondary wall surrounding the palace grounds. The homes and few businesses lining the streets this close to the palace were opulent affairs: two and three stories tall, built of white stone, and roofed with the same blue tiles as the palace. Somewhere along one of the many grand plazas was where Azerick would have had a home if he had wished it. Instead, he was now the owner of a decrepit ruin allegedly haunted by a vengeful spirit. He began to wonder about his own sanity and if the ghost could drive him mad if he were already insane.

He asked a few people he passed for directions to the Golden Glade. They looked from his travel-worn clothing to his plain horse before pointing him in the general direction of the inn.

Probably assuming I am looking for a job not a room, Azerick thought to himself.

The Golden Glade was located directly on the intersection separating the wealthy quarter of the city and the merchant quarter where much of the middle class lived.

The sign above the door was a painting of a golden waterfall cascading down into a pool of what was supposed to be beer or ale, surrounded by lush vegetation and grass. The paint was clean and fresh; probably touched up or repainted frequently to maintain the quality of the sign.

Around the back of the inn was a large, clean stable with three stablehands ready to take good care of the customers' horses. Azerick guided Horse through the gates that were now open but which were kept shut at night for security.

The three stablehands watched Azerick approach and conversed amongst themselves, deciding who was going to service the pauper and his worn-looking mount. They pushed the youngest boy forward, who was most likely the one forced to take the customers that looked least likely to tip.

Despite having drawn the proverbial short straw, the lad bounded forward with enthusiasm. "Take your horse, sir?"

Azerick dismounted and handed the towheaded boy Horse's reins. "Yes, thank you."

"Will milord be staying the night?"

"Do you know if there are rooms available?" Azerick asked.

"Oh yes, milord! The Golden Glade always has the best rooms available, except during winter festival, as they tend to fill up rather quick round the holiday," the groom replied helpfully.

"What is your name?"

"Peck, if it pleases milord." The boy then grinned broadly. "Of course Peck ain't me real name, but that's what everybody calls me on account of how small I am."

"Well, Peck, take good care of Horse for me." Azerick slipped a gold coin into the boy's small, grubby palm. "Brush him down real well and give him the best oats and feed you have. I'll probably be staying for several days at the least."

Peck looked at the small fortune in his hand. It would likely take him a year or more to save up that much if he did not spend a single copper on such necessities as food, clothes, or shoes.

"Aye, milord, I'll take special care of him, I will!" Peck shouted excitedly until Azerick put a finger to his lips and looked pointedly at the two older boys watching from the rear of the stable.

"Oh aye, milord, I catch yer meaning," Peck replied in a hushed tone.

Azerick had lived in the streets long enough to know that if a smaller boy came into any kind of wealth he would likely lose it rather quickly to anyone big enough to take it away from him, and it looked as though Peck knew such things as well.

Peck took Horse to one of the open stalls, removed his saddle and tack, filled the manger with fresh hay and oats, and began vigorously brushing the animal down. Wally and John walked over to the stall where Peck was busily brushing down the pauper's mangy horse.

"So did the raggedy man tip ya, Peck, or did he stiff ya?" Wally asked the smaller boy.

Peck gave a noncommittal shrug. "Just a single. Better than nothin', I guess."

"Ha, a single copper! I told ya the guy was a bum, Wally," John said and elbowed Wally. "I can smell a cheapskate a mile away, I can. Those are the ones we give to Peck!"

Peck just smiled as he brushed several hundred miles of traveling out of Horse's coat.

Azerick stepped through the solid yet decorative door at the front of the inn. A few well-dressed patrons watched him warily as he entered and approached the bar.

"Can I help you, sir?" the innkeeper asked casually.

"I need a room for a few nights, maybe longer," Azerick replied.

The man behind the bar looked at Azerick's clothes and the trail dirt covering his face. "I have a few vacancies, but you might find the rates in this part of the city a bit exorbitant. There are quite a few decent places in the lower quarter that can be had for a fraction of what I have to charge. I'd be happy to recommend a few of the more honest places if you like."

Azerick dropped a short stack of silver swords capped with a gold crown onto the highly polished cherrywood bar. "No thank you. I think this will do just fine. If you could point me to my room, I would like to get settled in. I would also like a hot bath drawn and directions to the nearest tailor."

The innkeeper's face became even friendlier at the sight of the coins stacked on his bar. "Of course, sir! We'd be glad to have you at the Golden Glade," he cajoled as he swept the coins off the bar and into his hand.

An hour later, Azerick had eaten, bathed, and gotten directions to a clothier. He purchased a few well-made outfits of dark material and set off toward the bank. Now dressed in his new clothes and having discarded his tattered garb, he received a much warmer reception at the bank than he had at the inn or the clothier's.

An attractive woman stood behind a marble-topped counter running the entire length of the back wall. "Can I help you, sir?"

"Yes. I would like to exchange these for coin," Azerick replied and dropped two small diamonds, an emerald, and a sapphire the size of his thumbnail onto the counter.

The woman's face flushed in excitement at the gorgeous, glittering gems lying on the counter in front of her.

"Of course, sir. Just one moment, please."

She turned and walked back to a man seated at a workbench visible through an open door behind the long counter. The man got up and went out to where Azerick was patiently waiting.

"Good day to you, sir. Let me see what you have here, if I may."

He examined each stone with the jeweler's loop pressed into his right eye. He held the gems up to the light and studied them in detail. "Very nice, no inclusions, good color and clarity," he mumbled half to himself as he studied each gem.

The jeweler and Azerick haggled on the value for a few minutes before coming to an agreement. The woman exchanged the gems for a pouch of coins once they finalized the deal.

"Is there anything else I can help you with, sir?" she asked pleasantly.

"Yes, is there anything deposited for safekeeping for me? It should have been left here for me by a man named Zeb," Azerick informed her.

"One moment, sir, and I will check the vault."

The woman returned with a heavy pack Azerick recognized. He paid the fee for his precious books, happier now than he had felt for some time, and returned to his room at the inn. He set up his books on a shelf built into the wall of the furnished room he had rented, pulled one out at random, and passed away the hours lost in its pages.

When Azerick looked up from his book and saw that the sun had set some time ago, he closed its pages, picked up his staff from where it was leaning in one corner, and left the inn.

He retrieved Horse from Peck who got him saddled and bridled for him, and headed for the eastern gate. The large main gate was still open to traffic, as a few people were coming and going. One of the guardsmen held up a hand as Azerick approached.

"Good evening, sir. Will you be returning tonight?" the guard asked.

"I certainly hope so," Azerick replied.

"If you do and the main gate is locked, just pound on the sally port there and we'll let you in."

Azerick thanked the guard for the information and rode out through the gate. He pointed Horse to the northeast where he rode until he could just make out the shape of the tall main tower of the ruins. He dismounted and tied Horse to the branch of a maple tree before proceeding on foot.

A chill ran up his spine and his hair stood on end as he drew nearer the ruins. Azerick came upon the first tumbled blocks of stone once comprising a section of the outer wall and caught a glimpse of movement out of the corner of his eye.

He snapped his head around, but he did not see anything there. The sorcerer walked through the breach in the wall and saw several buildings in various states of disrepair. Some stood nearly intact while others were open from one or more collapsed walls. None had a roof any longer. The timbers once supporting them had long ago rotted away and turned to mulch.

Another flash of movement caught his attention, but whatever it was disappeared in the fraction of a second it took him to look in that direction. Azerick picked through the ruins of what had once been a smithy. A rust-covered anvil still rested upon a granite block, an aged steel sentry left as an icon to the inevitability of decay.

He departed the ruins of the smithy and worked his way past various buildings. Few of them gave him any clues as to what purpose they once served. Azerick slowly walked toward the open maw of the central tower which looked like the large black mouth of a huge stone beast.

Another flicker of movement drew his attention away from the fallen remains of the heavy wooden doors once securing the entrance to the tower. He spun around in an attempt to spot the elusive figure, but he saw only more stone blocks and deep shadows. Azerick turned back toward the tower entrance, released a strangled cry, and took an involuntary step back as a wispy, lucent figure hovered in the dark entranceway.

"My children! Where are the children?" the plaintive voice cried out.

Azerick stood dumbfounded and his blood turned to ice water in his veins. His heart pounded in his chest and his hands shook. The apparition looked like a woman in flowing, ancient robes. The once colorful patterns were nothing but washed-out shades of grey. She floated perhaps two feet above the ground, her hair drifting about her head as if she were underwater.

"Where are my children?" the specter begged.

Azerick cleared his throat in an attempt to loosen his tongue. "Lady, your children are no longer here. It is time for you to go."

The ghost moved forward a few feet toward him. "Where are the children? I must protect the children!"

"Your children are gone, Lady, as you must do. You must leave this world of the living if you are to ever find them."

The specter appeared to think for a moment, and then a look of pain and rage rippled across her ghostly countenance.

"I want my children!" the spirit wailed in a voice filled with fury and torment. Its appearance twisted to match its rage. The face and eye sockets elongated, the fingers lengthened into wicked claws that she stretched toward the creature who dared to mock her pain with its warm, living blood. Her hair became a tangled, writhing mass that seemed to have a life of its own.

Azerick stumbled back under the agonizing assault of the banshee's wail. He clapped his hands over his ears in an attempt to block out the mind-rending pain of the dreadful shrieking. It took all his concentration to reach out to the Source and shape the spell that was his only chance at surviving the sonic attack. His nose bled and his vision began to fade under the terrible assault. With a final burst of will, Azerick enveloped himself in a blissful sphere of absolute silence.

He clambered back to his feet, saw the banshee, and staggered away. Azerick could feel the air grow colder around him as his silenced footfalls pounded against the ancient flagstones of the keep's courtyard. He bolstered his resolve and forced himself to run faster as the air grew even colder. The air he drew in and forced from his burdened lungs came out in thick vaporous clouds. Icy pain flared across his back when the clawed fingers of the vengeful spirit raked across his living flesh.

The certainty of death if he did not escape fueled his sprint as he pumped his legs ever faster. It seemed only seconds had passed since he had faced the spirit when he finally reached Horse, who was chomping contentedly on the grass growing around the tree to which he was tethered. Ripping the reins from the branches, he vaulted into the saddle, spun the surprised Horse about, and put his heels into his mount's flanks.

Azerick rode Horse at a gallop until they reached the gates of the city a few minutes later. One of the guards must have seen or heard him coming, because the sally port opened for him as he brought Horse to a walk just before the gates.

"Ho there, sir! You look like you seen a ghost!" the guardsman called out to him jovially.

"You have no idea of the truth of that statement," Azerick responded as he let out a deep breath.

Azerick ducked his head as he rode Horse through the smaller gate and left him in the capable hands of Peck upon reaching the inn a short time later. Azerick let himself in through the small side door opening into the stables.

He ascended the stairs to his room and fell upon the soft bed without bothering to undress. It would appear that if he was going to make the citadel his own, he was going to have to fight for it. Could he fight without destroying? Azerick desperately wanted a home that was his, but could anything be built upon the ashes of destruction without eventually falling to the same fate?

Everything he was and everything he had was built upon someone's loss, usually his own, but also the lives of others. Not this time. Azerick would build something that meant more than what he could take by force. Somehow, he would find a way to put the tormented spirit to rest so he could make his home in the tower. Several minutes passed before he worked up the will to kick off his boots, and he stared up at the dark ceiling until sleep finally took him in its embrace.

CHAPTER 15

General Baneford sat in his command tent coddling a bottle of strong spirits. It was something he found himself doing more and more often. The longer this tedious campaign continued, the more he sought solace by imbibing the mind-numbing brew. The general was well into the dregs of his bottle when a sharp rapping sounded on the pole next to the tent flap.

"What?" the general bellowed.

A young, wiry rider stepped smartly into the tent and gave the inebriated general a sharp salute. The intoxicated Baneford threw up his hand and let it drop back to his side in return.

"Sir, I have a missive from His Grace, Duke Ulric," the rider informed the general. He handed over a folded sheet of paper sealed in wax bearing the duke's crest.

General Baneford snatched the message out of the rider's hand and dismissed him with a wave. He staggered over to the small field table and sat down heavily. The general used his dagger to break open the seal and began to read the contents through bleary eyes.

> General Baneford,
>
> I am swiftly coming to the conclusion that the rather simple retrieval task I have sent you upon may be beyond your ability to handle. While you and _my_ men have been roaming seemingly aimlessly across the kingdom, others are busily making moves of their own and the king becomes more tightly ensconced upon his throne. Your

reward hinges upon the successful completion of the mission I have given you. For several years you have ridden out with a large force of my cavalry and, more often than not, returned empty-handed and with fewer men than when you departed! I have allowed you to wear my armor to facilitate your success, but even with that help, you fail me and continue to lose more of my men. You have one last chance to prove to me that you are not completely inept before I replace you and have you digging the privy trenches. If I have not obtained that which I seek by the end of summer, you are finished! Return with my armor, or do not return at all!

Your Lord and Master,
Duke Ulric Stanbury III

General Baneford read the scathing missive twice more before he set it down on his field table. He knew it was never wise to respond to such insults, particularly to your superiors, while in a rage or intoxicated. Doing so often resulted in saying things you would likely regret whether you meant them or not. However, General Baneford's anger served to burn off much of the effects of the liquor. He grabbed his quill, dipped it into the inkwell, and carefully and deliberately penned his response.

He would have to speak with his men after this and make plans. General Baneford knew he could rely on the support of those with him. He was a good commander and respected by the vast majority of the soldiers under him. The general would have to act fast and put together the finer details of his plan later.

For now, he just needed to set this first part in motion. He blotted and sanded the ink so it would dry then sealed it with his mark. He then called for one of his most loyal men. A few minutes later, his man stood at the position of attention while General Baneford gave him the letter addressed for Duke Ulric's eyes only along with several verbal instructions. The soldier took the letter, put it in a waterproof tube, saluted, and departed camp.

General Baneford sat back down as soon as the messenger left his tent. He imagined the duke's response upon reading his reply and chuckled, quietly to himself at first, but it built to a loud, belly-shaking bout of hysterical laughter. He looked at the liquid in his glass, saluted the empty air, and downed the remains.

The rider rode through the gates of Southport without slowing. The guards had no trouble identifying General Baneford's colors and made no attempt to stop him. He rode hard until he reached the stables where all of the duke's cavalry horses were stabled. The lieutenant had strict orders from the general and hastened to ensure he carried them out.

"Remove the tack from this animal and prepare me a fresh mount!" the lieutenant barked at the stablehands who jumped up to meet the rider.

Lieutenant Desmonde strode into the barracks where he looked for the men General Baneford told him to seek out. He found two of the officers playing cards and motioned them over to where they could converse privately. After relaying the message from General Baneford, the two officers ran off in search of the other men on the general's list while Lieutenant Desmonde headed for the duke's treasury minister.

He found the minister in his office poring over tally sheets and accounting slips. He busily flicked the beads of an abacus as he wrote the sums in a thick ledger. When the minister finally looked up from his accounting book, Lieutenant Desmonde handed the hawk-nosed accountant the funds request signed and sealed by the general. The minister broke the wax seal and read the contents. His bushy grey eyebrows rose as he came to the sum requested.

"That is a rather substantial amount, Lieutenant," the treasurer said.

"His Grace is anxious for the general to complete his mission, and General Baneford requires these funds to do so. His Grace was most adamant in his latest missive, but if you wish to delay me, the general, and the duke even further with your dallying then let Ulric's wrath fall on your head." Lieutenant Desmonde showed him the angry letter Duke Ulric had written, clearly displaying his impatience.

The clerk looked over the second letter and made his decision. "Please wait here. I will get the gold the general requires."

The clerk returned with two men carrying an ironbound chest. He opened it with a large key that he produced from the inside of his shirt and lifted the heavy lid. Lieutenant Desmonde could not hide his look of surprise at the amount of gold the chest contained.

The treasury minister began piling gold crowns onto a large balance scale by the handful then set very precise weights on the other end until it balanced perfectly. The minister wrote the number down in his ledger, dumped the coins into a strong canvas sack, and then repeated the process several more times until he pronounced that the entire requested sum had been distributed.

The lieutenant signed for the withdrawal and, with four small but heavy sacks of gold tucked under his arm, returned to the stables where he found nearly a hundred men mounted and ready to depart. He distributed the gold between the two other officers before handing another sealed letter to one of the stablehands.

"You are to ensure the duke himself gets this letter no sooner than one hour from now," he ordered the groom. "If you cannot deliver it yourself, then get one of the duke's pages to bring it to him, but no one except the duke is allowed to read it. I have men watching you. If you try to deliver the message before an hour has expired, I have given them orders to kill you. Do you understand?"

The groom swallowed hard and nodded. The young man sat down nervously, and the soldiers rode out into the night. The stablehand waited nearly two hours before he moved from his stool just to be certain enough time had passed.

He walked slowly to the castle where a pair of guards stopped him at the large door leading inside. One of the guards called for a page and waited. Within moments, a young man came to the door where the groom gladly passed along the letter addressed to Duke Ulric.

The page sprinted down the corridor with the missive in hand until he came to a stop in front of the duke's study. Taking a deep breath, he rapped loudly three times on the dark mahogany doors and waited for permission to enter. The page pulled down on the polished brass door handle and walked in. Duke Ulric stood in front of a large stone fireplace that filled the study with its warmth. Another man was standing nervously a few feet away.

"My Lord Duke, I have a message for you from General Baneford," the page said.

Ulric motioned for the page to bring it to him and dismissed him with a wave of his hand. As soon as the page left and closed the door, Duke Ulric turned back to the travel-worn man.

"Now explain to me exactly how you and your men bungled a simple kidnapping," the duke demanded.

The bandit leader cleared his throat and shuffled his feet. "Everything was going exactly to plan, Your Grace. We disabled the coach and killed most of the guards within seconds, but then a wizard attacked my men and me. We tried to slay him as well, but he was exceptionally powerful, and he killed nearly all of my men with magical lightning and hellfire."

"Get out of my sight, you useless sack of excrement before I lose what little patience I have left and have you strung up and beaten to death!" the duke seethed.

The bandit leader made a hasty bow and fled from the room.

Duke Ulric hoped the general was going to tell him his mission was almost complete. He was in far too foul a mood to read anything else. He broke the wax seal and read its contents. The more he read the redder his face became. By the time he reached the end of the message, his hands shook and his eyes bulged in rage.

The guard raced down the hall in search of the duke's chamberlain. He pounded furiously on the chamberlain's door until it opened.

"What is all this commotion?" Alton demanded.

"Milord, the duke is in a rage, and we don't know what to do," the guard stammered.

"What has happened?"

"I know not, milord. The duke received a missive, and since then we have heard only shouting and destruction from within His Grace's study."

Alton lifted the hem of his robe and walked as swiftly as his old legs would carry him toward Ulric's study. As he drew near, he could

274 / Brock E. Deskins

hear the duke's shouts of outrage and fury and the crashing of furniture. Lord Alton was reaching out tentatively for the door handle when the door swung inward with a crash. Duke Ulric stalked out, cursing, tearing down tapestries, paintings, and kicking over planters as he unleashed his rage down the hallway.

The chamberlain crept into the study and gasped in shock as he beheld the level of destruction. Not a single book remained on the shelves. Several of the bookshelves themselves lay toppled onto the floor amidst the scattered books they once held.

The curtains and tapestries previously decorating the walls had all been torn down, paintings had been slashed, and the furniture had been hacked apart with the weapons that once hung on the walls but were now strewn about the destroyed study. Lord Alton saw a piece of parchment bearing a broken seal sticking out from under a pile of books and pulled it out. He recognized it as a missive from General Baneford.

Duke Ulric of Southport,

For fifteen years, I have been your ever-loyal commander of forces. In that time, I have carried out every command you have issued without failure or question, no matter how dubious that order may have been.

For the past six years, my men and I have scoured the countryside on your orders so that you may ascend the throne and rule over all of Valeria. I have raided tombs, delved through caverns, and killed the king's own guards to recover your precious armor so that you may usurp the king for his throne. I have watched many of my men die valiantly in the name of your cause, yet all I have ever received from you is complaint after complaint for how long it was taking me to secure your throne.

Well, no more. No more will I squander the lives of my men. No longer will I trek about swamps and *wastelands for <u>your</u> cause. I am close to completing the suit so that its full power may be used, but it will not be for your benefit. You want to be king? You are welcome to that headache, but you can do it on your own merits, without my help and without your precious artifact. I will use the power the armor provides to carve out my own little fiefdom. The only way I will ever give you Dundalor's armor is if I come back to Southport and shove it up your arse one piece at a time!*

> *General Ronald Baneford*
> *Commander, Baneford's Brood*

Lord Alton covered his mouth with a trembling hand at the words written on the parchment. He could not believe the general had turned his back on his lord and master like that. He had also not known the general had such artistic talent, for at the bottom of the page were several detailed sketches of the general carrying out his final threat. The likenesses were quite uncanny, although the chamberlain knew them to be physically impossible.

Lord Alton ordered the guards to round up some servants to clean and repair the study as best they could and warned them all to avoid the duke at all costs for the next few days until he was able to speak with His Grace. Even Lord Alton was not about to approach Ulric while he was in this state. The chamberlain sighed, stepped over the mounds of destruction, and went to mitigate whatever damage he could.

EPILOGUE

Six dark figures dressed in black robes with hoods concealing their features sat around a circular table somewhere deep underground. Crypts lined the walls holding the bones of those who had walked the lands a very long time ago. The air was dry and full of dust, and the only sounds were those made by the six gathered around the raised stone disc.

"How much longer must we live with this abomination upon the throne?" one of the cloaked figures demanded.

"Patience; all is continuing as planned, albeit not as fast as we had hoped. These things cannot be rushed. All of the pieces must be gathered for a smooth transition," another replied.

"I am growing less certain of Duke Ulric's ability to accomplish his task. What of General Baneford? His man holds several pieces of Dundalor's armor. What is to keep him from acquiring the entire set and seeking the throne himself?"

"His Grace has assured us that he has the general's utmost loyalty. Besides, without the backing of the church, any claim he attempted to make would be wrought with strife even with the artifact. Nor does he have the army needed to try to take the throne by force."

"With the armor he would be an army unto himself, if the legends hold true."

"The armor does not make one as invincible as the legends make it sound, although he would most certainly be a formidable force. Obviously, the last person to don the armor was defeated, hence it was ordered scattered throughout the realm. No, the greatest difficulty would be if General Baneford withheld the armor for ransom, and considering what is at stake, it would be no problem to grant whatever he wished, within reason. The general is a commoner, and anything he would desire would likely be common as well. Gold, women, a title of nobility; these things would be a small price to pay, and given his years of faithful service in fulfilling his task, I see no reason not to grant it. We might convince the duke to preempt such treasonous thoughts by hinting at the rewards awaiting him upon completion of his task."

"But how much longer must we abide this bastard king? He is an embarrassment to the kingdom! What if Duke Ulric fails? What if we cannot find the final pieces? Are our men in place to take the throne by force?"

"We have multiple agents already in place. We will continue to replace men loyal to the king with our own as swiftly as we can. When the time comes, the transition should be relatively bloodless as long as Ulric succeeds on his end. Should he fail, the coup will be more difficult, and much more blood will be shed, but it will be a small price to pay for our kingdom's dignity."

"Despite a few minor setbacks, we will accomplish our goals. It is the will of our sun lord."

"Speaking of our shining lord's will, what of these tales of the undead? Many claims have now been substantiated by our own people and can no longer be dismissed as folk tales."

"Indeed. Begin sending out our members trained to deal with such things. In the coming times, it is more important than ever for the people to see us as a symbol of strength and reliability."

"Blessed is the light of Solarian," everyone around the table chanted in unison.

To be continued in:
THE SORCERER'S LEGACY
Book Three of The Sorcerer's Path

FROM THE AUTHOR

I hope you enjoyed this tale and will try my other works. Feel free to look me up on Facebook! You can also check me out on my website http://brockdeskins.com/ where I write serial fiction, free for your enjoyment, and answer questions!

Author page:
https://www.amazon.com/Brock-Deskins/e/B005M6VQ1O

Facebook:
https://www.facebook.com/brocksbooks/

Twitter:
@brockdeskins

PLEASE REVIEW MY BOOKS (Especially if you liked it). Customer reviews are the primary means of enticing others to purchase them. I am dependent upon the sales of my books to earn a living that will allow me to continue writing stories that I hope bring you some measure of entertainment. Thank you for your support.

OTHER BOOKS BY BROCK E. DESKINS

The Sorcerer's Path is an epic fantasy series.

The Sorcerer's Ascension: Torn from a life of comfort and luxury, his family destroyed by political intrigues and aspirations, a young boy must quickly grow into a man before the deadly streets of Southport devour him. Follow Azerick through a page-turning adventure that pits him against thieves, thugs, murderers, and men of power that will stop at nothing to achieve their goals.

Azerick must fight just to survive, but for him survival is not enough. A hunger to avenge the wrongs committed against him burns deep within. But that is not all that lies within the young man. There is a power waiting to be unleashed that may be the key to achieving the justice and security he seeks--if it does not destroy him first.

The Sorcerer's Torment: Azerick flees The Academy but quickly falls prey to powerful beings that use his skills and power for their own amusement. What these creatures do not understand is the power of the young sorcerer's will and the lengths he will go to for vengeance. Despite becoming a prisoner, Azerick finds his first true love, but can he keep it?

The Sorcerer's Legacy: Azerick has found himself a home and tries to settle down. He takes on an apprentice and tries to put all the death and desire for vengeance behind him. But when the Rook finds him, Azerick is once again pulled back into Ulric's schemes. Knowing that all he has worked toward and everyone close to him is in danger as long as these schemes are ongoing; Azerick decides to put an end to it, once and for all.

The Sorcerer's Vengeance: After narrowly avoiding being killed in his own bed by the land's most feared assassin, Azerick leaves his school behind to find out who sent him and to put an end to the threat once and for all. Azerick's search will take him to the very pits of the abyss and back to unleash hellish fury upon those that threaten him.

The Sorcerer's Scourge: With the siege broken and Ulric dead, Azerick can finally relax, study his magic, and run his school in peace. Unfortunately, Jarvin's reign is far from uncontested and the true usurper decides to make his move. Jarvin escapes with help from an unlikely source—a vampire named Landrin who still clings tenaciously to his own humanity. While Azerick and a large force from North Haven race to save the king in exile, evil forces are preparing to unleash a nightmare upon the kingdom that may well destroy them all.

The Sorcerer's Abyss: Now the master of the Fifth Circle of the abyss, Azerick is challenged by another demon lord for supremacy. Azerick must face this threat as well as his innermost demons, all the while searching for a way to escape his hellish prison.

Ellyssa fears she is going insane as she plagued by nightmares of her capture and enslavement. Deciding the key to saving herself lies in the total destruction of the object of her fears, she embarks on a crusade to find and kill the slaver, Captain Jake, and eradicate the slave trade.

Ellyssa's nightmares and battles spill out onto the streets of North Haven and gains the attention of The Academy. Fearing Azerick's school is turning out rogue wizards, The Academy decides to hunt down and destroy the rogue and place the school within their control.

The Sorcerer's Return: Azerick has come back from the abyss in order to try to unite all the races against the return of the old gods who seek to destroy them and subjugate the few they allow to survive a brutal purging. However, fighting ancient gods may be the least of his troubles as he battles to save a fractured kingdom, a brilliant son traveling a dark path, and the splintered soul of his own humanity.

The Sorcerer's Destiny: Brutally purged of his demonic influence, Azerick continues the struggle of uniting the kingdom to face the coming of the Scions, ancient gods banished by the mortal races during the Great Revolution two thousand years ago. The fallen gods' prison is crumbling, and Azerick is powerless to stop them from breaking free and enacting their cataclysmic vengeance upon the world.

The humans must ally with the other races in a final battle against impossible odds while their entire world crumbles to the ground and is trod beneath the feet of an unstoppable foe. How can they set aside their distrust of each other when they fear the very person trying to save them?

Rise of the Order: Banished to the abyss after helping defeat the Scions and saving the world from eternal darkness, Azerick languishes in perpetual misery as Lord of the Fifth Circle. The denizens of his hellish realm view him as a usurper and outsider. The chaotic creatures form an alliance with one goal in mind: destroy Azerick Giles, but Sharrellan stands in their way.

A powerful spell tears through the demonic planes, and when the dust settles, the dark goddess is nowhere to be found. It is up to Azerick to return her to her seat of power, but he has a price: return him to his mortal form and send him home.

Back home, a vast empire is on a crusade to conquer the world, and it has set its sights on Valeria. Their goal is to unite the world under a single banner, eradicate the spawn infestation unleashed by the Scions, and replace the gods who they feel have forsaken them with their mystical rulers.

Can Azerick save the dark goddess from the clutches of her demonic subjects and become mortal once again? Will he have the power to protect his people from The Order if he does?

Descent Into Chaos: The Order has arrived in force, and the fate of Valeria, and perhaps all the world, is poised to come under their iron-fisted control. Azerick and Daebian are forced to flee Southport and make a contentious alliance when King Miles capitulates to the invaders. Reduced to insurgent warfare, Azerick and his allies attempt to battle The Order's vastly superior forces in a series of hit and run strikes, but the enemy legions may not be his biggest threat.

Princess Sylvian Attar, daughter to The Order's godlike emperor and empress, has taken a personal interest in Azerick. Herself a powerful sorceress, Sylvian hunts Azerick in hopes of removing Valeria's legendary hero from the battlefield thus sapping her enemies' will to fight. Azerick decides there is but one course of action he can take against this unstoppable foe. It was time to inject a little chaos into The Order.

Brooklyn Shadows is a modern-day vampire tale. Full of action and snarky dialogue, Brooklyn Shadows is an enjoyable read for anyone who enjoys the supernatural underworld and butt-kicking vampires.

Shrouds of Darkness (Brooklyn Shadows Book 1) Leo Malone has been a vampire for the better part of the twentieth century. Once a prominent Sherriff (vampire cop), he now earns his living as a private eye and occasional bodyguard for anyone that requires some serious protection. Leo is hired by the daughter of a mob accountant who has gone missing.

The fact that her father is also a werewolf has Leo following a trail of grisly murders that will lead him through a web of intrigue and conspiracy involving his fellow vampires and the local werewolves that make New York their home, all the while trying to keep one particularly determined cop off his back and himself out of jail. Leo is not some pretty-boy vampire that all the girls ogle over, but a hard-eyed, remorseless killing machine who does not take crap from anyone.

Blood Conspiracy (Brooklyn Shadows Book 2): While dealing with the aftermath of the failed vampire council coup, Leo discovers that the modified Cure has fallen into the hands of a black ops government project designed to create vampiric super soldiers. When the inevitable happens, the off-book Homeland Security operation forcefully enlists Leo to help them resolve the situation. Worse yet, he has to work not only with an antagonistic werewolf named Meat, he is reunited with his hated creator, Lesile.

Primacy of Darkness (Brooklyn Shadows Book 3): Jack the Ripper, sadistic madman of old London, once thought long dead, has returned to New York in an effort to quench his thirst for blood and mayhem. When the city's vampire enclave finds itself insufficient to deal with a madman of Jack's caliber, Vincent, the enclave head, enlists Leo Malone to put the maniac down before he reveals the existence of vampires as he throws the city into the throes of chaos and terror. Leo soon finds that Jack is not the only monster with which he must contend. A ghost from his past has also seemingly crawled from its grave and seeks to put an end to him and the rest of his kind.

The Transcended Chronicles is the story of an outlandish young man as he goes from being a troublesome youth to one of the kingdom's greatest secret agents. Blessed (or cursed) with an amazing ability to both fight and abuse his body with every conceivable vice known to man, Garran Holt is either the kingdom's greatest hero or its biggest embarrassment.

<u>**The Miscreant**</u> **(The Transcended Chronicles Book 1):** Garran Holt is a troubled young man. Unable to tolerate his self-destructive ways, his mother sells him into indentured servitude as part of a work crew building King Remiel's new trade road. When mercenaries sent to disrupt the road's construction attack his work camp, Garran discovers an inner power capable of turning him into a warrior of unparalleled ability. When the leader of his work crew recognizes Garran as being one of the transcended (a fighter able to slip into the swifter currents of time), he is trained as an agent, one of the kingdom's elite spies. Crude, abrasive, and deeply committed to destroying himself with drugs, alcohol, and debauchery, Garran might be the kingdom's only hope against falling to The Guild, the powerful trade cartel bent on becoming the true and undisputed power in the land.

<u>**The Agent**</u> **(The Transcended Chronicles Book 2):** The Guild rules the kingdom through their puppet monarch, and Garran must race to save the last living heir to the throne before the powerful syndicate's assassins complete their extermination of anyone who could oppose them. Garran and Prince Adam Altena struggle to find allies in hopes of rescuing Adam's sister, who was forced to marry the usurper in order to prevent even the thought of rebellion, and raise an army

capable of defeating The Guild. With The Guild now in control of Anatolia's powerful army as well as their legion of mercenaries, their future is grim. How can a disreputable agent and a deposed prince convince their neighboring rulers to oppose The Guild, an organization that has had them cowed for decades?

Empire of Masks is an exciting and explosive new series that takes place in the world of Hedon and takes you across the land of Eidolan where ships sail through the skies and men and women wage war with magic, swords, muskets, and cannons.

<u>**Highlords of Phaer**</u> (**Book one of Empire of Masks**): Born a slave, descended of kings, Jareen Velarius just wants to provide the best life he can for his family, but Eidolan is a realm that challenges even the most stalwart of souls. Caught between his masters and those brave or foolish enough to strike against them, Jareen struggles to reconcile his role as a dutiful slave with that of a man who desires to be free. His goal: to return his people to a life stolen by the highlords more than a millennium ago.

Auberon Victore, sorcerer, alchemist, son of a powerful overlord, and Jareen's master, creates an alchemic compound he is certain will change the world; he just does not know how. Jareen sees it for the weapon that could break the sorcerers' iron grasp wrapped around the necks of every lowborn in the empire. It will change the world, but not in the way his master desires.

Across the Tempest Sea, a mighty storm has raged for a thousand years, keeping a terrible, long-forgotten enemy at bay, an enemy whose cruelty knows no bounds. Only the perpetual storm and their fear of the sorcerer highlords keep the Necrophages from returning to Eidolan and cloaking the empire in death and darkness. But the tempest is waning, and the dissidents' freedom may well come at the cost of their total destruction.

<u>**Nightbird**</u>: The Great Revolution ended the highlords' tyranny two hundred years ago, but the legacy of that epic war, and that of the principal architects' descendants, lives on. With the highlords' death and their taking magic, as it was once known, to their graves, Eidolan

fell into a time of darkness and its cities lived in isolation. However, some people, dubbed arcanists, discovered a new form of magic and the airships returned to the skies, rejoining the cities in trade as well as conspiracy, but a new darkness, more dreadful and deadly than any they faced before, is coming.

Kiera is a fifteen-year-old nightbird, one of many who flit about after dark, stealing whatever they can find in order to survive. She lives on a derelict airship in the poorest part of the city with Wesley, a young man who plies his trade as an escort to wealthy older women, and his little brother Russel, an autistic savant who communicates only through sign but who could secretly be the most powerful techno-arcanist the empire has ever known. Deep in debt to the underlord Nimat, Kiera dives into evermore dangerous schemes that put her at the heart of a secret war that could spell the destruction of not just the city, but the very empire.

Kiera is caught in the center of several factions on the brink of war. When she can no longer tell friend from enemy, there is only one side she can trust—her own.

Mourningbird: A creature of darkness lurks in the shadows of Velaroth, wearing the skin of its victims, and grips the city in terror. Dorian, a Necrophage bent on sowing chaos and paving the way for his people's invasion, has declared war on the humans of Eidolan, and there appears to be no one capable of stopping him.

Kiera's world is shattered by those who hold power, and she is forced to seek an ally. The nightbird is coming into power of her own, but can she stay alive long enough to seize it? Russel's behavior has taken a turn for the worse, and his actions have drawn the attention of those who would use his amazing talents for their own gain...and everyone else's loss.

The battle for Velaroth, and perhaps the world, has begun. Who will win? Who will live to mourn the dead? Will there be anything left for the victor to claim as their prize?

Standalone books

The Portal is a fun and exciting story of some less than popular teenagers that accidentally open a portal to a mystical land during one of their role-playing games. Drew, a dour and anti-establishment teenager, is pulled through and captured by evil creatures lying in wait on the other side. Now it is up to his friends and older brother to rescue him, but who will rescue Drew's captors from him?

Amelia (Battle for Ardentia): Amelia is a precocious, ten-year-old girl with a powerful imagination. In her alter-ego guise of a demi-goddess warrior princess, Amelia fights against a powerful demonic sorcerer named Romut and his horde of monsters in a never ending series of battles to protect the people of her imaginary world. However, the true battle strikes home when Amelia is diagnosed with a brain tumor. Now Amelia must fight not just the evil living in her imagination, but for her very life.

ABOUT THE AUTHOR

Brock Deskins was born in a small town located in rural Oregon. At age twenty, he joined the army and served as an M1A1 tank crewman, dental specialist, and computer analyst. While in the military, he became an accomplished traveler, husband, and father of three wonderful children. His military career completed, attended college to brush up on his skills as a computer analyst and gain new skills as a writer. Brock received his degree in computer networking and is now devoting his full time and limited attention span to writing.

BIBLIOGRAPHY

THE SORCERER'S PATH
The Sorcerer's Ascension
The Sorcerer's Torment
The Sorcerer's Legacy
The Sorcerer's Vengeance
The Sorcerer's Scourge
The Sorcerer's Abyss
The Sorcerer's Return

The Sorcerer's Destiny
Rise of the Order
Descent Into Chaos

BROOKLYN SHADOWS
Shrouds of Darkness
Blood Conspiracy

THE TRANSCENDED CHRONICLES
The Miscreant
The Agent

EMPIRE OF MASKS
Highlords of Phaer
Nightbird
Mourningbird

OTHER BOOKS BY BROCK E. DESKINS
The Portal
Amelia: Battle for Ardentia

Curious about other Crossroad Press books? Stop by our website:
http://crossroadpress.com
We offer quality writing
in digital, audio, and print formats.

Subscribe to our newsletter on the website homepage and receive a
free eBook.